Bonding Weekend

DAVID RAVEN

2023, TWB Press
www.twbpress.com

Bonding Weekend
Copyright © 2023 by David Raven

Edited by Terry Wright

Cover Art by Terry Wright

ISBN: 978-1-959768-20-3

This book is dedicated to the memory of my mother, Sandra Lynn Beasley, who stuck by me when I was running with the devil. May we always remember "What A Wonderful Bird The Frog Are."

Chapter One

Jake Reece was a signature away from being a rock star when the world of magic snatched fame from his grasp. The vagaries of Atlanta's dark underworld had weaved through the drama in his crazy life to rewrite it all.

Now he was slinging drinks at *Medusa's* again.

Tonight, Halestorm's *Back from the Dead* blasted from ceiling speakers as he shook tumblers, poured shots, and sang along with a group of cooks who'd just gotten off work.

A decent-size crowd was already there to check out the unique Atlanta Midtown hotspot. Where else could you go and see a Medusa statue with panties and bras hanging from it along with archetypal pictures of powerful women through history on the aged brick walls? We're talking Madonna, Joan of Arc, Joan Jett, Marilyn Monroe, Marilyn Manson in his made-up androgynous splendor, Tori Amos, Valkeries, Lady Chablis, the Gorgon sisters, Amy Lee from Evanescence and even the seventies punk singer Wendy O. Williams from the Plasmatics.

Here Jake was in his gilded cage, making great tips even if everything else had gone wrong. He was known around town as "the bartender who almost became a rock star." Some called him a ghetto celebrity. He hadn't gotten anywhere, but he was well known.

Rumors of his writing a book had intensified gossip about him. Acquaintances were coming out of the woodwork to ask questions about his new confusing mystique.

"What is this I'm hearing about a rock opera based on your nightmares?" an actress asked then ordered a Cosmopolitan martini. "I know you give tarot card readings, but aren't you taking this Madame Bell psychic thing a little too far?"

If they only knew, he thought, having to filter a credible story out of his life of metal, magic, and mayhem. "Okay, listen. I am writing a book while I put another band together, and I've had some wild psychic dreams that have given me ideas. That's all. I'm not receiving information from aliens. About the rock opera, that's later on."

She cleared her throat and lifted the martini glass. "So you haven't given up on music."

He scoffed. *Do these rumor-mongers ever rest?* "No. Writing a book is just a side project like I've said a million times to everyone. The regulars around here need to start their own tabloid."

She laughed and got up to mingle.

The truth was, he was obsessed with the new project. He believed the rock opera based on the book concept would guide his future success. Failure with the record label had only given him more drive.

Tonight, he was writing frantically before the bar got too busy. An orb of candlelight flickered over scrawled thoughts in a journal that would be added to his laptop file later.

"Are you journaling on your past life or scribbling shooter recipes," a feisty cocktail waitress from the strip-joint, *Dancers*, asked.

He looked up at her and grinned. The sarcastic remark was the wittiest thing he'd heard in a while. "I'm writing about a terrifying world I've created from dreams."

Her eyebrows drew together at his vague puzzling response. "Terrifying, huh?" she questioned musingly. "Your attempt to be a horror writer is terrifying. Leave that to Stephen King. I thought you had a record deal."

"I did for fifteen minutes. The label told me I couldn't record a concept record. They said it sounded like too much *epic bombast.*" He made quotation marks with his fingers. "The whole deal got dropped."

"And what happened to your band?"

He couldn't tell the truth that magic and drama in his life along with his grand musical vision had finally demolished his band *Lost Angel.* "Everyone just wanted to do their own thing."

"So now you're going to focus on being a famous author instead of a rock star?"

He groaned theatrically without answering. She shrugged and

walked off.

On and on it went all night, the questions getting more and more annoying.

Between making drinks and shots, he returned to his journal flickering in candle goblet light. Candles were a big part of his "poet ritual," making him feel like an artiste from centuries ago. Everyone knew he was strange, and some thought he was ridiculous. He was used to it.

On the jukebox, the old disco song *Heart of Glass* by Blondie came on. The song brought drunks to their feet to disco dance. One girl swung her hair around, pretending to be Debbie Harry.

He wrote feverishly for about another fifteen minutes, but then a bevy of club girls came in the door. Good. He needed a break from his crazy thoughts.

Slapping the journal shut, he placed a dilapidated paperback novel on top of it, *Black Dahlia* by James Elroy. Hex, a Darkened who owned a bondage club called *the Dungeon*, had given it to him. Jake had never read any James Elroy, just crime noir writers like Mickey Spillane and Raymond Chandler, so he just devoured it.

He loved to read anything about Hollywood: hardboiled crime novels, eighties hair bands, Jim Morrison, even stories about dreams made and shattered on the Sunset Strip. Singing with a band at the *Whiskey A-Go-Go* or the *Starwood Club* would just be a fantasy. He'd love to be a bartender in West Hollywood.

"How about a shot on me," he called out to everyone.

The place went wild with audience mania. Welcome to *Medusa's Family Feud*.

He lifted his reading glasses off his uptilted nose and slid them over his famous head of shoulder length wavy hair, a russet mane streaked vanilla, total California. There in the gilded bar mirror was the prince of a face that could've made him an actor, model, or porn star. His eyes made him a poet.

He reached for a tumbler while tossing his hair a bit. Sometimes he had his hair pulled back in a ponytail but not on nights a lot of girls came in. Tonight he wore a black turtleneck to look sexy and mysterious. Tomorrow, when there were more rock n' roll guys at the bar, he'd wear his *Dream Theater* or *Slayer* T-shirt.

"Tonight, I want everyone to try my latest creation inspired by a murdered girl in the book *Black Dahlia*. It contains blackberry tequila, cream, and my special mystery liqueur."

"You're naming your stupid shots after a Hollywood noir icon?" Mr. Ruke asked, appalled. The pedantic, bitter old man was referring to Elizabeth Short, the struggling actress murdered in the forties. "Your delusions of grandeur are laughable."

Jake held up a hand in mock appeal. His acrid repartees with Mr. Ruke were legendary. Hearing them go at it was a big part of the total *Medusa* experience. "Hey, it's just my ode to a great novel."

"It's disgraceful," Ruke muttered and turned back to the Ian Fleming James Bond novel he was reading at the bar. "The girl was murdered and mutilated."

"Hey," Roxy Rachel blurted out. "I think naming a shot after a dead girl is cool as shit." Her dirty-water blond hair was thrown over one darkly tanned shoulder. She was the bar's resident jack-shop model princess, tawdry and loud.

Her drag queen buddy, Secret, smacked her on the head. "Stop yelling in my ear or the next shot could be named after you."

Much went on all night, but the drama centerpiece of the evening wound up being a stripper fighting with her gay best friend about who'd stolen dope at a party earlier. The argument was so intense it took them outside the bar.

At last call, the couple was still there. Jake chugged muddy black coffee only an alcoholic could appreciate while watching them. He finally offered to comp their huge tab just to shut them up and get them out of there. He felt like a referee on *Celebrity Death Match*.

That's when he felt it—a desperate soul reaching out to him in the night, a woman, headed his way.

He closed his eyes and saw a flicker-flash image of a lissome figure in black rushing down the sidewalk toward the bar.

Out of Piedmont Park, she emerged from between two parked sports cars. Rushing across the street, the windswept girl was like a goth debutante who was late to a ball.

When she came in, the fighting couple was headed out the door. They paused to regard her curiously as though they were passing a ghost.

Bonding Weekend

The mysterious visitor slid black lace panties onto the arm of the snake-headed Medusa statue. Then she flowed over to the bar and slid onto a stool.

She hadn't actually looked at Jake yet, busy swiping her phone on a music quest, a black fingernail tapping out a tune on Spotify. He recognized the symphonic metal as *Wish I had an Angel* by Night Wish.

He paused a moment, time stopping, taking in her ethereal beauty. She was the hottest goth girl he'd ever seen, yet the sight of her was unsettling. Was she somebody from his past better left forgotten?

He felt a trace of magic from her along with all her complicated emotions and dire wants. He knew *weird* was about to rush into his life like never before. He just wanted a few moments peace before simple eye contact let loose the floodgates.

The imperious *clack* of long, lacquered fingernails on the bar filled his ears as he wiped down brightly colored liquor bottles. "I've been looking for you," she said breathlessly and placed a purse that looked like a small coffin on the bar.

His eyes slid to hers, and he felt a rush only a sex drug should deliver, a wind blowing across his soul. A nameless bond came together without a word.

He couldn't help but gaze at her as though she were a portrait. She was all curves and leather, a femme fatale. Luxuriously long midnight black tresses veiled a doll face of preternatural pallor like raven's wings.

He lowered his eyes thoughtfully and then smiled, relaxing just a little. "I can't wait to hear why."

"Because I need you," she said in a flat low tone. "Would you make me a Long Island Tea while we talk?"

Rum, tequila, whiskey, and gin streamed into a tumbler. The rest was history. Topped with coke and sour mix, the top-shelf drink brought a look of triumph to her eyes. And what eyes they were, green stars set in her milk white face.

A black heart-shaped pendant hung in the creamy hollow of her throat as bar light reflected off a vinyl cropped top with a ring zipper. Her black skirt bearing a pattern of skulls hung over shiny studded patent-leather boots ready for war.

"I see you knew to pay homage to Medusa," he said.

"I've done my research on this place...on you."

He stepped up to her and propped his elbows on the bar. Her eyes were almost too much for him to handle. "May I ask your name?"

There was a sharp intake of breath. "Josephine."

His eyebrows drew together. "Have you been asking questions about me at the *Dungeon*? I think Hex was talking about you."

"Yes."

Hex had told him all about the girl he'd met who looked like Elizabeth Short in the *Black Dahlia*. He regarded her in fascination—the jewel eyes, the flowing black hair, and dark sensual mystique. He could see where Hex would make a connection between Elizabeth Short and this girl. The raven-haired goddess before him, though, was much more ravishing than any struggling Hollywood actress of the forties. Still, this had to be the girl Hex was talking about.

"So let me guess," he said. "You're an assisted living caregiver."

She smiled thinly. "I'm a stripper...and I'm a professional violinist."

He stopped wiping the bar and eyed her in dark speculation, chills rushing through him. That's why eerie connections were being made in his subconscious. He was developing a main character for his novel based on a dark-haired girl he'd seen in recurring clairvoyant dreams, haunting him. The girl in these nightmares was a violinist, one of several, playing for tips on a nameless neon strip. If you spiffed her up with goth gear and heavy makeup, the girl in his dreams and the one before him would be one in the same.

The psychic déjà vu was unnerving. He needed a shot to calm his nerves. He poured himself a shot of Jägermeister from a Jager machine featuring a stuffed bug-eyed lemur with its arms around the contraption like King Kong clutching the Empire State building. The Jager-lemur wore a tie and shades for full comic effect.

Down went the cold Jager with its numbing *deal-with-the-bizarre-girl* effect.

He wiped his mouth. "Have you played in a band?"

A faint smile passed over her lips. "Oh yeah. I play in the underground magic scene. There is a big market for violinists in the world of magic. Symphonic metal and goth music is all the rage."

"I'm glad you're not a bounty hunter sent to kill me," he quipped then set a bottle of Whistle Pig bourbon on a shelf above the cappuccino machine.

She parted her lips in slow deliberation, manipulating the barbell piercing in her tongue thoughtfully. "Even in music there is much danger."

His eyes widened. "Trust me. I know all about it." Then he raised a brow inquiringly. "Is someone after you?"

"Yeah. The problem is an ex-lover wants me back...at any cost. She was my dominant and a brilliant violinist. I was her *familiar*."

Jake listened intently. "Who?"

"Her name is Felicity. She fronts a goth act called Dire Portent. I was in her band...before I ran."

He tilted his head, appraising her. He was certain she had all sorts of dirty little secrets, but he had picked up on one thing. "Are you having trouble going through your rite of passage, your Darkening?"

She sighed, sounding relieved he'd realized this. "Right."

"And you believe I can help you tap into your unfulfilled power?"

Her kohl-lined eyes flared. "Yes." She gasped. "That's why I've come to you. Then I'll be too powerful for Felicity to control anymore." She smiled like a devious child as bar light ran along a lip ring. "You thought I was just approaching you for sex, didn't you?"

He did his best shocked expression. "You don't just want sex? What's wrong with you? Let me guess. You're celibate."

She rolled her eyes, grinning big. Her black hair, oh so long, fell over her bare arms, the tips resting on the black vinyl coffin purse (And the tips were silver, oh my). She emanated a dark sensuality like chocolate.

He thought of the Dark Lust that Marci experienced from demons and wondered if sex with her would give him the same thrill.

After a moment's thought, she lifted her eyes. "Since you've brought up sex, I must say it's like music to me. I have to have it." She regarded him like an unattained goal. "I've never done a rock singer before...especially one with your special talents." Her eyes fell to the Dual Serpent amulet around his neck. "Time is of the essence, though. You have invaluable connections that I need right away."

"What connections?"

"Marci Stone and her girls have quite a reputation. I've heard all of you stopped Ariel Celique, the succubus bitch with her sex ring and designer drugs." Her eyes fell to his chest again. "You're all the rage now in the magic world. I even hear you're being hunted for that amulet."

He grinned boyishly. "Rumors abound in the underworld, don't they? Do you know of anyone after me?"

"Oh sure. Felicity is not just coming to reclaim me. She wants you."

"For what?"

She chuckled. "Why, your voice. She uses illusions along with music in her show. She can create amazing effects with the magic in your voice. She knows you're a powerful hybrid. Plus, she has...a much greater purpose for you."

He gazed upward, rolling his eyes. "I have no plans to open my dark side."

"It doesn't matter. She can tap into your suppressed dark power. You and your friends need to stop her."

"How do I know you're telling the truth?"

She cut her eyes away momentarily and shook her head, hair shifting on her shoulders with a breathing sound. "Look. Another guy from her band will be after you soon. He's called Minstrel, and he's absolutely nuts. He has been following me, trying to convince me to run off with him." She laughed, a soft scoff. "No way."

Jake sighed, getting it. "Okay. You want to meet Marci?"

"My Darkening may very well depend on her."

He regarded her incredulously. "Even if she knew how to perform a Darkened ceremony, I doubt she'd personally advance your cause."

"Her name carries weight. She could find someone who would do it."

He paused, speechless at her determination, then: "Why haven't you gotten in with the Darkened in this town?"

"I have. No one will do it. Felicity's dominant scent is on me, and she's a well known succubus in the music world. The Darkened are scared of her here. I've had lovers afraid of being tracked down by her."

His eyes settled again on the heart-shaped pendant. "You're wearing an amulet yourself. Is that to mute your aura?"

She tapped it with a long, lacquered black fingernail. "This hides her scent and helps me with my addiction to her. But a powerful psychic knows I'm her submissive once they've touched me—one like you. I can't make progress."

"So, you feel blocked. Are dreams driving you crazy? I had them before my Awakening."

"I have ways to deal with nightmares," she said, showing him the tracks on her arms. "But all of this anguish is worth it if I can become a greater succubus than Felicity."

Oh, she wants to become the ultimate dark goddess of the violin—a sexy soul sucker virtuoso.

She was forbidden fruit, a black rose, dark delicious poison candy. Would he be able to resist taking a bite of her? Anything that could become an addiction usually found him. He really needed to think, though. He'd barely escaped Ariel and her scheme to keep him forever as a slave in that fucking mansion. Should he tempt fate again? He sighed and tossed a bar rag by the register. "Let me call Marci."

When his sexy partner in magic answered, she was in the dressing room of *Pandora's Box*, the strip club where she worked. He quickly explained the situation in a hushed tone.

Naturally, she was appalled. "You want me to come meet a girl who longs to be the ultimate succubus fiddler?" She laughed. "I can't wait to meet this new *friend* of yours."

"Oh, don't get jealous of my sexy violin virtuoso."

"Whatever, Jake. Whatever. I can already smell trouble." She groaned while fumbling in a gym bag. "Yeah, I'll meet her. Tell her tomorrow around midnight. I'll work out plans." Then the line went dead.

He looked at Josephine grinning like an imp. "She's willing to set up a meeting, but let me tell you, Marci's no pushover. I'm not guaranteeing you anything."

Her eyes flashed in a feral way. "When?"

"We'll meet tomorrow around midnight. Let me get with Marci about exactly where."

She slid a black leather book with a silver pentagram on it across the bar to him. After drinking deeply from her cocktail, she said, "Wonderful. This is a book of poetry. I want you to have it. My number is on the first page."

He flipped through the book, fragments of erotica passing over his eyes. "What are you doing right now...for money? It can't be violin playing."

"I'm dancing to survive. On nights off, I go out and play for tips on the streets. Sometimes I even play my violin at work when I'm feeling bold. I try to hold on to who I really am, you know. I want to feel like a violinist, not a stripper."

He thought of Marci's double life as both hunter and stripper. "I know all about girls with complicated lives like yours."

"I'm sure." She blew him a kiss. Silver bangles with crescent moons clattered on her wrist. "See you tomorrow."

She turned and headed out into the night. He watched her merge with the shadows, black cat getaway.

After cleaning up before Stephanie, the dining room manager, came out bitching, he stalked to the internet jukebox and played *Call Me*, another eighties Blondie song apropos to this situation. Calling Josephine would feel like seeking a prostitute for one long dirty, dirty night.

***

Jake slipped into Marci's loft apartment for the third night in a row. He'd been coming over here on-and-off for the last few weeks to avoid psycho bitch Clara, his latest fling. She'd convinced him that moving in with her was the money-saving opportunity of a lifetime. Now he just wanted to escape her neurotic text-stalking clutches—*Where are you, Jake? If you're drunk, I'll come get you. Don't go home with another girl.*

Oh, what had he done?

The other day, Marci finally gave him the code to get past security in the luxury loft apartment building, but he needed to get out of Clara's pad before his stripper mentor got tired of this. He couldn't do a couch tour forever.

He flicked on the lights, thrilled to be in her swank Grant Park crib: waterfall murals, pillar candles on pedestal tables, lush tapestries. Coolest of all was the view of the Oakdale Cemetery through the wall length windows where he'd curl up and write.

Tonight, he was determined to maintain his writing regimen and finish the latest draft of chapter eleven. The book was tentatively titled *Spell Island*. He doubted he'd sleep tonight, hoping to produce some decent writing out of restlessness. He couldn't write everything at *Medusa's*.

After taking a shower, he dried off, wondering when the girls would get home. Most likely they were clubbing after work. Of course, it could just be Marci avoiding him, annoyed with the whole Josephine thing.

He made camp by the window, lit candles, and brought a thoughtful forefinger to the stud in his lip. With no band or shows to play, he'd really thrown himself into the project. He wanted to get it done, along with a few songs written for his rock opera before putting together his fantasy band—a major undertaking.

There was another reason for his creative mania, though. The dreams that started a few weeks after his Awakening were intensifying. They were much like the clairvoyant nightmares of his Calling—the crazy dreams experienced when your inner-self was screaming to come out of magical dormancy.

Out of his nightmares came a tapestry of images: humans with the wings of demons and angels, half-beasts drinking in bars, sex shows beyond imagining. He felt like he should be writing the *Divine Comedy Part Two*.

He took the basic storyline he'd been working on for about a year, totally transforming it with these dream images. The more he wrote, the more vivid the visions became.

His confusion over what was real or fantasy was horrifying. He felt as though his book had *actually happened*, and the story was slowly unraveling in his mind and making its way to desperate pages—and his life.

In *Spell Island,* his main character is a runaway girl living on the streets of Hollywood. She is a prodigiously gifted violinist who learns that an otherworldly Hollywood holds great opportunities for a beautiful talented girl. A drug dealer obsessed with her finds a spell book that opens a magical doorway, sending her *Alice In Wonderland* style to a dark surrealistic world woven from Jake's mind—a dystopian world of magic, sin, and corruption.

The way he was fleshing the story out, his protagonist tries to make it legitimately by auditioning for several bands and erotic stage shows needing sexy musicians, but she winds up playing for quick cash like a vagabond on neon lit streets full of dangerous supernatural figures. She finally seeks the protection of a pimp. This character is a flamboyant incubus who finds her gigs playing music in goth sex shows, but for the most part, she's used for prostitution. Finally, her lover boy drug dealer comes after her and saves her. They wind up hiding on the streets of the magical island, running into the most unusual characters as they seek out a doorway to get back to Hollywood.

Jake loved the storyline.

He gazed thoughtfully out at Oakland Cemetery, its swaying Cypress trees throwing streetlight shadows over mausoleums. It, too, seemed like a place of dark imaginings, belonging in Bram Stoker's *Dracula*. He didn't really think Margaret Mitchell, author of *Gone with the Wind*, should be buried there.

His expression darkened. If a character from his dreams just walked into *Medusa's*, just what else from his book was going to turn out to be real?

Chapter Two

Marci called Jake at work that night, and everyone agreed to meet at a Midtown dive bar called *Strays*.

The dancer/hunter extraordinaire showed up at the place a few minutes after midnight. She was dressed to impress—slacks, leather stacks, and a cropped top that showed off her tan midriff and pierced navel. Her chestnut hair, highlighted with early dawn colors, was thrown over one shoulder.

She was the Caster who'd brought Jake through his Awakening into magic, so there was a sisterly protective air about her when drama entered his life. Lately, this was most of the time.

She spotted him at the bar and rushed over through a crowd of Buckhead girls and bad boys. I.P.A. beers were the specialty here. Promo-posters and neon signs for breweries like Creature Comfort and Slow Pour were all over the exposed brick walls.

"Where's your new obsession?" she asked, coming up to him.

Jake laughed. He was dressed in black lace-up leather pants, a leather coat with tons of zippers, and a Batman shirt. His vanilla streaked russet hair fell to his shoulders, teased and tousled, bedroom ready.

"She's at the other end of the bar," he said dismally, pointing at the withdrawn girl staring down at a martini like it was a dead friend.

Marci made her way through the crowd to her, Jake behind her, arms folded. The despondent violinist looked ecstatic when she laid eyes on the hunter. Then she returned to her morose demeanor, darkly thoughtful.

"There for a minute you seemed really excited to see me," Marci said, regarding her curiously. "I thought you were going to get up and hug me."

"You're so beautiful," Josephine said, eyes cast down at the bar. "I know you just see me as a problem."

"A girl who works in a strip bar usually is going to be a problem. I've seen you out clubbing. The *Dungeon*, I think. Don't you know Hex?"

"Yes. I've talked to him about all of you."

"I've heard. He knows you were searching for Jake. He's quite in demand these days." She gave him a playful punch. "He's getting used to being hunted. I guess you know a little about that, too, don't you?"

She nodded silently, her black tresses sliding over her shoulder. Marci understood why he wanted her—*she was hot*—but she would be bad news. He'd go after her with the passion he held for all his addictions and make a wreck of his life again. He lived out his lyrics—erotic sex and late night trysts.

He ordered a pint of Guinness and sat a few stools away to give Marci space to interrogate the poor depressed vamp.

Marci wasted no time buying them both shots of Don Julio tequila first to maximize stripper bonding. "Where do you dance anyway?"

"I'm a very private person," she said, lips to the shot glass. "I'd rather not go into it."

Marci went *hmmm*. "So you want help, but you don't want anybody to know anything about you."

The mystery girl shrugged. "I'm just paranoid."

Well, that was the end of the incentive shots, then. She ordered herself a Marci-tini (This was her signature drink with special ingredients like Jake's Dahlia shot) and sat silent a moment, singing along to the old Cheap Trick song *Surrender* on the house stereo.

"Okay, so you're secretive," she said finally. "That's cool, but I've got to know certain things. Like why exactly does a violin playing succubus want you back so bad? It can't be as simple as sex."

"You're right. It's not that simple. I'm a very good violinist, you see. I've played most of my life. It's hard to find really good violinists in the goth world. She didn't want to lose me."

"Let me guess. You wound up playing second fiddle to a crazy controlling bitch."

Josephine raised her pierced nose in virtuoso pride. "You're very intuitive."

"And you're certain this succubus is coming to town? Rumors abound here in South Hollywood, you know. I don't always believe them."

"She's definitely coming," Josephine answered. "She's doing a big show during Bonding Weekend here, and she needs me for it. Minstrel has already been sent here to drag me back to her...or at least that's what he wants her to believe. He has ulterior motives."

"Minstrel?"

"That's her righthand man, or so she thinks."

"Why didn't she come herself?"

"She does solo work too...makes a lot of money. Once she's done with her shows, her main concern will be fronting her band project Dire Portent for a long tour—that's where I come in...and Jake."

Her eyes went wide. *What?* "Jake is telling me she doesn't want you to go through your Darkening because you'll be even better than her at this whole violin thing."

"I am hoping," she breathed. "Felicity is so powerful. She could even feed off my dormant magic." The girl's eyes went distant. "Her illusions...her playing...are so unbelievable."

"Yet you managed to get away from her. How did you escape?"

"I had an amulet made that suppressed my craving for her—the Dark Lust for a dominant. Then I ran. The power of the amulet faded fast, though, and I wound up finding other ways to deal with the nightmares and all."

Marci's eyes slid from the heart-shaped pendant resting in the hollow of her throat to the faint track marks. "Okay. So how is gaining your power of succubus going to help your violin playing?"

"You should see what it does for Felicity. Sex magic gives her unreal finger dexterity and power over aural-triggered illusions. They're a huge draw at the shows."

"You're saying the violin playing triggers the illusions?"

"Yes. Well, glyphs on the fret board are triggered by touch and sound. The more complicated spells actually feed off the player's emotions and imagination."

Marci flared a brow. "Huh. Even Hex would be impressed with illusions like that."

"Felicity's also after the grimoires in Ariel's mansion," the girl went on. "Great books of illusion are rumored to be there...and there's talk of finding doorways to the Nephemera, too."

"The Nephemera? Who in the name of God, if there is one still, would want to go there?"

"If the lore is to be believed, there's big money for musicians there."

"I can assure you none of us are in any hurry to go back to that creepy fucking house. That's no fun retreat." She sipped her Marci-tini, nearly choking on derisive laughter at the thought of that big ol' gothic god-only-knows-who-died-there *Adams Family* mansion. "Now I've got a question. If you want your Darkening carried out so bad, why didn't you go directly to Hex? He thinks you're the bomb and compares you to famous dead people."

She sighed, rolling her eyes. "I'll have to fuck him to get any help. Surely, I don't have to explain to you..." She trailed off, eyes large in appeal.

Marci completely understood. "Alright. First things first. This Minstrel character is already in town. Right? Where does he hang out?"

"He's usually at the *Highlander*. Sometimes he follows me from bar to bar."

"Which bars?"

"Any place on Crescent Avenue or Ponce City Market. He's down on Cheshire Bridge Road, too, hanging out at Caster bars. He likes those gay hangouts."

"I'll put out my feelers for him and go chat with Hex about your...*ambitions*." Then she planted her eyes on Jake. "I'll see what I can do. I guess you two are headed off to blow the town up."

She downed her drink and headed out like a gunslinger who'd just won a fight in the Wild, Wild West. The rock n' roller in waiting slid down to the violin diva, and they both watched Marci leave like guilty desperados.

"Do you want to see my apartment?" she asked.

"Do I *ever* want to see your apartment," he exclaimed, eyes rolling to heaven. "But what's the hurry? Let's hang out."

Several rounds of drinks later found them at a fine/casual late night Roswell spot that had nothing to do with the club scene and the beautiful people. It was mainly out-of-town business associates and quiet married couples cherishing some time alone together. It was pretty posh, though. The waiters wore ties; the tables were set with silver and china. Jake thought it was a great place to woo a girl without the formality of true fine dining.

When Josephine's wineglass of Prisoner red blend was served, she said, "I started drinking when I was twelve. That was years before I realized I carried magic."

"You're a prodigy, huh?" He laughed. "I realized it when I was sixteen." His eyes fell to the chocolate cheesecake placed in the center of the table, a sumptuous symbol of decadence. Neither touched it for the longest time. It was as though the dessert was a moment not to be ruined.

"And I started playing violin about the time I started drinking," she added.

"I started playing piano in high school. There's definitely a connection between budding vices and budding talent."

She gave a faint laugh, regarding him with a deep thoughtful expression. "You're so pretty for a guy. Is there a girl who has your heart?"

Yeah, the girl who stuck me with this amulet. "Yeah. Well, maybe. She told me she was a fallen angel, but I don't know what to think of that."

The goth girl sipped her wine, nodding. "Angels are a mystery, period. They gave away the secrets of magic first, you know—not the demons. I feel like they cursed us and ran off."

"I can understand why you'd feel that way. They're really just as devious as demons." He wiped his mouth with linen, considering what he'd just said. "Devious As Demons—that's a good band name."

She laughed softly, velvet ripple. "You're right. That is a good name. We must remember there is a duality to our lives, the gift of demon or angel blood or ichor, I should say. But it is a gift, not a curse, no matter how dark...no matter how complicated our situation gets. Any price is worth it to feel magic in our veins."

The singer raised a brow, conveying that he was impressed. "I guess that's true. The bottom line is we're chosen by magic. It doesn't ask us." He rolled his wine around in this huge goldfish bowl wineglass and sipped. "So, have you been in any relationships?"

"Not really. Relationships have never been very important to me."

"What does matter to you?"

"Sex, magic, and music. That's what matters. All of it becomes one when I play."

Now there's a manifesto. "I assume you're on no quest for inner peace."

"I feel peace when I play violin. It's like a drug. No, better. I do love my drugs, though."

He laughed. "You're the girl-next-door I've always wanted."

"Maybe if your girl-next-door lives in a castle," she quipped.

"Or Marquis de Sade's roommate," he said. "Oddly enough, I'm writing a book about a girl who plays violin but winds up being the naïve victim of a dark magical world. She *really, really* reminds me of you." He wasn't telling her any more than that.

"I'm neither naïve nor a victim."

"You're being hunted. I think you're in more trouble than you want to admit."

"Yeah, but I plan on winning this game."

Game?

Ariel had called the battle between her and the demon a game. The dark world of magic was all about winning and surviving. Would his dark princess be a winner on the chessboard of magic?

Oh, the girl before him was nothing like his lost love, Charm, his fallen angel, who wanted to feel real love, chase butterflies, and remember a first kiss. This girl simply wanted nothing in her way as she headed to prima donna glory in the music underworld, a gothic lioness without equal on violin.

One thing he really did admire about her, though, was that her obsession with being a brilliant player was greater than her carnal hunger, her thirst to be reborn as a succubus. The darkness she craved was really just a means to an end.

At least until she tasted all that power.

Sipping wine, he just took her in: her nubile form, the dark plotting in her troubled eyes, her sensual mouth. She should've been a black cat of prey, not a girl.

"Are you going to let me hear you play violin?" he asked.

"Of course." She planted the wineglass down on the table. "I'll play my heart out, and then you can play me. After all, by the time the bow goes over the strings, I'll already be naked."

"Oh, those are lyrics to a great song."

They tag-teamed the cheesecake, four big luscious bites for each of them. Soon their timeless moment was just smudges and swirls on a plate.

***

They walked down a sidewalk of swaying Magnolia tree shadows to her apartment. The old brick tenement building was a few blocks from the corner of North Avenue and Spring Street on the outskirts of a rough neighborhood (The Bluff wasn't far off).

Her small apartment was swank with leather furniture—much too nice to be in a borderline ghetto area. The walls were decorated with gothic artwork bordering on erotica. Even the vases and statuary were sensual and flowing. It were as though she wanted to live in a nowhere area where no one would look for her. It was her secret lair, batgirl cave.

A thick grimoire was set as a centerpiece on an asymmetrical glass coffee table, accompanied by a black pillar candle. Hung on the wall above the sofa was a wrought iron pentagram fixture bearing votive holders. Swags of black velvet festooned the corners of the place.

"Let me light some candles," she said softly.

In the flickering light, he gazed down at a spill of black lace bras and panties amongst perfume, pentagrams, and sex toys.

She curled on the sofa and opened the tome with a faint creak. "I can't read this..." Her eyes shot up to him. "But I bet you can."

The singer looked at it and shrugged. He'd never seen the language. Then he tried tactile impressions, which was how he gained most information. As images flooded his mind, the amulet around his neck flared with life. He drew what he saw in his mind, a circular formation of magical sigils. It was a complicated pattern, but in a matter of minutes, he had it.

"I knew you could do it," she said.

"I honestly don't know what I just accomplished. I just know it's some sort of doorway."

She smiled slyly. "You've just drawn a door to the Nephemera."

"The fallen angel's world?"

She drew closer, candlelight in her green eyes. "I believe so. That's what they say, anyway." She considered him intently. "Is it true you're a direct descendent of Merek?"

Wow, word spread fast. "I'm stuck with this amulet. That's all I'm sure of." He shut the book and cleared his throat. "So, what inspired you to start playing violin?"

"My snotty parents up North expected me to excel at playing violin and get a scholarship to some high and mighty ivy league school."

He nodded. "That's what my parents wanted from me. I just don't work well within the box."

She lit a cigarette, blowing a plume of smoke, eyes faraway, a conniving mistress in a soap opera. "I knew I was going to be a witch, so I just ran from home. I never talked to my mother again, but I like to think my playing would make her happy. This dark world of sex and drugs helps me forget the abuse I went through."

"You were abused?"

"My stepfather. I never told mom. I feel like magic fills the empty part of me."

He understood such emptiness, but was becoming a succubus the answer? That was her way of being in control of her life. Wasn't relying on sex magic as big an addiction as drugs?

He looked deeply into her eyes as she began to undress. He didn't trust her. There was cold selfishness and manipulation behind her gothic beauty. Yet, he wanted her. She would be another addiction, another taboo pleasure he was unable to resist.

And was she ever a tease.

In her bedroom, she played ambient dark-pop by the new Euro-band, Dark. The song was called *Nightmare*. She slipped off her studded leather top, and then the tight black skirt was flung to the side. She rolled her creamy white shoulders like a dancing gypsy, sliding off a black lace thong. Then went her bra. The midnight hair slid over her breasts like flowing shadows over Greek statuary.

She reached for a crop stick amongst her toys. Cracking it on the floor, she crawled in a feline slink toward him.

After pulling the Batman T-shirt over his head, she probed her tongue into his navel. Then she shoved him down on the bed and dug her nails into his chest. She gently tugged the ring in his lip as though it would open a new world of pleasure.

"These nails can take you to heaven or hell," she whispered, her tongue manipulating the barbell piercing.

She then bent the crop stick back as though to smack him with it and then paused, lips parted. A faint shadow of dark amusement played over her face.

She reached for her phone and opened a music box. Ballerina music suitable for a little girl filled the candlelit room.

Reaching under the bed, she slid something out and then straddled him. What she brandished this time was not a whip or medieval weapon but a violin.

She positioned the vintage instrument under her chin, the bow poised like a motionless dancer. The polished wood bore cabalistic symbols. Breathing deeply, she drew the bow across the strings, producing a beautifully eerie effluvium that mixed with the sweet innocence issuing from the music box.

She swayed like a flower as she played, the performance symbolizing the duality of the talented girl. Sensuality faced virtuosity in the prize-fighter ring of her soul. She was a crucible from which these forces could not escape.

Engrossed in the music, she disentangled herself from him, playing feverishly with one knee on the bed. Candles threw her form over the walls. Her playing became even more crazed, the shadows harkening of a pagan forest rite.

He felt like a sacrifice, the bed an altar. The music displayed manic genius. Even in her latent state of magic, he felt her power coaxed from the strings. A chill passed through him like the fleeting possession of an erotic spirit.

The music stopped abruptly. "Raise your hands to the bedposts."

He did so, wide eyes flitting about.

She reached under the bed of surprises again. What she drew forth was no violin.

It was handcuffs.

Click-click.

"I like being in control," she said. "It makes me feel sexy."

"Ariel was a Dominatrix. That's why all this *concerns* me."

"As I've told you, I'm not used to being a dominant. I always wind up strapped to something."

"By Felicity?"

"By all kinds. I've lived the crazy life. In the circles I run, anything goes. I'm ready to be the ring leader of my own S&M circus. I've made a lot of money with sex and music, and not just onstage."

Not just onstage? he mused. Oh, she was a prostitute, but was bartending and waiting tables any better? "But you just dance these days. Right?"

Just then the phone rang. She answered, her breath catching in her throat. "I'm coming," she said to the demanding voice on the other end.

She gazed down at him, her hair trailing over his chest, his mane spread out like the nimbus of a deity. She unlocked the handcuffs, sighing. "There's something I have to go get, something to help me with the dreams. The Calling is driving me crazy, and smack isn't really cutting it anymore." She dressed hurriedly. "Let's meet tomorrow."

"I have a show tomorrow night," he said. "I'm singing with a local metal band. It will be fun."

"I will try to come to the show. Either way, call me afterward." She peered out the window and sighed. "I have to go. You can stay as long as you like. Just remember to lock the door when you leave."

He sat on the bed, listening to a car door slam shut. He then peered out the window and watched a shiny black dream machine slide into traffic with her in it.

From the shadows of an alley, a cloaked figure watched her go, too.

Chapter Three

Everyone hanging out at *Medusa's* knew Jake's band Lost Angel was done. He readily confirmed that he wrangled with the record label over a compromise between commercial metal and his prog-metal/rock opera ideas, resulting in the deal getting dropped. The guitarist, Nick Dryden, started his own blues-based band. The bassist and drummer took on new projects, too.

Here's what everyone didn't know. The truth was, Jake and the world of magic were more than what any of them wanted in their lives. He was too instable, and the situation was too dangerous. The artistic differences and contractual terms of contention served to give them an out. He was still good friends with Nick, but they were talking less and less.

This left Jake all alone. It was lonely at the top. He still wanted to sing while he finished his book without rushing to put together another band. His outlet was a local metal band called Burnt Offering that went through singers like razor blades.

These guys were all heavily tattooed with long black hair. They could've been Josephine's brothers. They contacted him from time to time when they didn't have a singer. He even wrote a few songs with them.

Tonight, they were playing at *Cat's Eyes* in Little Five Points. Tickets were a whopping twenty-five dollars. It wouldn't be any extravaganza like the *Buckhead Theater* show that brought all the label attention to Lost Angel, but it would be a very energetic fun time. Old friends would be here, and tons of fans, screaming their lungs out.

The band went onstage at nine o'clock to huge applause. Jake wore a tight mesh top and lace-up vinyl pants, complete with a glam rock gauzy purple scarf and silver bangles. He untwined the scarf from his neck and tossed it into the crowd, throwing back his head to sing a long note of dramatic vibrato that should've come from the pipes of an opera singer. He was *that* good. He'd grown out his hair from a pop poster boy blunt cut to flowing shoulder length hair. With the guys in the band playing like demons unleashed, he looked more like a metal god than ever.

Friends at cocktail tables called him all kinds of ugly names in jest. Even the old pedantic curmudgeon, Mr. Ruke, showed up to root for him (He was secretly impressed Jake had been offered a record deal).

Buddy bartenders and waitresses always got a kick out of mocking Jake's stage gesturing. With gothic crosses dangling from his wrists, hand gestures sweeping and dramatic, he looked more like he was performing in *Jesus Christ Superstar*. Most of the crowd did love his overwrought charisma.

In the middle of holding a high wailing note, Jake spotted the strangest thing. A figure in a velvet duster had entered the bar. He played a violin in great slashing strokes of the bow with a high sense of drama. He wore a poet shirt with lace ruff as though he'd stepped through a doorway from renaissance times. Long and greasy dark-brown hair, belonging on a wind-whipped pirate at sea, hung nearly to his waist. A ruddy face bore a scruffy beard.

He cavorted about like a court jester, playing manically in a fit of rapture. *That freak has stolen the show.* Jake flung back his head for another long note. He was singing a final verse about racing a car through midnight streets when it dawned on him that this showstopper must be Minstrel, the character Josephine was telling him about. He couldn't wait to meet the cavorting stranger, but the show had to be finished.

The band was playing with a vengeance and didn't give a damn about a crazy fiddler. The guitarist played a Flying V, video pretty-boy, riffs slashing through Jake's keyboard atmospherics. *Wolves' Breath*, a song about running through a dark forest from gypsy girls who'd shifted into werewolf form, showcased a bold acrobatic solo of ascending scale runs, shrieking string bends, and flashy arpeggio leaps. The driving bass thumped behind it all, finessed around the drummer's crashing cymbals and tumbling tom-tom attack, double bass drums setting the pace.

They played several more songs, all heavy. The guitarist slammed a power chord that rang out like a cry for help as Jake played a legato classical flourish, ending the show.

There was great applause as the band left the stage, and the macabre eighties metal sound of Mercyful Fate came on the house speakers. The eerie falsetto of King Diamond truly set the tone for confronting this violin throwback to the Paris streets of centuries ago.

A bartender was already pouring him a Guinness. He downed it and ordered another, sipping this time as he watched the outrageous violin vaudeville. Was this just a besotted musician having a bi-polar fit? No, it was all too contrived to just be a drunken spectacle.

The mad violinist finally made his way to Jake, dancing a jig as he finished a comical Bluegrass piece. "So you're the rock singer who's become the object of Josephine's amour?" The voice was raspy but the words were clearly enunciated, a European who spoke excellent crisp English. His overall air was that of a charming Euro-trash swashbuckler straight out of an Alexander Dumas novel.

Jake took a deep gulp of dark brew and raised a brow. "You must be Minstrel. Are you stalking her?"

Minstrel gave a mock look of outrage. "You don't have to say it like that. I know what's best for her. She needs to stop running from me."

"Why? So you can drag her back to the lovely band leader I've heard such good things about?"

"She can't run from Felicity forever, and I have some ideas, if she'll listen."

Jake gave him a hard look. He didn't know what to think. He sensed the same desperation behind his jovial veneer that he saw in Josephine. He bobbed his head to the double-bass pound and heavy riffing that poured from the speakers then slammed another big gulp of beer. "So what are you trying to get Josephine to do?"

The violinist smiled. "She needs to go through her Darkening and become the master illusionist and musician she was meant to be."

"And...?"

"Start another band with me. And you should join us. I know you're a hybrid. You need to go through your Darkening, too. I don't think you understand the extent of your power." He pointed at the amulet. "Word on the street is that you are the only direct male descendant of Merek, the first coven head of the Estranged centuries ago. This makes you the Keeper of the Dual Serpent amulet. Oh, the amazing music we could create."

"Why would I want to go through my Darkening and consort with demons?"

The stranger regarded him curiously. "You really don't know what it means to wear that piece, do you."

"I just know a little basic history. Wayward angels used magic that estranged them from God, creating the Estranged, and then the Darkened took it a step further, consorting with demons. Then a big mess ensued. The blood of the first two opposing coven heads is supposedly in it."

He fingered the amulet, twined with two serpents symbolizing the Darkened and the Estranged, one black, the other silver. The crimson vial with all its mystery gleamed in bar light, swirling with magic only his eyes could see.

Minstrel's eyes narrowed knowingly. "It's believed that Merek created the amulet, but the real story isn't that simple. Do you know that if rumors are to be believed, the magic of a very powerful incubus is within the amulet. He was so bold he forcefully compelled an angel to have sex with him. That's where the real trouble started. It is believed Sephera, the angel in question, used her ichor to create the amulet with Merek. She knew a hybrid would one day possess it who would be even more powerful than her seducer. Are you following me?"

Reeling from this revelation, he nodded. "Are you insinuating I'm supposed to confront this demon somehow?"

A chilling grin spread over Minstrel's face. "I think you've heard enough for now. Mark my words, though, you can tap into great demonic power if you go through your Darkening. Your powers as an incubus would be immeasurable. You'd be the sex god of rock."

"And be dead within a year," Jake added dryly.

Minstrel shrugged. "Possibly, but no guts, no glory. You would certainly enjoy the ride." His eyes gleamed with humor born of insanity. "And it certainly wouldn't happen before we put together one hell of a band with Josephine. I believe you would be able to best Felicity at illusions."

"This is all *too* bizarre."

"Bizarre but true. You also need to realize Felicity is coming for you as well as Josephine. She knows all about what happened at Ariel's mansion. She believes you found the hidden library."

Jake shook his head dismissively. "I'll deal with Felicity when she gets here."

"Not without going through your Darkening. She's too powerful. Do what I tell you, and we'll hit the magic club circuit together. I have enormous contacts. A goth metal band with violins would be a huge draw. Let's go before you become a slave to Felicity just like Josephine."

Jake cleared his throat. "First I have someone you need to meet."

Marci was across the room, hipshot, elbow propped on the bar. She and Moonshine had been watching the strange conversation intently.

He made a *come here* gesture, and they glided over to him like beautiful fish. "Looks like Jake isn't going to keep the crazy fiddler weirdo all to himself after all," Marci said. "That's so big of him. Oh, what has he gotten himself into now?"

"He is gonna have a ball Bonding Weekend," Moonshine said with her sexy southern lilt.

Marci's eyes went wide with jealous derision. "Oh, he's already found him a Darkened doll baby. She plays violin, of all things, and I do believe the guy we're about to meet used to play with her in a goth band." She hugged Jake and then gave the violinist an appraising look, brow arched. "Let me guess. You're Minstrel."

He reached for her hand and kissed it several times. "Yes, that's correct, and you are as lovely as I've heard."

She snatched her hand away. "That's enough. I don't need any more of your grandpa pecks."

He drew his hand back, laughing uncomfortably. "I hear you are the preeminent bounty hunter of the Atlanta area."

"What's 'preeminent' mean?" Moonshine asked in a low voice.

"I'm top dog," she muttered back. "Why are you interested in Jake, Mister Fiddler on the Roof?"

"I want to create an amazing band with Josephine and Jake."

"And make slaves of both of them, too, right?" Marci snapped.

He frowned, looking puzzled. "I need a band, not slaves." And then he resumed playing, wandering about the room.

She shook her head, eyeing Jake. "Where is your new girl, anyway?

His face went dark with concern. "I thought she'd come by here." He called her number, but it went straight to voicemail. An image went through his mind of her shooting up on her bed. He shuddered. This had not happened long ago. When he reached out with his mind to her, he couldn't feel her, though. Something was very, very wrong. Or had she somehow psychically shut him out?

"I make money all sorts of ways," she'd told him.

Perhaps an impromptu kinky midnight business venture was more important than seeing him, but that didn't explain why he couldn't sense her at all. He didn't want to be possessive, but he thought he'd better go to her apartment and see what was going on.

"I'm going to see her," he said. "I think something bad has happened."

"Don't leave me out of this," Marci said.

"Me either," Moonshine exclaimed in a country girl shout.

It took the guys about thirty minutes to escape old friends and fans, but finally they slipped out the back.

Minstrel was long gone.

***

Marci parked on a narrow street in the shadows of swaying Oak boughs. The gang walked around the corner, and Jake pointed at an apartment window glowing with candlelight. "That's her place." What he wanted to see—the curvy silhouette of Josephine playing violin—didn't appear.

They found the door to her apartment ajar. Candlelight flickered in the hallway.

He pushed the door open. "Josephine?" he called, voice laced with dread.

There was a half full glass of wine on the coffee table along with two empty beer bottles. The place was hazy with cigarette smoke, but the party was over. Nobody was there. He picked up one bottle and went inward, calling on Sight. A candlelit exchange of money and dope flashed through his mind.

"She just *used*," he said. "She's probably passed out."

Deep down, though, he really knew it wouldn't be that simple. He didn't want to open the bedroom door to find some nameless horror out of a Lovecraft tale waiting for him. For a moment, he just stood there, time suspended, listening for sounds, a stir of sheets, a moan, anything.

Marci came up behind him. "Let's do this." She pushed the door open.

All eyes fell on the bed.

This was no splatterpunk scene of a noir crime novel. This horror had a name like none other, evoking images of his mother's funeral and crematoriums.

"Shit," Marci said, Moonshine gasping behind her. "You're new girl is..."

Ashes.

Wind blew through a window like a sardonic sigh of the night.

Actually, it was what was left of Josephine's ashes. Someone had removed most of it—and in a hurry, too. Her dormant magic resonated from scrabbled, finger-scored remains, her dying anguish an indelible signature.

The scene surrounding the tousled sheets was reminiscent of a B-Horror movie about a jilted psychopath. This was total drive-in fodder: *Die, Violin Girl, Die.*

Handcuffs were fastened to the bed and rose pedals were spread across the sheets, tumbling in faint wind, lost souls.

The pedals came from a bouquet of roses on the bedside table. There was even a box of candy next to it draped with rosary beads and then crowned with a burnt spoon and an empty dope baggy—modern art to a heartbroken addict.

He read the card on the flowers: *To Josephine, my love.* An image flashed through his mind of a trembling hand writing feverishly in crazy lust mania.

Under a pillow, he found a bag full of whatever she'd cooked on the spoon. "Purple powder? What is it?"

Marci inspected it, her expression darkening. "I think it's Rapture, a sex magic designer drug. You don't see it very often because it's expensive. It's no mere street drug. Covens with a lot of money will pay big bucks to have it made. Spellbooks with the recipes for such drugs are sought by hunters because of their demand. But..."

"But what?" he asked.

"It's only deadly to mundanes, I thought."

"It was certainly deadly to her," Moonshine interjected.

Marci nodded. "I'm calling the council," she said, taking out her phone. The Athens-based Council of the Estranged ran the show in the Atlanta area. She had a five-minute talk outside and came back. "They're telling me a dealer has probably gotten his hands on the recipe with the intention of cooking up a ton of it and selling it Bonding Weekend."

"Do you think it's that Tom Alderman drug dealer who was helping Ariel?"

"Oh no, I've gotten word he's dead. Rumor has it one of Kitty Dreadlock's buddies tracked him down. I should've finished the job myself." She sighed, shaking her head. "Even if he were alive, I don't think he could make a drug like that without Ariel."

"Who's now a statue in an abandoned mansion thanks to the demon she never should've conjured," Moonshine added.

"Exactly."

"So, does the council want you to do anything about this?"

"Oh sure. That drug was not meant to be on the streets. We don't need dead out-of-town mundanes everywhere Bonding Weekend. This will draw the attention of paranormal divisions everywhere. Even the Darkened Council would want something done about this."

"Did you take on the case?"

"I told him I'd look into it. I really don't like jumping every time the council wishes I'd do something unless they pay me up front."

"You didn't get your usual hunter's fee?"

She shrugged. "We're just speculating, you know. There's no telling how she got that dope."

He touched the card with the flowers. A vision surged through his mind of a man with a tattooed bald head flipping through the pages of a grimoire. His profile was highlighted by candlelight...that nose...like a vulture's.

"There's a big-time hustler behind all this," he said. "A

Darkened, I believe. I want to try and catch this guy. I feel bad about my very own...Black Dahlia. She was a girl out of my book."

"If you catch a big dealer handing out a drug like Rapture, I will most certainly introduce you to the council and get you paid." She shook her head. "You know my attitude, though. You're gonna get yourself killed going solo."

"I will call for you in time of need, Scooby Doo."

"We sure *could* star in our own cartoon, couldn't we?" Moonshine said.

"Yeah. Life has been a black comedy since I got stuck with this amulet." He gazed down at the bed as tears welled in his eyes. Oh, her lush bottom lip, those long fingers on the violin, her tongue piercing a hidden jewel in a treasure chest of sensuality—it was all gone. How fast someone he really wanted to know could come into and go out of his life. It was terrible, fleeting like a great book he'd read too damn fast. Or worse, a great book he'd read a little of and then left somewhere—a lonely subway, a bar, a nowhere diner—gone forever.

Her story was over.

Or was it?

This knot of mystery hadn't even started to unravel. Did forgotten pages of her life wait to be found in the shadows of bars, old motels, and dangerous streets?

Jake didn't doubt it for a second.

He reached down, trailing his fingertips through the remains of her, and saw her life with cinematic clarity: dancing on tabletops, violin flourishes onstage, nights in bondage, the sweaty sex for money.

He felt her pain and adventure as though it were his own.

Then in his mind he heard violins followed by a gauzy vision of a cloaked figure rushing about in shifting shadows.

"The mad violinist," Jake said, opening his eyes. "He was here. I believe he took the ashes, but I don't think he had anything to do with the...overdose."

"Who could've given her dope like that?" Moonshine asked.

He picked up the card again, inner-eye coming to life. "Now I'm seeing somebody besides the bald hawk-faced guy, a real low life. He's got money, but he's a loser."

"A secret admirer?" she mused. "Lots of secret admirers are

losers."

"This feels more like a stalker."

"A stalker with big bucks?" Marci laughed. "Every stripper needs one. I'm jealous. Anybody who ever stalked me was just plain crazy and broke."

He scowled in frustration, focusing hard on his clairvoyant vision-flashes. "I see two or three figures carrying on and drinking in this place, but I think they're just dope-boy flunkies with no power." He was silent a moment, then: "They've been here many times...and they've ripped her off. I'll bet they've taken her violin."

"Drug runners do that," Marci said.

"After they've taken your money and your soul," Moonshine added.

"So, if we find these dope-boys, they can lead us to the vulture-nosed dealer."

"Yeah. But the best place to start this investigation is with Hex at the *Dungeon*," Marci said. "That weasel will certainly know if someone is selling Rapture in his club."

Wind from the open window suddenly rushed through the room as though taking all Josephine's secrets away. Rose pedals settled back on the bed like drops of blood.

He suppressed a faint sob. "It would really help me if we just get the hell out of here."

Both girls ran their fingers through his hair. "We'll hook you up at the *Dungeon*," Marci said. "We both made a ton of money last weekend."

Chapter Four

In the downtown hotel district stood a neon-lit black brick building that was probably a hotel a hundred years ago. It should have been a turn-of-the-century landmark that ghost hunters died to explore.

Instead, it was a goth/bondage club.

There might be ghosts haunting the *Dungeon*, the premiere magic underground goth club of the Atlanta area, but it was hardly a historical dump where one would find a Discovery Channel documentary being made. The crafty entrepreneur, Hex, had turned this place into a high-end operation where Casters blended in with the goth and fetish crowd. For those who thought they were hot stuff and had money and dark fantasies, this was the place to be.

The last time Jake saw Hex, the club owner slipped him the novel he was reading now for the second time, James Elroy's *Black Dahlia*. He'd just gotten thrown out of a limo by the strip bar owner Alexis who'd foolishly attempted to take the Dual Serpent amulet off his neck.

Even though this was mainly a Darkened hangout, Marci and Moonshine were in here quite a bit. They gave hugs and high-fives to club scene kindred (other strippers mostly) as they made their way up three flights of candlelit stairs. Masterful demon/angel murals—scenes of sex and the bouts of supernatural titans—were showcased on the walls.

On the third floor, they walked down a long hallway lined with pillar candles clasped in the gnarled grasps of gargoyle statuary. Near the end of it, their leather heels clickety-clacked over illusion-triggering runes, which sent a flock of illusory ravens down the hallway. The macabre birds passed over their heads and flew out into the main dance chamber.

A big crowd of goths, gays, and bold mainstream revelers watched the night birds soar over the dance floor and shriek past a hanging candelabra before dissolving into mist and shadows. Many cast their eyes on Jake and the girls as they entered the dance chamber, the spectacle a dramatic harbinger of their arrival.

This main three-bar chamber was comparable to a decadent Roman extravaganza boasting beautiful velvet furniture arranged around the dance floor, darkly lit booths for darker conversations, and bondage artwork across walls painted black. The DJ was playing trance music laced with Gregorian chant and choir vocal looping.

Club owner Hex, sitting at the bar with ravishing bartender Abagail, eyed the gang. Surely, they had fascinating news. Watching them slide free of the crowd and reach the bar, he folded his arms and smiled knowingly like an amused smug psychic whose precognition never failed him.

The girls ordered drinks and shots for everybody, even Hex and the bartender, in the Bacchus club.

"I've met Josephine," Jake said, elbow propped on the bar. Abagail handed him a shot of Rumpleminz.

"Yeah," Marci said. "She was the all-time evil girl of his dreams. He'll write metal songs about her for ten years, at least."

Hex smiled triumphantly, his matchmaking complete. The strange little man came across as the complete German intellectualist poser package—a goatee, a silly director's cap (marking him as the great impresario of the goth circus), a black turtleneck, and dark hair slicked back to accentuate his widow's peak. He'd missed his calling to be a pro wrestler's sidekick manager.

"Ah, what a hot little dish she is. Did you two make beautiful music together?" Then he frowned. "What do you mean by '*was* the all-time evil girl of his dreams'?"

With a solemn country lyrical lilt, kind of comical (she hadn't meant to be funny), Moonshine said, "She's died under mysterious and dire circumstances."

Hex flared a thinly plucked manicured brow. "Oh really? Mysterious and dire, huh?"

"She took a drug that turned her to ashes." Marci showed him the full baggy. "I feel sure it's Rapture."

His eyes flicked to the baggy and went wide. "Oh it sure is. Our plot certainly has thickened. That's no street drug. That's arcane rich party shit. I don't even know of anyone using it in Atlanta. I have heard of bounty hunters from other areas getting their hands on it and selling it here and there from time to time. It's so expensive only high rollers within the kinky magic sex circles get it. For a two-bit local drug dealer to be selling it on the streets—"

"Somebody who wanted to woo her bad sure knew how to get it." Marci tossed back her shot. "We think she was getting stalked."

"Yeah. Did you ever see anyone following her around? A weirdo geek flashing money, maybe?"

Hex rolled his eyes. "This place isn't short of weirdos who would be after a girl that hot. Usually, though, she was alone or with this one blonde girl from her work. And as you well know, she mainly talked about wanting to meet you." He refilled everyone's shot glasses, Killer Bees this time (Jager and Rumple). "The few men she did come in here with were conservative money guys who were either tricks or sugar daddies." He scoffed, shaking a tumbler of Marci-tini ingredients. "They wouldn't have known where to get Rapture."

"Speaking of prostitution, she wasn't just hooking and playing sex games to pay for drugs. She was struggling to put together blood money for her Darkening. She thought she could bribe somebody to perform the rite."

Hex shrugged. "She could've. Why didn't she?"

"I don't know if it was simply a money issue or if it was because everyone feared her spurned master, this succubus goth violinist named Felicity. Apparently, everyone thought the bitch would come after them." Then she gave Hex her best schoolgirl smile of mischief. "I wouldn't be surprised if she'd approached you about all this. Did she ever talk to you about performing the Darkening rite of passage?"

He raised an eyebrow then finally tossed back his own shot. "She'd ask questions about my knowledge of the Darkened rite, but then the conversation would get back to our rock celebrity here. God, she'd reminded me of Elizabeth Short, mysterious and desperate...our Black Dahlia. That's why I thought I'd done great things by sending her his way." He smiled at the singer like a snake. "What exactly did she want from you?"

"She mainly wanted me to run off with her before Felicity got to town. Do you know anything about her band Dire Portent?"

"Yeah. Her act is quite huge in the magic/illusion circuit."

"Felicity was obsessed with having Josephine back in the band by any means necessary."

"Ah, no wonder she was scared as hell."

"To be honest, I might actually have put together a band with her, but she would've eventually wanted me to go through my Darkening. I wasn't about to do that." He reached for a freshly poured shot and went on reflectively. "The whole idea that I'm hybrid really turned her on. It seems to be the biggest deal to anyone who learns about me. I'm such—"

"An enigma," Hex finished, making a thoughtful face. "My guess, though, is once you open up your Darkened appetites you would fall apart rather fast."

"That's the smartest thing I've ever heard you say." Marci patted his arm. "I'm so proud of you."

He smirked, and then his eyes flared with sudden realization. "Oh, here comes Bonding Weekend. That would certainly explain the demand for rare drugs, and Felicity is sure to be at the battle of the bands show. You better hope she doesn't know about you."

Jake shook his head, groaning. "Josephine told me Felicity wants me in her band, too. She intends to kidnap me and make me sing, in fact."

Hex's hands flew together in a loud celebratory clap. "Oh, this is all too good."

Marci made a gesture like she'd slap him. "You're supposed to be on our side." Then she nodded ruefully and cleared her throat. "We're not here just for kicks. We want to stop the Rapture dealer behind all this. The problem is we really didn't learn much about Josephine before she died. Did she ever mention to you where she danced? She wouldn't tell me."

Hex slipped two orange slices on a sugar-rimmed martini glass. "Yes, but I can't remember. I would try *Shadows* or, oh yeah, *Pulse*. Darkened girls are really getting into the scene there. I do remember a few things now about the blonde girl Josephine came in with a few times. She always wore jerseys like a college cheerleader. She was a total girl next door, never wearing club gear. One night, she was arguing with an attorney who talked a lot about his trips to Vegas, drugs, and hookers. He seemed to know them both pretty damn well." He thought a moment and snapped his fingers. "Peter was his name. I wouldn't be surprised if he were the blonde girl's sugar daddy. Anyway, those two talked a lot about her borrowing his car on the weekends and the wild constant partying at his house. My guess is some escort service may as well set up shop there."

Marci chuckled. "Do you remember blondie's name?"

"I want to say Amy. It started with an A. What I do remember was a cool snake and apple tattoo above her ass, that Garden of Eden kind of thing. Maybe that'll help you find her."

"Well, it's a lead." She ordered more shots and proposed a toast. "Here's to new quests." Then she, Moonshine, and Jake clinked double-shot glasses of Killer Bees.

Well, here was what was on the mystery platter: A musically brilliant goth girl who'd destroyed herself before she could be hunted down by her Dominant, a mystery blonde college girl who was probably far from being any mere girl-next-door, and a pimp daddy attorney who probably ran his posh pad like a brothel. Oh what a cocktail.

The investigation would begin with a forbidden apple. It made sense to Jake.

Chapter Five

J ake and the gang weren't the only ones on a quest. Minstrel was on a mission, too.

Hopping out of a cab, he moved purposefully down a dark side street toward club *Pulse*. In front of the neon-lit building, he paused to play violin for a small crowd of cheering street rabble just for kicks. One homeless man danced a jig to it like a court jester, hoping someone would tip him. A bouncer who was sick of it all finally tipped the derelict five dollars and told the bunch to scram.

The violinist breezed past the bouncer and strode into *Pulse* with the air of an aristocrat looking for a wayward mistress. Was he ever the coolest cat at the club with his hip modern day vagabond street look: a deep purple velvet frock coat over a Nox Arcana T-shirt, the print in calligraphy, and a sheer black scarf twined around his bristly throat. There was even an artful rip in one knee of his jeans. The look was topped off with studded boots bearing big silver buckles, pricey Doc Martens.

He rushed dashingly up to the girls, playing hypnotic flourishes as he gazed into their eyes. Oh what charm. What panache. It was as though a mad fiddler had been sent by the devil to claim souls in the Atlanta strip bar scene.

The get-up should've been comically absurd, yet he aroused serious intrigue from onlookers. Was he a famous magician? A performer in Cirque du Soleil? Such questions were typically posed about him.

Indeed, he was a magician, but he was no Chris Angel. He was a Darkened Caster, and music and illusion were his dice in a supernatural game.

He wandered about the place, his bright smile a masterpiece of social artifice. He really did enjoy this strip bar, though, even if he were here on serious business. The sprawl of girls on slick leather furniture, awash in eerie crimson light, imparted the sleazy comfort of the brothels he frequented in Europe. The girls even looked like bored hookers, watching cars go by.

This feeling of lazy decadence was enriched by the DJ's current set—the heavy lush sound of the band Ghost doing their version *It's a Sin* by Pet Shop Boys. The music was being played for a swaying girl with an expression of druggy languor on her face.

She was one of many Darkened who danced here, as this place was a bastion for Darkened dancers in this city.

He headed to the bar, gazing at himself in the mirror behind tiers of top-shelf liquor. He primped, movie-set ready, tossing his long ropey hair back. He had a profile that belonged on a coin, his nose an arrow, stubbly chin bearing a slight cleft.

A girl came up to him, asking to hear his classical wizardry, but he had no time for virtuoso histrionics at the moment. He'd play for her later if he were in the mood. He might even use an aural hex on her to sway her to bed. It remained to be seen what the night had in store for him.

He ordered a martini then ran a silver-ringed finger over the lip of the glass as he plotted out his night. He didn't need anything else to go wrong. His time in Atlanta was turning out to be a complete misadventure full of lonely late night wandering and bad midnight trysts.

And now Josephine was dead.

His eyes slid along the bobbing heads of dancing girls, searching for Abbey. He spotted her during a dance pop set with Katie Perry and Brittany Spears songs in it.

In this place of gothic drear, she was different with her girl-next-door look and esprit attitude. Blond hair bouncing, she came across as too much of an all-American cute thing to be dancing here. He knew, though, she was not innocent. Sordid stories got around, mainly involving Josephine.

Oh, and look at that tattoo. There's was nothing like snakes and apples.

"Womanizer" was playing when he met her eyes. Parading over to her platform, he began playing a violin accompaniment to the sassy song, flinging his long hair in pop dance star mockery.

Many of the girls got the biggest kick out of him, but Abbey was not one of them. The sight of him quickened a look of fury on her face. When she finished her set, she pattered quickly with the guys who'd tipped her and headed straight over to him.

He rushed toward her, arms outstretched in appeal. "Abbey, love, how are you fairing?" His loud strident voice was like a sloppy discordant note he'd play drunk.

She folded her arms, scowling. Hair thrown over one shoulder, she looked like a sorority girl mad at her boyfriend. "I'm not *fairing* well at all." Her lips snapped together, a grim line forming. "Can you tell me where Star is?" This was Josephine's stage name.

He flared an eyebrow then drew the bow over the violin strings. He was plying no magic, but the fluidity of the dulcet tones still drew attention. "No, dear heart," he lied.

She scowled, eyes burning. "You may have freaked her out so bad she left town. She won't even answer my texts."

He played a quick flourish on his violin. "For a shot of tequila, would you mind telling me where her...uh, connections hung out? I have a feeling they know where she is."

She groaned, rolling her eyes. "I-I don't need a shot, but if those guys have done something to her..." Then against her better judgment, she told him where the dead stripper often met her dope boys.

He nodded, a big smile spreading across his face. "Thank you. I've been needing to speak with these gentlemen for a while."

She straightened her thong, sighing in despair. "Don't come in here and bother me again," she said, eyes ablaze, and moved on to do a table dance.

***

Minstrel showed up at a dive bar on Ponce called *The Spot*. He was ready for a showdown, his gun a violin.

College kids shot pool, played darts, and swilled pitchers of cheap beer. The walls were covered with signed rock posters and neon beer signs. *Hotel California* by the Eagles played on the jukebox. Who'd think runners of arcane dope were hanging out here?

A drunk sorority girl looked at him as though he were a famous actor. Then a group of them started arguing over who he could be.

"Are they filming an X-Men movie in town?" a girl asked.

"Yeah, but that dude belongs in *Pirates of the Caribbean*."

The violinist overheard it and chuckled, posing like a celebrity at the bar. One girl was particularly drawn to his mystique. They made eye contact, and he approached her, playing a quick flashy piece that made the girl clap. Jealousy was in the eyes of the guys around her.

She leaped up from the table, throwing herself at him. "Hi, I'm Katy. I tried to learn violin in high school and couldn't get anywhere with it. You're amazing. What were you playing?"

"Ah, what you just heard, my dear, is Niccolo Paganini, the greatest virtuoso of all time."

"Hey, wasn't he rumored to have made a pact with the devil for his talent?"

"Yes, my dear." He slung a shot down his throat and winked. "You never know who's gone to the dark side for forbidden gifts."

Her eyes grew wide in little-girl terror.

"Care to hear more?"

"Um, yeah." She looked back at her table of buddies. "They can wait."

This girl was already in his web. He played dulcet enchanted tones like a spider ensnaring its prey. She listened, mesmerized.

Everyone at the table laughed at her because they didn't realize how truly spellbound she was.

"I'm staying at the Highland Inn in Little Five Points," he told her, lowering the instrument. "Room sixty three. My name is Minstrel. Just drop by and I'll play some more for you."

She ran her teeth over her bottom lip. "I'd love to hear some more music." And he had every intention of making beautiful music with her.

Sliding his eyes away, he turned his attention to the beach bum bartender. "I'll take a vodka martini."

The bartender gave him a curious look and then smiled broadly. "Are you in theater? You know it's not Halloween."

"The world is a stage, my dear." He drank by himself at the bar until three guys came in. They were the ones he'd seen at Josephine's apartment many times. They'd used her for sex—he'd felt it in the deep of night by her window—and ripped off her violin he'd given her to pay for dope. That was outrage he would not abide. Plus they'd brought her the Rapture—that made them murderers in his book.

And the blood of her murderers was what he needed for his ritual to bring her back.

He drank while he watched them shoot pool for the longest time. Finally, he just couldn't help himself. He began to play.

The balls on the pool tables began to swerve and zip about erratically the faster he played.

One of the scruffy guys eyed the violinist. "Do you think that goofball over there has something to do with this?"

"Yeah, he's watching us. There's something fucked up about all of this. Let's get out of here."

They paid their tabs and headed out to a back parking lot. They were in their cars when the violinist slipped out of the shadows.

"Here's a little tune for my three blind mice," he exclaimed, playing frantically, sparks flying from nimble fingers as he whispered an incantation.

Spectral gossamer floated in a loose wreath from the strings like trained cobras. Glyphs flashed on the instrument like lights in Vegas.

It was show time!

The conjured spirits took the form of hags out of Shakespeare's *Hamlet* and raced madly across the parking lot like prisoners escaping a dungeon after untold years. Their ragged flowing garb trailed behind them like morbid kites.

And were these demons ever hungry.

Minstrel laughed hysterically, a keening banshee cry, as the three rushed for their cars in blind hysteria. Oh, this was better than being at the drive-in on Labor Day.

The first dope-boy was so coked out of his mind he had a heart attack at the sight of the monstrosity. He never even reached his car. He just collapsed in a paroxysm. The second punk managed to jump in and screech out onto the street, but a wailing hag spirit smashed through the windshield and ripped through him, exploding out the back of the driver's seat. Entrails streamed from the mouth of the flying zombie bitch as it left the demolished flipping car. Never try to outrace the devil.

The finale was a fine spectacle of demon-starved butchery. The chump was struggling to get the car door open as the demon swept down. It surged into his body in a flash of pulsing iridescent light, possessing him, eyes bulging and then exploding, body and soul ripped apart. The guy crumpled like a razed building as the dark spirit rushed out of empty bleeding eye sockets in an inky effluvium. Balls to the wall!

Minstrel reached into the victim's gory remains and picked up a cell phone dripping with blood—perfect for his ritual.

Shouts came from the back of the bar, prompting him to make a dramatic exit. Playing a flashy lick, he vanished into thin air.

Blocks away he reappeared, prancing off like a leprechaun, playing the devil's solo part in *The Devil Went Down To Georgia*. He always did think the devil should've won that contest.

Minstrel called an Uber that dropped him off next to a row of condemned buildings. His destination was a playground near there.

He kept the stripper's ashes in a silver box nestled in the branches on an oak tree near a swing set. There was a young girl sitting there when he arrived—or rather the ghost of a girl.

"My friend disappeared when you showed up," the girl said. "I wish you hadn't scared her off. She's my only friend."

Minstrel smiled. "Oh, your friend will be back. I assure you. She's just waiting on me to...pull a few strings." He cleared his throat. "Would you like to hear me play?"

"Oh yes."

He played in a wild frenzy. She danced like a wild gypsy girl to the music, laughing merrily. "Will you bring back my friend?"

"Soon she'll be back for good. For now, though, you must run along. What I have to do right now is *scary*...even for the ghost of a girl."

She ran from the playground, the patter of her feet dissolving in the shadows along with her body, claimed by the night.

On a crumbling sidewalk shattered by encroaching roots, he drew an elaborate sigil with black chalk. Within a circle, he drew a pentacle, the sigil at the center of it. Then he placed ashes at all six points of the star. He then buried the silver box containing the rest of her ashes under shards of concrete. He then placed the bloody cell phone over the sigil.

"Ah, the death of your murderers should sway your will," he

whispered to the night.

He spoke an incantation in Latin that brought a great wind through the complex of old burnt buildings. Thunder rumbled and lightning flashed across the sky.

Smoke rose from the center of the pentacle, thickening into a writhing black mass of serpentine grotesqueries. This was followed by a rush of sound that was not the wind, but the conjuring of a spirit. It, too, entered the circle though it was invisible.

A roiling shadowy mass morphed into the form of a girl. It was like artwork slowly unveiling itself, sliding free from curtains of darkness, a butterfly woman emerging from a dark metaphysical chrysalis.

She floated upward, clad in studded leather and velvet, her ghostly nubile form turning the sky into a gothic masterpiece. For a moment, she merely hovered like a super heroine (Get the first issue of Demon Babe Mutant!) becoming one with the night. Then she floated to the ground as she took form in flesh. Glyphs of magic shimmered around her and then faded away.

"Oh, I have indeed brought you back to the flesh," he said in hushed awe.

She left the circle and floated over to the swing. She clasped the chains and swung like she herself was a little girl.

The demon overtaking her spirit was to be applauded. It truly did look like Josephine. The dark spirit used her soul and its magic to bring her back. Was he seeing her or a demon, though? Who knew how a lost soul and a devil would mix.

"Oh, I am alive again," she called out. Her face held an expression of addled ecstasy. "It's wonderful, yet you are not one to be trusted. You have bound me to a demon."

He shook his head in dismissive frustration. "You would've wandered the world as an angry spirit forever."

She vaguely nodded. "Now I will be hunted forever while I cling to this world."

"Are you serious?" He gasped. "You have experienced a rebirth that other spirits—"

"Would die for?" She laughed, stopped swinging, and ran bejeweled fingertips over her arms, gently tugging at strands of her hair. Then she looked around, smiling wistfully. "I wrote poetry here. There's a special little girl who comes to see me here. She'll return if you leave."

"Yes, I will leave you for now," he responded indignantly. "I'll go and retrieve what was stolen by those dope-boys. Do you still have your books of poetry?"

She sighed. "I feel sure my journals are all at my place. No dope-boy wants something from your heart he can't sell. They should all be stacked next to my psycho letters."

"What psycho letters?"

"They came from a crazy secret admirer. He was the one getting me Rapture. I don't know why that loser wanted me so badly."

"So you know who this is?"

"I have a pretty good idea about this and many other things, but you don't need to be concerned with any of it."

Minstrel's eyes darted about as his thoughts raced with possibilities. "Okay, you don't want me in your private affairs. Is there anything else I should know?"

Her eyes went distant. "I gave Jake Reece a journal. I wrote poetry and prose about many things including this playground. If he's good at explicating verse and prose, he could find this place, my secret sanctuary."

Now this did alarm Minstrel—forget stalkers. "That rock singer has it? He most certainly doesn't need to be privy to the whereabouts of this ritual site. He and those stripper girls are going to be enough trouble as it is. Felicity will be very unhappy about this."

She swung again gently, chains creaking. "I don't see where I have a use for Felicity anymore."

He raised his eyebrows. "The demon hosting in you is not so powerful. You may need her magic to pull through to this world completely. You'll see soon enough when your new flesh becomes hungry."

A druggy pleasure spread over her face, and she swung harder, her interest in him gone. "Very well."

In disgust, he left to get drunk and make further plans. He'd enjoy this private victory without her at his side.

***

Toward dawn in his darkened motel room, Minstrel sensed

her presence before the rattling of furniture began.

"Josephine?" he whispered.

Demonic energy asserted itself, and Josephine strained for the physical realm. She was part flesh/part ghost, ectoplasm becoming a firm body with delicious curves, flowing darkness becoming black tresses. She tore off her clothing, black lace panties and a bra falling to the floor.

Those green eyes were fixed on Minstrel, feral with lust. "You always wanted me. I'm here now for you. My new flesh needs you."

The succubus slinked toward him. Without another thought, he fell prey, pushing everything off the bed so he could lay prostrate to this beautiful dark creature. Whether it was a demon or femme fatale mattered little to him.

"I feel like some fallen city." He laughed, as he was used to the role of seducer in sex games, not submissive.

And seduced he was. A heavy sigh rippled with giddy laughter as she peeled away his frippery. Would Marquis de Sade be envious of his ghost sex? Maybe Minstrel, too, would wind up in an asylum after this, and the great libertine of lore would feel vindicated.

Her fingernails dug into his chest, and pleasure and pain became the same as she rode him. Now she was very, very solid, supple, and moist. He exploded into this lush revenant of a girl who would've never been with him in her former life (She detested him). It was euphoria opening doorways to new addiction.

Before her curves reverted back to spectral mist and dark shadows, she whispered, "Jake will read every line of that journal to find me..." And then she was gone.

He got dressed, body thrumming with sex magic, his mind racing with anxiety. Jake and those girls needed to be dealt with, but all he could think of was having that sexy nightmare again.

Later, he went back to the playground to set up wards around it. Children, both ghostly and living, could come here and play, but no psychic would ever find it.

Chapter Six

Benjamin Crow was sketching illustrations for a new fantasy role playing game when his phone rang. It was none other than Thorn. "Hello?" He was already on edge.

"Benjie boy, you've got trouble. I highly suggest you come see me right away."

Benjie boy? Ben felt panic coil in his gut. "What? I've paid you for everything. What's—"

"Just get to *The Basement* pronto."

He dressed and rushed out. He was glad to see Peter wasn't home yet. The tension between them had been bad lately.

He raced away from Peter's house in the red Camaro he'd just bought with his recent inheritance and made it downtown as fast as possible.

The Basement was just that—a basement bar at the bottom of a dumpy hotel on Spring Street. Local blues bands played there, and third-rate girls came in off the street to hustle free drinks and tricks. It was a cool hangout joint for restaurant/adult entertainment industry people who wanted to avoid mainstream bars. This meant everyone from hard-drinking strippers to fine-dining booze-hound waiters came here every night to whoop it up. Many were here to find dope.

It was Seventies Disco Night, and Donna Summer was blaring through the door at the bottom of a metal staircase. Benjamin trudged down the steps to the dimly lit bar, knowing it would be crowded as disco hell. Nevertheless, he would spot Thorn right away. His dramatic appearance of striking glam menace was unmistakable. In his thirties, he was bald with a tattooed crown of thorns around his head, smoldering eyes accentuated by eyeliner. He held a humped beak nose high in the air that belonged on a vicious bird of prey, the ultimate king pin Raptor. He wore a fur coat that was stolen in a heist along with black latex lace-up pants. Girls loved him, but he was ruthless, a gay playboy with a bad temper.

Benjamin found him in a back booth; his brooding face flickered in candlelight. Groaning, Ben jostled his way through the retro-crowd across the bar. He was scared to death of Thorn, but the man was too dangerous and powerful for him to ignore. Still, he felt like the drug dealer's bitch. He even looked like he should be Thorn's toady. A failed gamer with a ratty shock of dyed black hair and a noir Joker Rising T-shirt, he came across like an overweight goth-misfit comic book collector. The truth was he dealt with the dealer as little as possible.

Thorn thought the wannabe high-roller was annoying. He was too paranoid and nervous, as his habitual high-strung finger tapping underscored his fidgeting demeanor.

The anxious loser had been in and out of drug rehabs since high school, a complete loner who knew nothing of real friends or popularity. He *truly* was a genius gamer, illustrator, and board game concept creator, but his partying and bi-polar behavior had sabotaged all efforts to succeed. He was considered to be crazy, and jokes of his nerdy neurosis abounded about him.

Even the losers get lucky sometimes, though. He had fallen on an ace card: a big inheritance from a rich uncle (no one else in the family talked to him) who passed away. He'd finally won in a big, big way.

Tonight, he was more nervous than usual, rocking back and forth in the booth when he sat down like he was geeking on meth. "What's going on?" He felt like his life was a rollercoaster about to fly off the tracks.

"Your interest in sex magic romance compelled you to approach me about getting Rapture for you. Correct?" Thorn asked in his velvety voice of prim condescension. He was filing his fingernails, shooting glances up at Benjamin.

"Yeah, sure. You never front me anything, though. Why are you acting like I owe you?"

"Oh, it's not the money. It's the situation you've put me in. The fantasy girl you wanted so badly has met her demise."

"What?" He gasped.

"Her dope-boys watched her turn to ash. They even brought a pinch of her back to confirm her death." He bounced a small baggy of ash in the air. "Only a full-blown Caster can take Rapture with little risk. She wasn't any witch, Benjie boy. You got Rapture for a girl who either didn't know or care that it could kill her."

Ben threw out his hands in frazzled appeal. "I had every reason to believe she was magical. I've seen her play violin. I saw sparks fly from the strings while she played. How was I to think she wasn't a witch?"

"You saw sparks fly," Thorn repeated musingly. "Trust me, Benjie boy, she hadn't gone through her rite of passage into the real deal. That means she was still in dormancy." Clearing his throat, he ordered another cognac without offering anything to Benjamin. "Now I can understand why you wanted this girl bad enough to get a magical horny drug, but your obsession has caught up with you. Here I am an up and coming dealer in the arcane drug scene, and I've made myself look like a fool for trusting you. The spell cookbook containing the Rapture recipe was consigned to me to make a batch for a select circle of Darkened. It was meant for a big party Bonding Weekend. This is a wealthy bunch that will have no problem sending hunters after me if they find out I'm making money on the side with my own batch. Are you getting the picture?"

Benjamin was shaking. "Yes, yes, I get it. What now? What do I do?"

Thorn sipped from the fresh snifter and then went back to work on his haughty fingernail project. "Here's the biggest problem. I've gotten word that some bad hunter chicks are on my trail. They're asking questions around town. The girl you were stalking was apparently schmoozing with a metal singer boy who knows these bad bitches real well, especially Marci Stone." He dropped the fingernail file and reached over the table to grab Benjamin's wrist. His gaze was withering. "I'm hearing all this grandiose mythological shit about this singer that totally and completely freaks me the fuck out. You need to get them off my trail. Quick. Before I stop trying to convince myself not to kill you."

Ben snatched his arm free, trembling hand flying to his mouth. "I'll handle it. I'll find a way. I've got money. Just give me time."

"Bonding Weekend is coming up. I intend to make a lot of

money with Rapture that weekend. I don't need interference. I'm giving you three days to deal with those girls and that singer, or your show is over."

"Oh don't worry. I'll put together a plan."

"Alright, Benjie baby. Now's your chance to prove you can run with the big dogs...or else."

***

Benjamin went back to this room at Peter's house, turned on music, and collapsed on the bed. Fuck. What had he done?

He listened to Queensyrche's *Operation Mindcrime* over and over: a prog-metal eighties concept album about a heroin addict used by the government, a corrupt priest, and the hooker he loved. The epic *Suite Sister Mary* was a syncopated operatic piece of heavy metal mastery, punctuated with dark reflective interludes.

It seemed his life should be stitched into the storyline somehow. He listened again and again, dwelling on it. The music echoed his strange life and desperation.

Through the pound of power chords could be heard a faint stirring sound. He shot up from the bed to behold a sketch pad floating in the air. It suddenly flopped to the floor, and then a closet door creaked open.

When the first curvy shadows slid over the walls, he felt her. He knew.

He packed frantically, grabbing everything that mattered to him. He'd find a motel room and never come back here.

Peter could have this haunted house to himself.

In his new flashy car, he scrolled through his contacts, seeking the number of the amulet dealer he met a few weeks ago.

Chapter Seven

Medusa's was full of the ragtag regulars that Jake knew so well he could make their drinks the minute he spotted them coming in.

"Oh Jake," Mr. Ruke said. "When will you be done with your hit novel?"

"When are you going to drown in one of your martinis?" he retorted while writing furiously on his manuscript. His writing had become more driven than ever. The book was the only way he could really hold onto her. He dropped his pen when another shout for a drink came, though.

The late afternoon was another sing-a-long bar festival of wild late night portent. There was a chorus of drunken servers and bartenders singing along to *California Dreamin'*. Strippers were getting up on the bar. Roxy Rachel and Secret had already been thrown out for fighting with each other and then let back in when they showed up at the door together, crying. Some guy was even caught looking at porn in the bathroom stall. If things kept up, tonight could make history in the chronicles of crazy nights.

A waitress regular he called "Hippy Chick" because she only listened to early seventies music played an old Doors song Jake loved. "I'll tip you ten if you'll drink a shot out of my navel," she said, lying across the bar in front of Jake. She stared over at Mr. Ruke, who was regarding her like something he'd step on.

Jake poured the *Black Dahlia* shot he was famous for into her navel as a small crowd cheered him on. He lowered his head, and as if bobbing for apples, he slurped up the sweet concoction while she ran her fingers through his mane. He started laughing and spewed most of the shot onto her stomach.

"Damn, Jake, you're losing your touch." She slid off the bar. "I should've gotten Secret to do it."

"Secret wouldn't get near you with her mouth," Mr. Ruke

remarked disdainfully and returned to whatever thick, deep intellectual book he was reading. It appeared to be *Fountainhead* by Anne Ryan.

Jake made a row of *Black Dahlias*, telling everyone again about the twenties actress Elizabeth Short who was murdered, the killer never found. Mr. Ruke went off on a pontifical tangent about the murder, but Jake upstaged him, reading pages out loud from a fifties pulp fiction novel about gambling, drinking, and damsels in distress. He made sound effects with glasses and ice, turning the bar scene into a vintage radio show. Even some of the girls who normally didn't listen to him gave him rapt attention. Girls always liked to hear about other girls getting in trouble.

It was nice to have fans in this place. He felt like this bartending job was all he had after the whole record deal fell apart. Jake was a modern day Jim Morrison as far as many were concerned, but he was also constantly being told how bad the dining room manager, Stephanie, was talking about him when he wasn't there. Some said everyone was jealous of him, his success just a matter of time, but he still worried his destiny was waiting tables and slinging drinks until the day he died.

He recalled reading in a psychology textbook that depression and low self-esteem were the two most common psychological problems in American society. This wasn't difficult for him to believe. He had a bad case of both. What pill do you take to treat "rock singer in ruins" syndrome? Did fallen angels feel like this? What drugs do they take?

Failure to reach stardom was the least of his problems right now, however. Marci finally cracked the whip about his couch surfing, so he'd forced himself to go back to Clara's. He took the attitude that as long as he came home really drunk he could handle her.

And did he ever handle her.

He wound up banging her, and she told every-fucking-body. Was it ever time to get the hell out that apartment *for good*. The imperious wine connoisseur was going experimental-sex-psycho on him, wanting to play all sorts of kinky games. He was going to wind up like that poor guy in Stephen King's *Misery*. Josephine had given him a big enough taste of bondage.

He wrote a few more pages to pass the time. As he feared, the night turned into an exhibition of Roxy Rachel's druggy antics, heavy drinking drag queen drama, and rowdy waitresses gone wild. It was starting to look like he'd never get the place cleaned up so he could escape.

He heard the clatter of dishes in the dish room and cringed. One shattered, followed by hyena laughter from the dishwasher. He loved the insane dishwasher, but he didn't need any comedic delays stalling his night plans.

An annoying text from his live-in stalker roommate came around midnight. He ignored it.

At last call there was the usual tableau of drag queens, drunken waitresses, and gay couples with stories of twisted romance. He listened to their sordid stories as he wiped off pictures of female icons the place was famous for. Then he extricated panties, scarves, and ties from the poor Medusa statue.

Finally, it was New York last call time: "Alright, everybody, you don't have to go home, but you've got to get the hell out of here."

After locking up, he headed out like a lovelorn vampire on the hunt for sex, thrills, love and adventure—whichever came first would do. The point was, the night scene was calling him.

His cell phone rang. The music was a snippet from Dino Jelusic's band Animal Drive, their metal version of the eighties song *The Look*.

"Are you about to get off from work?" Marci asked.

"I just left."

"You need to meet me. There's been a murder, and Fred is at the crime scene."

***

One of the main reasons Jake was excited about this night was because he finally had a car again after handling his D.U.I. hassles. It was a clunker he found on Craig's List, but he knew when he saw the car, it was for him. It bore decals by a Seventies throwback. The dented bumper displayed a Jefferson Airplane sticker on one side and Black Sabbath on the other. Early heavy metal and psychedelic music was a great balance of taste. He had to have the car.

He drove to the crime scene, metal music blasting. Fred

Waters was waiting in the bar parking lot with Marci at his side. Yellow police tape was everywhere, though the paranormal forensic team was long gone.

Jake got out of the car. "I can't wait to hear this."

Fred nodded in disbelief, blowing out a sigh. "What was described to me by someone from the bar came right out of the nightmare world of magic. It had to have been spirits or demons or whatever. This is the remains of one of the three victims." He pointed at a mound of ashes. "Forensics is waiting on your input before they bag it. Please don't touch it if you can help it."

The singer squatted and held his splayed hands over the ashes. A vision of a shadow-veiled figure in the throes of feverish violin playing surged through his mind. A clairaudient streak of dazzling notes came to him with such vivid force he shuddered.

"Our violinist has struck," Jake said. "I do believe he has avenged the death of Josephine."

"Josephine?" Fred asked.

"A girl from our *nightmare* world."

Fred just nodded, straightening a fedora. "I see." He was a diminutive bulbous-nosed troll of man who was often called a clown without makeup. He was ugly in that strange way that conjured thoughts of caricatures. There was a theatrical air about him that detracted from his passionate desire to be taken seriously. He might belong on South Park, but he did run Fulton County Paranormal Investigations. Marci was who he called when he was at wit's end.

"I'm certainly counting on you to help me with this," he said to both of them.

Marci nodded. "The fun's just started. Trust me."

She and Jake walked away to talk a moment. "How did that violinist do this?"

"I think he conjured demons with music," Jake said and started crooning lyrics to *The Devil Went Down To Georgia.*

She cut her eyes toward Fred. "Let me go deal with Dick Tracy. We'll meet later at the *Dungeon.*"

He hung out at a few party spots off Pharr Road before heading to the bondage/goth hot spot to meet Marci. He breezed in the door like a star, no cover, no hassle. It was the first time he'd felt like a million bucks in a while.

He heard pounding industrial dance music that was tantamount to hell's soundtrack blasting through its gates, but it was a sound his night-starved heart welcomed.

He saw this dark subculture as a modern counterpart to the old noir Hollywood days, so he felt like he was doing research just by heading into the entrance. The goth world was the juncture where romance and nightmares merged, and intellectualism met dark poetic thought—all of it stemming from lost searching souls expressing themselves through fashion, literature, music, and art. The darkest parts of the soul could bring the greatest revelations.

In this fantasy world, he could find himself. Darkness opened doorways to sinful adventure.

Tonight, the club was very eclectic in clientele. It wasn't just a leather and latex bondage crowd. On the first floor, throngs of girls and guys who looked like they stepped out of a soap opera sipped martinis on groupings of leather furniture.

Above them was a Vlad the Impaler mural—a hazy castle on a rocky precipice surrounded by the vague eerie suggestion of bodies impaled on stakes. Armored horsemen were galloping across a drawbridge through a pall of mist toward it. No one seemed to think anything of it.

The flickering shadows of go-go cages thrown by candlelight covered the mural, lending a lurid eroticism to this image of medieval brutality. On a platform beneath the cages, tattooed dancers twisted and twirled as though they were enacting some exotic ritual.

He jostled his way to the bar, eyes reflecting sensual shadowy faces full of dark promises. Calling out a drink order to a morbidly thin bartender with dyed dreadlocks and a nose ring, he tossed down a twenty. The bartender poured a Red Bull into a glass of Skyy vodka. He snatched it up and chugged it. Then he made his way to the manic dance floor.

He slipped into a velvet chair next to an alcove where a gay couple made out. The dancing was like a mosh pit of frantic sensuality.

He closed his eyes, feeling the music going inward. For a while at least, he forgot all his problems. His annoying life was chased away by pounding beats. Lights danced behind his closed eyelids, and the mix of incense and cigarette smoke wafted around him, pleasantly intoxicating.

Opening his languid eyes, he spotted a group of waitresses from the sushi bistro down the street from *Medusa's*. They were ogling gay guys and laughing.

He headed over, hearing, "I'd let that one queen do me on the pool table." She was pointing at two muscle-bound men in leather harnesses.

One of the girls rushed up to him. "Where have you been? I haven't seen you out in weeks."

"Oh, I've been out *a lot*. I'm dealing with psycho-bitch codependency."

She giggled.

"That's the best kind of codependency," one said, eyes lighting up in mockery. "They call it true love."

"Love I really can't handle."

Everyone laughed at his self-deprecation but looked him up and down all the while. He might not have a record contract, but the label certainly didn't take his looks from him. He was forever the conceited fop, all that beautiful hair crowning a face made for headshots. He was slim and cut, wearing a sleek black leather coat over micro-mesh, lace-up Doc Martens and vinyl slacks. A rock photographer's dream, he was just too pretty to be a guy.

The girls were talking about going to the new gay bar on Cheshire Bridge Road when his eyes met Josephine's doppelganger.

The femme fatale leaned hipshot against the bar, holding a tube of lipstick as though it were a weapon. She wore a black trench coat and a fedora, tilted rakishly, her mystique stolen from the fantasies of film noir. Crime novelist Mickey Spillane would've envied the sight of this girl, those black clad curves of cream shrouded in cloak and shadow, long raven hair thrown to one side.

In the neon light, her piercing green eyes were verdant portals to a world she held enthralled.

Their eyes met, and as he fell into that fiery verdure, an overriding cold sensation washed over him. An eerie tingling trailed behind it.

Was she a ghost? How?

He didn't see how. He'd never seen such a complete physical

manifestation or seen such eloquence in a spirit's eyes, a commingling of want, hurt, and a siren's drive to seduce.

There was a play of pierced tongue between parted lips, and then she beckoned him with a single slender finger, a black lacquered fingernail reflecting laser light.

"Come to me," she mouthed silently.

And he was hers—a possession.

He floated across the floor, his pulse quickening as the music's tempo increased, throbbing faster and dragging his pulse rate with it. A group of girls flounced in front of him, blocking his view. He skirted them in irritation and found...

No one. She'd vanished into thin air.

He nodded with growing certainty. She was most likely spectral, but that just made this situation all the more intriguing.

"Did you talk to a really pretty girl with long flowing black hair?" he asked at the bar.

"Where?"

"Standing right here."

The busy bartender shrugged. "Nope."

It didn't appear anyone mortal could see her. Yeah, the ghost theory was holding up. Still, he wanted to find her. There was nothing like a good ghost hunt. Besides, spirits never came to him with seduction in their eyes. They normally just tore his furniture up and taunted him with his addictions.

He emerged from the club, windswept, feeling a vague sense of failure. He was pleasantly loaded, though, and felt playful.

Neon light threw his shadow across the sidewalk. On odd impulse, he lifted his coat like a cape. Now his shadow belonged to the Phantom of the Opera.

He loved anything theatrically macabre, but he didn't need to look like a fool out here. With his luck, he'd get arrested.

Deep in thought, he found himself wandering aimlessly. He was headed past the Five Points Marta station when he spotted his night club noir siren again.

Her garb was different now, a windswept gauzy black dress pressed against the curves of her body, laced bell sleeves fluttering. A studded choker around her alabaster neck made him think of some ethereal heavy metal queen, yet she was really too elegant for such a description. It didn't do her justice. She belonged to another century, a world of debauchery run by Marquis de Sade.

Then to his dismay, the girl melted into the shadows as though all she'd ever been was a shadow herself.

He raced into the Marta entranceway like a thief on the run, the clack of his Doc Martens echoing throughout the station.

She's in here, he thought desperately. *She has to be.* He rushed up to a turnstile and jammed a slew of quarters into the machine; several clattered to the concrete. Then he rushed down a flight of steps to an empty platform in time to see the ghostly vamp enter one of the cars just as the door slid shut behind her.

"No," he exclaimed, running up to the window. "Talk to me," he pleaded with the ethereal beauty, but her face was one of inscrutable pallor, her eyes cutting from his.

The train rumbled off, taking his heart with it and leaving the rest of him in the desolation of the echoing Marta station.

He turned from the tracks and walked away, feeling abandoned. This was all he needed in the wake of his lost love Charm running off, leaving him with only an amulet and that damn letter.

Then he spotted something sparkle in the station's lighting. Frowning, he walked several feet and leaned down to pick up the piece of jewelry. It was a large ornate silver crucifix suspended from a black crushed-velvet choker.

He held it up to dirty sodium light, reading an inscription on the underside of the cross.

Josephine...

And then it vanished from his hands, turning to mist just like the girl who'd worn it.

***

Back at the *Dungeon*, Jake did two shots of Jägermeister and downed three-fourths of a Guinness. He had just chased the ghost of a stripper through the Marta station. *How does anyone top that?* And how could he tell anybody without sounding insane?

Behind a hulking leather-clad queen-meat package he spotted Marci and Moonshine. They were a sight, too. Moonshine was dressed like a kinky schoolgirl—thigh high boots fit for stage, a short plaid skirt, hips hung with a thick patent leather belt and a crop top that read "Bad Kitty."

Marci wore a stretchy top with a ring zipper, stacks, and a snug leather skirt with lightning bolts on it. It was too bad the name Storm was taken by the X-Men.

They joined Jake at the bar. Hex was pouring. Jake had already told Hex his ghost story when he returned from the Marta station.

"Our Jake has been chasing ghosts around the block like a maniac. Maybe she has come back to haunt everyone. How do you feel about those dope-boys getting demon-slaughtered anyway?"

He shrugged. "Actually I think Minstrel had the right idea."

"Maybe so, but now you've put yourself in the middle of all this drama. You really need to avoid these strange codependent relationships you seem to have a penchant for. First, you obsess over a fallen angel calling herself Charm who comes to you in the guise of your deceased girlfriend. Then you find a Black Dahlia look-alike who winds up dead herself. And by the way, it should be obvious why nobody helped that girl Josephine with her Darkening. All this town needed was for a crazy young girl to become some kind of premier violin virtuoso succubus. God. Why don't you find yourself a kindergarten teacher?"

"A weirdo only wants a weirdo," Moonshine quipped, accent like hot syrup.

"Actually, opposites do attract," Marci said. "I've seen Jake go after sensible girls. Anyway, do you think there's a chance this fiddler Minstrel has gotten involved with the Rapture dealer we need to find? Maybe that drug lord sent our violin avenger to kill those dope-boys so they couldn't run their mouths."

"Anything is possible," Hex said. "But my guess is that your *violin avenger* is probably just plain mad that his plans were ruined by losing her. He may have done it just to placate Felicity. I'm sure she's furious about the girl's death. She's who you really need to be worried about. Jake the urban myth and his amulet are prime rib. You're wanted like no other."

Jake started singing an eighties hair band song by Ratt: "I'm a wanted man..."

Marci pulled her stool closer to his and clutched his face, her early dawn streaked hair falling over her shoulders, softening the intensity of her expression. "I can't protect you constantly, and you aren't much of a fighter. The main reason I wanted to meet you tonight was to tell you about a guitarist named Snow and his coven. His band is going to be in the Bonding Weekend battle of the bands. It would be a chance for you to sing and play live in front of a big crowd again."

He threw back a shot. "I'm a leader and a loner."

Her eyes flared. "What you mean is you're good at leading yourself into hell alone."

He nodded silently. It was true.

"This could be good for you. You'll be part of a magical union, but still have your personal life, your job and music, and that book idea."

"This is about that Zowie girl, isn't it? You want to do an exchange?"

She shrugged. "It's partially about her. The power of three is very important to me. I need two beside me, not just Moonshine. Zowie is a very skilled fighter. She needs to be with us instead of Snow. You would fit in much better in his world." She paused, sipping her drink. "He lives in the coolest fucking old house. It's supposedly haunted, which is right up your alley. Plus, you need a place to live. I think you should join his coven. It'll get you off my sofa and away from that crazy bitch Clara. He's told me he needs a keyboard player for his goth metal band Dark Promise. The bass player, Muriel, writes dark poetic lyrics that you would die for. They're beautiful and eerie. It will be very enlightening."

"I always thought my comics were enough enlightenment. Should I go to a séance, now that I'm seeing the ghost of Josephine?"

Her face darkened with fascination. "Oh yeah, tell me your ghost tale."

He told her the whole story. "I watched a piece of her jewelry vanish in my hands."

She raised her eyebrows, nodding. "You never have met Sophia. She owns *My Hot Sister*. Her psychic magic is like no other. Ghosts will communicate with her. We'll see her as soon as possible. Tomorrow night, though, we need to go meet Snow."

Chapter Eight

few blocks from the King Memorial Marta Station, Marci pulled into a parking lot featuring a new-age bookstore and a trendy coffeehouse. Between these two stood a vine-swathed brick building. A sign read "Stygian Showroom."

She used the key Snow had given her to open the door and then led Jake through a small gallery lined with the work of local artists. At the bottom of a dusty staircase lay a huge backroom set up like a nightclub. About a hundred chairs were arranged before a stage opposite two bars.

This place was all the rage in the underground art scene. A lot of cutting edge plays were performed here along with spoken word performances. Tattoo shows and even raves went on here, too.

The owner also rented out the venue for bands. Dark Promise used it as their weekly rehearsal spot.

They were one of the big names playing Bonding Weekend using magic, namely illusion. It would be the greatest desire of any band to upstage them.

Felicity and her act, Dire Portent, would certainly be one of them. Rumors of Felicity's competitive animosity toward Snow had prompted him to seek Marci's help. This wasn't the first time he'd used her gang as bodyguards.

"Snow?" Marci called out.

The guitarist separated from shadow and placed himself in stage-lights. He looked like he belonged in a burlesque show from the twenties. Long hair bleached white hung over a black velvet dress, gaudy costume jewelry sparkling, pears around his neck. He was tall and lanky, long face ending in a cleft chin. Full glossy lips and thick dark eyebrows lent him a diva sensuality. He could've been a laboratory experiment to turn Lurch from the Adams Family into punk singer Iggy Pop—with some success.

Jake couldn't wait to hear his voice. Would it be a creepy

butler basso profundo voice made velvety by sex change drugs?

"Hey, honey," he cried out in a nasal whine to Marci.

A heavy metal guitarist with a voice like Liberace—how could this get any better?

Flaring an eyebrow, Snow began to play, backlit, transvestite metal goddess. He played a fast neo-classical passage and then shifted into raunchy wah-wah mode before slowing down to play a highly emotive eerie passage with rich shrieking sustain. It made Jake think of Ariel's screams before she turned to stone.

Glyphs flashed on the stage as he played a flash of notes, and then gargoyles rose from a thick purple mist. They roared, took flight then lost form, reduced to shards of light.

Marci gasped. "I thought they were real."

"Yeah, for a minute."

They applauded. Snow did a curtsey. Then an expression of fun confrontation came over his face. "I brought you here tonight to play, too. If you're good, you'll meet the band at the house." He gestured at a piano next to a massive drum kit.

Hours ago Marci had handed Jake a demo tape of songs with keyboard parts he needed to learn. He'd listened a few times and gotten the gist of it.

There was no way he could play it note for note, so he took off with a spirit of improvisation. He overplayed really, showing off, slinging his head like the crazed composer of a brilliant concerto. Ending with a dazzling run down the keyboard, he lifted his fingers from the keys and made a "ta-da!" gesture.

Snow came at Jake as though to grasp some precious object. "You are Chopin reborn. You're even better than I heard." His gaze dropped from his face to the Dual Serpent amulet. "Oh, and you'll have unimaginable power as an Illusionist."

"See..." Marci said, "he can add new dimensions to your talent. It'll matter later once you're solo again."

He hugged Jake, who blushed. "Solo? Why would he ever want to leave me?" Then he laughed, a wild and witchy shriek.

"What is it with everyone wanting me eternally?" Jake asked.

"Ah, Ariel," Snow said in a musing tone of horror. "You're recent exploits are legendary already."

"Whatever. What I want to know is why you're called Snow."

He gave Jake a sly look. "You'll know soon enough."

"What's truly legendary is his love of cocaine," Marci whispered in Jake's ear.

His face brightened like the sun. "Oh really? That's not necessarily a bad thing. Now let's talk about that dress. You aren't really gonna walk around like Norman Bates impersonating his mother all the time, are you?"

"Actually, I do this for Halloween shows or an occasional cabaret appearance. I just wanted to see how you'd react."

"Your playing is phenomenal, but I deal with enough drag queens at *Medusa's*."

Snow turned serious. "I'm not any bar fly. I've paid my dues in the music/magic circuit." A faint smile played over his lips as he peered down at himself. "Let me lose the dress and this cheap ass jewelry."

He went to the back and changed into black jeans and a sleeveless latex top. The funky skull-buckled boots he came out wearing made him look even taller, towering, hippy Frankenstein in club gear. As strange as he was, Jake kind of liked the guy.

He could see crow's feet etched in the corners of his new friend's eyes even with stage makeup. He was in his forties, seasoned, no doubt, in life as well as music. He reminded him of his actor friend David.

"I need a backup singer and keyboard player," Snow pressed on. "If you'll help me out, the fringe benefits will be mind blowing." He made a snorting sound as he pantomimed doing a line of coke. Then he gave a sharp trill of laughter, a rich drunk girl laugh.

"I'll think about it," Jake said then made a gulping sound of dread.

Snow rolled his eyes. "You don't know a good thing when you see it, do you, honey. While you're thinking about it, let's go out. Zowie awaits us."

***

They all agreed to meet Zowie at the *Hellfire Club* lounge. It wasn't disco night, but the DJ was playing great seventies songs by Parliament, Rick James, and the Bee Gees to a small but mighty crowd.

At the moment, KC and the Sunshine band was pumping.

Marci couldn't help herself and leapt up on a dance platform. She shared the stage with a stripper in her fifties who crushed beer cans with her tits.

Marci was bent backward, hair a colored waterfall, when Zowie walked in the door. She was a certified razor girl with California flair. Wearing disco retro gear, she styled through the bar to the dance floor, where she did a quick series of complicated dance moves with graceful ease. The moves almost seemed choreographed, Vegas cabaret level, but she moved with natural flair. Marci loved it.

They made eye contact, but Zowie still didn't approach her. Marci liked that, too. The girl wasn't desperate. Why should she be? Everything she wanted was surely drawn to her like media attention.

"I'm gonna make the first move," Marci said.

Moonshine crossed her arms, blond honey hair thrown over one tan shoulder. "Does she realize what an opportunity this is?"

A hint of a smile played over Marci's face. Was she a tad jealous? "She's probably just trying to be cool about things. This is like getting a date to prom. She's just as nervous as we are."

The country girl made a face like she saw her point. "She needs to be nervous. We're what it's all about."

"Maybe you're the one with attitude, not her," she retorted, giving her a playful push.

"Hmmm. Maybe so. But I'm right."

Marci vaguely rolled her eyes and headed toward the dancing girl. She felt like she was filming a cheerleader movie where the girls all hate each other. *She has to be cool if she's with Snow,* Marci thought. *Let me just get this proposition shit over with.*

Zowie surged right up to her in a sensual flow, slinging long platinum hair belonging to a sexy Cyborg in a dark, advanced future. Moonshine watched intently from the side, jealous cat eyes. She was ready to throw her Thai Basil margarita at her.

Marci pressed up against her, undulating, their midriffs pressing together, connected navel rings clicking. "Did you dance professionally?"

"You must have seen me on *Dancing with the Stars,*" Zowie said sarcastically. Her voice had that resonant West Coast lilt that movie producers of erotica loved—just a little raspy and tough.

"Actually, I've danced in L.A. and did showgirl work in Vegas. I did a fire and sword act there. To be honest, I *would* like to be on *Dancing with the Stars*."

Marci laughed. "You're a star already. You just need to change stages."

Zowie did a sensual twist with her hips, twirling. "Snow wasn't kidding about my joining you, huh?"

"He sure wasn't. How about a drink while you hear me out?"

Moonshine joined Snow and Jake at a cocktail table. They waved at the two girls as they headed to the bar.

"You belong with us," Marci said and ordered her a Marci-tini. "I know all about you. You're a fighter, not a go-go girl for a metal band"

Zowie nodded, running her hand through her silver tresses, nose ring glinting in bar light. "I thought the dancing would keep me out of trouble, but I'm bored with it. The acts I did in Vegas involved some challenging choreography, at least. Yeah, I'd rather fight."

Marci responded with a single emphatic nod, very impressed. There was a poised, classy assured air about her, yet she didn't come across like a cocky bitch with vainglorious stories of epic battles. She was tired of apocalyptic wannabe warrior girls who should've been in *Escape from New York*.

Marci regarded her thoughtfully for a moment, sipping her signature drink. "I'm glad you feel that way because trouble is coming. I'm sure you know all about Felicity. What's more, I really need a third member. I've just lost a great girl, and we need to fill a void. It's not easy finding the caliber of talent we need."

Zowie listened intently, close to ecstatic. "Okay. I'm all for it. Let's meet at the house as long as it's cool with Snow. We'll have a great time. Nobody can throw a party like Muriel."

Across the room, Snow watched the conversation, his arms folded smugly. "Why fight destiny? My plans always prevail."

Jake took a big gulp of Guinness. "Just don't plan on seducing me because *that* won't prevail."

Snow snapped his head around and started singing *You're So Vain* by Carly Simon. Then he ordered a round of Don Julio '42 shots for everyone.

David Raven

Chapter Nine

At *Medusa's* the following day, lunch was slow. The wild menagerie of regulars who filled Jake's nights with laughs and drama wouldn't show up until about the time he was leaving.

He wrote when he could, watchful of dining room manager Stephanie. The sharp-dressed saucy girl was always up in his business.

In this particular chapter he was writing, the struggling violinist was meeting a talent agent for dinner, not realizing she would soon be kidnapped by a crime lord. He was really starting to get the hang of capturing her voice and the whole dystopian feel of the narrative.

His dark thoughts settled on Josephine. Hex had told him to begin his investigation at *Pulse*, but there was an adult novelty store that sold posters and postcards featuring pictures of local strippers near here. Often the name of the club they worked at would be noted. It was something to check out before following Hex's lead.

It was a rare treat to only work lunch. After helping the ululating dishwasher finish cleaning up the back, he drove his hippy dream machine over to *Mary Mac's Tea Room*. He was served a plate of steaming homemade vegetables from a prim server, southern cuisine served with a lisp.

"Did you see *Dracula* at the Fox last October?" he asked.

No, I was too busy running from a succubus. "Actually, I didn't. Is it true those classically trained ballerinas look like they're masturbating onstage?"

The server's eyes went wide. "It comes so close," he said in an appalled breathlessness.

Jake laughed, nearly strangling on sautéed spinach.

Slowly extricating himself from the clutches of girl patter

about night life and fashion, Jake joined an eddy of corporate workers strolling back to their cars. He passed Blondie, the famous *Clairmont Lounge* dancer, as he neared the shop *Hot Nights*.

His eyes met with the legendary dancer's momentarily. Her preoccupied expression flickered with recognition, but she kept going. He thought nothing of it. Most people in this city needed to stay strangers.

He laughed, thinking about Atlanta's misconceived identity. This was no true Southern city. With all the pop stars, models, and actors heading for stardom in what had become South Hollywood, the place was like New York or L.A. in drag as a Southern Bell.

All women had their secrets, though. The world of magic in which he belonged was certainly one of this city's darkest.

He headed another block, and the neon lit sex emporium came into view. This wasn't any hole-in-the wall perverts slipped in and out of incognito. It was the local sex market's answer to Wal-Mart. All it needed was retirement-age greeters up front, directing the flow of sex addicts.

He knew more than a few girls who bought toys here, and the girls who worked here were porn stars in their own right.

He walked in on a porn star promotional. It looked like a scene out of an independent movie doing a spoof on the porn show business. Movies were being hawked at the door by girls with bright smiles. They acted like they were glad he could make it to church.

The focal point of all this hoopla was a photo signing session for a black female porn star. She didn't have anything on but the tie she pulled off the banker who'd come to see her. The Medusa statue at work would be jealous of this girl.

"Where are your stripper photos?" he asked a cute movie hawker.

The sexy redhead with a lip ring focused her large eyes on him, directing him toward a rack of gag cards. "Rock star boy, over there," she exclaimed over the throbbing drone of trance music.

He smiled bemusedly, never knowing whether someone was being sarcastic or not about his band getting signed. He breezed through the gag cards before moving on to the local photography section next to it. Most of the photos were brought in by photographers working for the local skin trade magazines, but amateurs brought in all kinds of risqué and racy shots.

He rifled through the photos, recognizing several of the girls from *Pandora's Box*. He wouldn't be surprised if he saw Marci in here. She didn't turn up, but after going through about fifty of them he saw a photo that looked like a movie poster for a gothic version of *Gone with the Wind*.

It was Josephine.

She stood under the marquee of the Fox Theater, raven hair flowing. The stellar glitter of her emerald eyes projected dramatically from her porcelain poutiness.

"There's my ghost." He laughed to himself and found more photos of her. Annotated on the back of them was the location where they had been taken. Hex's intuition was correct. *Club Pulse* was written on several.

His remark drew the attention of a floor girl. "What were you saying about a ghost?"

He looked at her distractedly and then his eyes slid back to the photo. "Let's just say this girl belongs in a ghost story," he quipped. He was oblivious of several employees watching him warily from the register, his reaction to the photograph oddly melodramatic. "Who took this photograph? Do you know?"

The group of girls glanced at each other in a conspiracy of amusement, and then one of them said, "I could find out. Hold on."

Minutes later, a preoccupied manager came up to him, wearing an artificial smile Jake used all too often himself. He was a preppy nerd type with horn-rimmed glasses. It always amazed Jake how often such people ran places like this—an evil dork leader who never gets laid but finds control through the business end of prurient desire.

"Yes, how may I help you?" he asked crisply. He had that look in his eyes like he'd just love to pick Jake's mind apart, taking what he needed to be sexually successful in life.

"Sorry to take up your time, but do you know who took these pictures?"

The manager studied the picture and looked up, grinning. "Great picture of a hooker, huh? Especially if the hooker is doing Broadway." He laughed. "You want to know who takes these headshots, huh?"

Hooker headshot, Jake mused. *That's hysterical.* "Could you tell me?"

There was an amused searching look in his eyes. "Yeah. A guy named Scott Walden took it. He comes in once a week with new ones."

"Could I get his phone number?"

The manager shrugged, a saboteur's gleam in his eyes. "I can't, but if you're willing to leave your name and number, I'll see whether he's interested in getting in touch with you."

Jake stared dumbly at the guy. The offer was fair, but the demon of impatience within him clamored for more. Some cooperation was better than none, though. "Please make certain that he gets this." He scribbled down his name and number.

The manager took the slip of paper, nodding. "Oh no problem." His eyes met Jake's, a wry smile crossing his face. "I wanted your autograph anyway."

The singer smirked. He never knew where obsession rested.

Chapter Ten

O ur loser/gamer Benjamin walked into the strip bar *Shadows* with an air of purpose. He made sure he wasn't too drunk and wore a black turtleneck sweater and a new leather jacket. He slicked back his dyed hair with mousse, which he never used, a big loop in one ear like he belonged in *Pulp Fiction*. Now he was Agent Sexy Noir, or at least looked intriguing and successful. Tonight, he needed to be persuasive.

"I've got a problem," he said to a girl twirling onstage.

"What's that?"

"I need a hitman."

"Are you serious?" Her brow flared.

"I really mean I need a hunter...someone who is a bad ass with magic. Can you help?"

"A hunter?"

"Yeah. Someone who won't mind when things get messy."

"What kind of money are we talking about?" She tossed her hair about, long tresses like a whip.

"How about ten thousand dollars?"

She scoffed. "That doesn't seem like much. Good luck with that one."

He tipped her a fifty and shrugged. He thought the Darkened girls in here would have contacts. Surely somebody wanted quick money.

He went back to the bar and had several rounds, sinking into the muck of despondency.

Oh shake it off, he thought. He had all that inheritance money now. He was out of rehab, and he'd never be a *nobody* again. Girls and power would finally be his.

Jake Reece and those strippers weren't going to stand in his way.

Ben drank through several stripper song sets, and he was

about to pay his tab when he felt a tap on his shoulder. With a sharp intake of breath, he looked up.

"You're in luck," the dancer said. "Just go into the alleyway behind the bar. I've arranged a meeting for you." Then she flounced back to the dressing room.

He skulked around back, lit a cigarette. In the shadows, a small creature thrashed through the weeds behind a rusty trashcan. He gasped as he was slammed against an alley wall. Clumping footfalls ceased before him. He opened his eyes with a nervous flutter and didn't know whether to laugh or scream.

The stocky figure before him had missed his calling, not being the lead in *Springtime for Hitler*. He wore a leather duster emblazoned with a swastika over a Slayer T-shirt and a studded choker around his thick neck. Amber hair was blown back theatrically (total pompadour) as though he were a fat opera singer who'd taken a foray into heavy metal. A Nazi cap was set rakishly on his head. His fingernails were painted black. German crosses dangled from his wrists, and a leather belt clattered with silver rings, completing his kinky fascist look.

"Who are y-you?" Benjamin sputtered.

"The Prince of Darkness," he answered with radio personality resonance. "Actually, they call me Drake Omen. Or just Omen."

"Is that a stage name? I can't see you stripping."

Omen just smiled. "I'm more of a prostitute, really. I hunt things for a bounty." He paused a moment, assessing Benjamin, who was still shaking. "I understand you've got a proposition for me."

"Yeah. If you won't kill me, I'll buy you a drink and explain."

At a cocktail table in the corner, a waitress brought them both Long Island Teas and shots of Grand Marnier.

Omen was one of those gays that girls just loved. They fondled the piercing in his plucked eyebrow and asked about the tattoos on his muscled arms. To judge by the thick silver rings on his fingers, one would think he'd just pillaged Rome.

"Where did you get those *beast* rings?" a girl asked.

"Quests," he answered simply and turned his attention to Benjamin. "So who exactly are you after? And why?"

He sighed and then told his story. "I fucked up and gave

Rapture to a girl who couldn't handle it. I thought she was a witch, but she needed to go through her—"

"Her Darkening."

"Yeah. It killed her...turned her to ash. Now she has these mighty friends trying to avenge her. My dealer wants them out of the way before they cause him trouble."

"And just who are these people?"

"One of them is a rock singer, and the hunter girls are strippers. I heard the name Marci Stone."

"Oh really?" His tone was arched. "Would the rock singer's name just happen to be Jake Reece?"

"You know it."

"He must think he's the god of rock after what he did to Ariel."

"You know more than me."

Omen shook his head. "I must tell you I've seen your kind before. You don't know anything about magic, but you're handing out dangerous candy to look like a big shot."

"I didn't mean to kill her! I mean, I didn't..."

"You just wanted to have sex with her and she wound up dead. How do you think that looks in our world?"

"Okay. Okay. Will you take care of the opposition?"

Omen gave a chest heaving robust laugh. "You really think there's nothing to it?"

Benjamin started his signature blubbering of desperation.

"Alright, alright. Take me to meet your dealer."

***

"This cigar is from my humidor," Thorn said. "You'll enjoy it immensely."

Omen knew little about fine cigars, but he lit it and puffed on it with great relish. It looked like a scene out of *The Godfather*.

The trap house was in the *Bluff*—Atlanta's roughest drug area. When Omen roared up to it on his motorcycle, he gave the dilapidated lair a hard look and just about turned around and left. Then Thorn rushed out onto the porch in all his fur-coated glory, insisting he come inside and chat.

The interior was the exact opposite of the shabby exterior— swank leather furniture and breathtaking cityscape artwork. A huge print of Atlanta's skyline hung over the sofa. Any up-and-coming hipster would dream about having this place.

By candlelight, Thorn scraped together lines of coke with a Platinum American Express. He doled out several lines to his men and call girls before offering a thick line to Omen. Then he picked up a fingernail file and began his persnickety self-absorbed preening.

Omen snorted the line with a big gasp and leaned back in a well-cushioned leather chair. He sighed theatrically. What hospitality.

The retinue of gunmen watched Omen warily. Thorn remained silent. Girls watched from flickering candlelight shadows with curious feral eyes.

Omen cleared his throat, beginning this touchy conversation with an urbane confident tone. "Were you aware of the risk you were taking letting that fool bring me to you?"

"I've already made my calls," Thorn answered evenly. "You're who you claim to be."

"That's true. So, just where did you get the Rapture from? That's no common street drug."

"A coven head called me who wants to throw a big party Bonding Weekend. I'm known for my *cooking talents*." He made quote signs with his fingers. "They even gave me their grimoire cookbook. The result? They're going to have a fucking blast Bonding Weekend."

Omen chuckled. "I'll bet they don't know you made your own batch for private use. I can see how selling it Bonding Weekend could make you a lot of money, but you sure fucked up selling to this Benjamin idiot."

Thorn nodded ruefully and sighed. "He's come into a lot of money and offered a huge price for the Rapture. I knew he was just being a fool, but I thought the girl he was obsessed with was a full-fledged Caster who knew what she was doing. Now the fucking Partridge Family wants me dead."

Omen laughed at the absurdity of the situation. "I don't guess you can get help from the Darkened Council because they'll kill you for selling it to some idiot in the first place." He leaned back, smirking, appraising Thorn. "I'm surprised you didn't just do away with this loser."

Laughter rippled over Thorn's following words. "I have thought about emptying his account and slinging him in a ditch, but he brings me a lot of business. I sell dope in strip bars I've never even heard of thanks to his endless carousing. But if things get worse, I *will* kill him."

Omen leaned back in contemplation. "This is no small thing. I don't underestimate Marci Stone. She's well connected with the Council of the Estranged. I could wind up in more trouble than you."

The dealer blew a long plume of cigarette smoke. "Benjie-boy has about a million dollars in inheritance money. He'll be willing to pay you anything."

"Really? What does he think I was going to do this for, anyway?"

"He was talking ten grand."

"Try fifty thousand."

Thorn was stunned a moment and then released wheezing laughter, cigarette smoke streaming from his nose. "I'll get our inheritance poster boy on the phone now."

An hour later, Benjamin showed up with a stack of money in his trembling hands.

Omen counted it then gave Benjamin a look of amused speculation. "How did you meet this girl, anyway?"

"My highfalutin attorney friend throws a lot of parties. She was hooking there. I found out she was a stripper and worked at a place called *Pulse*. She went by the stage name Star. I went there and met her and started buying dances. I tried to get her to meet me later for a thousand, but she wouldn't take it. I kept trying to talk to her but nothing worked. After a few weeks she stopped talking to me even to do dances. I saw her playing violin one night, and I noticed symbols on her instrument. I asked around and found out she was into that magic stuff."

"So you stalked her until you found out she was a Darkened."

Benjamin winced, shaking his head. "I just couldn't stop thinking about her. The more she ignored me, the more I was intrigued, particularly when I saw how well she played violin and the attention she drew. I wanted to really know her, but I didn't know how to get her attention. I heard she was into drugs and came up with the idea of sending her Rapture. I thought it would get her attention."

Omen's manicured eyebrows flew up. "Oh, you got everybody's attention. You're an overnight sensation."

Benjamin blushed with anger and frustration. "Why didn't she know the drug was dangerous to her?"

Omen scoffed. "I guess she didn't know what she was getting into. Rapture is not that well known because it isn't a street drug." He looked over at Thorn doing his nails nonchalantly. "You must be pretty big in the Atlanta arcane drug scene."

Thorn crooked a brow. "I'm one of the best sex drug alchemists around."

Omen nodded. "I don't doubt it."

"Can you stop these people who are after me...after me and Thorn?" Benjamin interjected with spiraling alarm.

Omen gazed down at all that money. "I'll try to handle this Bonding Weekend. I must say, though, facing Marci Stone is against my better judgment."

He headed out to his Harley-Davidson and found Judas Priest's *You've Got Another Thing Comin'* on Spotify. Singing the famous eighties metal tune at the top of his lungs, Omen roared off into the night.

Thorn watched the bike vanish over the horizon then went back in the house to divvy up more powder.

Benjamin already had his money out.

Chapter Eleven

J ake was in the middle of arguing with Mr. Ruke about whether Stravinsky was as great a composer as Bach when his cell phone rang. It was the photographer, who would be more than happy to see him. They talked a second before dining room manager, Stephanie, came out front. Then he had to hang up fast.

He cleaned the bar as fast as possible. Regulars wondered why he was so quiet and focused—that was a new one.

"Where are you going in such a hurry?" Stephanie posed in annoyance, frowning as she watched his flurry of action.

He made himself stop and turn around. "I'm off early today for the first time in months. It's my big chance to get a few things done before my singing gig tonight. I might even check out a second job."

The hostess, poised behind a stand with her hands laced behind her back, blushed. Several waiters doing side work pretended not to listen.

Stephanie smiled coolly. "Okay. Do what you want. Have you done liquor inventory?" She fiddled impatiently with a pen.

He started working his way slowly toward the front door. He was getting out of here if it killed him. "I'll come in early tomorrow and do it, okay? See ya." He left behind a giggling hostess. Stephanie, arms folded, had a dark look in her eyes.

In thirty minutes, he was at the intersection where Euclid Avenue met Moreland in Little Five Points. He slipped in a Sevendust CD and sang along with the vocalist's soulful pipes. Didn't that singer work at the Fellini's across the street before he made it big? Listening to it made him feel tapped into the city's soul.

The sidewalks of Little Five Points were teeming with hip shoppers going from one jewelry kiosk to the next. Skater punks ran riot, gliding down the strip, cigarettes dangling from their mouths. A windswept girl outside a tattoo parlor was giving tarot card readings. He hoped he wouldn't need her to find Scott Walden's apartment.

Scott was apparently a well-read Bohemian type who sold photographs to survive one week and then pot the next. Jake hadn't met a true hippy in a long time.

Turning off of Euclid Avenue, he twisted through a series of shadowy narrow back streets, canopied by overhanging oak tree boughs. The streets were flanked by quaint bungalow homes.

When he reached his presumed destination, he pulled over to the curb and frowned. This place looked rough. He reread his directions and shrugged.

He strode down a weed infested sidewalk toward a red bricked two story apartment building. Potted plants and wind chimes hung from balconies in dire need of painting.

He was looking for apartment thirteen but found two apartment threes. One of the doors had two screw holes in front of the second number.

He knocked on the door with the empty nail holes. This felt like the kind of photographer he'd find, a broke genius.

There was a shuffling noise and the sound of feet padding across carpet accompanied by the squeak of a wooden floor. A dead bolt slid free, and a hippy wearing spectacles, a Grateful Dead T-shirt, holey jeans, and flip flops came to the door. The reek of marijuana wafted past him into the hallway.

Scott took one look at Jake and his dull expression bloomed into bright recognition. "Hey, you're the bartender at *Medusa's*. Aren't you in a big local band, too?"

"I was. There'll be another one."

"Come on in. You're the closest thing to a celebrity I've had in here unless you count old famous strippers."

Scott's apartment was sparsely furnished with flea market furniture. Bags of weed and drug paraphernalia lay on a scuffed-up coffee table.

The centerpiece of the place was an imposing stereo system that Jake could have mistaken for a U.F.O., boasting four speakers that were taller than totem poles—gods of thunder.

There was even a vinyl record player amongst the arsenal.

Several towers of compact discs surrounded it along with a vinyl collection that would make collectors of seventies rock blush.

"I don't know what you're into, but check all this out."

He flipped through the collection: original copies of *Exile on Mainstreet* by The Rolling Stones, *Machine Head* by Deep Purple, and *Demons and Wizards* by Uriah Heap. There were boxes of these collectibles.

"I buy and sell them at thrift stores and conventions."

"This is killer," Jake said, checking out recent Japanese imports of prog-metal bands. "So, what's making you the most money?"

Scott gave a lazy lopsided grin. "It just depends. I do a lot of freelance work. Sometimes the local adult entertainment magazines pay pretty good for strip bar shots. I also go around town just taking pictures of girls. Let me show you some." He tossed Jake a beer and then ducked into one of the bedrooms. Several minutes later, he emerged with a manila envelope. "Here you go, man." He handed it to Jake.

"I think you'll find what you want." The scraggly bohemian flopped down in a beanbag chair and lit a cigarette. "Lots and lots of pretty Atlanta women."

Jake shuffled through the photographs quickly. Most of them were sexy pictures with an urban backdrop, but none of them featured the raven-haired beauty he sought.

"I'm looking for photos of this girl." He showed him the Josephine photos he bought at *Hot Nights*.

Scott's eyes went wide. "Oh. Have I ever got a story about *that girl*." He blew a plume of smoke and looked at him curiously. "Why are you interested in her, anyway?"

"She's a friend, and she's disappeared. I'm trying to find anyone who might know anything about her."

"I know she used to dance at *Pulse*. Go talk to a girl who goes by the stage name Abbey. I believe they party a lot together."

"When did you take this picture in front of the Fox?"

"About two weeks ago. This brings me to my story. She disappeared."

"Like a ghost?" Jake laughed.

"Actually, just exactly like a god damn ghost." He dashed in the back and returned a moment later. "Look at this. It still gives me the fucking creeps."

There were two photos of the windswept girl in black, lips parted sensually. In the third one, she seems to be fading out of the photograph, her hair becoming black mist, her porcelain skin reduced to the reflection of moonlight. The image was haunting, erotically surrealistic.

"I've never seen anything like it," the photographer said.

"Can I have these?"

"You sure can."

They made some small talk about the strip bar scene, and then Jake headed out the door.

Dusk was falling on Atlanta, the sky beautifully bruised. He considered the mystery of nightfall, and then he turned on the overhead light in the car to gaze down at the photo of Josephine.

"I think you're the most beautiful ghost ever," he confessed as though a priest was listening. Then he headed out into a wild new night.

***

Omen rode down International Boulevard, a fat knight riding a metal beast. He parked across the street from the *Dungeon* in a warehouse parking lot and placed wards around his bike. He wore his best leather bondage gear. No one was going to out-style him here.

Word around town was that everybody who was anybody in the Darkened/goth world came to this club to catch up on filthy magic gossip. He'd get the scoop on the hunter here.

At the door, he paid a cover to a studiously indifferent girl who was reading a huge literary hardback by candlelight. Then he forged ahead.

The illusions here were just as amazing as he'd heard. He stepped on a rune trigger that filled his eyes with a phantasmagoric montage of black-and-white sensational sixties horror imagery: roaring man-lizards from lagoons, zombies rising from graves, a screaming vamp in a monster's grasp.

Exploring the different floors, he found where they played mostly industrial-dance music and goth rock. He found himself dancing—attempting to dance—to Sisters of Mercy, twirling his rotund form around, making funky zig/zag gesticulations with a cigarette.

Finally, Omen spotted a group of girls radiating Darkened magic. Clad like go-go dancers, they were most likely strippers. He approached them, flaring a thinly manicured eyebrow. "Hi, ladies."

Wary kohl-shadowed eyes slid to him through cigarette haze. "We don't have gay daddy issues," one of them said.

Omen cleared his throat. "Just hear me out. I'm a booking agent for New York sex shows featuring Darkened performers. I'm looking for a girl named Marci Stone. Do you know where she dances?"

The girl scoffed. "You're a talent agent for Darkened girl sex shows, and you want *the* Marci Stone?" An expression of dark amusement passed over her face. "Do you even know anything about her?"

He shrugged. "Not really. I know she dances."

"She's total angel magic, an Estranged girl, not Darkened."

"Why are you really looking for her?" another girl asked.

Omen gave them a sly look, creepy charm, and slipped each of them a hundred. "Just tell me where she works."

They looked at each other guiltily. Then one said, "I think she'll be at the Burnt Offering show. The guy she runs around with has been singing in that band."

"A singer?"

"The dude everybody thinks is a metal god. Jake Reece. He wears that amulet I'm hearing stories all about."

"Where is this place?"

"It's a bar out in Little Five Points called *Rock Bottom*. It's right across from the *Vortex*. You'll see."

***

Omen roared into the *Rock Bottom* parking lot, singing Meatloaf's *Bat out of Hell* at the top of his lungs.

Unabashed, he walked into the bar like he owned it, cap tilted rakishly, smoking with his head held high. He paused to check out the posters of local metal bands plastered all over the walls around beer signs. Vintage metal blasted from the speakers, something like Fates Warning. The double bass drum attack was like angry fists pounding the walls. Pool players wailed the lyrics with anguished passion. Omen loved it.

"Are you in a Billy Idol tribute band?" a loaded vacant-eyed girl asked artlessly.

He thought he'd heard everything now. "Yeah, I'm a back-up singer."

He strode up to the bar, medieval crosses on thick bracelets clattering when he placed his chunky hands on the bar.

A purple haired bartender, pouring a line of shots into plastic cups, gave him a wide-eyed confused look that resolved into hilarity.

Who was this queen?

"Can I help you?" she asked.

"The most fucking expensive vodka martini you can put together in your finest plastic cup." He slid a fifty across the bar. "Keep it."

She lit up like the dawn of a new day, big revelatory smile, nodding. Omen's charm, wit, and loose wallet worked wonders on a jaded bartender used to cheap drunks. She poured heavily the best top-shelf shit she had into a tumbler and handed him a stout drink with olives floating in it.

He drank deeply, eyes floating over the smoke-hazed room. This was definitely a metal crowd: leather clad dolls and shaggy guys sporting obscure European metal band T-shirts, i.e. Kissin' Dynamite. However, this place held a great duality. There were also a lot of people here who seemed to be in the restaurant business or theater.

He moved deeper into the crowd, spotting a tawdry blonde having it out with a drag queen. Well, what do you know? Maybe he would fit right in. "You're here to see this band?" Omen asked when the two stopped arguing to order fresh drinks.

"I'm here to give emotional support to the dumb singer. Jake, poor thing, needs all the help he can get. Bless his straight heart. I wish he'd give up on girls and give me a whirl."

"So, how do you know this *poor thing*? Does he come to your cabaret shows?"

"He never comes to any of my damn shows. Me and this trashy bitch right here drink ourselves half-blind at *Medusa's* where he pours." Her eyebrows drew together, and she looked him up and down. "You must be from out-of-town. Mars maybe. He had a band called Lost Angel that almost got signed."

Lost Angel—the name echoed in Omen's mind. Yeah, he had heard all about this hot guy. Now he was actually curious about the show and not just the kill. There wasn't anybody in the magic/music scene with major record company interest. It was very much underground. Jake Reece was fabulously singular, a one of a kind. It was too bad Omen had to kill him.

Finally, three guys with long black hair hit the stage. The guitarist let a power chord ring like a death knell and then out came Jake—fucking fop—Reece, shrieking this long theatrical note tantamount to a banshee cry. He wore vinyl pants and a mesh top, a sheer black scarf twined around his neck. A princely mane fell about the shoulders.

The kid has got it, Omen thought. He could see why Jake was being sought in the world of magic for all sorts of reasons. He worked the stage like a seasoned performer doing an acclaimed musical, half-artiste/half-lion.

You look so young. You could be a fucking teen idol.

It was clear, however, this guy wasn't singing for teenyboppers. He was belting out this metal machismo shit with the fervor of a possessed opera singer.

He then noticed two shadow-veiled figures watching him intently from a far corner. They had their energy muted, but they were definitely Estranged Casters, probably hunters. In fact, he was almost certain one of them was Marci Stone.

Omen hung out for a few more songs. The bar crowd energy was unreal, as the band played like they were in a coliseum. He was aware, though, the girls were moving closer to him, sneaky vamp vigilance.

He left while he was ahead of the game—but not before writing the name *Medusa's* on a bar napkin.

Chapter Twelve

When Jake showed up for work the following day, he sensed that something was very wrong. The smell of death lingered in the air like old gun smoke. The general manager Al gave him a great big smile—which he rarely did—that was artificial and brittle, as though someone had paid him to act like he had a real personality. Jake knew better.

A number of the waiters who were normally very loud and obnoxious seemed inhibited. A few of them mumbled a polite hello as he paced back to the office, wondering whether the F.B.I. was waiting on his arrival.

"Remember the dipping oil gets three dots of balsamic glaze," Stephanie stressed to a new waitress passing her. She smiled coolly and then averted her eyes.

Jake's pace quickened, and so did his pulse. Everything else moved in slow motion as though a denouement of dark judgment were unfolding.

In the Roman arena within his mind, snide waiters cackled hysterically from their lofty seats. *It's over, asshole! Gladiator Al is going to flail you to death!*

He was a nice guy—just a little fucking stupid!

Ha! Ha! Ha! You idiot! Overrated dreamer! Go get your meaningful literature and hit the road!

The echo of laughter rattled his brain until he nearly screamed before he made it to the office. Even the Hispanic dishwasher gave him a funny look and walked off cursing under his breath. That was nothing unusual, though.

Shutting the door to the office, heart racing, he asked, "What in the hell is wrong with everyone?"

Al looked up from the calculator he was banging on. His fake smile faltered a little. "Um...I can't be sure."

But Jake was sure. The house of cards in his mind that

represented his fragile life trembled and then mercifully became still again.

His impending doom wasted no time in presenting itself. At one o'clock that afternoon, Jake was seated at a back table, Al and Stephanie opposite him.

Al took off his glasses and appraised Jake, eyebrows drawn. "Jake, how do you feel about your performance here at *Medusa's*? Do you feel that you do as well as you could? That you give it your all?"

"What?" he scoffed. "Give it my all? Half the regulars in here would stop coming in if I weren't here. I'm practically doing the bar manager's job, inventory and everything which I never had any intention of doing."

"We told you that was a part of it. You can't just make money. There is responsibility as well."

"You have to earn your position, Jake," Stephanie interjected in her tart condescending way as she pulled a lock of strawberry blond hair behind an ear.

Jake kept his composure, though, taking on a patronizing tone of his own. "Whatever. Compare my sales figures with the other bartenders."

There was a moment of silence. He listened to the distant clatter of silverware beneath his measured breathing.

Al raised his eyebrows, pushing his pen up and down in that fidgety annoying manner he had. "This is true, but you walked out on inventory yesterday, and Stephanie had to complete it."

Stephanie folded her arms, relishing the coming retort.

"Sure, but—"

Al raised a palm. "That's not all." He leaned back, closing his eyes a moment and then cleared his throat. "I've gotten word you're giving away shifts. Why?"

Even Stephanie looked genuinely curious. She'd no doubt overheard regulars talking, those who knew he'd gotten nights covered to go interview at some other clubs.

Jake shrugged. "I didn't really want to quit here. I just get the feeling you need someone with...more of a corporate vision."

"So you thought you'd get trained here, and then dump this place in favor of one of those late hours bars that you trawl through?" This was Stephanie's snide remark.

"I'd never thought about it quite like that."

Al leaned forward and sighed while studying him intently. "Jake, I'm afraid..."

Jake saw an arm in his mind, coming down at his house of cards like a pendulum.

"That we're going to suspend you for two weeks."

There it was. The arm smashed through the cards, sending them downward into the abyss of his mind.

Oh, but ironies abounded. He closed his eyes and smiled. The sensation of warm honey suffused him as though he were experiencing a religious euphoria. His eyes opened to the two managers, prisoners of their own houses of cards. *Yours will never topple*, he thought. *You two are prisoners forever.*

He focused on Al's drivel again. Apparently he had no idea Jake hadn't been listening. "...will be happy to let you wait tables again. You were a great waiter. You are by no means fired, but I do feel you should be doing dining room service instead of working behind the bar."

Jake just shook his head at Al's vague smirk. 'Doing dining room service' and being in servitude to this prick were tantamount. As Robert Plant would say, it was time to ramble on.

Jake stood up like a lawyer about to deliver his final triumphant bit of evidence and leaned over the table. He looked Al square in the eye. "You know what? I'd rather panhandle than be in this place another day." Both of their faces blanched. Jaws dropped. "I'll tell you something else. I can have a job downtown bartending just like that." He snapped his fingers. "I don't want a reference. I'd be embarrassed to tell anyone I ever worked here, anyway."

Without another word, he left. Wide-eyed waiters stared in shock from every shadow and crevice of the restaurant, which was deathly silent except for Jake's light-hearted whistle as he strolled coolly out the front door. They could almost hear victory in his voice.

"Take this job and shove it!" the Hispanic dishwasher sang in his best southern drawl, then cackled. He was proud of Jake, for once.

Jake wasn't distraught like the time he was run off for drinking behind the bar. Walking out into the parking lot, he lit a cigarette, blew a plume of smoke, and held the cancer stick high in the air as he howled a primal cry of liberation. He was sick of it all—the newfound corporate mentality and the putdowns about the band and his personal life. They just didn't want him moving on to bigger and better things.

And you watch, he thought. *My goofy regulars will follow me like sheep* (although that might be a dubious victory).

Now it was time to execute Project Alcatraz—in other words, escape Clara's wine-supper-club clutches. At this time of the afternoon, he'd have no problem snatching up the rest of his stuff and hitting the highway without fear of hurled wine bottles and cutlery.

He careened wildly around every corner as he sped home with teenaged recklessness.

It was three thirty in the afternoon. Clara would be home by five, and he wanted nothing to do with her. *Goodbye, Clara. Parting is sweet sorrow.*

Pounding up the staircase, he pulled out two big travel bags and stuffed them with jeans, shirts, and a hodgepodge of smaller items. He threw them over both shoulders so that the straps crossed like Mexican bandoleers. He was down the staircase and halfway across the foyer when the thought occurred to him that he should leave a note for Clara.

In the kitchen, he ripped off a paper towel and scrawled a heartfelt message: *In every life the winds of change must blow. Well, I must be leaving you. I hope that doesn't blow. It's been real. Peace out.*

He leaped into the car and barreled out of the driveway, feeling reborn. The highway of life just split into wild new possibilities.

Back in the city, night drew the curtain on Atlanta's hectic daytime drama. The freaks would come out now like vampires awakened.

First, it was time to play super sleuth (He told Marci never to call him Secret Squirrel again). He headed to *Pulse* to see what he could learn about Josephine. That meant seeking out the blonde "apple and snake tattoo" college girl dancer.

On Cheshire Bridge Road, he zoomed past a galaxy of strip bar and sex shop neon lights to arrive at *Pulse*. The sign flashed as though throbbing with pleasure.

He liked the place. The club was a solid second-tier strip joint with hot girls who'd left the very top joints because they'd gotten too stuffy (Plus the magic scene was big here). The bartenders looked like big smiling coke burn-outs who weren't fast enough to deal cards in Vegas anymore.

He planted himself on a bar stool and pulled out the photo of Josephine. A sultry jazz tune took over, wailing saxophones leading the way. It was a smoky sex tune his Russian cab driver would love—that *Shaft* seventies porn feel. He ordered a Long Island and turned toward the stage.

A high heeled dancer in a black gown burst through the curtains and slinked toward the front of the runway. It was time for role playing games. He was a detective, and she was a manipulative dame of Hollywood noir.

He went to the stage, tipping her fat. "Have you seen this girl?" he asked, showing her the photo.

The sensual languor fell from her face, replaced by concern. "Not recently. Is she okay?"

"I'm worried she's in trouble. Do you know of a blonde girl who hung out with her?"

Her eyes took on a searching cast. "Abbey? Let me go check in the back." And then she finished her set and left the stage.

Time plodded by. A slew of Long Islands later, he was so drunk and bored that he pulled out a deck of tarot cards. "Who has questions about sex, drugs, and...oh yeah, life." He wound up doing three readings for girls who were just astounded.

"You're a regular Madame Bell," the bartender said. "Here's a round for giving the girls a thrill."

"Cool." He slid the bartender a twenty for a tip.

"So, are you really psychic?"

Jake shrugged. "I wish I could answer my own questions about life." He showed the bartender the photo. "Do you recognize this girl?"

He gave it a quick glance, frowning. "Yeah, Star. She danced here until about a week ago. Then she just disappeared." He handed back the photo, giving Jake a hard appraisal. "Are you her boyfriend?"

"I'm just a friend who wants to find her. Do you know any

girls here who knew her?"

"Abbey, I think." He was shaking a tumbler, looking around the place. "She's here. I don't know where, though. I'll tell you if I see her."

I'm tired of going in circles, he groaned inwardly. What now?

In the meantime, he moved toward a cocktail table near the main stage, hoping to see his jazz girl again. A stripper cast a heavy-lidded gaze at him, blond tresses spilling over enormous silicone breasts, nipples pink and swollen. She moved her left shoulder in a sensual circular motion to techno throb, inviting him to move closer.

His eyes moved to the tuft of blond pubic hair and then slid down an oily thigh to her garter belt. She did the rest. With a single finger, she stretched the belt inches away from her thigh.

Jake grinned. "Do you want me to fold the money any particular way?"

She batted an eyebrow. "Just stick it in."

Snap went the garter belt. She gazed down at him curiously, a goddess studying a creation. "You're too cute to be in here," she said with a lilting voice made distinct with a peculiar cigarette rasp. *Caramel meets sandpaper.*

"I guess boredom overcame my pride," he said, thinking he needed to write that thought down.

She leaned in and ran her fingers through his tousled mane. As paranoid as he'd become of magical peril, he was worried he'd turn into a frog.

"You're too pretty to be a guy."

"I'll bet you say that all the time." He gestured toward the smoke-filled room of sex-starved men.

He was just getting a round of drinks when he felt a tap on his shoulder. He turned to behold an apple pie blonde who had to be the girl he'd heard all about from Hex. "Are you...Abbey?"

"That's right." She smiled brightly, starry eyed. "Aren't you the singer in Lost Angel?"

"Have you ever seen us perform live?"

"No, but I know a lot about you." Her eyes took a tour of him. "And I know Marci Stone."

"So you know all about magic."

"I know Star...Josephine was going to be a witch. I loved her, though. She was so talented, and now she's just..."

"A ghost?"

Her eyes flared wide. "You've seen her, too?"

"Yeah. She got her hands on Rapture, and it did her in. Do you know who'd be dealing a magic drug like that?"

Her face went flush with anger. "I'm not sure, but you need to find that jerk with the violin. He has something to do with this...even if he didn't actually get her the dope."

"I know all about Minstrel. Have you seen him lately?"

"He came in asking the same kind of questions as you, wanting to know who brought her drugs. I told him about a bar where she used to meet her dope-boys. Did he go?"

Jake laughed. "He sure did. You must not read the newspaper much."

"What do you mean?"

"Uh, poetic justice has reached that bunch. They're dead. Still, we need to find the big honcho. Those punks were just runners."

Nodding, she sighed and pulled back a strand of hair from her lips. "What you really need to do is talk to Peter."

"Peter, huh? Give me the rundown on this guy."

"He's a regular playboy, a really successful attorney. He handles drug felonies. That's funny, huh? He's got all kinds of contacts and always has strippers and girls from escort services at his parties. I don't know if he'd talk to you or not. He thinks he's bigger than life."

"Did you and Josephine party with him?"

"Yeah. We used to go all the time. Josephine got freaked out by that weirdo Benjamin dude and stopped going."

At the utterance of that name, Jake lowered his drink, shuddering. A shadow-veiled figure opening a briefcase of money flashed through his mind. The vision immediately dissolved.

This weirdo was definitely connected to all this somehow.

"Do you think Peter could lead me to this guy?"

She rolled her eyes, making a spitting sound of distaste. "I think the loser still rents a room at Peter's house. The moocher should be easy enough to find. Just go to one of those parties."

He nodded, lifting a fresh Long Island. "So this loser *lives* there and rides the playboy gravy train. I can't wait to meet this guy."

"I'll give you Peter's address. Hey, you've got a better chance of getting in with that cute girlfriend of yours."

"Marci's not my girlfriend. I don't have one."

"Oh really?"

"I don't have time for one. Plus I just escaped a very toxic relationship."

She tilted her head inquiringly, blond hair sliding over her tan shoulder. "Can you find time for sex and casual companionship?"

He grinned devilishly. "It seems to find me. Anyway, back to the script. Who else parties with Josephine who might know where she was getting her shit?"

Abbey tucked back all that sexy cheerleader hair, eyebrows drawn together. "Have you ever gone to *Final Destination*? That's where that weird old drag queen hangs out. She's rich, too. She used to run an art gallery and a fancy antique store. She has this house that ought to be a horror museum with creepy old weapons and hidden rooms. Josephine and that drag queen bitch go way back. She actually *lived* in that horror house for a while."

Could this get any better? He finished his drink, ice rattling. "Okay. I think I know where that is."

He wound up getting a couple of dances from his new friend. She did indeed have the apple and snake tattoo on her back. She was the girl-next-door who could turn out to be the devil.

"I want to see you again," she said, eyes full of dark plans.

"Maybe we should go to one of Peter's wild parties together."

"We could, but we don't need Peter for a good time. Before we go out, you really should visit Peter. Every first date deserves a good story."

After another dance, they exchanged numbers and he left, feeling confident, mane flowing.

Well, what now? The specter of reality was throwing its shadow over his fun night of investigator role playing. He had to think about what to do next. He was done camping at Clara's, but he needed to get a motel room until he had a better plan. This would most likely wind up tantamount to a major life decision.

He found a cheap seedy motel on Highland Avenue flanked by an Indian restaurant and a skateboard shop. He couldn't help but laugh. Surely a droll psychopath ran this place.

Swinging the dirty motel office door open dramatically, he received a wan, lopsided smile from a stringy-haired woman who looked as if she'd recently been saved from the streets. He could have counted the number of teeth in her mouth.

"Hi there," he said in drunken cordiality. "I need a room."

She nodded slightly and dropped her tired eyes to a clipboard. "Okay, hold on."

Paying fifty for a single night, he pulled his car up to room 112. Rap music blasted from a black Trans Am full of raucous teenagers howling like marauders in an anarchic world as the car screeched out of the parking lot.

In the room, he flicked on a light. How far he was from Dunwoody hit him squarely in the face. Each dingy wall featured pictures of small town carnivals. Around these prints were scrawled numbers, the sordid appeals of addicts and prostitutes dancing around visions of cotton candy. *Call me for a good time...*

He turned on a television. The troubled soul at the desk was pleased to tell him it picked up Playboy and other porno channels. He surfed through several channels and then turned it off.

The bathroom was filthy, rust trailing from faucets, dirty tears. The mirror was spattered with dried toothpaste, tile cracked and crumbling.

He pulled back the bedcovers and discovered pubic hair on sheets that smelled faintly of sex and desperate sweaty nights. These sheets, washed a thousand times, would forever be an olfactory echo of wanton passion.

There should be mirrors on the ceiling, he thought and found *Hotel California* on YouTube. The live version had a flamenco flare evoking images of Caribbean Island dusks, bikinis, and unbelievable herb. If only this dump was in Jamaica.

"...the pink champagne on ice," he sang, going back out to get his laptop from the car.

For about ten minutes, he swigged from a Grey Goose vodka bottle like a besotted pirate, pantomiming playing frantic Flamenco guitar chord strikes while he flung his hair. Then collapsing on the bed, he gathered his thoughts and read aloud a few paragraphs from his book:

#

She was lost in this dark magical world. She knew as little about this place of debauchery and danger as it knew about her. She loved the anonymity, though. It made her feel free and wild.

Her sense of mystery and adventure about these streets drove her to stay up for days on end. There was just so much here, unearthly pleasure in thrilling disguise. You could be dancing with a demon or having sex with an angel and not even know it. The possibilities were endless.

She was also quite aware that this world hungered for her, too. Everywhere she went, men approached her with drinks, drugs, and promises. Even girls, dressed in leather, called like sirens from the shadows...

#

He paused, nodding slowly in dawning approval of the passage. It bore the noir romantic feel he was after. He would have written more, but he was just too drunk and exhausted.

After staggering to the shower, he fought with knobs that screeched with rusty resentment. Vibrations sent small shards of tile into the tub. They felt like sea shells under his feet.

He smiled faintly as he heard the banging of a headboard in the adjacent room. The hot water hit him. Who needed a porn channel?

When he passed out, the copulative banging next door bled into his dreams.

He was sixteen, thrusting into his fifteen-year-old girlfriend in an abandoned barnyard. She giggled in mock complaint about the straw scratching her back and ass and then matched his rhythm, pink fingernails pressing tightly into his back.

Shrieking in delight, she rolled him over, tufts of his hair in her fists. Then the girlish pink fingernails turned long and black, and the straw morphed into black satin sheets.

"I'm coming back," Josephine whispered with a voice like none other, dead stripper sexy voice. The nails dug into his chest, drawing blood.

He awoke with a gasp, expecting a leather-clad angel of death to be straddling him, but there was nothing to behold but the motel room ceiling. It was quiet except for faint city sounds. Even the banging of the headboard had ceased as though a possession had ended, bored demon moving on.

Had it only been a dream?

He exhaled sharply as a subtle chill—like one accompanying an erotic memory—passed over his skin. It was like the faintest sensation of sex magic.

Shadows slid across the wall, appearing to take human form, but then the shadows were lost to the night.

A breeze filled the room from an open window by the bedside table. For a fleeting moment, he was certain he smelled Josephine's perfume, an aroma of alien goddess pheromones. Then it was gone as though dispelled. He was alone again with his haunting speculations.

He fell back on the bed, sighing heavily. Out of the silence, the rumble of a motorcycle filled his ears. He shuddered as hostile Darkened magic rippled across his flesh. This was not a case of mere eerie possibilities. His amulet flared to life.

An image rushed through his mind of a heavy figure riding a metal beast. A showdown was coming like the one on that fateful night with Kitty Dreadlock—the night he felt his true power for the first time.

What now? Should he ward himself in here? The whole idea of being trapped freaked him out. No, he needed to get the fuck out of here.

He raced out the door and headed toward the back of the motel.

***

It was Zowie's night out with Moonshine and Marci. Their goal was to keep count of how many guys they blew off while having the time of their lives.

They headed to *Ponce City Market* like college girls after taking midterms—loose, laughing, free-spirited. After fried calamari and Silver Oak cabernet, they wound up at a dive bar across the street for a rowdy time.

A goof ball was stumbling toward Marci like Frankenstein to ply his drunken charm when her phone rang, a sound snippet of trap music. "Jake, why are you hyperventilating?"

"I'm being chased."

She threaded her way through the crowd toward the

bathroom. "What do you mean *chased*?"

"I'm staying at the Highland Motel. This biker just showed up who, I feel sure, is hunting me. I even recognized the Judas Priest reject from the show. My guess is he's been following me since then."

She couldn't help but giggle. "You're staying at that dump?"

"Beats Charm's couch."

"You'll be glad to know we're right down the road. We're coming." She charged back to the dance floor and jerked Zowie away from a man in a business suit who might have actually been a legit catch. "Jake's got trouble. You get to take out a biker as your initiation. What luck, huh?"

"How 'bout me?" Moonshine pouted.

Marci scoffed. "Oh, you can lead the way, hot thing."

***

Jake stood in the shadows of an alley behind the motel, heart racing. The Harley engine thunder was getting louder. Marci and the gang would never get here before he had to face this chunky tattooed titan on wheels.

He was actually trying to remember the lyrics to Steppenwolf's *Born to be Wild* when the roaring sound of death heralded the arrival of the biker at the end of the alleyway. The bike reared up like a creature of myth as the rider reached over his brawny shoulder and drew a sword from a sheath harnessed to his back. Shimmering glyphs of magic floated about the bike as he surged down the alley with the soulless passion of the headless horsemen.

Going inward, eyes closed, Jake willed magic out of his soul where it lay coiled, flooding his flesh like a drug shot into his veins. His eyes turned to starbursts, and tendrils of magic arced between his fists.

The confrontation looked like a scene out of a Japanese horror movie. Poised to sling a roiling sphere of light, the singer watched in horror as the bike rose into the air like a bounding beast. On impulse, he threw all his will into a spell of telekinetic power.

The bike froze in midair. His attacker flailed the sword at the magic-charged ether until finally Jake's psychic hold on the bike faltered.

The metal beast crashed to the street, and Jake took off, thinking of his next play. How could he beat this death rider straight out of the apocalypse?

The bike's engine shut off, and Jake looked back to see big boy coming after him on foot. *This should be fun*, Jake thought, rushing down another dark alley.

He leaped onto a fire escape ladder, rusty and vine draped. An eerie light illuminated the graffiti-ridden walls as the hefty leather boy appeared beneath him, weapon brandished, glyphs on the blade glowing. He looked like an overweight Roman gladiator lost in time, searching for a lion in the city streets.

Jake was crawling into the window of an empty studio apartment when streaming hair and dangerous vinyl-clad curves dropped past him from the roof. The rocking babe rescue unit was here.

The alley became an arena of battle, biker monster pitted against Greek pantheon heroines. The only thing missing was a stentorian and cheering crowd.

Omen's sword morphed into a spiked flail, and he came at them with all the fury of a raging Cyclops. The girls threw spell bursts that were met by a spiked iron ball, swung in a great arc from a heavy chain. The roiling orbs of light were reduced to useless sparks.

"Impressive," Marci said, sliding daggers free from thigh-strapped sheathes. "But I've got this."

Moonshine backed her, ready to throw silver stars.

"Let me take him," Zowie said. "I can deal with flails." She slid a sword free from a back harness, the blade ringing in the night like a death knell's steely cry. She circled Omen, lunging and swinging. He rushed at her, swinging the iron ball to no avail. She flipped and whirled, her agility overmastering his might.

Backing away, he grumbled an incantation. His bike appeared, rumbling down the alley as though ghost-ridden, coming at her.

She leaped out of its path. The bike turned around and rumbled up to Omen like a metal hellhound to its master, the warlock's metal familiar. The biker leaped on it and took off down the alley.

"That's quite a trick," Marci said. Her eyes slid up to Jake, coming down the fire escape. "Did you fight him?"

"I held him off. It was pretty cool watching that bike float in the air."

The three girls raved about getting to see such a spectacle as they headed off.

***

At the twenty four hour diner, *The Majestic*, they devoured rich late-night breakfast food while they listened to Jake's crazy sleuth stories.

"First, the good news." Jake chugged coffee then speared a scrambled egg clump with his fork. "I met a girl named Abbey at *Pulse*. She's got the forbidden apple tattoo Hex was talking about. She told me about a wild playboy attorney. A guy named Peter. Apparently, Josephine and my new friend Abbey hung out at his place a lot until a creep named Benjamin started to bother Josephine. I've picked up on him psychically. He's definitely involved in all this. And it gets better. He actually rents a room in the attorney's house." He shrugged, twisting a strip of bacon around his fork. "Anyway, this house is our next stop."

"Do you think this guy is our Rapture and Valentine candy boy?" Marci asked.

He sighed deeply and put his cup down so hard that coffee sloshed on the table. "When she said his name, I picked up on demented criminal energy and desperation. Plus I saw some kind of shady transaction I can't fully explain. My vision was too murky. Anyway, I certainly think he's Josephine's killer."

"Did she tell you where this attorney lives?" Moonshine asked, sipping orange juice. She'd ordered egg whites and wheat toast with no butter.

"She sure did. She's even willing to go over there with me."

"Oh," Marci said, "you've even made a date of this with your *new friend*. That's good news."

"The bad news is you have a bounty hunter after you," Zowie stressed. She was the drunkest of the girls, ordered a chicken salad with several of the vegetables picked out (Meg Ryan would've been proud of her—the waitress wanted to scream). "Wasn't that the freaky gay leather guy at the show standing up front?"

"I feel sure," he said.

Marci grimaced. "He's coming back for more. Trust me. Did your new friend give you any other leads?"

He scoffed. "Yeah. This might be even better than the playboy story. Abbey thinks a drag queen who hangs out at *Final Destination* might know her drug connections. This is some rich old queen who ran a really successful antique shop specializing in macabre oddities and weapons." He placed the coffee cup—his link to life—gently on the table this time. "It appears she lived with this strange female impersonator. Why can't I find somebody with money to move in with?"

Marci rolled her eyes. "Nobody needs to be taking care of you. You've spent enough time with me, couch surfer."

"Oh whatever. The point is, there's no telling what all happened in that house between those two. Abbey said the guy's house looks like a creepy museum. Plenty of kinky fun went on there."

She made a smirky "I'm impressed" face. "I knew you'd be good at this investigator thing. Weird knowledge just naturally comes to weirdos, in your case magnetically. Speaking of strange houses, you're still meeting Snow's gang tomorrow night, aren't you?"

"That's right. I might soon be living with a cross-dressing coven head. I can't wait to meet his gang."

There were warm giggles from the girls as Marci's phone came alive with rap music. It was Hex. "Well, if it's not the devil." She listened intently, eyebrows raised. "Let's go to *The Dungeon*. Hex has got an earful."

***

Around the bar at *The Dungeon*, they watched Abagail pour long streams of Skyy vodka and Peach schnapps into a tumbler. Hex, talking in his haughty heated way to security, came right over at the sight of them.

"Yeah. A stripper from Tryst came to me about you." He waved vaguely at them all. "Some burly leather queen came in here on the pretext of being 'a sex show talent agent,' hoping to track you down."

"He found us," Marci said flatly then lifted her shot glass.

"We just fought him. What I want to know is *how* he found us."

Hex smirked. "Well, those girls weren't going to tell him anything until he flat out paid them a handful of cash to talk. I think the stripper told him about your show with that band Burnt Offering."

Marci groaned. "That's how he found us. Dumb bitch. We ought to find her and kill her."

"He paid her a hundred dollars. She didn't know what she was doing," Hex said. "So, what's your next move?"

Marci cast him a dark speculative look. "Hex, you wouldn't hold out on us about a dealer hanging around here would you?"

"No, Marci. Holding out on you doesn't go too well. Did you ever check out *Pulse*?

"Yeah, I met a girl named Abbey," Jake said. "She told me about an attorney named Peter. I've got his address. She even sent me a photo of him." He held out his phone.

Hex's eyes went wide. "Oh yeah, that's the guy. He's got a reputation for throwing one bitch of a party. One is probably going on tomorrow night."

Jake threw back the Hollywood shot. "I'll tell Peter that you three are hookers. That should hold the key to his heart."

"I don't think so," Moonshine said.

"Oh, we're going to have a ball," Marci assured her partner, dropping twenties on the bar.

"Come back and give me the dirt," Hex said, watching them leave like performers heading to the stage. "I can't wait to hear about your wild night of drama."

Chapter Thirteen

The attorney's flashy modern crib, a contemporary Hollywood Hills dream home, was on Lenox Road right around the bend from Phipps Plaza. There were so many limos coming and going from the place that one would think a huge movie premier was underway.

But no, this was just another party for Peter Forest: call girls, high-rolling clients and local celebrities—every weekend.

"This attorney runs quite a show here," Marci said as they headed toward the door. She'd parked along the road like a thief casing the joint.

Moonshine groaned. "I'll bet we need to be on a list to get in there."

"Just tell the door guy you three were sent by an escort service," Jake said.

Zowie shoved him. It wasn't so gentle. "No. You tell them you're a gay porn star. How about that?"

"Whatever." He held out a splayed palm in that prissy "block you from my life" way divas and queens loved. Even Zowie laughed under her breath.

At the door, they all clamored to get in, but sure enough, the doorman said, "This is a private party. You need to be on the list."

Marci got in his face. "A friend of mine got killed who comes to these little *parties*. Just tell the attorney I'm a friend of Josephine's."

Concern darkened the doorman's expression. "Josephine? You mean Star?"

Oh, her stage name. "Yeah. Star."

Seconds later, out came a handsome middle-aged man with thick grey-streaked blond hair, combed to the side, soap opera svelte. He wore a blazer with jeans and a T-shirt that read "I Love New York." In his hand was a glass of expensive scotch he downed as he shut the door behind him in dramatic fashion.

"What do you know about Star?" The question sounded like an accusation.

"She's dead," Marci said flatly.

His eyes narrowed in disbelief. "What?"

"She overdosed on a drug called Rapture."

"Rapture? What the hell is that?"

"It's a sex-magic drug, one you need a spell to create. Do you know of a supplier who could get their hands on something like that? Or create a drug like that themselves?"

"No," he said indignantly. "That's absurd. I wouldn't deal with any fucking witch."

"She had a secret admirer who was crazy enough to give it to her." She showed him the note.

He read it and scoffed. "I have no idea who could've done this. It's just so bizarre."

"Think hard. Do you know of anyone who would stalk her? Maybe someone who had a history of bothering strippers? This person would need a nice sack of change to buy a rare drug like Rapture unless he was screwing the drug dealer."

They saw it in his eyes—a dark realization born from great anxiety. Still, he stuck to the script. "I've got no idea. I think now would be a good time to leave."

"Thanks for everything," Marci said. "You might find it interesting to know the drug turned her to ash."

This mix of horror and outrage overcame his face, and then he marched back into the house and slammed the door.

***

Coke was tantamount to the nectar of gods at Peter's parties—it was *that* important. There was no other local source more reliable at supplying nose candy than an unforgettable dope runner extraordinaire who'd earned the nickname Dennis the Menace. Most people just called him Dennis these days, but his real name was anybody's guess. Stage names and pseudonyms—they weren't just for strippers and writers anymore.

Dennis sat amongst a hard drinking, coke loving bunch in a living room decked out with slick leather furnishings and ostentatious Mediterranean artwork. He was oblivious to what was going on around him, though. Martini in hand, lips pursed, he just wanted to hear what Peter had learned outside.

With hippy long dirty blond hair, huge gypsy cool silver loops in his ears (Cher would love them), he was a Bohemian Midtown Queen if there ever was one. He was well known in the gay cruise bar scene of Midtown, but he even got invited to a lot of big Buckhead parties—straight ones, at that—because gay connections brought great drugs.

Peter loved having him at his house. Wild stories and flamboyance added comic relief to the drama and too serious sex games around there. The truth was, he wound up talking to the dashing dope-boy more than he did to the powerbrokers that came here.

When the door opened again, Peter stormed back in. Dennis rushed like a courtier to his service. The attorney motioned for him to join him in a small room lined with leatherbound law books.

He poured a glass of Macallan 18 scotch from an ornate beveled bottle set on a gleaming sideboard. After downing it and filling the glass again, he released a long sigh, shaking his head. "I can't believe what I just heard. Truth really is stranger than fiction."

"Star's dead, huh?"

"They're telling me she was turned to ash. What damn drug turns you to ash?"

"Ones with magic," he answered tartly. "I knew something from the dark side was gonna make its way in here sooner or later." His big Betty Davis eyes rolled about in wonder at the hideousness of it all. "Let me tell you about those girls who just left. They're witches and stripper bitches. Forget *Charlie's Angels*, those three hunt demons. The hot guy was the singer in the band Lost Angel. He's involved in this Josephine thing somehow, I'm sure."

"Alright, alright. This magic stuff is real. I believe that. Still, why would Star who'd stick anything in her arm take something that dangerous."

"You just answered it. She was miserable and would try anything. You know how desperate she acted. Bonding Weekend is coming up, and these festivals bring in all sorts of dangerous designer drugs that nobody knows enough about." He shrugged then sipped the martini. "I've heard Rapture is used in sex rites. It's expensive as shit. I don't know how she got it."

Peter filled the glass again. "They think somebody stalking her got it for her. You don't think Benjamin..."

Just bringing up that geek's name elicited a hardy laugh of disdain from Dennis. "Oh, I'm *so* sure he has connections in the drug underworld of magic. Sure, money talks, and he just inherited a little nest egg, but still." He sipped deeply from the martini, thinking. "Really, Peter, why don't you get that loser out of the house?"

Peter agreed, pondering Benjamin's inheritance, which was much larger than what people thought. He didn't want to bring up those strange occult books he saw in his room. He shook his head, sighing. "I probably will wind up throwing him out. Let's get back to the party before people think we're involved."

"Hey, I'll give you a whirl," Dennis exclaimed, the laugh dying in his throat from the withering look on Peter's face.

***

Outside the door, Benjamin listened intently to Peter's conversation with his favorite punk dope-boy—his precious pet Dennis. Then he darted up to his room before they came out.

There was a sprawl of books on his bed. The Bible was turned to Enoch, passages on Nephilim underlined. Next to the Bible was the Apochrypha, which topped a stack of grimoires he'd recently purchased.

After lighting candles, he got on his laptop and logged into YouTube. He selected *Operation: Mindcrime* by progressive heavy metal band Queensyrche, an awesome but twisted eighties rock opera/concept record loosely about government corruption and perversion in the church. His favorite song was about a priest who used a prostitute for sex in exchange for shelter from the streets.

He toyed with the beads of a rosary Josephine—Star—had left at a party one night. He pressed it to his face, sighing. Then he let the beads slide off of his fingers like serpents being freed.

After listening to *Suite Sister Mary* several times, he drank deeply from a bottle of Crown he kept under the bed. Then he called Thorn, anxiety rippling through his voice. "What are we going to do? Those witch stripper girls along with that singer dude were just here at Peter's fucking house."

Thorn scoffed. "'We?' 'We?' Are we French now? *We* aren't going to do anything. You need to pay Omen more money."

"Tell Omen I'll give him another ten thousand. I'll do anything to get rid of those people."

"I'd tell him twenty, my friend," Thorn responded. "Your life depends on it."

***

Minstrel's college girl quest landed him in a downtown motel with a nymph like no other. She rode him like there was no tomorrow. She called her friends between sets in the fuck-fest to tell them she was banging the "violin pirate dude."

The girl was on her phone, delirious with sex magic, when shadows started to shift and thicken in the room. Then a black cat appeared next to the bathroom door, crouched, watching.

"I didn't know you had a cat," she exclaimed in her euphoria. She had no idea what was really going on. She just knew she'd never had sex like this in her life.

"Oh, don't worry about that cute little cuddly thing." He laughed while running a finger between her breasts. "The little darling just wants its Meow Mix."

He'd known for a few minutes that demon magic was in the room. His flesh rippled with it, decidedly pleasurable.

The girl slid from the bed and pulled on panties as she argued with her girlfriend. "I need to go meet Cynthia. She's out with some guy whose driving her nuts." She rolled her eyes. "Plus, she's jealous of you."

The cat padded to the middle of the room, glittering eyes fixed on Minstrel. "By all means, go to your friend. I'll be in town a while. Come back when you can."

Fastening a mini skirt and snatching up a tank top from the floor, she said urgently, "I'll come back. I promise." She slid her feet into sandals then headed for the door.

The faint sound of a car cranking met his ears as the cat shifted in shape, roiling mist chrysalis, and then rose up to female form, a curvy silhouette filling the far wall.

Studded leather, creamy skin, and midnight black hair materialized as ectoplasm hardened like cooling candle wax.

David Raven

The demon/Josephine hybrid was close to the physical plane, longing to be fully fleshed. She straddled him, and he tasted the breath of a dead girl given life once again. A warm wind rushed through the room as his fingers explored her body. The tactile adventure was eerily erotic. Her skin was so supple in spots while in others he felt only the struggling force of magic.

Dark Lust filled him like a drug, and he knew before they even got started that making love to the Josephine demon would give birth to new addictions.

"You always wanted me so badly," Josephine breathed. "Now you can have me. I need your power to finish pulling me through to flesh."

"Yes, I would love to consummate your return and run away with you. I fear, though, you will need Felicity to be brought back fully." He tugged strands of her hair, sighing at her beauty. "Regardless, all those who were stealing from you...who brought you that drug...well, I've killed them all. I have your violin and jewelry."

"Good," she whispered. "To hell with them all."

Handcuffs materialized in her hands. He held out his wrists willingly. This wasn't the first time he'd played games with a demon.

Chapter Fourteen

It was raining the night the real investigation fun started. Topping off the noir mood for the evening, Jake dressed in black to look dangerous—a leather coat with countless zippers, a turtleneck sweater, stretchy lace-up pants, and shiny black Doc Martens. On his wrists, he wore entwined silver beads. He even wore his fedora, tilted rakishly, so *Pulp Fiction* cool. Damn if he wasn't the sexiest detective ever.

He was passing through the hotel district, *Hard Rock Café* on his left, when Marci called. "How is your sleuthing going, hot stuff?"

"I just headed out. I have a lead in a jack shop of all places that I'm going to follow up on before I head to *Final Destination*. I'm about to chase down a valium with a few shots of vodka. That'll really put me in the mood for all this."

"You certainly have a cocktail for success. Just call me if you see trouble coming."

"Don't I always?"

She scoffed and hung up, pounding background music clipped from his ears. Now, he heard only city sounds: blaring horns, shouts from the streets, car stereo music—the soundtrack of the night.

Watching businessmen rush to Uber rides from big hotels, he had to laugh at the misconception held by so many that this was a big cow-town. He couldn't even remember the last time he drank sweet tea. Of course, he was an alcoholic who'd trade southern hospitality for valiums or cocaine anytime. The point was, the underbelly of the city was a huge dark secret in a town known for historical battles fought with cannonballs, Margaret Mitchell, and writers like Pat Conroy.

He knew a world that came to life when the normal unknowing people went to sleep—an underground scene meant for addicts, divas, dealers, and wielders of magic, all of them playing steamy roles.

And which role did he play? He felt like he played all of them. Was he a diva? Gay guys sure thought so.

He pulled up in front of a lingerie shop on Cheshire Bridge and parked his car behind a small purple building that made him think of Prince and rushed to the neon lit front. Rain pelted him as though it had a grudge.

Jake felt he'd entered Wal-Mart's sexy sister. Dildos in all sizes were displayed behind a counter along with lubricants, love oils, candles and bondage gear—a dominatrix fantasy world emporium.

And then his eyes fell on the model.

She smiled in a way that could subjugate a man, exhibiting full-lipped knowledge of all male weaknesses. He sensed that more than a few men had bowed at her feet.

"Hi," she said with a voice of sultry opiate languor. She was curled on a velvet chaise lounge like a leather clad cat, a lush spiral of hair falling over one eye. She knew the moves, her sensuality contrived. "Love that hat. What brings a good looking guy like you here?"

"Are you Chloe?" he asked, an eyebrow raised, fedora tilted in a charming way.

"You know it. One of my following must have sent you to me."

"Well..." He cleared his throat. "I'm looking into the death of a friend." He showed the picture of Josephine on his phone. "Do you recognize her?"

Chloe sighed, staring at it a minute. "I think I've seen her in a strip bar somewhere. And *Final Destination*, too, I think." She handed the phone back to Jake and regarded him incredulously. "You came here just to show me that photo?"

"No. I got word you know a guy named Jazz who bounces at *Final Destination*. It's my understanding he could tell me about the scene around there. Talking to him could help me with my...quest."

"Yeah. I know him real *wild sex story* well. He's a big black guy with a heavy accent. I believe he's from Jamaica or someplace like that. Anyway, I feel sure he works tonight."

"Okay great. Is there anything about him—weird or

whatever—I need to know? The last Jamaican I met thought he was the reincarnation of a voodoo priest."

She shook her head, laughing. "No, he's just a cool guy who shoots pool and smokes a lot of weed. All the night people know him."

"Night people," he repeated musingly. "I like that. It's as though we're all revenants—Party Zombies."

She grinned at his droll humor. "Well, good luck. You're cute, but if anyone's weird, it's you. What's your name, anyway?"

"Jake Reece. I'm a singer."

She gave a slight nod. "Oh, that metal band. That's where I know you from. You're strange, but I get good vibes from you. I'll call Jazz and tell him you want to talk." She reached for her phone on a porn magazine. "Come back when you have time for a thirty minute session. For you it's just fifty dollars." She smiled slyly. "You'll be whipped."

"It won't be the first time." He headed back out into the night, rain over, air thick and heavy.

A long drive down Piedmont Avenue brought him to a cluster of gay bars on the corner of Juniper Street and Fourteenth—a thriving scene made up of every night crawler in the city. *Final Destination* was a block from the corner.

Everything from flashy sports cars to beat up vans was parked bumper to bumper for blocks around the club. Party people headed in droves to hot spots. There were even a few drag queens strutting down the sidewalk like they ruled the night.

After parking his car under a windswept Magnolia, he rushed by two men holding hands and joined the short line to get into the club. The young girl in front of him gazed up at the club's sign like it was the radiant manifestation of a deity. This was probably her first time in a nightclub, which meant tonight could be her first time for a lot of things. He just knew he couldn't wait to get in and hang out. Rob Zombie music ran berserk in the streets when the metal doors flew open like Hell's soundtrack blasted through its gates. He loved it.

He took out the photo of Josephine, moonlight and neon dancing across the phone's surface. The wind gusted, and once again he swore he could hear her call him.

He spun around, eyes sweeping the street. There were only a

few night freaks and shadows. A tingle ran down his spine. Was he losing his mind? He then entered a black painted antechamber lit with lurid red light, music racing like a cracked-out pulse. Maybe Satan's notion of disco hell awaited him.

"Twenty dollars," a preoccupied goth girl said offhandedly, hardly making eye contact with him. She was too busy reading *Wuthering Heights*. Jake imagined she was just like the haughty girl Heathcliff fancied in the book.

He ducked through an archway with a beaded curtain, feeling like a cheesy lounge singer going onstage. Before him was a crazy mix of aloof strippers, wild Buckhead girls, amused drag queens, and bold gay guys. And then there were always those odd people who looked like awkward tourists.

He ordered drinks at the bar, wondering how he'd ever find this Jazz character. Then he remembered Chloe say something about Jazz playing pool.

He scanned the area and headed over to where three tables were nestled in the corner of the room. A couple of guys looked like hustlers, but he didn't see anyone who met the description of Jazz.

Jake suddenly felt a rapid, insistent tap on his back and spun around, ready to fight to the death.

"Wanna shoot pool?" his friend asked with a honey thick conviviality. "My name's Mitch. I've always wanted to fuck a straight singer. You're a hard rocker who could rock me hard."

He was facing a guy who needed to be doing salon commercials. Cheekbones jutted proudly under a dark tan, and thick brown hair lay moussed back in blow-dried splendor, eyebrows neatly plucked. He wore a T-shirt that read "Paris," and designer jeans worn very tightly. Converse sneakers completed the look.

Jake blushed and then started laughing. He was used to gays, but this was so abrupt and aggressive. "How about if I let you buy me a drink. There is something maybe you can help me with."

Mitch tweaked a brow. "There's little doubt that I can."

Just as Jake was about to ask his worn out question about the photo, a girl slinked out of the cigarette haze to meet Mitch's new acquaintance.

"Oh, I've seen you onstage, pretty boy," she crooned, then bit

Jake's ear and drew circles on his neck with the tip of her tongue.

Mitch pulled her away. "Stop, Constance. That's rude. I mean, really girl. I've told you not to drink so much."

Jake backed against the railing that surrounded the pool table area. Constance reached for him again, lightly clawing his face, tugging on his lip ring.

"If he's not straight, he will be," she asserted with a giggle.

Mitch was thoroughly annoyed. "He's straight already, Constance. He isn't in need of your converting." He clutched her shoulder and petulantly shoved her away from him as though she were an incorrigible child he knew of no other way to deal with her when she got this plastered.

"Anyway, didn't you tell me you need help or advice or something?" Mitch asked, hungry eyes back on Jake.

Her arm free, Constance moved in for the kill again. Feeling as though he were fighting off a leopard, Jake asked, "Uh, do you know a guy named Jazz? I was sent..."

She started licking his face again.

"By a friend who thought he might know a few things about a girl I met."

"You need dirt on a girl? Oh, hanging out here is better than working for a tabloid." Mitch didn't seem to notice that Constance had finally stopped pawing at Jake. "Everybody who's anybody knows Jazz. Wait, here he comes now." Mitch gestured theatrically.

Jake will never forget the first time he saw Jazz. The large well-muscled black man moved jauntily through the crowd around the bar like a wrestler on *RAW*, strutting to the stage. He smiled expansively, gold teeth sparkling, a red bandana around his head. A weed pendant hung around his neck; big loops dangled from his ears.

"Hello, beh-beh!" He was saying "baby." His accent was islander thick, consonants full and ripe like exotic fruit, his enunciation flawlessly crisp. "You must be Jake." Then he just started laughing, a resonant chuckle.

"How'd you guess?" Jake could certainly see why everyone thought Jazz was from Jamaica. He later discovered Jazz was actually from St. Croix in the Virgin Islands. "Have you seen me live?"

More booming robust laughter, then: "Seen you live? Who are you, Bob Marley? No, that crazy bitch Chloe called, talking like god was on his way to see me." His face went serious. "So you are a rock n' roll singer?"

"Yeah, I guess you'd call me that."

Constance was dripping off his arm again, nibbling his ear.

"A regular Elvis?"

"God I hope not." Then they both laughed.

"So...why are you looking for me?"

"Do you..." He trailed off. Constance was really beginning to annoy him.

Mitch saw it, dragged her by the arm off into the crowd.

Jake had never been so relieved. "I was hoping you could identify someone for me."

He showed Jazz the Josephine photo. He examined it, thick eyebrows drawn. Then his customary smile spread over his thick lips once again. "Ah, I have talked to her many times. She is a very spooky woman. I haven't seen her lately."

"She overdosed. She's dead."

The expression of alarm gave way to a dark hooded look of speculation. "You want to avenge her death. I can see it in your eyes."

Jake sighed. "I'm not working for the cops."

"I know." His eyes rested on the amulet. "You are some kind of...vigilante."

Jake moved closer to him, whispering as though at confession. "I'm a friend trying to avenge her death. She overdosed on something she never should've taken. She reminded me of myself. I'm a little obsessed with the idea of bringing her drug dealer to justice."

"Obsessed, huh, beh-beh?" He laughed and then regarded Jake seriously. "You are going to get killed. You can't just hunt down drug dealers with so much hocus pocus going on these days. And she was definitely involved in the dark side of things—magic, shall we say?" Jazz looked around the room. "Maybe the weird old man who cross-dresses knows what's up. They actually *lived* together."

"Where is this guy...woman?"

Jazz chuckled as if he knew a dirty secret. "Beh-beh, I believe you are as crazy as that old man is. Over there. Look." He pointed through the crowd.

It took a moment for Jake to spot the dour wizened face at the end of the bar. He sat alone in his own cynical world, his very aura seeming to repel those around him. He was like a wicked grandfather watching over his hedonistic children with a baleful gaze.

Jake glanced over his shoulder at Jazz. "I have to go talk to him."

"Have fun, beh-beh. You are crazy as hell."

Jake felt a nightmarish sense of dread as he made his way past night freaks to the bar. He felt like he was going to visit Crypt Keeper. Jazz's laughter behind him didn't help matters.

Jake strode up behind the shriveled up old man. He didn't seem like much of a threat. He was a frail thing, bald except for a few wisps of silver on a liver-spotted head. He was slumped over, his shoulders doing little more than providing a hanger for a black overcoat.

The old man was gripping a walking cane, the handle of which was an ornately carved head of a snake. There were cabalistic symbols on it Jake thought he'd seen before.

As though sensing Jake's presence, the old man spun around in his seat. Jake almost wet his pants. He saw madness in those bloodshot eyes and, scarier, unnerving wisdom.

"I was told about you," the old man rasped, his voice conjuring images of dank cellars and cobwebs, centuries old. He lifted the cane several inches off the floor and brought it back down—*crack*!—with a hammer of the gods vehemence belying his appearance. Jake shrank back in horror.

The old man's hypnotic eyes cut away, a serpent interested in other prey. Rising from his stool, he swept the overcoat around him in a theatrical way, becoming a vengeful wraith of old radio shows. The snake's head was gripped tightly in his gnarled fist as he moved through the crowd with surprising speed. At the sight of him, everyone stepped anxiously out of his way.

Jake shuddered at the thought of the old man's words: *I've been told about you.*

How would he know about me?

Unless...

He dashed into the crowd, determined to beat the old devil at his mind games. He burst out of the exit in time to see the cane slip into the door of a cab as the car pulled away from the curb.

Jake cursed, rushing to another cab. Conga driven Latino club music issued from it. "Follow the cab ahead of you," he said breathlessly. "I have no idea where it's going. Follow it at a distance."

The Hispanic driver gave a scoffing bark of laughter. "So, you want to follow that crazy old man who likes spooky bitch hookers."

"Spooky bitch hookers?"

"Witches, man. That one girl he used to takes home is spooky as hell."

"Could you describe her?"

"She has long ass *Adams Family* black hair. Hot but evil, you know?"

Jake showed him the picture.

"Yeah. That's her. Shit. Even the fucking picture is scary. She was always wearing pentagrams and talking about spells and creepy books, all that shit. That bitch was into the magic you hear all about these days."

Jake broke into drunken song: "Do you believe in magic in a young girl's heart..."

The driver laughed. "What was in her heart was no Valentine card shit." He pointed ahead of him. "That old dude was paying to get whipped or even kinkier shit. I heard him calling that girl *master*."

Now *that* was creepy. "I see your point."

"You'll really see my point once you see his creepy house. We're almost there."

Jake's driver followed the cab to the Candler Park area. He wended through a series of twists and turns until the cab ahead was spotted going through a wrought iron gate flanked by leonine pillars. Beyond the brick walls lay a huge pink Victorian house.

Jake gestured sharply for his driver to pull over. "How much do I owe you?"

The driver turned the club music down. "Twelve dollars."

Jake handed him twenty. "Now, I want you to do me a favor and wait for me. I don't think I'll be long, okay?"

"I will wait ten minutes," he said, anxiously ripping the plastic off the top of a pack of cigarettes and tossing it irreverently out of the window. "You should come running back soon enough."

"Okay. What more could I ask?"

Both of them flinched when the sound of shrieking tires filled the night. The cab driver who took the old man home sure wanted the hell out of there. The cab raced off like a bat-out-of-hell, the gate slowly creaking back. Jake gave a shuddering laugh, heading toward the place.

The huge pink mansion looked like something out of Alice in Wonderland. If this guy was an antique dealer who specialized in the macabre and danced in drag, he felt sure this place was a regular chamber of kinky horrors.

Rejecting all common sense, Jake took a deep breath and clambered over the brick wall sequestering the house from the world. He wondered whether wild dogs waited to shred him on the other side.

Well, close enough. Two Dobermans ran around the house. "Oh, oh, the hounds of hell." He laughed hysterically.

He threw magic, staving off the racing dogs long enough for him to make it around the side of the house. Leaping up the steps to a terrace overhung with swaying oak tree boughs, he conjured a swirling shield around himself. The dogs bounded up the shadowy steps, leaping and barking at Jake ferociously. The wards held them at bay, though.

"Release," came a commanding voice, and the dogs headed off. "Nice evening, eh, Jake?"

From open French doors, the old man was studying him with beady, piercing eyes, a glass held tightly in his gnarled hand, the cane in the other. He rolled the ice around in the glass and brought it to his mouth. He was backlit by candles, throwing flickering shadows.

"Vodka is my second dearest passion." The old man's tongue ran across his cracked lips as his eyes bore deeper into Jake.

For a few moments, there was nothing but the wind and the old man's raspy breathing that betrayed decades of smoking. A life of hard drinking was also evident from the spidery veins on his nose and cheeks.

Finally, Jake broke the silence. "And what is your first

passion?" he asked, unnerved. At least the dogs had run off.

The old man threw back his drink, eyes wide as though he had the most delicious secret. "Oh, I dare not tell you." He released a howl of sardonic laughter, a maniacal super villain's laugh.

I'll bet he'd look like the Joker in drag. Jake imagined him with blown-back red hair.

"Why have you come here, my dashing singer? Or do I have to ask?"

A wicked witch's cackle was accompanied by a knowing glint in his eyes. He tapped the cane on the terrace tauntingly as though at any moment he'd strike Jake with it. That moment never came—just the *tap, tap, tapping* like a raven at a window in the dead of night.

He smirked devilishly. "Well?"

Jake breathed deeply and pulled out his phone, holding up Josephine's photo. "Do you know this girl?"

"Oh yes." He tittered.

"She overdosed on a very dangerous sex drug and is no longer with us."

"Oh really?" the old man shrieked in derision. "You fool! Josephine is everywhere. She is the night itself." He brandished the cane high in the air as though to stab the moon and harness the elements of nature.

She is the night itself, he mused. *I could use that in a song.* "So you know her spirit now haunts this world. I just want to find the dealer who is responsible for her death. Did she ever mention a dealer who dealt Rapture?"

The old man calmed as though a bi-polar storm had passed through him and left. "I've read her books of magic...those grimoires and her journals. Her time here is something I'll never forget. As far as her life away from me went, though, she was very secretive. You act as though you love this girl. You don't even know her. To love her you would have to see the beauty in evil and her selfish brilliance. Why, she only cared about music and torture." His fingers caressed the snake handle, thumb running over the symbols of magic. Then he smiled. "I have something to give you if you want to know her so badly." He went back into the candlelit house and returned with a black book, her diary. "Here. You can read all about her life." He tossed it to Jake. "And do catch that dealer. He needs to die a terrible death."

"On that we can agree."

Oh, I got my hands on her diary, Jake thought, looking out for the dogs as he rushed down the steps.

His crazy host for the evening ranted behind him. "She's coming back, and she'll be with me forever."

Jake ran toward the stone wall like he was escaping a haunted house. A heavy wind stirred the oak boughs around him as though upset about his leaving.

"You'll never be able to take her from me," the old man shouted. His howling laughter echoed through the night. "She's going to use you, and then come back to me forever."

At the wall, he grasped a thick rope of ivy and slung a leg over, bits of brick clattering downward. He heard the glass of vodka hit the terrace and shatter.

"She'll use you up and then come back to me," came a maniacal cry from the house.

Finally, the ranting was swallowed by the distance between them. Jake sprinted up the street, thrilled to see the cab driver waiting for him.

In the cab, he flipped to the middle of the diary—near the end of the entries—and read by the light of his phone:

#

Dear Diary,

I will be the greatest violinist in the world of magic once I go through my Darkening. Tonight, I will practice in the playground where the little girl waits. She always appears when I play, homeless, yet so beautiful.

#

Gasping in fascination, he read and read until the driver let him out a block from *Final Destination* where his hippy dream machine was parked. Then he went back to his motel room and read until dawn.

Chapter Fifteen

T**he** goth club *Rivals* was the new rage in Midtown Atlanta. "Classy Gothic Hot Spot" was the blurb a Creative Loafing critic gave it. It featured a mad list of martinis and sensual chocolates set on all the bars, flickering in the light of pillar candles. The music was everything from eighties and nineties stuff—Depeche Mode, Shadowcrux, Ministry, and Type O Negative—to Ghost, Black Veil Brides and New Year's Eve. At the moment, new Evanescence was playing, ethereal but heavy.

The darkly lit place was festooned with lush black swags. Huge candelabras hung above every bar. Showcased in a lurid red pool of light behind the main bar was a breathtaking mural of a demon and an angel drinking wine together in a dark forest. The winged creatures were surrounded by gauzy figures in the throes of lovemaking on plush beds of leaves and huge gnarled roots, a sex rite of opposing beings of myth. Throughout the club, there were murals with similar depictions.

Many believed the angels and demons partying together symbolized gays and straights coming together in this high-end cruise bar where both came looking to hook up.

Those versed in the world of magic knew the truth of the matter, though. While the crowd's diversity was great for business, the owner wanted to unite the Darkened and Estranged. Many thought it was preposterous and downright dangerous to draw both crowds, but there was a growing trend toward harmony and even sexual interaction between the factions. Why not bond the groups with cocktails and sexual excess? This was a great spot to meet someone taboo. During Bonding Weekend, the club would make a fortune.

Minstrel strode into the club like a proud suitor heading to meet an anxiously waiting princess. In suave and cavalier form, long coat flapping, he rushed up to a waitress about to drop a drink and clutched the Martini glass with a flourish, holding it steady.

"Would you care to hear a sweet melody?" he asked, drawing a bow across the strings of his violin.

She laughed, flattered. "I wish I had the time."

He darted about, slinging charm and promises like a bard stolen from centuries ago. People thought he'd been paid to perform here, but as always, there was an ulterior motive.

"So, do you take tips for playing?" a girl asked.

"I take whatever you desire to give me," he answered suggestively. "But what I really want is a little information. Who would know about the rock-band scene here in Atlanta?"

"Elise. She works the bar on the roof. She's your metal head social butterfly."

"Why, thank you." And up he went like the fiddler on the roof.

Elise was clad in tights and a studded leather top, bartender batgirl, making Bay Breeze shots when Minstrel glided up the stairs. She was putting limes on the drinks when she set eyes on him. She giggled, holding the bottle of Grey Goose vodka in her hand as though she might have to defend herself. She shot security an amused glance. The guy looked like he was ready for Broadway, but these magic types could really be dangerous.

He stalked up to her, sweeping his coat about dramatically. "My lady, may I introduce myself? I am Minstrel. You are beautiful—a mortal but beautiful nevertheless. Lovely women are some of the few things that matter to a man who's been around as long as I have."

She smiled slyly, amber hair streaming in the rooftop night breeze. "How long have you been around?"

He flared an eyebrow. "There were no cell phones, I can tell you that." He placed the violin on the bar and reached into a deep pocket. "Care to see a card trick?"

"You're a regular Houdini, huh?" She watched him shuffle, his showmanship enthralling.

"Because you have the key to my heart, I want you to pick one special card from the deck."

She pulled one card out. "Ah, it's the Queen of Hearts."

"And the Queen of Hearts is always your best bet," Minstrel said in a singsong way.

"I've heard that song by the Eagles." She grinned.

"Okay, so why don't you do this Desperado a favor and hold the card behind your back. Have you ever heard of the band Motorhead? The British metal singer Lemmy?"

"Sure. Everyone has. I don't listen to it, though."

"And what is their most popular song?"

Her eyebrows drew together. "That...uh..." She snapped her fingers. "A song about poker."

"The Ace of Spades," a guy at the bar told her.

Minstrel smiled. "Now check your card."

She peered at it and gasped. "It's now the Ace of Spades."

Then he tossed several cards from the playing deck into the air, what drifted down to the bar were tarot cards.

Everyone was astounded.

"You're an important girl around here, aren't you."

She smiled, shrugging. She was into this—into him.

"I think you are very crucial to my task here." He pointed at the card she still held. It, too, was now a tarot card: The High Priestess. "That's you, my dear. And being the High Priestess, perhaps you can answer a few questions for me."

She folded her arms, her wrists clattering with skull charms. "What questions?"

"I'm looking for the guitarist in Dark Promise. Do you know where his house is?"

She frowned, puzzled. "Why?"

"I'm interested in playing with him."

"A lot of musicians want to play with him. He's a genius. What makes you so great?"

Minstrel sighed, slid the cards into a pocket of his velvet coat and then picked up his bow and violin. He began to play a dazzling series of arpeggios, the runes on the violin flashing as though spellbound. "This is off the *Twenty Four Caprices*—Niccolo Paganini's greatest work."

"Okay, so you're amazing. Let me call him."

Snow picked up: "How is my bar vixen?"

"Your vixen is talking to a violinist who wants to play with you," she said in a low tone. "I'd be careful. He's interesting but very weird."

Bonding Weekend

***

Snow canted an eyebrow at Jake. They were exchanging songwriting ideas and drinking—mainly drinking—at a dive bar on Ponce De Leon Avenue. "I think your violinist is at *Rivals*." He led the way past security and down a hallway lit with candles on shelves of ornate stonework.

They headed straight to Elise's bar. Snow, all that bleach-blond hair thrown to one side, a leather duster flowing around him, looked like a cross between a Nordic god and a villain in a Bond film. Jake, wearing a turtleneck and three-quarter-length leather coat, was forever the spy seeking a movie role.

"Where is this fool?" Snow asked Elise. Then he spotted him playing violin for two girls curled in a velvet wingback settee.

"Snow, don't cause a scene."

"I've always wanted to meet one of Felicity's minions."

Snow and Jake approached Minstrel, who leaped up, twirling away from the girls. Effulgent light trailed from the bow. "I'm here to talk, not fight. Don't make me pull a few tricks. I might surprise you."

Snow regarded him with amused disdain. "What do you want to talk about?"

"I want to confirm what I'd heard, that Jake is joining your band."

"Why do you care?"

"Don't you want a fabulous violinist in your band? We'd be unstoppable."

"I've heard you want to leave Felicity," Snow said, glancing at Jake. "Why don't you just run? What's holding you back?"

"There's a small market for violin soloists. Plus, if I'm leaving her, I need—"

"Protection? Whatever. What kind of ruse is this?"

Jake nodded. "And what do you know about Josephine's death?"

Minstrel's face reddened in indignation. "I didn't want her dead. I wanted her to run off with me."

"Yeah, but you've done something terrible to her," Jake said. "You collected the ashes from her apartment. What have you done?"

Minstrel looked outraged, palms out in appeal. "She was one of us. I couldn't let the police get her ashes. Besides, I desperately needed her essence..."

Jake gasped, ritualistic images rushing through his mind in a montage. His eyes rolled upward in realization, and then he said flatly, "You've bound her spirit to a demon."

Minstrel shook his head in frustration. "She would've wandered through this world as an angry ghost forever. There was no other way. Now she can't wait to return to the flesh."

Chills rushed through Jake. "What exactly do you mean?"

The violinist scoffed. "I mean to bring Josephine back to the world. The demon is not quite powerful enough to bring her spirit completely into the physical realm, though." He threw back a shot for courage and pointed at the singer. "I believe you could bring her back if you slept with her. You hold great magic you've never used. The demon could tap into your dark side."

"You want me to sleep with a ghost to bring her into this world?"

"That's right. If you don't do it, Felicity will, and then our demon girl will be the bitch's slave forever."

Jake was speechless, watching the violinist dash off into the crowd. He started to go after him, but Snow grabbed his arm.

"Forget it. The violinist might be out of his mind, but who are we to stop a dead girl from having a second chance at life? We all get used by demons sooner or later."

That truth Jake fully understood.

***

Just a few blocks from the corner of Memorial Drive and Moreland Avenue stood an old brick bar swathed in ivy. This well kept secret was called *The Escape*. The place drew mainly artsy types and misfits who lived in their own worlds, avoiding mainstream crowds.

A jukebox in the corner was covered in rock band decals. *Fascination Street* by the Cure was playing.

The members of Snow's coven were hanging out on a grouping of cool retro vinyl furniture. There were even lava lamps on low tables.

Cameo had a boy's head in her lap. Muriel had her feet

propped on a coffee table, writing lyrics by candlelight. Even Zowie was there (Everyone knew she would officially join Marci soon enough), drinking more than anybody and playing the most music. They were a motley crew of Casters, to say the least.

"I'm playing The Beatles." Zowie stuffed a dollar into the machine.

"You're trying too hard to be deep and philosophical," Muriel said.

She was the band's bassist, singer and primary lyricist. She had long earthy-brown hair that was draped over an Avenged Sevenfold T-shirt, her flowing hippy skirt covered in cabalistic symbols. Her black lace-up Doc Martens were propped on a velvet ottoman.

Huge sixties cat girl glam horn-rimmed glasses were perched on her high-bridged nose. She just finished reading a passage aloud to a small audience. Tonight it was Mary Shelly's *Frankenstein*. She was forever the erudite showboat.

"Whatever," Zowie retorted after a moment's thought. "I thought you'd want to hear a song off *Sgt. Pepper's Lonely Hearts Club Band*. So just what do you want to hear?"

"Play Slayer."

"Fuck no. That's too wicked. I could drown in all that evil shit. Here we are basically the spawn of angels..."

Muriel threw back her head and laughed at the irony of it all, the worn out book sliding off her lap to the floor. She snatched it up, crescent moon charms jangling.

Coven member Cameo was sprawled like a princess on an elegant chaise lounge, her head in the boy's lap. He was playing with her golden blond tresses.

"Don't laugh at her," Cameo called out. "Battle Bitch Barbie will think you aren't taking her seriously enough and beat your ass." Speckled with silver glitter, she was the quintessential cosmo-blond Caster. She danced onstage with the live band, go-go girl extraordinaire, trained ballerina to boot.

Zowie never responded to her barb, engrossed in song selections. Cameo regarded her slyly, a small hand with electric blue sparkly fingernails poised thoughtfully at her candy mouth; pink and black plastic bangles hung on her slender wrists. "We're doing karaoke tonight. I'll always be able to beat the shit out of you at that."

Slayer possessed the place, frantic power chords merciless, vocals roaring. "Why are you acting so competitive? I don't think I'm Ms. Special," Zowie said. "You'd throw me out on the street in a heartbeat to get Jake Reece in the band."

"Maybe not out on the streets," Cameo said. "But I might kick you out of bed for him."

Zowie feigned a shocked look. It was priceless. "You mean you would really fuck out his brains? *Noooo.*"

It was Cameo's turn to laugh now.

In the midst of the repartee, Brice came back with a round of drinks, placing them on the coffee table. He was the drummer, twenty-five, but he could've just gotten out of high school with his long brown "Emo" bangs. He was no callow youth, though. Several lip piercings and major tat work—mostly skulls and snakes—on his arms and neck made him look more like the cross between a teeny bopper idol and a demented cult leader. "I'm not going to hang out if you two argue all night."

Muriel's phone rang, horror ambient sounds. She picked up, listened intently. "Let's go to the house. Snow's got a story."

A small group from the bar went with them. It wasn't just the drama that drew them there. A night at Nightmare Mansion—Snow's house—was a paranormal spectacle that would put the Adam's Family out of business. Everybody wanted to see the place.

The gothic Victorian revival house was a few blocks away from the Oakland Cemetery in a hip area of historic Grant Park. The *God only knows who the fuck got murdered here* house was a century-plus survivor of Atlanta development and gentrification.

The multi-gabled vine-covered house needed all sorts of work done to it, but the years of neglect just seemed to add to the mystique of the place. With peeling oriels, candlelit turret windows, and a shadowy wrap-around porch where flowing figures of velvet hung out, the weather-beaten masterpiece just screamed house of horror.

"I bet Rob Zombie would love to buy this place," Snow often boasted. And eerie stories abounded to support this assertion.

The centerpiece for most of the stories about the murders and paranormal drama surrounding the house sat in the front yard. This single enormous tree looked like something out of Tolkien's *Mordor*. This leafless, bone white spindly enigma was called the "Bone Tree" because it was permanently denuded as though stripped by magic. Rumored to glow on full moon nights, it reached for the sky like some cursed creature begging the gods to reverse a spell of damnation.

"I think the House of Usher needed that goddamn tree in its yard," Brice once said musingly, regarding the Bone Tree as he smoked.

"Don't bring Poe into your world," Muriel said. She loved Poe and read him often on the porch to her literati. "But I must admit," she added jokingly, "the Usher house would've been impossible to rent, too, if that damn thing had been up front."

Snow had gotten a great deal on the house because it really was stigmatized property. It didn't just look spooky. It had the history to back it up.

Twenty-five years ago, a metal singer who went by the stage name Devi Darkness owned it. He fronted a very popular local goth metal band called The Masquerade. He had it made—or so everyone thought. Management was shopping demos around to major labels, and they already had an indie deal with Forbidden Records. The band was hot. Even the state-of-the-art basement recording studio in the house was sought by other Atlanta acts. Devon was making a fortune just producing other people.

The house became infamous for the band's wild parties. During the recording of *Nightmare,* their second CD with Forbidden Records, he threw a huge bash, drawing New York rock journalists, porn stars, and all manner of moguls from Los Angeles.

It goes without saying there were girls, girls, girls.

And with groupies came jealousy.

On the night of the big bash, there was a drive-by shooting. Devon's entire band was killed. The police found their bodies strewn around the Bone Tree (the shooters were believed to be ex-boyfriends of girls at the party, but nothing was ever proven). Some believed that's why the tree appeared dead. The death of the members killed its spirit.

Devi threw a band together to finish recordings and then immediately moved from the house. Weeks later, right after the release of *Nightmare,* he committed suicide. He was buried by friends in California.

Songs from *Nightmare* went viral on the internet amidst lurid tabloid sensationalism. It was thought that maybe the singer, known to be bi-polar, orchestrated his band's demise. There were even rumors their bodies had been buried on the grounds around the house.

It wasn't rented for years. Tales of strange lights were reported by neighbors to the police. Others saw ghostly figures walking around the property. The place became so notorious that ghost hunters came to check it out, declaring the place "teeming with spirits."

An art gallery owner from New York eventually bought it, and then terrified, he sold it a few months later. A bold restaurateur who didn't believe any of this "ghost buster shit" turned it into a French bistro. It was successful at first, but reports of ghost sightings finally brought the stylish place to an end.

The house sat like an unwanted orphan for many more years.

Then Snow and his coven came along. Now the ghosts were just part of the big happy family.

***

The partying group trudged up a hill from *The Escape*, Muriel telling everyone about the Bone Tree like she was hosting a ghost tour. Their guests marveled at it. Silhouetted in moonlight, the spindly branches looked like capillaries radiating through the night sky.

"Just look at this beautifully evil thing," Muriel whispered. Huge boughs creaked in the wind, their moon shadows thrown over the candlelit porch. "Those branches go on forever like veins in the darkness as though they give the night the life blood it needs." Everyone nodded at the dark profundity.

The ghost tour went on. She led them up the shadowy porch steps and into the living room. Brice already had booze laid out like a master plan.

First-timers were always in awe of the eccentric house. "Where did you get all this cool stuff?" one asked.

In a tour guide tone, she said, "When the restaurant owner abandoned the place, he left the furniture. All this velvet furniture was here when Snow took the place over. The velvet wingback sofas had most likely been set around a grand piano or cocktail area." There were even big oval booths set along one side of the wall—all this stuff just left behind by a terrified owner.

The mantle above a fireplace featured an array of morbid clown and eerily elegant gothic dolls that Muriel had custom made by a San Francisco doll maker. Each doll held a classic horror novel in its arms. Her favorite figure embraced *The Castle of Otranto*.

Cabalistic symbols, painted in flowing script, adorn the walls, flanked by pillar candles in sconces of iron scrollwork. Gay erotica and gauzy cityscape prints were placed amongst it all.

Cameo danced about in her short party dress, sparkling ballerina, invoking the scripted spells on the walls with whispered conjurations and elegant hand motions. Runes flashed and wind rushed through open windows carrying spiraling leaves.

Spectral ribbons of light issued from the walls like escaping ghosts, carrying images of misty forests, purling streams, and frolicking winged creatures. Some of the magic carried erotic scents. One could take a deep breath and have an orgasm.

"So, tell us about the ghosts," newbies demanded like kids around a campfire.

Brice smiled mischievously at Muriel. "Are you ready to tell a ghost story to our friends? We could..." He trailed off as the awaited duo was heard charging up the porch steps.

"You're partying without me?" Snow exclaimed, flinging the door open with a theatrical flourish like he was late to a talk show. He struck a haughty pose, nose high, lips pouty. His eyes, though, betrayed great worry.

Jake was right behind him, pulling his metal mane free from the collar of a leather coat. The coven had met him earlier in the day. They couldn't wait to party with him tonight. Snow was jealous.

Zowie was doing a split on the floor, a wine cooler tilted to her mouth. "Snow, you looked perturbed. Did some guy turn you down?"

"Oh yeah, Zowie, I was out begging for sex and no one wanted me. No. I just encountered that crazy violinist who's been running around town, harassing everyone."

Cameo twirled and floated over to Snow, then handed him a glass of wine. He downed it like a shot.

In Muriel's ear, Snow whispered, "This lunatic wants Jake to have sex with a ghost to bring her back to the flesh."

"Josephine?"

"She's the one."

Nosey Cameo overheard it. "Would you do it?" she asked Jake, eyes like an ecstatic child's.

He shook his head. "I don't know what to do. Talk about getting used for sex."

She grinned. "What's wrong with that?"

"That demon will turn to Felicity to reach flesh if Jake refuses," Snow said.

"This is going to get nasty." Muriel made a sweeping gesture toward everyone in the living room. "In the meantime, we have fresh faces amongst us who want to hear about the ghosts."

Snow nodded at the assemblage. "Make no mistake. Our spectral friends will come out the night of the big party of Bonding Weekend."

"I can't wait," newcomer Rachel shrieked. "I feel like everyone has seen the ghosts but me."

"Is it true they were members of a band?" another asked.

"Yes," Cameo said. "Beautiful long-haired boys." She lit candles. More runes were invoked, illusion effluvia moving like spirits through the house.

Muriel smiled. "Don't you love it? Everybody drink and enjoy the show. Magic is all around you. And who knows? Maybe even tonight the dead will join us."

"They're dying to party," Brice said dryly.

"And they're dying to dance," Cameo said. "I've danced with all of them."

"Death can't keep them from the dance floor," Muriel whispered in poetic musing.

"Isn't that an old goth band called Dead Can Dance?".

"Brice, all those rock history books you've ripped off from me to read, and you have to think about it?"

"I'm sorry. A lot of that dreary shit bores me. I'm not going to read about something I don't give a fuck about."

"You should give a fuck about Dead Can Dance and bands

like Bauhaus—they're goth institutions."

"Oh yeah, you've lost—"

"Alright, that's enough pitter patter," Snow said. "Let's talk about the ghosts. They are most definitely real. I've seen the whole band in the recording studio. At the Bonding Weekend party, I'll take you down there."

Muriel opened a book of poetry: *The Work of Keats.* "Now don't just come to see ghosts."

"Come to be eternally young," Cameo interjected, forever dancing, candles in her hands, twirling firefly girl.

"Exactly," Muriel said. "Tonight, everybody just hang out and have cocktails. It will be a nice preamble to that night of festivities."

Snow came up behind her, whispering, "I'm calling Dennis. Just give me fifty."

She gave him a hundred and fifty. There were several more outrageous contributions. Dennis the Menace would be doing a highly profitable coke run.

The dashing dope-boy showed up at the house about thirty minutes later. Jake watched from the candlelit porch as the long-haired blond dealer handed a package to Snow.

"Weren't you at Peter's the other night?" Dennis called out to Jake as he headed back to his ride.

"Yeah. Is that attorney ready to talk?" He tilted his head quizzically, eyebrow flared. "*We* need to talk first." And then he slid back into the cab and left.

Jake had heard much about the infamous flaming dealer who slung coke all around town. Girls, especially strippers, loved him. The few times he was in *Medusa's* he was aloof, though. Word had it that the whole idea of making buddies with Jake was beyond his ego threshold.

Aloof or not, Dennis had great stuff. White lines were snorted off mirrors, tables, and body parts. Jake fell back on a velvet sofa, eyes rolling upward. The high was like a mental slingshot, sending reality to Mars.

Everybody started making out then. A guy came on to Jake, but he pushed him away, laughing. Snow, though, had found a lover, and Cameo was kissing a girl. Brice just kept doing lines in his own world. Now there was an addict in the making.

The sexual dynamics were really no more bizarre than what went on late night at *Medusa's*, but the magic here was like nothing he'd ever seen.

Snow drank wine and did this snaky-undulant ritual dance to Gregorian Chants while images of castles streaked from his palms. Apparitions of robed monks encircled him and then vanished.

The music changed to dark racing electronica. The place changed like a stage set into a nightclub. Furniture was shoved out of the way, and dancing began. Couples headed upstairs.

Muriel grabbed Jake's arm and pulled him out to the porch. The scent of Myrrh filled the air. "I hear you are trying to write a novel. I want to read to you something I wrote. You know I write song lyrics, but I want to write literary horror. I love vampires. What I'm about to read to you is about a couple who've been bitten, and now they're sharing a dream from vampire magic. I call the story *Inverted Heaven*." She sat with him on the porch swing and arched an eyebrow. "Ready?"

"Ready."

Candlelight flickered over pages of flowing cursive. Muriel in that moment looked terribly sexy, a dirty librarian. She was a little nervous, a hand absently fondling a vine-festooned trellis.

With a sharp intake of breath, she read aloud: "The vampire queen Agatha drank deeply from Jason, and then he collapsed next to Sarah on the motel bed, laughing giddily. They drank beer until the bottles slipped from their hands. It was as though they'd been drugged. Jason was the first to start dreaming."

She stopped reading aloud and gently squeezed his hand. There was a warm glow between their palms. She mouthed the prose silently, his mind becoming a stage for the dream. Vividly, he could see it all.

In the dream, the drunken couple went out into the night. They panhandled on street corners, hustling every way imaginable. Jake sensed the girl would sell herself to get what she wanted: heroin. Her boyfriend might even do it. They were both so desperate.

A police car screeched around the corner. The couple took off running, faces of primal fear.

Then the dream morphed into a long dark alley in a grim dystopian world. Running for their lives through neon and shadows, they heard heavy footfalls and wild banging on brick walls, raucous gang sounds. They looked back from their flight to behold zombies chasing them. They ran faster, gasping for breath.

The alley then morphed into a dark forest. Now they heard the howl of wolves. They were running so hard that huge gnarled tree roots became death traps.

They spotted a black building with a neon-lit sign among the trees, shadowy swaying giants. Trance music, dark and eerie, pounded from the structure.

A metal door to the place swung open, revealing a fanged figure in velvet, beckoning them inside. They rushed through the door, the snarling of wolves devoured by the pounding beat.

Agatha and the others sat around a dimly lit bar, syringes in their long pallid hands. They drank wine while gargoyles perched in their laps like pets.

"'Welcome to our bar, *Inverted Heaven*. You're safe from the wolves here,'" Muriel said aloud once again, assuming a vampire voice. "'You can stay forever. We can satisfy your every want.'"

"The bartender shook a bag of dope tauntingly," Jake said aloud, the words flowing from her mind to his.

After lowering the journal, Muriel ran her nails over Jake's wrist. He didn't open his eyes until she gently tugged at a cross-studded leather bracelet.

"Wow." He gasped. "So, the vampire's club, a stronghold of sin and addiction, became their heaven...an eternal bastion from the real world."

"Heaven and sinful pleasure were one and the same there, hence the name."

He tucked an errant strand of hair behind his ear, eyes taking on a searching cast. "The concept is really thought provoking."

Muriel blushed as Cameo burst out of the house. She planted her eyes on Jake. "Kiss me," she demanded. "You're so beautiful."

Jake reached for her, lips parted, eyes half-lidded in dreamy languor. He barely noticed Brice charging toward them.

Brice jerked her by the arm, whirling her around. "I knew if he joined, you'd run to him like some groupie." He scoffed. "I mean, already." Jealousy burned in his candlelit eyes. "Why don't you two just run off together? Better yet, why don't I get the hell out of here?"

Chapter Sixteen

Muriel watched Brice storm off, shaking her head. "I'll bet he dared her to go hit on Jake, thinking she wouldn't really do it. He shouldn't play these games if he's going to get jealous."

"Games?" Jake rose from the swing.

"The sex games," she said. "I play house mother-slash-mistress quite a bit. It adds an interesting dimension to my life of music, illusion, and poetry." She smiled. "Sometimes I get directly involved."

"Oh really?" Jake laughed. "You run this place like a brothel?"

She sighed. "I guess you could say that. There's several rooms upstairs for sex-capades. This place is considered to be very romantic. Sometimes I even read poetry to lovers before they go upstairs. All sorts come here to live out fantasies."

"Brice isn't living out any fantasy. He's furious. You keep talking about games. What happened?"

Muriel and Cameo grinned at each other. "You don't realize it, do you."

"Realize what?" Jake's expression was one of puzzled annoyance.

"Brice is bi-sexual. He wanted to seduce you before Cameo could get her claws in you. He put money on getting you first."

"Brice? You're kidding."

They nodded, grinning.

Jake rolled his eyes. "I don't know why anybody thought I wanted to try that."

Muriel took a sip of wine, journal in her lap, moonlight in her eyes. "Everybody wants to fuck a sexy front man. You're a local star."

Cameo smiled in her devilish artful way. "You're almost too

pretty to be a guy. You truly bring androgyny to an awesome level. You've never thought about it?"

Jake tilted his head quizzically, eyebrows stitched. "Did Marci put you up to this?"

The girls laughed, co-connivers, naughty schoolgirl laughter.

"You're telling me Marci wishes I were gay? Listen, I think I should go after Brice."

"To fulfill his rock star fuck fantasy?" This was Cameo's quip.

"To calm him down. I might be living with him, after all."

"Oh, he'll come back," Cameo said. "He's just obsessed with me. Ironically, the more he has sex with me, the more he realizes he's gay. Still, he wants more. It's so strange and beautiful."

Candlelight reflected off glitter on her magazine face, a supermodel self-assurance about her. "You're a secretive singer," she said, almost teasingly. "Why don't you talk about yourself? How do you feel onstage? I feel like a goddess when I'm onstage dancing."

He didn't know how seriously to take the question though he'd been asked it a thousand times. "The crowd can make you feel like you're a rock god, or they can make you feel like you're nobody. Every night onstage is a risk. It's kind of like your party house games."

She looked at him wistfully. "Sometimes I wish I were a musician instead of a dancer. I feel like all I do is twist the minds of perverted boys and twirl through life."

He shooed a bobbing firefly from his face and pulled back his tousled mane. "Snow tells me the show is nothing without you. You're a big part of the draw. Plus, you obviously do much more than dance and seduce."

She cut her eyes skyward, and then a look of great relish came over her face. "Oh yes. I'm an Illusionist."

He tilted his head thoughtfully. "Can you make castles appear?"

She smiled in smug triumph. "My trick onstage is stardust." She ran a hand through the air, wiggling her fingers. Magic trailed behind them, glittering gossamer streaks, weaving and roiling, coruscating like a disco ball. With ceremonial hand motions, she manipulated the streaks into a double helix, a dragon, and then the magic spread out like the stars of the night.

"You needed to be on the *Jetsons*," he gasped. "Here's Planet Janet. She's a galaxy girl. You'd be fun to be with on acid."

"I am a drug," she said.

"What kind of drug?"

"Sex magic." She grinned like a cat with a secret. "Sex and magic is everything. You're a rock singer and a magic one at that. Are you addicted to sex?"

"I'm addicted to a lot of things. Yeah, sex is on the list. Sex has caused me the least problems, though. I'd like to think I'm not your typical rock guy."

"So let me guess. You are looking for the meaning of life through deep lyrics, poetry, and literature. It's no wonder you're fascinated with Muriel."

Arms folded, Muriel listened intently, a faint Mona Lisa smile on her face. Jake shot her an amused glance. "I like to think meaningful words hold the answers."

Cameo was silent a moment, running a hand with glittery nails over a slender wrist, toying with rainbow bangles. "I believe you can find most answers if you stop running from yourself."

He frowned. Candlelight glinted off a lip stud. "What do you mean by that?"

"Embrace what you are and enjoy life no matter what your addiction is. If it's helping get through this dark world then fuck it."

He frowned. "Even if the addiction leads to death?"

Wild merriment filled her eyes. She opened her mouth as though to laugh but said, "Don't party yourself to death. Just go to the edge and then return to real life. My next challenge is sex with a Darkened, which is supposed to be out of this world from a galaxy far away like in Star Trek. Of course, I've heard of these succubi. I won't mess with one of those. That's a death wrap."

He laughed, windswept hair clinging to the silver hoops in his ears. "I thought danger was your thing."

Her eyes widened. "It is, but not getting loved to death. Rushing to the arms of a succubus is suicide."

Muriel tapped him on his arm. "I have a surprise for you."

"What's that?"

She grinned victoriously, pointing toward the yard. "You

have your first bona fide groupie here to see you."

Up the porch steps came a windswept Darkened princess, a pentagram nestled between the swell of her breasts. She wore a leather skirt and a corset, nose pierced, a thick studded leather belt around her waist. Her long blond hair was thrown over a tan shoulder, the tips dyed black.

She nearly straddled him on the porch. "I've never fucked a metal singer much less one from the angel-powered Estranged side of magic." Desire burned in her eyes.

Cameo laughed. "Did you take your Viagra?"

"She'll do anything to have you," Muriel whispered. "She's paid cash for this night."

"What?"

Cameo stuffed money in Jake's pocket. "Congratulations! You're a male prostitute."

"And of course I got my little cut," Muriel muttered in his ear.

"You bitch," he said, then started giggling.

Cameo's eyes were full of wanton joy. "A hybrid has never been fucked here, you great pioneer."

Jake had been with so many girls that this really wouldn't have been any big deal except she was a Darkened. He did want to experience Dark Sex—especially since his chances with Josephine had been stolen from him.

His prearranged paramour wasted no time. She rushed up to him and kissed him roughly. He swooned from waves of dark magic as he ran his fingers through her hair. Then she took his hand and led him into the house.

"Room One awaits you," Muriel said, pointing upstairs like Charon guiding riders across Styx.

Up the creaking stairs they went. His craving for sexual adventure burst out of the shadows of his soul where forbidden desire lay coiled. They rushed with teenaged abandonment to the room.

The love nest was a plush playboy dream. There were glyphs on the wall in the shape of a valentine. *Illusions for lovers*, Jake guessed.

"Everybody wants to fuck a rock star," the girl breathed, eyes becoming black stars. She threw him on the bed, one fist full of his hair, lacquered nails running over his lips. "But I'm no wannabe. If it's a star I want, it's a star I'll get."

As the aggressive girl ripped off his shirt, he thought he heard a violin, but he was just reliving the night he nearly slept with Josephine. He would never regain that night, so there was no way he could let this opportunity slip through his hands.

Velvet curtains blew in the wind as she ran a pierced tongue down his chest, serpentine sensual, that flooded him with a deliciously feverish sensation. She whispered filthy promises that were never meant to leave this bedroom. This was like fucking in Vegas.

The runic valentines flared to life, ignited by the airborne sex magic. Spectral sheets of erotic images solidified above them, carrying a vanilla scented sex spell. He felt deliriously uninhibited.

She straddled him. Upon penetration, he experienced a head rush of dark magic that took his breath away. Then the magic filled his body like a toxin.

As she rode him, he thought vaguely of the succubus Ariel and her spidery familiars, her tarantula pets. Would their countless tiny bites have brought on such pleasure? Would he have loved the taste of her whip had it come to that?

Who knew? It was the secret of derailed fate.

Still, the rough and tumble sex with this hot Darkened diva was plenty wanton enough. Demons of unearthly pleasure were released, ones Jake could never recapture. If Dark Sex became an addiction, no drug would ever satisfy it. The very thought of it was terrifying.

When he lay spent, he stared up at the ceiling, sweating profusely, feeling poisoned in the most decadent way. He could understand why this would turn Marci, who was sensible as strippers go, into a nymphomaniac. She'd told him all about her bouts with Dark Lust.

"I feel drugged," he said softly.

"It just feels like peace," she whispered back. "Don't get me wrong. I've never felt anything so euphoric, but fucking you is the closest I'll ever get to angels. I feel...oddly sated."

They came down a spiral staircase to a staring delighted crowd. He felt like he'd passed a fraternity initiation. The Darkened girl ran out to join Muriel and Cameo on the porch.

On the dance floor, Snow was twirling spheres of light containing ravens. He threw them at the floor, and the black birds flew upward, becoming angels and then mist.

"How was it?" he asked, the gossamer of airborne magic coalescing in his hands. "Was it the sex of a lifetime? There's nothing like Dark Sex. Do you feel like you've been with a goddess?"

"It was more like having sex with the devil," Jake quipped.

Sex with a goddess, Jake mused. He wondered what it would be like to have sex with Charm, his admitted obsession, the fallen angel who'd given him the Dual Serpent amulet. She would be the closest he would come to any god.

This night had been too dirty a pleasure to have been imparted by anything other than magic twisted and dark. This night was the forbidden apple.

"What would God have to do with the Darkened?" Jake posed.

Snow blinked. "What do the Estranged have to do with God?"

Jake supposed this was true. Their existence was the result of rebel angels—not God. He gave a faint laugh. "There is a fine line between the Darkened and the Estranged, just like love and hate. We're all just demons, really, aren't we?"

Snow laughed insanely. He'd had a lot to drink. "We are the result of angels giving away mystical secrets. Why, we were inspiration for those who wound up consorting with demons, which gave birth to the Darkened. We can't fucking talk about anybody." More eye rolling, shrieking laughter.

The singer smirked, a new girl coming at him. "And you know our angels partied like demons."

Snow almost choked on his liquor. "Oh, they partied like hell. Just look around you."

It was quite a sight. Look what the loose angelic tongues of wayward angels had brought about. It was dark comedy and debauchery to a disco beat.

He beheld lovers floating in midair, candles and other objects floating right along with them. They didn't seem to be aware that they were drifting through the living room like beautiful sea creatures luxuriating in deep dark watery depths. Runic tattoos glowed with magic, furthering the impression of the effulgent pulsing of exotic fish.

Cameo, Muriel, and the Darkened girl were French kissing each other as they danced on roiling mist, orgiastic images streaming from Muriel's graceful hand flourishes.

Jake was about to get completely caught up in the spectacle when he felt a hand clutch his shoulder.

"It's Brice," Snow said in an urgent whisper. "He's in trouble."

***

Brice headed to an East Atlanta bar where he did one shot after another, sulking about Cameo. He just couldn't handle living in the shadow of Jake Reece.

He eventually got drunk enough to start showing off. Alcohol brought about an epic sweep in him from withdrawn manic depressive to telekinetic showman.

On a bar napkin, he scrawled a circle of glyphs, muttering an incantation. "Place your drink on the napkin," he said out loud in a circus ringleader voice.

The couple next to him shared a look of amusement. Behind them, others were watching raptly.

"Sure," a girl said.

She placed a margarita glass on the napkin, and the glyphs flared to life.

The glass rose into the air like a carnival ride, a gondola-rita, twirling and flipping. Beach scenes and images of erotic sex rose like ghosts from the napkin and spiraled around the hovering glass.

"Margaritas make you think of a nice vacation, huh?" Brice asked rhetorically as the glass floated down to the bar.

Several gasped. "Oh my God."

"Not God," he answered flatly. "It's magic."

"Who are you?"

"I'm the drummer in Dark Promise. We play all over town. Come see us Bonding Weekend. We'll be in the battle of the bands."

"We can't wait to go," she said.

The couple ordered another round.

It was then that hostile Darkened magic rippled over him. He turned around, eyes stabbing the night through a wall-length window by a cocktail table. The figure of a biker could barely be made out in the shadows of an alley just beyond neon light.

He slung a drink down the back of his throat and then slapped down a stack of cash. "Tom, let me out the back. I think I've got trouble."

"Sure," he said. "You look like you've seen a ghost."

"Something worse."

The bartender took him through the kitchen and let him out the back door. He ran across the street to a convenience store. Milling around a few panhandlers, he called Snow: "I believe that biker is after me."

"Where are you?" Snow asked loudly over the music in the house.

"I'm in East Atlanta. You know the abandoned house across from *The Trojan Horse*?"

"That trap house? Sure. Hide in there and show him a few tricks. We're coming."

He raced down a shadowy narrow street, running beneath swaying boughs to a screened-in porch. Snatching a black Magic Marker out of his coat, he scrawled illusion trigger glyphs in the doorway, on the wall next to a vine-covered window, and on a graffiti-ridden wall. He weaved his dark twisted imagination into a series of incantations.

Darkened magic hit him palpably. He cursed as the rumble of a motorcycle engine met his ears.

In the foyer, he scrawled a few more trigger glyphs and headed up the rickety stairs, shadows swallowing him.

He slipped into a room strewn with broken crack pipes, empty lighters, and candles. He lit one taper candle jutting out of a dirty wine bottle. In the flickering light, he scrawled warding glyphs, incanting feverishly. That's when Snow called back.

"Help's coming. Is big boy there yet?"

"Not yet. Maybe he's afraid to come in here. He needs to be. My illusions are gonna turn this fucking place into a house of horrors."

"Killer," Snow said, cackling. "So, why did you run off?"

Brice gave a shuddering sigh. "I-I needed space. Cameo was pissing me off."

"You don't like Jake, do you."

Brice was silent.

"And in a jealous spate you ran off alone. I warned you that right now it's dangerous to be alone. We're not popular."

"I'm never popular."

"We all love you, Brice."

From below he heard steps creak. His breath caught in his throat. He'd never been alone in a situation where he was being hunted. From below there was rattling and then a smashing sound.

"What the fuck!" came a cry from downstairs.

Brice laughed giddily. "I love it."

***

Omen swung the front door open and stormed inside, flail wielded. There was nothing and no one. He lit several candles on the floor. Drug paraphernalia was everywhere in this dump along with empty beer cans. It was quiet...too quiet. "Where for art thou, punk," he called out, realizing his prey had to be upstairs.

That's when the freak show started. As glyphs flashed like lights in a pinball machine, the house became the fantasy world of a gamer. Crackling light running along the floor gave birth to a seething mass of snakes. Winged grotesqueries materialized from shadowy corners. Giant spiders emerged from shimmering holes in the ceiling, descending to the staircase on threads of web like rappelling eight-legged demons.

Omen stared at it all with a mix of shock and awe. *Fuck,* he thought. *What have I done?*

A shrieking winged thing, swamp witch's pet, swooped down at him. Several followed it. Their huge wingspans cast larger than life Batman shadows, comic book dramatic.

Omen swung his spiked flail in a wild arc. It missed the attacker but smashed a hole in the wall. Another wild swing shattered several stair banisters.

The flail proving worthless, he threw several well placed spell bursts, reducing the magical winged constructs to inky black gossamer.

In the meantime, the snakes had surrounded him. A cobra reared up, hissing. It recoiled when he swung the flail at it.

As another serpent reared up with sea monster fury, he raced for the staircase. If he could just get to the top, the nightmare would end. Or he hoped.

The spiders had turned the stairway into a gauzy silken trap of web befitting a Lovecraftian vision of hell. He stormed up it, slashing furiously.

Halfway up the stairs, a closet door at the top of the staircase swung open. A zombie sprang out like a rotting toy and charged down the steps at him, wielding an axe.

Omen made a circular motion with an open hand, forming a huge ball of roiling light. He hurled it at the morbid life-sized video game avatar. The orb slammed into the zombie; effulgent construct shards rained down on the hallway floor.

His eyes flitted nervously around the candlelit trap house. What else would be freed from the kid's imagination?

Steeling himself for a showdown, he strode down the hallway, flail ready.

***

Heavy footfalls echoed down the hallway. Brice heard whispered curses and a throaty chuckle.

"I'm dead," Brice said to Snow in a low tremulous tone.

"Make no mistake. Marci is coming," Snow said.

"Okay. Cool." He hung up.

The footsteps stopped at the door. "Why don't you come so we can chat? It's not you I want. It's Jake Reece." There was a pause. "There's no way out, and you're constructs aren't beating me."

"Fuck you," Brice shouted, whispering incantations to strengthen the wards.

"Fuck me? You shouldn't talk to a one-man demolition team like that."

There was a moment of deathly silence. Then the door shattered as though a bomb had gone off in the hallway. The apocalyptic biker-leather-boy stood there, held back by the wards. He idly swung the spiked ball from the heavy chain as though it was a pocket watch.

"Next go the wards. Why don't you just join me for a cocktail or two. Maybe some dancing. I need a young handsome escort. If you'll spend some time with me and answer a few simple questions, I'll drop a grand on you, cat daddy."

"Shut up," Brice muttered.

Omen made a tsk-tsk sound. "I've just been through an ordeal of your making, and you won't spend time with me even if I play sugar daddy? You make me feel like an unwanted old queen."

"Hear that car outside?" Brice asked with a note of pride.

Omen was raising the flail when headlights passed through the window. The Gestapo cap gleamed in the light, face outlined dramatically. He was motionless, throwing out his senses, then took on a shifty-eyed tense air.

Brice smirked. "Here come those bad bitch girls. You can feel it in the night."

"Why don't you just tell me where Jake is?"

"I don't know a goddamn thing about that prick, okay?" The phone rang. "Marci's here, motherfucker."

Cursing, Omen took discretion as the better part of valor and took off down the stairs, his feet like manic hooves. He stormed out the back door and rushed to his bike hidden in an alley.

Marci shrieked up to the front curb, Moonshine riding shotgun. They were leaping out of the car when Brice burst out of the house.

"That dude's gone like a freight train. Get me out of here."

"You've been a bad boy," Moonshine said.

"Spank me when we get back to the house. I already feel like a bitch."

Marci turned up the music, Queen's *Bohemian Rhapsody*, and headed back into traffic. "I'm sure you love Freddie Mercury."

He scoffed, nestling between the girls, stick shift between his legs. "How could I not?"

Marci grinned, turning it up louder, hair streaming. City lights flew by them. "Okay. What happened?"

Brice took a big sip of vodka from a plastic cup Moonshine filled for him. "I almost got kidnapped is what happened. He wants to find your precious Jake so bad he was willing to pay me for a night out."

Marci giggled. "Precious Jake, huh? How did he find you?"

"He showed up outside my favorite spot in East Atlanta. I guess he'd been following me."

"Do you think he knows where Nightmare Mansion is?"

Brice downed the drink and motioned for Moonshine to tilt the bottle his way, cup poised for more. "I don't think so, or he would've crashed our party as bad as he wants Jake."

Marci nodded in agreement, zooming down Memorial Drive. "This guy is obsessed with Jake. If he finds the coven house, this could get really, really bad."

***

From the woods down the road, Omen watched Brice leap into the car like a crazed bandit. Marci Stone had saved the day once again.

It was time to talk to that idiot Benjamin. This situation was going to take longer to resolve and be a lot more complicated than he had initially thought.

Cranking his bike, he roared up an embankment, singing *Bat out of Hell* by Meatloaf. He felt free, a god on his chariot. His desire, though, to take out that dashing singer had reached a level of obsession, and that wasn't freedom at all.

Chapter Seventeen

Benjamin counted money in a motel room, plotting and waiting. There would be girls at Peter's party tonight, girls who would listen to his money talk even if he was a nerdy gamer who'd been in and out of rehab.

Candles were lit throughout the room as he sketched a board design for a dark fantasy game concept. Next to it was a tome of spells he'd secured through the underground arcane market.

Queensryche played on his laptop. One of the main themes of *Operation: Mindcrime* was the corruption of government and religion. The concept album made him dwell on the twisted Southern Gothic nature of the Christian Rehab scene where he'd done so much time and dealt with so much shit. Those religious camps were for low-grade morons. He was a gamer genius.

A long dark epic song came on about a hooker who was being used by a priest for sex. Benjamin knew all about getting used. Those losers in those glorified shelters couldn't even put together a simple resume. He'd do all the writing for them for cigarettes and small fees.

Next door, he could hear rough lovemaking. He couldn't stand the sounds of ecstasy, tossing sheets, the bed squeaking frantically. All that should be coming from his room.

He checked his wallet. He'd get a hooker here before the big party and get some blow. He needed to get tweaked anyway to do more work on his fantasy game.

His dark thoughts settled on pretty boy Jake Reece, who got all the girls—and Josephine. She'd loved him.

In this town, he was a pop icon, a sex symbol. A guy like that thought he was better than other people. Could he really become a worldwide rock star? It made Benjamin shudder. He couldn't help but be insanely jealous of a star in the making that had the power of magic in him along with music.

Surely Omen was going to put and end to him and the others before he lost his mind.

A rap came at the door. It was the dealer with his coke, a scruffy young dude with a scar across his cheek. He placed the dope in Benjamin's hand in a stabbing motion, took the money, and moved right along. Nobody seemed to want to be around him for any length of time.

Doing a quick line, he lit more candles and turned up the metal bombast. This particular song featured a choir for theatrical grandeur, double bass drums like a fear-driven heart, power chords ringing out ominously. The singing was operatic and anguished.

His ritualistic role-playing began. He ripped his shirt off, a rosary clinging to his perspiration moist body. He was a rock god, pantomiming guitar licks, throwing his head back and forth in vocal histrionics, his fist holding an imaginary microphone.

Shadows shifted and thickened around him. Spectral lights passed across the mirror like storm-lit clouds.

"Don't you want me?" the ghost whispered. "I'm finally here for you. Let me feed on your lust. You could bring me back to flesshhh..."

He shuddered, reaching for a bottle of whiskey stashed in a twisted nest of sheets. He chugged like a pirate, wishing the bitch would just go away.

The darkest irony abounded. His greatest obsession—an unattainable stripper—was now his greatest fear. He tightly clasped the amulet he'd paid thousands for while reading an incantation from the spell book.

He hoped it held ghosts at bay like the book said. A shadowy female form slipped over the mirror and then trailed across the wall before vanishing. Maybe the amulet really was working.

Another knock came. He rushed to the door, peering through the peep hole at a rakishly tilted cap bearing a swastika. It was his fat leather boy savior Omen. For a while, he wouldn't be alone with the dark spirit.

Omen waved sarcastically. His troubled eyes reflected streetlight.

In the room, he kneaded his fists in manic thought. He appeared to be a god-of-war, contemplating the next move.

"Did you find Josephine's heartthrob and splatter him?"

Benjamin asked.

"He's protected," Omen replied. "And I don't just mean by those girls. Do you know what a coven is?"

Benjamin's eyes moved about searchingly. "Yeah. A coven is a group of them bound together by magic."

"Exactly. I've got to get him when he is unprotected. That's the challenge."

Benjamin nodded that he understood. He lowered the liquor bottle onto a cluttered nightstand, brushing a chewing gum wrapper onto the floor.

He reached for a porn magazine, *Barely Legal*, spreading out a line of coke on a photograph of a girl posing on a picnic blanket, the page gleaming in candlelight.

Omen pulled up a chair, the legs raking over the stained carpet. He leaned over the bed to do a line, his splayed fat fingers pressing into the mattress.

"I have to follow him until he's alone and vulnerable. That means time and more money. The good news is I'm starting to take this whole thing personally, which means I'm definitely following through with this."

Benjamin hurriedly chopped up a line with a credit card. This poor overused card was well on its way to the limit.

"That's good to hear." Out of a briefcase, he grabbed a stack of hundreds. "Just take it."

Omen counted it with a faint smile, eyes gleaming. "Okay. This will do for now."

Benjamin slipped another baggy out of a drawer. "Just do whatever it takes to get rid of our...music celebrity."

Omen gave a huff of a laugh. "I know you wanted that stripper, but you seem to *really* hate this guy on a deep personal level."

Benjamin tapped coke onto a girl's glossy paper midriff. "He thinks he's a rock god." He did another line. "I think all gods should die."

***

Omen stalked into a downtown twenty-four-hour diner, drawing the stares of two truck drivers. They were laughing it up with a stringy-haired waitress, but when Omen swung the door open, at the sight of him, they stopped laughing.

He slid into a back booth, counting the money in his lap Benjamin had just given him. The waitress watched him warily. The truckers just glowered.

She crept over to him, saying in a low tone, "What can I get 'cha, mister?"

In his signature urbane tone, he said, "I'd like coffee and a stack of pancakes with bacon and scrambled eggs."

Watching the grubby cook work furiously over the grill, he contemplated the desperate idiocy of Benjamin. Talk about delusions of grandeur. He was really crazy.

The nutty gamer wasn't a complete fool, though. He would get rid of the singer if it was the last thing he did.

Herein lay the problem. Omen had never met a Caster like this singer. His power was immense for someone who didn't really know what he was doing, which, in Omen's eyes, made him more dangerous. He needed to catch metal's answer to Elvis alone one more time. Even then, he would have quite a task taking him out.

He was sopping up syrup with a ragged slice of pancake when he felt the magic of Darkened kindred out in the night. Just what was coming? *Oh, pancakes and confrontation—what a combination,* he thought.

A figure emerged from the shadows, velvet duster flapping, a violin held in the air like the prize of a vagabond.

The bow slid over the strings, and then his preternaturally nimble fingers took off. He cavorted about like a jester who'd slipped through his place in time to the streets of Atlanta. He slung his hair about like a heavy metal god, striking poses as though he were going to be on the cover of Rolling Stone.

In a whirling dervish of fiddle mania, he ceased all motion and pointed the bow dramatically at Omen. Then he grinned, hair in his face.

Omen chuckled, toying with the gaudy silver pentagram ring on his big fat thumb. Just who was this? He'd met plenty of homeless insane Casters with no money but a world of stories about bizarre exploits. These raconteurs were usually harmless, but he never knew when he was going to meet a downright dangerous eccentric.

The violinist swung the door open, slowly drawing the bow

across the strings. Magic surged through the instrument, runes glowing, airborne symbols floating like tiny spirits in the early spring breeze.

A drunk from the bar went to the jukebox, slapped in some change, and then *The Devil Went Down to Georgia* by the Charlie Daniels Band came on. The gum-smacking waitress finally found her sense of humor and shook her head, chuckling, watching the spectacle. The night would always bring in freaks.

Minstrel danced about the coffee house as though filming a music video, playing the violin parts of the song. Omen reached beneath a stack of dirty plates and snatched up a dollar. He approached the violinist, waving the dollar tauntingly. The crowd in the place became an audience in a small concert theater, clapping along.

Minstrel stopped playing. "Ah, you are the one who needs the tip. We must have a little chat."

A mix of suspicion and amusement spread over Omen's face. "And just who are you?"

Minstrel played a crazy flourish of notes and then joined Omen at the booth. A final legato run finished his late night diner performance. The show was over. People looked disappointed.

"I'm Minstrel. I've followed you here from *The Dungeon* many times. I know all about you. You're going in that club under all kinds of ridiculous pretenses, but I know you're hunting Jake Reece, the rock singer with the coveted amulet. I do believe I have information that will lead us to an understanding."

Omen sipped coffee, pudgy pinky finger in the air. "Do tell."

"First, why are you after Jake? Is it the amulet you seek?"

Omen raised his eyebrows. This violinist might be worth taking seriously, after all. "No, I'm not interested in the amulet. He's causing difficulty for a...certain business connection." He gave the violinist a deep speculative look and then pulled out a cigarette. "I've heard the rumors, though. Do you believe it's the legendary Dual Serpent Amulet?"

Minstrel's smirk was smug and knowing. "The magic in his voice is unmistakable. He is the direct descendant of Merek, the first coven head recorded in the annals of magic. It was his destiny to have that amulet. I don't think the singer knows the magnitude of his latent power."

Omen certainly believed that. "I'm not on a treasure hunt. I was hired to kill him. Why are you after him?"

"I want him in my band, not dead."

Omen let out a bark of laughter. "You want him to sing while you fiddle away. I love it. You're going to coerce him into doing pop versions of Jean-Luc Ponty pieces?"

"Oh no. I'm part of the preeminent goth/illusion act Dire Portent. We'll be at the Bonding Weekend festival. We need him to win the battle of the bands." He sat back, drawing the bow over the strings. "Our leader, Felicity, will not be pleased if you slay our potential *singer-slash-keyboard player.*"

Felicity? Omen mused. He'd heard of a succubus in the music circuit who was powerful, talented, and insanely ruthless.

"I suppose she sent you here to collect him." Omen pushed the pancakes aside.

"This is true. I wanted Jake and Josephine to form a band with me, but the singer scoffed at me, blaming me for her death. As for Josephine..."

"I know exactly who you're talking about. She overdosed." Omen gave a faint derisive laugh. "A dead stripper in your band would be a great gimmick. I'd love to see that."

Minstrel scowled. "You might be surprised at what you'll see. Let me ask a rhetorical question. Who wants Jake dead? Let me take a wild guess. There is someone hustling Rapture who fears getting connected to her death. I happen to know Jake and those hunter girls are trying to get to the bottom of things. There's no chance someone has paid you to stop them before they learn too much, is there?"

Omen chuckled, eyes rolling upward at the absurdity of it all. He wanted to be able to tell him the Council of the Darkened or a great coven leader had sent him on a daring mission. What came out was, "A poseur gamer dork is paying me to take out that singer."

Minstrel laughed. "I do believe I've seen that clown following her. He was stalking her, buying her candy and dope and sending it to her as a secret admirer. He's really the reason she's dead, I'll have you know, and here you are helping him. What motivated this loser to hire a bounty hunter?"

Omen smiled like the Cheshire cat, his bejeweled fingers

sparkling in the diner light. "Let's just say you should watch what kind of party favors you give a girl you're obsessed with. If you get reckless with magic, it could make a drug dealer look bad. And that's dangerous."

Minstrel tilted his head thoughtfully, nodding. "So, my intuition was pretty well spot on. This gamer stalker is under pressure to get a dealer off his back."

"A lot of pressure," Omen stressed.

Minstrel sighed theatrically. "So, now we've come to our little conflict of interest."

Omen smiled faintly. "You need a singer, and I need him dead."

"Maybe we can reach a little compromise. Why don't you capture him and give him to Felicity when she arrives. She would most definitely pay a generous bounty for him, more than you'd ever get from your desperate friend. And it would get Jake off the mystery dealer's trail."

Omen sat back and thought about it. If he got rid of those girls, too, he could collect twice. This could turn out to be quite a coup. "How can I communicate with Felicity?"

He pulled out a phone from the deep pocket of his cloak. She answered right away: "Felicity, I believe the bounty hunter is open to suggestions."

There was a brief discussion with periods of silence punctuated by the faint clink of plates, the clattering of silverware, and the rolling sound of a cash register drawer.

Two Buckhead party girls tumbled drunkenly into the door as Minstrel hung up. "Felicity wants you to join us Bonding Weekend. We'll party like bored royalty." His face darkened. "If you go through with your designs of murder, though, you'll have to deal with her. I would not want to be in that position."

Omen stabbed a piece of egg. "What I'd like to know is why don't you catch him? And where is Felicity, anyway?"

A haughty air overcame Minstrel. "I'm not a fighter. I'm a violin-illusionist. I honestly don't believe I could capture him. As for Felicity, she is doing solo performances, but she and the rest of the coven will be here soon enough."

"Okay, all that sounds fantastic, but I must tell you, the singer and those girls are not easy prey."

Minstrel made a genteel dismissive gesture. "I've met Marci Stone. I know what you're up against. I still believe you'll pull this off."

Omen closed his eyes, breathing a deep sigh. "If it's the last thing I do."

They exchanged numbers, and then both of them went their own ways.

Chapter Eighteen

There was a small gathering at Nightmare Mansion the night after all the drama—no wild party, just Jake, the girls, and the coven breaking bread.

"I propose a toast," Snow said. They all held up shots of Don Julio '42 Anejo tequila. "May the burning bridges behind you light the path ahead."

On the candlelit porch, incense of Myrrh and Frankincense swirled around like gentle spirits. They clacked shot glasses together and threw back the smooth tequila.

Brice wiped the liquor from his mouth. "You know I gotta laugh about last night. When that biker knew you were coming, he hauled ass."

Marci smiled, pouring herself another shot from a bottle set in a rocking chair. "He needs a well thought out plan to have a chance of beating us."

"Why exactly does Jake have so many enemies?" Brice asked. "Is it all about the amulet?"

She tossed back the shot and sighed, then leaned her head against the vine-covered trellis. "The current problem is that the Rapture dealer we're searching for probably wants him dead, hence the biker. Then there are haters who don't want hybrids around. Plus, he could be a rock star, and there are those who just can't stand it. They either want him dead or enslaved."

Brice scoffed. "I still don't see why everyone wants him so bad. Didn't he realize what he was getting into when he took that amulet?"

Marci gave him a long considering look, and then glanced at Jake, who was pretending not to hear any of this. So that was it. He *really* was jealous of Jake. Hopefully this was going to pass.

Windswept, Muriel lowered the thick fairytale she was reading. "He didn't want it. He was bamboozled by a demon and a fallen angel."

Muriel and Brice started arguing.

Snow listened a moment, amused by all the insecure egos. He handed Jake another beer. "You truly are a wanted man, outlaw cowboy."

Jake rolled his eyes, shaking his head. "Oh, what have I done with my life? I'm notorious for all sorts of reasons. Somebody who thinks I look too much like Bon Jovi could put a bounty on my head. I'm surprised an ex-girlfriend doesn't want me killed."

Snow lit more candles around the porch. "Still, your problems seem to center around that damn amulet. Tell us about finding it. I'll bet you have a story comparable to *Treasure Island*."

Jake sat on the porch swing next to Muriel, who was pouring wine. The moon shadows of swaying Bone Tree branches played over him, and he became the cover for a gothic romance novel.

"A demon manipulated me into searching for it. The demon promised a spell called a "flesh ride" which endowed me with the power to project myself in spectral form into the bodies of others."

Cameo gasped, wide eyed. "I've heard of it. It's all about experiencing others' sexual pleasure and addictions. Can you still do it?"

He shrugged. "Maybe. Even though the demon freed me after we beat Ariel, I really didn't want to fool with any dark gifts anymore. I felt like doing so would draw the demon back to me."

"Yet you're still bound to the amulet," Snow said, pointing at the blood filled pendant, twined with the two jewel encrusted snakes, the silver one representing the Estranged, the black one symbolizing the Darkened.

Jake shook his head. "This amulet doesn't want to let me go, demon bound or not."

"So, an angel in human guise gave it to you?" Muriel asked.

He sighed. "Yeah. She went by the name Charm. She had been holding it in secrecy from her kidnappers."

"Marci told me about Tricky Mitch and Kitty Dreadlock. They were a colorful pair of hunters."

"I won't ever forget those cat eyes...or gangster boy with his slicked back hair. What a widow's peak. The little creep was actually kind of cool looking." He sighed, beads on his wrist rattling when he sipped the beer. "They're dead now, though, along with my sweetheart succubus Ariel Celique."

"I hear you had a crush on Charm, the fallen angel," Cameo said, doing this big exaggerated wink. "What happened to your little love affair?"

"She ran off and left me a bizarre letter telling me she had very little time here and that I...was meant to have this amulet. I was meant to protect it. I feel like I've got this magical gameshow prize." He leveled a very dark and serious look at Snow. "Do you believe in the Nephemera?"

He nodded. "Oh, the Nephemera is real. I've encountered angels in human form that make it out of there from time to time, usually running from hunters...or simply wanting to be free of that dark dangerous world for a while."

"I think that was one of the main reasons Charm is here," Jake interjected.

"Probably. It's apparently true that they have to go back eventually, however. They can only go so long without the magic there. The same goes for demons. They're all like exotic animals out of their element when they leave that place."

"How do these angels appear human? It can't possibly be some kind of illusion or glamour spell, can it?"

"No, it's not an illusion. They bond with souls, using magic to assume flesh. Some will merge with a ghost...others can merely touch something a human has and tap into their spirit. I've even heard about the ghosts of dead Casters being able to take over other spirits to reach the physical plane. I haven't seen that, though."

"This girl looked like my old girlfriend who was killed in a wreck. How do you think the angel bonded with her soul?"

"Who knows? Maybe the angel tapped into your memories to form the guise of her."

"Unreal. Tell me more about the Nephemera."

Snow sipped his wine and then held a candle to his face, the ghostly raconteur as wind blew across the porch. "Fallen angels created the Nephemera to escape the wrath of God, and then all manner of magical creatures wound up there, including demons. I've heard it's an island made up of a series of concentric rings with urban sprawl within each one. All manner of adventurous mundanes make their way there to experience wild fantasies, sex shows, and prostitution. And it's dangerous. Big time. Angels and demons play both predator and prostitute. The arcane black market scene is like the Wild West. Crime Lords run these nine worlds. The House of the Fallen is at the center of the angel's hideaway. Rumor has it there are nine angels in this bastion just like there are nine rings, but I don't know if there is a connection. My intuition is that this dystopian angel's world of pleasure and danger is a few hundred years in the future. Where, you wonder? I've gathered a cataclysm occurred and what's left of California becomes this fantasy world."

Everyone was drawn around Snow, engrossed in the story. "Do you think an earthquake destroys California?" Marci asked.

Snow's eyes narrowed. He was mystified like a child about all this, too. "Or from war?" He shrugged.

"This sounds like a great place to put a new Disney World," Cameo said.

Snow's eyes flared in mad delight. "This place is the darkest Disneyland. Life is a movie." He took another sip of wine, then filled his glass again in a sloshing pour. "Anyway, there are spell books with incantations to open doorways to the Nephemera, but I haven't seen them. I wouldn't doubt the library in Ariel's mansion holds such books." He sipped thoughtfully. "Did that demon really turn her to stone?"

Jake raised his eyebrows. "It sure did. She never should've summoned that demon. Apparently it was from the Nephemera, and angels there weren't too happy about her conjuring it for a spell. They pitted her and the demon against each other. And did that demon ever win."

Snow laughed, nearly choking on wine. "I heard the angels put up barriers around that fucking sex mansion until one beat the other. It was like a celebrity death match." Snow mimicked an announcer: "In this corner, the premier psycho succubus of the South: Ariel Celique!"

"And in the other corner, the demon that turned on her." Jake laughed, blowing a plume of cigarette smoke. "We escaped, thanks to the demon, but we didn't get to find the hidden library."

"You should go back," Snow said. "I bet there are grimoires holding all kind of secrets on the Nephemera. Just the value of those old books..."

"How old would the earliest grimoires be?" Jake asked. "Marci tells me the first covens date back to early medieval times."

Snow nodded. "The Knights Templar was searching for them, so I'd say so." He paused, sipping a drink that reflected moonlight and candles. A moth spiraled around the flame and then darted off at the swish of his hand. He held the candle to his face again. "There is an interesting backstory to the first two covens." He paused as everyone drew near like the moths. "The first coven of the Estranged worshipped an angel in the guise of a beautiful goddess. The first Darkened coven worshipped a demon in male form, possessing long black hair. It is said that the air about him was imperiously feminine. Both *deities* were so heady with power there was a showdown between the two beings, and then the most bizarre thing happened." He paused for theatrical effect.

Muriel said dryly, "The suspense is killing us."

"The demon used a sex spell to woo the angel. It was the first time sex in human guise between an angel and a demon occurred."

"How good was the sex?" Cameo asked, grinning.

"The sex between the two was such ecstasy other angels and demons followed suit. Okay. Here's where many get confused. Sure, it was an abomination for the angels to have sex and share magic with humans, but consorting with demons really did the trick. This caused the Nine Elders to go into exile before God's wrath came along. Here's what is really strange, though. It is believed that the angel and demon that started all this drama were fused into one being, by God, as a curse. Even weirder, the angel used her ichor to plant *angel seeds* within a pregnant girl of the Darkened coven before this *fusion* could happen. The father was no other than—"

"Merek," Jake exclaimed.

Everyone made gameshow bell victory sounds.

"That's right. Out of three children, only one was born a human, a hybrid of both magics. Two angel spawns hijacked two unborn souls to take form and left the womb long before the third baby was born. That child is the reason you're here all these centuries later, Mr. Jake Reece." He pointed in mock condemnation at Jake. "What's more, the amulet contains not only the blood of Merek and his Darkened lover in the other coven, but—"

"The ichor of that angel," Muriel finished, truly in awe this time around. "And it most certainly had demon magic in it from the sex."

"All that dual magic in one amulet," Snow said musingly. "And you wonder why everyone wants you?"

Jake just shook his head. "I don't want to believe any of this is real."

Snow huffed. "You can feel the magic. You know it's real."

"So, what happened to the demon?"

"It's my understanding that somehow they hauled it off to one of the darkest corners of the Nephemera where it dwells in a castle like a condemned crazy aristocrat. The demon rules a district in one of the rings, but it can't go beyond it for whatever reason, probably magical barriers. I'm sure the debauchery in this dark corner of angel world is beyond imagining. The whole affair makes me think of the lunatic libertine Marquis de Sade, who spent much of his life in asylums."

"Kinky," Cameo said.

"Anyway, Jake, you hold the power of the first two covens and that creature's within the amulet. And you are the one meant to tap into its power, the only one who should, anyway."

"He needs to go through his Darkening to truly reach his true power," Muriel said.

"No way," Jake exclaimed. "I'll end up like Ariel."

Snow shrugged. "Either way, there is plenty of magic within you. That makes you a wanted man." He shot a glance through a window at Brice to make certain he wasn't listening. Then he whispered, "By the way, I'm sorry about him. That's the most talented but frustrated misfit I know. He wants to be straight in the worst way. It bothers him that Cameo likes you, obviously."

"The terrible part is I like him," Jake added. "I didn't want this drama. I hope I don't ruin the band's chemistry. What's he doing, anyway?" He got up from the swing and peered inside. What met his eyes was the strangest sight.

Brice was curled on the couch as fluttering magazines floated about him, along with an ashtray, the petals of flowers from a bowl of potpourri, and beer bottles. He was like the anguished center of a chaotic universe.

Jake stepped inside and approached him. "You know, a lot of

girls ask about you. I wouldn't be so concerned with Cameo."

Brice regarded him with bleary drunken eyes. "I want to be like you. I want to be a star. Everybody wants you. Stars attract other stars. Cameo thinks you're a god."

"Oh, she's just a little ballerina prima donna. Look, why would you want to be me? I don't have a band or a record deal, and I'm being chased for this amulet that I don't even want. I had to leave the apartment I love because I was being persecuted by spirits. All my money is coming from slinging drinks and two-bit tarot card readings. I sure don't know anything about being an Illusionist."

Brice just stared blankly at the ceiling. "I'll never get the girls you do."

"If you help me learn to be an Illusion performer, I'll help you get girls."

Brice's expression brightened. "Uh...okay. Sure."

Cameo rushed through the door and threw her arms around Jake.

Cussing, Brice leaped up from the sofa and stormed upstairs.

"Thanks, Cameo. I was just getting somewhere with him. You should cool it with your games."

"Games are what make life fun, that and sex and dancing."

Still, tingling with the remnants of Dark Lust, he was easy prey for her. She might come across as a shallow tart, but she was actually a shrewd girl.

She pushed him onto the couch.

Here we go again, he thought.

Spectral light slid across the ceiling.

"The ghosts...they're here," Jake said.

"Yeah. The ghosts of the murdered metal band," Cameo whispered. "It could be they're drawn to you. Who knows? Maybe they think you should be their new lead singer."

"You're morbid," he said before she slid her tongue into his mouth.

Chapter Nineteen

Dusk had turned the sky into smoky apricot bourbon as Dennis flew on a skateboard down Peachtree Street like a gliding bohemian satyr. Posing like a pro, he sported cutoff jeans and his favorite Betty Davis T-shirt. If the dead star were reincarnated as a gay prima donna, she may very well find herself stuck in the confused confines of this devious hustler (Rumor had it he'd done a drag show as the dead diva).

There was nothing Dennis loved more than wheels under his feet and the feeling of power as passersby gawked at his traffic defying antics. A pizza held high above his head, nose held high with it, Dennis looked like a fast food icon, a skating Statue of Liberty basking in insolent glory.

He outraced several cars, giving the finger to one guy in a Porsche who whizzed by dangerously close to him. *Screw 'em,* Dennis thought. He despised cars and traffic.

He glided by several cafés and zipped around the corner, a roller boogie Mercury, sex on wheels, dealing with rush hour traffic was like blowing off somebody in a club.

He glided several more blocks and then relaxed his pace. His apartment, shared with his on and off lover Stephen, was across the street from the Art Center Marta Station.

Skateboard over his shoulder, Dennis trudged up the carpeted stairs to the second floor of a three-story apartment building tucked between a high-rise parking deck and a Russian bistro.

Finding the door unlocked, he flung it open and held the pizza like a conquistador brandishing ill-gotten spoils. "I know I should have been home earlier but don't be a bitter bitch," he exclaimed in his tart prissy way, gay feminism down to an art. He tossed the pizza on the dining room table. "You see, I can redeem myself. I've brought nourishment, a fabulous redneck Italian meal."

The walls of the apartment were covered in provocative prints from Stephen's days as a model and flashy wall ornaments. A grimoire was set on the coffee table along with a spread of *Rolling Stone* magazines. He dealt with so many Casters, he'd finally started reading about their world.

The maudlin music of Morrissey was playing from the bedroom or maybe it was The Smiths. Either way, it was pretentious *slit your wrists* pop music that told Dennis Stephen would be dealing with some melodramatic sense of failure. He would have some story about how he was all alone in the world and nobody wanted him and nobody loved him. It just made Dennis sick.

He strode down the hallway to the bedroom and swung the door open. There Stephen was asleep, probably wishing he could just die.

He clasped Stephen's shoulder, shaking him vigorously. Dennis once described Stephen as "the devil meets Elvis." He had long brown sideburns and a pompadour, a devious glint to his blue eyes that you wouldn't find in any Memphis southern boy. He had desires only the dark bowels of this city could meet.

"Wake the hell up," Dennis shouted. "It's getting late. We have a fun, fun night that begins at Peter's."

Stephen groaned pitifully and turned over, pushing Dennis away.

Dennis smirked, slinging back the drapes. "Your lunch date with that girl must have gone really well. If I were capable of being jealous, I just might be. Of course, no fish could replace me regardless of hotness."

Stephen dragged himself out of bed and rolled his eyes at him. "You need not worry about being upstaged by the opposite sex," he drawled sarcastically. "My date went terrible. No, worse than terrible. I just can't think of another adjective."

Sympathy softened Dennis's expression of annoyance. "Tell me about it while I get you a cup of coffee."

"There really isn't much to tell," he called out to Dennis who'd gone into the kitchen. "The date wasn't going so bad until she caught me looking at a guy, and then she got sassy with me. I mean, really nasty. We got into an argument in the restaurant, and she wound up going back to work in a huff."

Dennis paced back into the room with the miracle of caffeine and a plate of pizza. "Here, have some pizza with your coffee." Dennis tore a piece free for himself and devoured it whole. "See Stephen, you're not about girls. You never will be, I don't think."

"Great. Now say something that will bring me joy."

"How 'bout if I show you somethin'." Dennis drawled in a mock Southern accent. He pulled an insanely large bag of cocaine out of a backpack. "We were fronted all this to sell over the weekend. And if we sell it all, we'll get twice this for Bonding Weekend."

Stephen was reborn. "Oh yes. The white girl has arrived in all her glory."

"A girl you can get along with who won't care if you look at guys." Dennis chuckled and licked tomato sauce from his fingers. "Now get ready so we can go to Peter's. No more whining about women and your thwarted exploits at being a heterosexual silver-tongued demon." He lit a cigarette and smiled slyly. "Besides, tonight could get very interesting. He wants to talk to me, and I think I know what's up. Subject on tonight's show: Ghost strippers and the attorneys they terrorize."

"I love it." Stephen laughed.

Thirty minutes later, they burst out the front doors of the apartment building with studied indifference for the neighbors. The boys were too busy getting their look together to care about stares. Dennis was putting his wild frizzy hair back in a pony tail as Stephen fastened an enormous silver loop into his ear. After a little more primping, they were ready. Dennis waved at a cab parked at the High Museum café.

Stephen breathed an agonized sigh. "Now please tell me we aren't going clubbing with Peter. Okay, please?"

"Oh heavens no. Where's your faith? We're just going to do business. I need to find out what he *really, really* wants, though. Then we'll have to engage in idle chatter for a half hour or so. It'll build your character, tolerating someone who nauseates you."

They leaped into the cab, and the black cab driver, who knew them all too well, gave them a knowing smile as he cranked the car and pulled into traffic.

"I'll tell you something about Peter," Stephen said. "I know everyone says he's straight, but I'd swear he makes eyes at me. Don't you notice? Or am I being swept away by vanity again?"

David Raven

Dennis lit a cigarette and blew a plume of smoke out the car window, his nose held regally in the air. Clad in black, he felt artsy and irresistible. "The answer to your questions is...well, maybe. He's a bored, rich attorney who might want a boy toy. Why do you think I'm so well paid for the coke? It's pointless speculation really. Here are the cold hard facts. We, the young and hip, are exploiting the rich elite. Peter and his ilk are even more corrupt than we are."

"I think I understand now," Stephen said, clearing his throat solemnly. "We may be brazen drug addicts, but at least we aren't lusting pigs who dine on abused power and court fascist delusions of grandeur."

Dennis smiled primly. "Very good, Grasshopper."

"Thank you, master." Stephen rolled his eyes at Dennis while lighting a cigarette.

Buckhead traffic was terrible, but by the time they'd plotted their night out, Peter's playboy mansion appeared around the bend of Lenox Road.

After tipping the driver lavishly, they slipped around back to go through an entrance that led to the swimming pool. Then they snuck in through a sliding glass door. Oh Peter. With all his surveillance, he never locked any of the damn doors.

"Surprise!" they shouted together, and then a look of alarm came over their faces. There in the living room stood Peter with a gun in his hand. He was plum red from drinking and stress, his hands jittery.

At the sight of them, he breathed a deep sigh of relief. "God, it's just you guys."

Dennis scoffed. "You knew we were coming. We always come around the back like Batman and Robin."

Peter sighed, flopping down on a thick cushioned leather sofa. "I know. This ghost thing is driving me crazy."

"Peter darling, who is it?" a party girl—probably a call girl—named Jennifer asked, descending the stairs. The girl's eyes swept the room, eyes flaring at the outrageous scene. "Jesus, Peter, don't kill our valuable connections."

"My sentiments exactly," Dennis exclaimed and handed Peter a full envelope.

"Hey, guys, get yourselves something to drink. I'm going to

talk to Jennifer about something and be right back."

"You go, girl," Dennis exclaimed. "Tend to your lady friend."

It was time to pillage the village. Stephen and Dennis rushed into the kitchen like crazed rats or perhaps marauding Vikings, knowing Peter would do all the blow he had in his possession like a maniac before joining them again.

Dennis attacked the liquor in the refrigerator. Holding his head back, long blond hair reaching for the linoleum, he poured Belvedere vodka directly into his mouth until the overflow sluiced down either side of his face, dripping to the floor. Stephen guffawed at his reckless indulgence. He couldn't help it.

He snatched a bottle of cola out of the refrigerator and made himself a very stiff cocktail. Stephen found a bottle of Dom Perignon and guzzled most of it as though it were soda pop. His tolerance was high, to say the least.

"There's one swallow left," Stephen said with a sense of allure. "Sure you don't want some sparkling bubbles to go with your vodka?"

"Are you trying to make me puke? Oh, what the hell? Give it to me."

The bottle slipped from Dennis's grasp and shattered on the floor. Stephen fell against the counter, holding back hysterical laughter. They picked up the bigger pieces, the smaller ones Dennis kicked around the floor to various corners of the kitchen. They needed to be Peter's first gay housekeeper team.

"Dennis, you're a regular Hazel."

"I'm much cooler than Hazel," Dennis said, pushing spectacles up the bridge of his nose, lips pursed.

Their banter was interrupted by Peter returning to the room. He was so geeked out, his face could snap apart.

"She's upstairs. We can talk now." He was nervous, perspiring. "First, here's your grand."

All that money plopped into Dennis's hot little hand like it was nothing. "Thanks for paying our rent, but you're about to have a heart attack. Have you been up all night?"

"That ghost. I saw her in a mirror. Josephine." He threw back a golden shot of Whistle Pig whiskey and then poured for everyone. He was certainly a generous playboy.

Dennis would never tell Stephen, but he really kind of liked him.

"Did you say you know these magician people?" Peter asked.

Dennis smiled like he'd swallowed a mouse, the tail hanging out of his mouth. "I sure do."

"Alright. I need help. I guess I should've been nicer to that gang the other night. I'm just so—"

"Snooty and isolated," Stephen interjected.

Peter shrugged. "Could you help me? Drink and hang out all you want. Then see about contacting your ghost gang."

They all did shots like frat boys for another hour, and then Stephen and Dennis headed to Nightmare Mansion.

***

Cameo received the dynamic duo in a gale of girlish laughter. Her fantasies about gay men were quite quixotic. She thought of Dennis as a flaming Romeo in need of her seduction. One of her greater purposes in life was to convert as many gay men as possible to heterosexuality. Dennis thought she just might be capable of it—for a night, anyway.

Cameo hugged Dennis like he was the last guy on Earth. "Everyone is looking for you, boy," she rasped.

"Why? You know I'm coming over with the sugar."

Fluty laughter spiraled upward and then down again. "Did you know a frilly looking character with a spellbinding fiddle is in town? Jake believes this guy has cast a spell on some stripper's ghost. Didn't you know a girl named Josephine from Peter's parties?"

He chuckled deviously. "Oh yeah. I know all about the paranormal drama at that place. Peter is about to have a coke binge nervous break down over ghost sightings of her there."

"Really? I love ghosts. What's the big deal?" She giggled. "So, why exactly did you call me to come over and not Snow?"

Dennis's eyes rolled about in plotting thought, and then a Cheshire cat smile spread across his face. "You know you're my favorite of the bunch. I thought you could introduce me to Jake."

"Why?" she asked suspiciously, eyebrow flared.

"I need a ghost hunter to get that girl out of Peter's house. She's going to ruin the party scene there."

Cameo laughed. "You should really think about calling

Sophia. Now there's your ghost hunter."

Exciting possibilities flashed over his face. "Yeah, she probably could help, but I've never met Jake. Is he here?"

"No. He works at *Final Destination*, tending bar."

Dennis howled. "A metal singer two-timing on *Medusa's* by working in that crazy queer bar. Now I've really got to meet him." He went and told Stephen, who was still on the porch, sending messages on Facebook. "We're going to *Final Destination* tonight."

"You just can't live without drama, can you."

He called Sophia and explained the situation.

"I can't wait to meet Jake Reece," she said. "I hope he's ready for his first ghost hunt."

"You might have to school him, girl," Dennis said, and then they made plans to meet at the club.

"I'm not really into this ghost and magic stuff like you," Stephen said while the two waited on their cab's arrival, "but I really must ask whether this Josephine you keep talking about is that fabulous raven goddess I met a few times at Peter's."

"One and the same."

Stephen gasped, hands flying to his mouth. "That poor girl is dead?"

"Drugs. Overdose. I'll bet she'd call it murder. I can't imagine anything worse than a ghost diva who wants revenge."

***

Jake had gone back to *Final Destination* to tell Jazz and Mitch about his wild time with the cross-dressing antique dealer. Things happened quickly from there: a conversation about Jake's bartending experience landed him an interview with the manager of the place. In just days, he was bartending in this nuthouse of debauchery.

Things were just beginning to go really well on the night Dennis and the others met him. He made change from the cash register, shouted for the barback to bring him more ice, and made four gin and tonics, three shooters, and one Margarita. His Black Dahlia shooters were such a hit, regulars were calling him that as a nickname. The dance mixes of his last band Lost Angel were constantly requested, pounding relentlessly like rough sex.

And did this place ever rock. It was busy as hell. This was supposed to be the slow bar? He vaguely remembered Tim, the manager, leisurely ambling by about three hours ago, patting him on the back, and guffawing at his struggle to keep his pace up. Jake mumbled an obscenity and walked away, which made Tim laugh even harder.

There was even Mitch's input: "Come on, old thing, work. How can we maintain a respectable cruise bar with a slow bartender?"

"How can I work with you hitting on me all night?"

Jazz laughed his ass off.

And then there were all the girls. Strippers and Buckhead Barbies were coming here just to meet him. He slopped a drink on one girl who instantly forgave him and slid him her number. Through the course of the night, several slipped him the seven digits. By three in the morning, Jake was feeling like a regular bottle twirling Tom Cruise.

He was tightening the spout on a bottle of Bombay gin when the hideous signature voice of the old man sounded behind him.

There he stood, dressed impeccably in a double-breasted black suit and striped tie. A white handkerchief flowered out of the coat pocket resplendently. He gazed at Jake like a serpent, his expression one of supercilious pleasure.

"You look flawless," Jake said, thinking he looked like the funereal parlor director in *Phantasm*.

"And I feel absolutely divine. And why shouldn't I? Tonight is a night for celebration. Josephine is even closer to becoming flesh again." He held his cane up as though it would draw lightning.

Okay, Jake thought. "Uh, can I get you a cocktail?"

"Why, yes. A martini. Dry. Grey Goose."

Jake poured the drink, his hands shaking. He couldn't help it. He'd never met anybody so creepy in his life. His eyes darted about for a familiar face. *No one.* He placed the drink on the bar and snatched his hand back as though he were feeding a shark.

"Hey, princess, I need a drink," a shrill insistent voice called from down the bar.

Jake snapped his head around. "What?" At the sight of Dennis and his entourage, he couldn't help but chuckle. The smug purse-lipped hustler was his savior. He rushed to the gang with great alacrity. "You saved me from that maniac," he said in a low tone.

Dennis appraised the old man and laughed. "You've met Josephine's crazy queer sugar daddy. Don't tell me you're listening to his bullshit. She's probably beaten him senseless with that whip of hers."

"Or maybe her violin playing sent him over the edge," Stephen said.

Dennis jumped in. "He was already quite mad before he met her."

Sophia shook her head. "You are both so mean-spirited." Then her eyes rested on Jake. "Marci has told me much about you. We've needed to meet."

Jake reached over the bar and shook her hand. The silvery-haired medium did look like Stevie Nicks. She even dressed like a gypsy.

Then his eyes shifted back to Dennis. "So we finally meet. You're one of us, aren't you? I guess I should've realized it."

"I'm dormant, but angel magic runs in my veins. The fun's on the way, though."

"I'm just a regular fag," Stephen said but laughed.

"There's nothing regular about you," Dennis assured him then ordered drinks for everyone.

Industrial rock was playing, a raucous Nine Inch Nail remix of *Sin* that sounded like feverish sex on a rollercoaster. A lot of mesh, velvet, and vinyl headed to the dance floor.

"We need to talk about Peter," Dennis said. "He's about to lose his mind with Josephine haunting that place. I'd heard ghosts are drawn to you and thought you might like a ghostbuster job."

Jake handed a Long Island Tea to Sophia. "Don't you do this kind of thing professionally? Why come find a frustrated artist?"

"Yes, but I would love to see your talent at work. Marci tells me your potential is unbelievable. Wasn't there a sexual attraction between you and this violinist?"

He shrugged. "I have a thing for girls I've seen in dreams."

She chuckled warmly. "Okay. You have a bond with her. Let's make plans to meet Peter. Oh by the way, I own a bar called *My Hot Sister*. I need a parttime bartender. Could you work one night a week?"

"Is it a lesbian bar?"

"Yeah, but they'll love you there. Just think about it." She sighed, thinking hard. "Don't you have a diary that belonged to that girl? Marci was telling me about it."

"I have a few journals of hers. One is in my coat." He reached in his leather coat and produced a small journal with filigree gold leafing.

Sophia grasped it in both hands, closing her eyes. She whispered as images rushed through her mind: old weapons ...dungeons...mistress." After a moment, she came out of her trance and uttered a single word: "Thorn."

"Thorn?" Jake questioned.

"That name just echoes through my mind," she said, unnerved. "This man is at the center of it all. He's very, very dangerous."

Jake took time to tell her about the bounty hunter after him. "We feel sure the drug dealer behind all this has paid him to come after me. We're trying to find him first."

Sophia closed her eyes. "I'm seeing a playground. It has something to do with this girl."

"I've seen this place in my mind, too," Jake said. "Her remains are there, ashes buried somewhere. I'm sure of it, but I can't get a hold on where it is."

"Who do you think put her ashes there?"

"Her bandmate Minstrel. He wants her back from the spirit world to *play* with him once again."

She nodded. "May I keep this for a few days? Let me see what I can draw off of it."

Jake thought a moment, hating to part with anything of Josephine's. "Alright."

Sophia nodded appreciatively, realizing how strong his connection was to Josephine. "In the meantime, let's see if we can get in touch with her ghost at this attorney's house. She may very well aid your quest."

"Call tomorrow," Dennis said, sliding his number across the bar.

"Sure. I just need a cigarette and a cup of strong black coffee. Then I'll call."

The three of them moved on, the enormity of this situation leaving Jake lightheaded. Taking a break, he headed for the restroom. He would find privacy in a stall to do a line.

Nightclub bathroom stalls were nothing but malodorous tiny citadels for the addicted and sex driven, but if one could stand the stench, countless pleasures could be administered in their confines.

Locking a stall door, he used his car key to scoop out coke from a baggie, snorting it deeply into both nostrils. For a moment, he just listened to the world around him. Music from the dance floor vibrated the walls like a demonic force. Beer bottles clattered, and the drone of a thousand conversations was punctuated by laughter and loud cursing. He read several numbers scrawled on the stall just for the hell of it, finding an obscene yet witty verse of poetry. Then his thoughts drifted back to a huge question in his mind.

If Josephine does return to the flesh, what will happen between them?

Chapter Twenty

Racing down Lenox Road, Jake was so engrossed in the Hollywood metal band Black Veil Brides he nearly missed the resplendent driveway in front of Peter's flashy house. The rattling dream machine careened up behind a Porsche, shaded by a huge Magnolia with big waxy flowers. The whole place just screamed power and sex—a great place to do a rock video.

Idling a moment, he changed the music. *You're So Vain* by Carly Simon was playing on the old classics station he'd found. He had a feeling this could be Peter's theme song.

A tall beautiful girl answered the door. A knowing smile played over her face, and then she slid the chain lock off the door.

"Who is it, Jill?" a voice called from upstairs.

She looked Jake up and down, fluttering a well manicured eyebrow. "I think it's your...gentleman caller."

"Very funny," Peter said, heading down.

They all wound up in the living room where the anxious playboy lawyer wasted no time doling out the party favors: thick lines of coke for everyone. The raconteur launched into his conversation as though he was in a courtroom, boasting about big wins for felons, trips to New York, and all the partying. Jake did think he was rather entertaining, but finally Jill, looking bored, left the room. An awkward silence took over.

Jake cleared his throat. "I'd like to talk about Josephine."

Closing his eyes, Peter nodded. "There is some fucking weird shit going on here. I really do think that girl is haunting this house. I'm at the point of desperation." After saying this, he divvied up more powder.

Jake snorted another small line. "If she's haunting this place, there's a pretty good chance I can draw her to me. We'll just see. In the meantime, I'd like to ask you a few questions. I don't know what all you've learned from Dennis, but she overdosed on a magic demon-drug. Do you know anyone who would sell Rapture to her?"

Peter did a long line and chased it with Scotch. "No. Her thing was coke and heroin."

"Rapture is in a whole different league."

His eyes narrowed. "She was in a whole different league. Not too many strippers played violin. What exactly was she after? I know she was hooking to score dope, but there was something else that she really wanted. Dennis told me she dealt in the *arcane market.*"

"Let's just say she was after her true magical power and freedom from a certain controlling bitch. Was she at your parties a lot?"

"All the time, but she was a very private person. I used to pick up on snippets of her conversations with Dennis, but I never overheard much that made sense to me. It was just all so weird. Even things I'd ask her directly were met with cryptic responses." He chopped up more dope with a Platinum American Express. "She loved secrets."

"Often ghosts divulge secrets," Jake said. "Is there anything you'd like me to ask her when I make contact?"

"Questions?" He scoffed. "Just ask her what it'll take to get her the hell out." He fell back on the sofa, sighing heavily as he gestured toward a polished sideboard laden with top-shelf liquor. "Help yourself and come outside."

A big party was in the works with party girls around the pool and couples going in and out of the sliding glass doors. Many were headed upstairs for sexy extracurricular activities. This place only needed a camera crew to film the follow-up to *Boogie Nights.*

Set up by one of the bars was a tarot card reader. She was giving a reading to a girl in a bikini.

"Did you hire her for entertainment?" Jake asked, astounded.

"Exactly. Party people loved that shit."

"Is she any good?"

"How should I know? I found her on the internet. She might be a fraud, but I did talk to her about my ghost problem to see if she could help." He chuckled. "She was clueless, but she gives these melodramatic readings, and then her *clients* do more coke. It keeps Dennis busy."

Jake walked over to meet this probable charlatan. He felt magic from her, however faint. She looked like a frumpy unemployed bookkeeper with huge coke-bottle glasses and a plain blunt cut, a cartoon channel psychic.

When the reading was over, she smiled up at him. The bikini girl leering over her shoulder at him headed back poolside.

"You look like somebody I would've worshipped when I was a teenager," the hoaxer said.

"And you look like the cool teacher I never slept with."

"I bet you say that to all the washed up hags." Her face darkened speculatively. "I'm Dora. Are you...?" She touched him and drew back. "Such magic. Are you here for the ghost hunt?"

"Yeah. Are you here to be part of a reality show?"

She shrieked with laughter. "I usually do birthday parties. This place is *wild*."

He grinned, his head tilted thoughtfully. "Do you believe a spirit infests this house?"

She made a wincing expression. "I don't know. Maybe. People who have fantastic houses always think they're haunted. It's fun, though, being a part of this."

"You should have a ball meeting all these hookers."

Dora looked around in awe. "I was sort of a coke whore back in the eighties, but I've never seen anything quite like this."

Night was coming. Heaters and Tikki torches were placed around the pool area. There was a group playing drinking games. In the pool, volleyball was going on.

"To be young," she said wistfully.

"Hey, you're young at heart."

He went poolside and approached the bar.

"Hey, I know you," the bartender said. "I'm Robin. How's that band of yours going?"

"We broke up, but I'll eventually put together another one." He plopped down on a barstool. "Do you believe these ghost stories going around?"

He shrugged, filling a glass with ice. "I wonder. Some people who've had experiences here won't come back. And the stories only get better." He gave Jake a wary look and then smiled. "I've heard about you and those girls. I know that magic stuff is real."

"Do you know of anyone dealing in magic designer drugs?"

He sighed heavily. "Not really. You should talk to Dennis." He looked over Jake's shoulder. "Speak of the devil."

"Did I hear my name?" Dennis asked, taking a seat by Jake.

"I thought we'd meet here, and you'd introduce me to Peter. Where have you been?"

"I'm always fashionably late. Besides, you two needed some private time to break bread." He lit a cigarette and smiled slyly. "Has there been any fun ghostly gossip I've missed?"

The sky was a dark bruise. Shadows of tree limbs played over them like spirits who'd come to listen, as well. It was a perfect time for ghost stories. Across the pool, two girls watched, whispering in girlish conspiracy.

Robin poured everyone a shot of Jägermeister. "I've never seen anything, but I've heard stories about things moving mysteriously in the rooms upstairs. Couples don't go up there to fool around like they used to. As nervous as Peter has been, something is definitely up."

Dennis tossed back his shot, holding out the empty shooter glass for another. "I truly believe I saw Josephine in a window the other night. She was actually dancing to the music being played out here. And I've seen lights...weird spectral stuff. And I've smelled her perfume." He slammed the second shot, then wiped his mouth. "And there's something else."

"Don't hold us in suspense, drama queen." Jake laughed.

"I've been feeling demon magic along with it. I don't know whether we're dealing with a demon or a ghost. Now that really is scary."

"Yeah. It sure is," Jake said. "I think we're dealing with a demon that took over a ghost. The demon wants to take physical form through her."

"Ah, brilliant," Dennis exclaimed. "Snow was talking about a crazy violinist in town who bound a demon to her spirit."

"I believe it. So just what have you seen around here?"

Wind blew through the trees, spirit whispers. "I actually saw a dark form move over a bed upstairs. At first, I thought it was the shadow of a bird, but then it got weirder. Music came on in the house, and I swear I saw dancing shadows. The bedspread even slid onto the floor. I even felt fingernails claw my arm. I heard about a sighting of her walking around the pool in the middle of the night."

A bikini clad girl rushed inside, buttocks jiggling. She had a beer commercial festive air about her. This was definitely a cool place, and he wanted to check it out further. Jake got up from the bar. "Let me make my rounds. I'll be back."

He milled about the party, running into a couple of waitresses from the sushi bistro near *Medusa's* and a manager from *Pandora's Box*, Marci's workplace, partying with a group of strippers. There was small talk about his next band and life at *Medusa's* and then he excused himself and started exploring the house.

His every instinct told him to head upstairs. He found a staircase featuring a balustrade of filigreed ironwork, prints of Paris leading the way up. The second floor held a legal library, bedrooms used as sex parlors, and an entertainment room with pool tables, bars, and flatscreen televisions. The sounds of sex and laughter could be heard behind one closed door.

Then he came to a door where he felt magic, faintly but there. He pressed his fingers to the door and received a surge of impressions—the cavorting of a misfit, Bible pages fluttering in candlelit ritual, money changing hands—

"Jake." Peter's voice came from behind him. "You're getting something. What is it?"

Jake, startled slightly, turned to behold the attorney with a girl on each side of him. "I'm feeling magic."

"Magic?" Peter said incredulously. "The only thing magic about Benjamin is his inheritance. He pays me a thousand a month for this room. I'm tired of him living here. The girls hate him."

"May I see it?" Jake asked.

Blushing, Peter hesitated, his complexion already flush from drinking. He was obviously a little embarrassed for him to see it.

Jake understood why soon enough. The room was a teenager's shrine to rock music. Peter stood in the doorway with a forced gameshow smile on, annoyed with the faint giggles of derision from the girls.

"I love it," Jake exclaimed. "There's the star child." He was referring to Paul Stanley of Kiss. There were pictures of Hendrix, Zeppelin, and modern bands.

On the bed lay a Bible, a used bag of coke, and...a grimoire.

He snatched it up, staring down at a spell on dispelling demons. A letter on cream stationery fell from its pages like an angel from heaven.

#

Josephine,

You aren't like the other girls. I know your talent and beauty hides great magic. What would it take for me to have you?

#

Jake dropped the letter, eyes rolling upward. It took a moment for him to catch his breath.

"This is her stalker without a doubt. Benjamin's directly connected to the drug dealer I'm looking for. I'm sure of it. I don't think he realized what he was getting himself into. And now the obsession of his life is dead...perhaps chasing him now, a ghost wanting vengeance."

"The last time I saw him he was wearing something weird," Peter said. "A charm."

"Like mine?" Jake smiled.

"Not quite that...detailed. Is that blood in the thing? Anyway, I've known for a while he was obsessed with the whole witchcraft thing."

Jake nodded. "I think that's one of the main reasons he wanted Josephine so bad." He continued checking the room. The tangled bed spread was a mock-up symbolizing the dark desires of the misfit's soul. Designs for a board game were drawn on paper and spread out on the bed, and the lyrics to all the songs on *Operation: Mindcrime* were scrawled on pages strewn about the board game plans. The songs about the corrupt priest and the girl he saved from the streets were written over and over, maniacally.

On a pillow rested a Bible.

Is that what this goofball thought? He was going to save Josephine? Did he think saviors and murderers were one and the same?

"Tell me about this guy. Is he a gamer? How old is he?"

"I think forty-three. He had ideas for all these dark fantasy games. He'd worked for these companies that fired him because he couldn't handle his partying. He'd go in and out of rehab. Finally, he got this inheritance and hasn't stopped buying hookers since. He even goes to Vegas to gamble. And Atlantic City."

"Bright Lights, Big City," Jake responded musingly.

"Good book."

Jake grinned and began running his hands over things. "Let me see what else I can pick up."

"Sure. Just don't mess up his—"

"Altar to the gods of rock?" Jake finished, grinning.

"Yeah. Exactly."

Fingertips to the posters, he saw Benjamin in air guitar form, empty hands impassioned with stage histrionics.

On a chest of drawers, he found a photo album. He flipped it open.

What? It held pictures of Jake, photos of him onstage, but that wasn't what was most disturbing. He had photos of him at work. He'd been stalking Jake, too.

One photograph of Jake had a question on the back of it written in feverish script: "This is who you've left me for?"

Flipping through the Bible, he found runic symbols scrawled on pages with annotations like, "no real God would give this life to me."

Jake looked back at Peter in astonishment. "Here's what I want to know. Why did you let him live here?"

Peter shrugged, disgusted. "I felt sorry for him. I met him in a strip joint and bought him a few drinks. We started talking. He tried to impress me with his gaming knowledge, which meant nothing to me, but then it came to my attention he'd gotten a big inheritance and wanted to meet girls at my place. I thought better of it. It didn't bother me so much that he was nerdy. He just seemed mentally...*off*. Anyway, I let him come over. He started spending money on girls like I hadn't seen in my life...like he'd never seen a girl. He eventually told me the whole rehab story and how nobody wanted to have anything to do with him, especially after he'd gotten all that money he really didn't deserve." Peter sighed, downed expensive Scotch. "Anyway, I had an extra room, and the rest is history."

"Do you expect to see him tonight?"

"I doubt it. He's so strange. Even having this room, he'll get hotel rooms and not come back for days."

"He's probably busy stalking another stripper," Jake said. "So tell me more about these ghostly appearances here."

The attorney sat down with him in the living room, everyone else outside. "I've seen shadows sliding over the walls and heard things rattling. I've even seen that girl in the mirror. She really scared me."

"And it was Josephine?"

"Oh yeah. Nobody else looks like that goth girl...and that damn violin. I could hear her playing it. There's more. I want to show you something in one of the guest rooms."

Peter led him down the hallway to a door he unlocked. He jabbed a finger at the bed. "See how the sheets are twisted?"

"Wild night in the sack, huh?"

"This happened without anyone sleeping in it."

"With all that goes on in this house, are you sure one of your buddies didn't go for a fling in your bed?"

"Nobody has a key to this room. Nobody. And there's something else." He pulled back a fold of sheets to reveal a black lipstick holder that looked like a coffin. "This was hers. How did it get here?" He handed it to Jake.

A surge of imagery slid across the back of his eyes. He saw Josephine sitting before a makeup mirror. She was applying eyeliner as a woman behind her with tresses of platinum and blue caressed the luxurious curve of her jawline. A thick silver-ringed submission collar bound Josephine's neck. It was linked to a chain fastened on the other end to a leather bracelet on the woman's wrist.

"The show is about to begin," the woman said softly to Josephine, a voice from space, and then the scene vanished from his mind.

"May I keep the lipstick case? I want to meditate with it. Where can I be alone for a while?"

"Get yourself a drink and go in the library."

Jake brought a glass of wine into the dark-paneled room, lit some candles standing about, and closed the door.

Clasping the lipstick case tightly in his hands, he saw three figures on stage, playing violin and viola. He was hit with the strong realization that Felicity was most definitely coming for Josephine.

And for him.

Jake leaned back, sighing heavily. He reeled at the

possibilities. Could she complete the spell on Josephine?

Visions bloomed, flowering into orgies. He saw Josephine chained to a bed floating on roiling mist. Voyeurs watched.

Felicity poured candle wax on her, the wax running like tears over her breasts and the swell of her hips. Blood in a chalice was passed around, and then the vision dissolved.

Suddenly, several books flew off a desk followed by a window sliding open. Wind rushed in; candles guttered. He gasped as shadows slid along the walls of books, coalescing into a writhing nebulous form.

The lipstick case rose and floated in the air, going end over end. "I will be with you again," the signature velvety voice of Josephine whispered.

A violin materialized from spectral gossamer. The spirit began to play an eerily mellifluous passage, pulsing with light like a morphing insect as it strained for corporeal form, as though a painter was fleshing out an image on canvas.

There was a flash of flowing velvet, a staccato burst of lithe midriff, a glittering navel ring. Inky strands of ectoplasm solidified into flowing black tresses. But no hold would last. She just couldn't quite make it over...

The beautiful creature of half-light/half-flesh straddled him. He was rendered prostrate to a moon goddess, bent on sacrificing him to the night.

"I will be with you," she whispered.

Then she fell apart like a broken doll. Spectral shards dissolved. Pallid flesh and black leather were lost to the night's shadows.

His breath caught in his throat, and he closed his eyes. He shuddered in the fear that she would return to take him to some dark heaven forever. Only the wind remained, that and flickering candlelight.

***

"I couldn't wait to get out of that house," Jake said, recounting his night at Peter's. "I fed him a line of bullshit and took off."

"Ghosts that want to return to the flesh are not good news," Marci said, watching a hostess mouth a snide remark to a smirking waiter. They were at a high end New York style diner on Fourteenth Street. "Are you ready to go meet Sophia, or do you need more to drink?"

"I'm as ready as I'll ever be," he said, downing a glass of wine. "Actually let's get another round of shots."

"Alright, this is it," she said, texting Sophia after she ordered two more shots. "We'd still be here at last call if it were up to you. We need to deal with this ghost crisis."

An hour later, Marci pulled up in the driveway of Sophia's house, the medium standing there amongst wind chimes. Windswept, she looked spectral herself.

She rushed down the steps, lacey bell sleeves snagging on vines twined around the railing. Marci and Sophia hugged like old dear friends who hadn't seen each other in years.

Sophia tugged back Marci's dawn-streaked hair in a motherly way, bangles and charms on her wrists clinking and clattering musically. A searching cast overcame her eyes. "What's on your mind? A dangerous hunt you need to talk about?"

"Oh no. I just did a successful run for the council," Marci said. "I'm mainly here about this whole ghost business and the possible trouble to come Bonding Weekend with that evil violin bitch Felicity on the way and magic designer drugs on the streets. We need to catch the Rapture dealer before the party starts."

"Even the world of entertainment in magic is dangerous," Sophia said. "This is why I love my house, full of powerful positive energy." Her eyes settled on Jake. "I was waiting on you to call me. Did you go to Peter's house?"

"I sure did. And the ghost came to me. It was scary. I don't want to do that again without you. Did you draw any impressions from the journal I gave you?"

"Yes, but I only get confusing images of a ritual in that playground. I'd really like to reach the ghost directly."

Jake took out the lipstick coffin case and tossed it into her hand like it was toy. "I can assure you that can be arranged."

She smiled. "I'm sure. Let's have some drinks first."

"You're speaking to his heart," Marci said.

"Hey, let the lady work her healing magic."

Ethereal wave music floated like aural spirits through her mystical place. They went inside, and Sophia poured everyone a glass of wine.

Jake eyed the candlelit shelves of oddities. Amongst roots and dried herbs were monkey skulls, desiccated bird claws, and terrariums of exotic frogs and spiders. "I take it you run an apothecary."

"I do tarot readings, séances, and make all sorts of spells."

"She makes all my amulets," Marci said. "And no one is a better alchemist. We need more people like her in this world instead of fighters and bounty hunters."

She smiled appreciatively, her silvery hair otherworldly in the candlelight. "Now tell me Josephine's story. I'm confused. Why do these other two violinists want her back from the dead?"

"It's morbidly simple. The succubus bandleader, Felicity, needs Josephine back to complete her trio act. Josephine was a huge draw for Dire Portent. Irreplaceable, most likely. She ran from the dominating bitch, though, to pursue her Darkening, which Felicity wouldn't allow. I believe she was worried Josephine would be more talented than she.

"Anyway, she came to me mainly because she thought I could help her go through her rite of passage, the Darkening. She was doing all kinds of dope to cope with the misery of her Calling nightmares and wound up taking a demon drug, Rapture, that her stalker gamer-guy gave her. Now she's a spirit wanting her life back."

"And she's tied to a demon that will *bring* her back," Marci interjected.

"She's nearly there," Jake said. "I saw it."

"I see." Sophia nodded, her eyes settling on his amulet. "I do truly believe that is the Dual Serpent Amulet of lore. It was meant to be yours."

"You believe the whole bloodline thing? I am a direct descendent of Merek?

"I can feel the chemistry you have with it. I can't come to any other conclusion." She sipped her wine, regarding him as though he were an enigma. "How did you get it?"

"A fallen angel came to me in the guise of an old girlfriend."

"She just gave it to you?"

"A demon sent me in search of her. When I found her, she slipped it to me before her captors knew what was going on."

"Captors?"

They filled her in on the Ariel vs. demon drama and the Kitty Dreadlock hostage situation.

A puzzled look came over her face. "The demon let you go when it won the game, right?"

Jake laughed. "Yeah, but fate doesn't want to let me go. Sparks fly if someone tries to take off the amulet."

Her eyebrows stitched together. "Where is this angel now?"

"She ran. She seems to think she is protecting me by staying out of my life. I brought the letter she wrote me, so you could see it. My mystery girl called herself Charm. I thought maybe you could provide some insight. I couldn't gather anything...maybe because she's too close to my heart."

He handed the letter to Sophia. She read it and then closed her eyes. "She's running from a terribly powerful demonic force. I feel this dark being is from the Nephemera. He'll be in the guise of a man, and he'll wear a hat...a top hat. Bizarre. And the demon wants your amulet for its own designs...and you *dead*."

He sighed. "Another hater. Do believe in this angel world?"

"Oh yes."

Fuck me. He didn't want to believe any of this. Shuddering, he said, "Okay. Let's get back to the task at hand. Look. Josephine might not have been a Darkened, but she wasn't evil. Just scared. I want to free her spirit from the demon before it's too late. I don't want her to wind up being a soul-sucking succubus."

Sophia sipped her wine thoughtfully. "Let's hold our séance."

In a room lined floor-to-ceiling with grimoires, jars of grotesqueries, and cabalistic tapestries, Sophia lit pillar candles on pedestal tables and tea candles on a huge round table with a black velvet tablecloth.

She placed Josephine's journal topped with the lipstick holder in the center of a summoning circle and lit incense around it. They held hands around the table, and she began to utter a flow of Latin. Chills rushed through Jake as shadows thickened and the candles guttered.

Sigils glowed on the table, and the journal floated into the air along with the silver holder.

In Latin, she uttered: "Josephine, we summon you with the combined will of our souls."

A spectral mass of leather and lace solidified into a shimmering apparition of the girl. "I can't stay long. My master doesn't want this."

"Who is your master?"

"Nix..." And then she trailed off in a gasp.

"Were you forced into this?" Sophia asked.

"Minstrel wanted it more than I..."

"And who do you believe is the cause of your demise?"

"My secret admirer..." Words melted into wordless breath. "And Thorn. He's the dealer. Find Thornnn..."

That Benjamin freak and Thorn are definitely connected, Jake thought.

"Josephine," Jake asked. "You knew Charm. Right?"

The wind blew. Candles guttered and the spirit writhed. "Yes. She knows much."

"Do you know where she is?"

"Savannah."

"Doing what?"

"Using her beauty and wiles for personal gain."

"Would she know where Thorn is?"

"Maybe. She knew him. And she *really* knew Peter."

Then she was gone.

Jake slumped in the wingback chair, cringing. *She'd fucked Peter?* Revelation brought with it much pain.

There was a great rattling as though from an earthquake and then the journal burst into flames.

Sophia's hands flew to the book, smothering the flames but not before many of the pages were destroyed.

"The demon doesn't want this to exist. There's something written that would've led to her remains. If you find the playground, you can break the spell."

She rifled through the smoldering pages, read an entry: "*I will eventually find someone to perform my Darkening, and then I'll realize my true talent, Felicity be damned. Tonight, I will go to my secret place at the abandoned school and read and write poetry and swing forever if I want to with my young girlfriend. I'll even be able to hear music from the homeless blues guitarist who sits at that old empty church. Then maybe I'll go down the street and dance and play violin for the antique dealer.*"

Jake's eyes gleamed with a scheming boy's sense of adventure. "I'd read about the secret place but not a passage that intriguing. I feel like I'm playing a game of Clue, a swing behind a school, a guitarist, and church nearby, and an antique dealer down the road. I know the antique dealer."

Marci's eyes widened. "Is that the creepy man you met at *Final Destination*?"

"Yeah. I thought maybe Josephine's secret place was that pink fucking house because she had a room there like this goofy Benjamin guy has at Peter's." He gave a faint laugh. "You've got to see that big pink Victorian house. It looks like something out of Dr. Seuss. Anyway, there's no swing set at that old man's house...unless it's part of a sex fantasy setup in one of the rooms." After a moment, he nodded dismissively, downed the wine. "She keeps talking about a seedy neighborhood with an abandoned school. Forget the pink house possibility."

"That's too far fetched," Marci agreed.

"Let's get back to Peter. Based on what we just heard, he surely knows this Thorn guy, yet he hasn't mentioned him at all in our conversations. One wonders. Do you think he hated to destroy a beautiful underworld partnership by running his mouth?"

"He's not going to tell you about his *major dealers*," Marci stressed. "He's worried about getting killed. Between Thorn and the ghost, he probably doesn't know who he fears the most." A look of resolve came over her face. "We need to find that biker bounty hunter and make him talk. I'll bet he knows where we can find Thorn."

"I think we all agree Thorn hired him," Jake said.

"Or Benjamin did to get Thorn off his back. That's more likely," Marci said.

The singer nodded. "What we really need to do first is find Charm. She probably knows all about Josephine. And when we find her, I bet the biker won't be far behind."

In the flicker of candlelight, Sophia poured more wine. "There's much to do. We still need to do a purging of spirits at Peter's, no matter what. Tomorrow night, I'll be at *My Hot Sister*." She smiled invitingly at Jake. "If you want to work, just come join me."

Chapter Twenty-One

The following night, Jake picked up a bartending shift at *My Hot Sister*. Sophia's music played—everything from symphonic metal to New Age music—unless a guest played the jukebox.

The breathtaking murals of beautiful fairy girls on the walls were renowned in the club scene. Candles and incense lent an ethereal ambience to the place. Sophia even gave tarot card readings in a dark corner of the bar.

Probably the biggest draw to the place, though, was Agnes Scott College students across the street. The all-girl liberal arts school was where *Scream* was filmed. Sophia warned Jake, around midnight, girls would pour in here.

At eleven-thirty the crowd consisted of tired waiters, girlfriends of Sophia who'd been partying in Midtown, and strippers who were just starting their night. On the jukebox, the reflective music of Tracy Chapman played. Then the waiters played sing-a-long Jimmy Buffet songs.

Finally, a bored stripper got up and played *We are the Champions* by Queen. This song seemed to precipitate the whole crazy night ahead.

In sync with the Freddie Mercury bombastic victory music, Agnes Scott girls made a grand entrance. They poured in the door as though a college girl home invasion was being used as a rock video storyline.

Jake witnessed this infiltration in amused awe. He'd never seen so much long hair draped over cardigan sweaters in his life. The imaginary rock video could easily become a porn movie. Would his working here cause the college to crumble? He'd heard stories about these girls. They hardly needed his corrupting.

"We all want to try this Black Dahlia you're all the rage for," a girl exclaimed, slamming down a stack of books on the bar—to hell with school—and slinging her long hair out of her face in a cute flounce. "But first a beer."

When Jake handed her a pint of Harp, she downed half of it then slammed it on the book stack like a crowning achievement.

Seven girls lined up. Black Dahlias for everyone? *Oh Jake you genius!* He smiled like the Cheshire cat. *Here we go!*

Herradura Silver tequila streamed into a tumbler along with his mystery blackberry liqueur. He shook it as though doing a magic trick then poured the concoction through a strainer into a series of shot glasses. The first shot went to a girl in a tank-top that read *Bad Kitty*. Then the rest snatched theirs up for a toast.

Oh fame.

During a break, he browsed over his manuscript. The violinist was playing for tips on the streets of Spell Island, and she came to the cold realization that the sex shows were where the money was at, that and prostitution with magical beings. Magic and sex were everything in this dark world.

He considered the desperate actresses of old Hollywood like the Black Dahlia. Would they have taken the risk of going to a dangerous future world of magic to become famous? Josephine sure would've done it.

He turned back to the wild college crowd. It would be a long night, and there was so much ahead of him over the next few days. He had to find Charm and move into Nightmare Mansion. Both would come with a lot of drama.

Still, he was thrilled to be working tonight. He needed money and loved meeting new crowds that didn't haunt *Medusa's*. It was a chance to talk about his bands, his book, the streets, the clubs, everything.

As he was telling stories about one of his rock shows, a dazzling violin riff met his ears, carrying an erotic rush of dark magic. From the end of the bar, Minstrel smiled broadly, eyebrow flared.

"Your aura is like none other," the violinist said. "I tracked you here quite easily. May I try this Black Dahlia shot I've heard so much about? Let me buy you one. Too...for a toast."

"A toast to what?" Jake scoffed.

"New beginnings. After all, you'll be consummating Josephine's return soon."

Jake made a shot and slid it toward the strange violinist. "You've lost your mind. Why don't you just break the demon's spell on Josephine and leave her be?"

Minstrel made a reproachful clucking sound and then downed the shot, looking impressed. "Leave her be? She'll be a wandering angry spirit with no purpose. You shouldn't want that for her." He played a flashy lick and added, "By the way, I didn't come here to whine about your having sex with a ghost. That's an eventuality. I actually came to tell you what I've done for you in all my generosity."

Derision filled Jake's eyes. "What's that?"

Minstrel tilted his head, eyes sliding thoughtfully over liquor bottles. "I've met your nemesis, the bounty hunter who's after you."

Jake froze. "Oh really?"

"I believe I've convinced him not to kill you, but you really must stop looking for the dealer who's selling Rapture. This particular entrepreneur intends to make a lot of money Bonding Weekend, and he has no intention of letting you stand in his way. You and your girl dream team really should give it up. It's not worth it." He paused to play a mesmerizing creepy piece of music.

Chills washed over Jake as an image rushed through his mind of Minstrel in front of a summoning circle, playground monkey bars behind him. This segued into an image of Josephine sitting in a swing, writing poetry. Then everything dissolved like hot wax.

Minstrel flared an eyebrow. "Why, you look like you've seen a ghost. Did my playing cause that much disquietude?"

"Why would you summon a demon to possess Josephine?"

Minstrel sighed. "She needs to return to the flesh however she can. I didn't want to make a deal with a demon, but what can I do?"

Sophia walked up behind Jake, shaking her head. "Demon deals rarely go well."

Minstrel shrugged and then played a looping riff of arpeggios. "Josephine was already on a path to self-destruction. One drug or another was going to be the death of her. When she is back with us, we should all run off together before Felicity arrives."

Jake changed the spout on a bottle of Grey Goose vodka, his expression a puzzled scowl. "I think I've told you I'm not selling myself into slavery. I'm not gonna be some fiddle playing weasel's singer bitch."

Minstrel made a tsk-tsk sound. "I don't want a slave. I want a front man. I need your talent. By the way, I prefer *violinist extraordinaire*."

"I'd rather stay here and deal with Felicity."

Minstrel nodded ruefully. "I don't think you understand what's coming. Okay. Fair thee well." He walked out with a nonchalant air, playing a melancholy piece in the night wind. Girls surrounded him, listening and laughing. He was certainly a gifted weirdo.

Jake turned to Sophia. "When he played a minute ago, I saw a clear image of him summoning a demon in a playground. Did you see or sense anything?"

Arms folded, she'd been listening to the whole conversation. Her eyes went distant, thoughts and feelings going inward to wrap around it all. "This playground...he's placed powerful wards around it, blocking psychic intrusion. That's why it's so hard to get a grasp on the location. Felicity would kill him if the spell on Josephine was thwarted."

Jake sighed. "I can't wait to find Charm. We'll get real answers from my fallen angel."

***

Moving into Nightmare Mansion turned into a hysterical ordeal. It wasn't the actual moving that was the challenge. It was listening to Clara's spurned tongue. She regarded Jake, Snow, and Brice in horror as though a cult had broken into her place.

"You're a loser," she said to Jake caustically, arms folded, imperious queen. "I tried to get you away from those Midtown bottom feeders. I'll bet you're shooting dope again."

"And I'll bet you've got another terribly exciting wine tasting party with your corporate cookie-cutter buddies," Jake retorted. "Sure wish I could sit around and have the shit bored out of me about bad stock investments and bitter divorces, but I've got to move on."

"Jerk."

After grabbing a final suitcase and a stuffed animal Lemur, he made a dramatic exit, nose held high (Snow was proud of him), singing the song "Moving Out" by Billy Joel.

The other guys waited by a rented van. Cameo, who didn't help with anything, was drunk and threw her arms around Jake when he made the final run to the van.

Clara scoffed at this fit of rapture. "What kind of a bleach-blonde slut is that?"

Cameo's eyes went wide at the nerve of the haughty bitch, her mouth making an indignant O. "Oh really? Really?"

Jake tightened his brows. "Clara big shot, this girl can dance like she's pro. We're talking Atlanta Ballet level. All you're good for is running your foul mouth."

Clara rolled her eyes. "Whatever. What would you know about dancing and art? My friends think you're boorish, and by the way, that music of yours is racket. I don't know why you're so full of yourself."

"You sure liked having sex to that racket," Jake shot back.

She gasped. "You pompous little..."

He was no longer listening as he leapt into the van amongst juvenile laughter. Cameo gave her the finger like a little redneck firecracker in a *Smokey and the Bandit* rip-off movie.

Last but not least, the gang went by the motel where Jake had been staying. He bid farewell to the drug dealer whom he'd gotten to know quite well. They did a quick goodbye party, wildly indulgent, thick lines of coke snorted on motel furniture and shots of whiskey drunk like vainglorious sailors.

The real party continued back at Nightmare Mansion. Muriel greeted them with drunken effusion, arms outstretched, loose velvet sleeves flapping in the night wind. "Cries of the liberated," she shouted from the porch with a Joan of Arc furor. "Our Jake is free."

The house was quite a spectacle. Candles floated in the air like spirits on fire. The French prog-metal band Adagio pounded from ceiling speakers, setting off illusion bursts, a storm of erotica. Cameo twirled up and down the staircase to the music, an improv audition of rapturous abandon. Jake tried to dance with her and wound up tumbling down the stairs.

After a few toasts on the porch, everyone went to the gallery to jam together—an unofficial underground show. There was a crowd of about thirty, selected mavens there to see Dark Promise with Jake for the first time.

The show began with Jake playing legato runs on his piano, triggering the illusion runes Snow had placed on the ivory keys. The visual effluvium was astounding, tapping into Jake's mind: a beautiful naked girl on horseback, lovers in twisted sheets, and then two girls on a rollercoaster, making out with pierced tongues.

The band joined his intro. The music carried a heavy note of orchestral suspense, slow at first, and then it took off. It sounded like eerie indie soundtrack music, and in fact, the song was about a young girl on the streets, punctuated with sparse whispered lyrics about drugs, alienation, and hardscrabble life. Snow's guitar playing was morose but virtuosic, the riffs like a requiem. Muriel's plodding bass notes were like heavy ponderous feet headed to the gallows, double bass drums racing through it all.

After a few sets, they headed to *Pandora's Box* to see Zowie dance for the first time. There was a fair crowd there for a Thursday, not overwhelming. Moonshine and Marci were at the bar, dancing. A group of businessmen was transported by carnal fantasy, corporate dreams displaced by curves, music, and moves.

On the main stage, Zowie was dancing. Even stripping, she came across like she was doing an exotic Vegas act, platinum hair of a glam cyborg. She was too exotic for this world, alien hot, a timeless beautiful creature that would return to the cosmos.

When the girls got off work after midnight, they went back to Nightmare Mansion with the gang. They drank heavily, but the mood was mellow. Cameo danced from time to time through the night, listless and drunk, a lonely spirit turning the porch into a dance stage.

"I wish the ghost band would show up," she said, balancing on the vine-festooned railing and twirling, nimble toed. "Then I wouldn't have to dance alone."

Snow scoffed. "You'd be having sex with all of them. We'd never get you out of the house."

Shrugging, she kept twirling, a languorous dance of eternity.

Around noon, they awoke like cat burglars who'd passed out in drunken ineptitude. They'd crashed in crazy configurations— porch chairs, velvet furniture, the swing.

After drinking a little hair of the dog (and snorting a few white lines), they staggered to a pancake house on Memorial Drive and took up a big sticky table like hungover council members.

Cameo, full of playful erotic thoughts, talked about pouring syrup on herself. "I would make the cutest pancake for some Darkened boy."

"You've certainly been eaten for breakfast before," Muriel said dryly, slicing into an omelet with artichokes and portabella mushrooms.

Cameo laughed, dirty bad girl laughter, and planted her saucy eyes on Jake. "So, are you going to join the coven?"

He sighed. "I move in and join the band, and now you want me strapped to you forever."

"It's just a thought." She speared a slice of bacon with a bent fork.

"We'll talk about it after Bonding Weekend," Snow said then slurped coffee. "We have a wild weekend of drama coming up, and Felicity, who is most certainly on her merry way, will be a formidable opponent, musical and otherwise."

"She won't have a dancer girl like me," Cameo exclaimed, fork in the air like a trident. "I see a weekend of domination, both musically and sexually."

"I do like the sound of that," Muriel said. "There's a poet beneath that dancing slutty façade."

"Exactly. I'm a ballerina illusionist sex addict and a closet poet to boot."

Muriel nodded. "I love it."

Zowie cleared her throat, rolling her eyes. "Whatever. Let's get back on track." She gave Marci a look of inquiry, flaring an eyebrow. "You are letting me go to Savannah for this *fallen angel* quest, aren't you?"

"Of course," she answered, eyebrows stitched. "Not to find Charm, though. You have to complete your rite of passage into our group. Believe you me, that biker is going to follow us down there. I want to see you finish that guy off."

***

Marci led the way to Savannah in her Miata, Jake striving to keep up with her in his clunky car. Since he'd just gotten his license back, he was thrilled to be driving instead of riding shotgun with the girls.

Moonshine and Muriel rode with Marci, so he had quite a captive audience: Cameo, Brice, Zowie. In control freak mode, he ruled the radio like the DJ host of an MTV music show, playing songs as varied as *Brain Salad Surgery* by seventies art rock band Emerson, Lake, and Palmer, and *My Girlfriend's Girlfriend* by nineties goth rockers Type O Negative. He even played the United Kingdom industrial metal band Cypher16. They liked most of it, drinking like groupies.

"I'll break out some great west coast weed if you'll play some reggae," Zowie said. "This shit just makes me want to drink beer and fight."

Jake laughed. "Drink beer and fight? I don't listen to redneck rock n' roll." Jake found Bob Marley on Spotify nevertheless. "Your weed idea does sound good. I should start smoking more and mellow out." She passed him a joint, and he took a drag, nodding in approval. "So, Zowie, didn't you live in Hollywood?"

She smiled, the joint to her mouth. "Oh yeah."

"Have you seen Jim Morrison's house?"

"I have been all over where he used to hang out. Motels...everything."

"We've got to go," Jake said.

"I'll take you all over Hollywood if we make it through Bonding Weekend."

"And if I don't run off with Charm when I find her. I might take her to Hollywood."

A strange silence took over the car, then Zowie said, "You really seem obsessed with this girl."

"Which one?" Jake asked. "My runaway fallen angel or my overdosed Darkened girl?"

"Both," Brice said. "Tell us more."

"Tell me more. Tell me more," Jake wailed, mocking the old *Grease* soundtrack song with Olivia Newton John and John Travolta. "Charm came to me in the guise of my deceased girlfriend Cierra, which makes her hard to forget, to say the least. Josephine, on the other hand, looks like a girl I've seen in visions of the Nephemera, a great mystery that completely freaks me out. The point is, both girls are pretty darn obsession worthy."

"So this angel came to you as an old girlfriend in order to...seduce you?" Zowie asked.

"Aside from wanting to be alluring to me, she wants to experience being young, wild, and free in this world. This is her chance to be free from the Nephemera for a while. I think of her as a beautiful enigma."

"And Josephine? Elaborate on why she's so unforgettable."

Jake's eyes narrowed. "Her story is fascinating. She thinks...thought she needed to be controlling and ruthless to make it in a dark world. The sad truth is, she probably did need to become a succubus to realize her full talent. Her situation was...is as desperate as the struggling violinist in my book."

"So you're more fascinated with the idea of her as a character than her as an actual person."

"Yeah. I guess that's true."

"You want her back, though, don't you," Brice said.

"I just wish I'd never lost her to drugs. I don't want her coming back from the dead, though...a revenant demon puppet."

"If she does come back somehow, could you resist her?" Brice asked.

Jake sighed. "Who knows? I haven't been able to resist a demon yet. They seem to fulfill fantasies that gods can't."

"Well, then. She might not capture your heart, but she'll sure get your body," Cameo said.

"And your soul," Brice added.

"And suck you dry of magic," Zowie finished.

"Thank you everyone for telling me about my succubus sucking fate. I'll be a desiccated shell. I have so much to look forward to."

"I think great sex is worth death." Cameo laughed, stoned out of her mind, swigging vodka and eating chocolate.

Born to be Wild by Steppenwolf was the first song they all sang together. Oh, the sixties hippy spirit abounded. Brice wailed with the most anthemic furor.

Cameo played old Madonna songs, mimicking the pop star's high pitched voice in *Holiday* quite well. Everyone was so fucked up, they tried to hit the diva notes with loopy feebleness. It was pointless but fun.

Along the coast, they spotted a motel with a greasy spoon diner across from it. Jake rattled up behind Marci and parked under a tree draped with swags of Spanish Moss. The hazy-headed gang

Bonding Weekend

poured out of the car like Halloween misfits in search of debauchery behind motel doors.

The clerk was a middle-aged bleached blonde with a sailor's mouth. She made him think of big-mouth Gwen at the Speedy Trip near his old Midtown apartment.

"Is the circus in town?" she exclaimed, turning from a black-and-white television set.

"We're tourists from Atlanta," Cameo said. "We're here to see your fine city."

She ran her eyes over them, taking in the black fingernails, dark kohl eyes, exotic piercings, velvet and leather gear. "Tourists? Are you sure you're not a cult?"

"We're a band."

"That's the same thing." She chuckled. "What can I do for you folks?"

"We need a room for the weekend."

They wound up with two rooms, one for the girls, one for the guys. The furniture was thrift-store fodder, but the prints were noteworthy, framed photos of marine life straight off the Discovery Channel. For a while, they all sat quietly in hazy meditation, staring at whale pictures. Cameo found a whale song video on YouTube to complete their oceanic spiritual experience.

"This whale shit is creepy," Brice said. "Let's start drinking and hear some *real* music." He took a chug of Jameson while Jake broke out the tequila. "So, tell us what lies behind this whole Black Dahlia shot success story of yours?"

"Yeah," Muriel said. "When you're finally famous, you could market your own liquor as part of your branding."

"It's hard to believe tequila and blackberry liqueur taste that good together," Zowie said.

He cleared his throat, waxing philosophical. "The shot is symbolic of the noir thriller/struggling sexy girl duality angle. The blackberry liqueur represents dark sensuality and the tequila just makes me think of the hard drinking and poker playing in noir crime thrillers. The two together make a great shot."

Cameo nodded hardily, pouring liquor into a plastic cup. "So, give us some dark Hollywood history."

Candles were lit around the room. Jake became a raconteur of noir fiction as shadows fell and trees whispered outside, moss streaming like flowing garments from branches.

"Elizabeth Short is the Black Dahlia. There was a lot of speculation over her life, but I believe she was a desperate girl who wanted to make it in acting. She was poor, met the wrong men and went to the wrong parties, sort of like Josephine. She's really like the main character of my book. Now there's a desperate girl wanting fame who's headed for disaster."

"So the dark romance of being a struggling druggy artist lies behind the shot and the book," Muriel said after a moment's reflection.

"Exactly," he exclaimed, tequila held high in epiphany. "And I'm inspired by the parallel I see with the world of the forties and fifties noir fiction...desperate girls, hard partying, corruption. I love it."

Moonshine tilted her head thoughtfully. "It seems you blur reality and fantasy. Josephine is no book character. A confused girl who didn't deserve to die just overdosed because she was too miserable to think things through."

He nodded emphatically. "Exactly. She was overwhelmed by her circumstances just like Elizabeth Short. This is one of the reasons I want to avenge her death."

Moonshine's eyes narrowed. "You see yourself in all these people, don't you. You feel like you could easily wind up like them."

He grimaced while pouring more shots. "It's a possibility."

"The 27 club," Muriel said musingly.

Zowie shook her head. "You just seem to have a bad habit of messing with demons. I know we need to find the drug dealer, but I wouldn't be obsessed with the return of Josephine."

"No." He laughed. "That's not it. I'm obsessed with freeing her spirit from the demon so that she can't come back. We need to find the playground. I don't want another succubus in my life."

Marci made a cut-the-shit chopping motion with her hand. "Let's stop arguing about returning spirits and start looking for Charm."

Jake smiled deviously. "Another round, and then we'll hit the streets."

***

Jake followed Marci through the misty night until finally they found a neon drag off River Street. Cruising past a huge liquor superstore and a brightly lit porn shop, the cars slipped into the parking lot of the strip bar *Pentacles*. This was where their fallen angel quest would begin.

The strip joint attracted Casters who traveled up and down the coast. As a staple in the underground magic scene, this bar could easily be a place Charm was working.

The smoky interior came across like a gambling house: girls slapped down cards, laughed loud, and shots were poured heavy. High rolling, middle-aged men coveted eighteen-year-olds, nubile trophies that kept them immortal.

Figures around three pool tables watched with hooded eyes as the group headed to the bar. A bartender came over who was lost in the world of Cosplay, dressed like a piggy-tailed princess.

Drinks were ordered, and they turned to the main stage where a girl twirled a pearl necklace. Panic! At The Disco was on, but she needed twenties swing music playing.

Jake headed up to the stage and stuck a twenty in her garter. "Come chat with us when you get a chance. We want to ask you about somebody."

The dancer had a bemused smile on her face when she left the stage, fidgeting nervously with her pearls. She plopped onto a barstool next to them. "Why do I feel like I'm on Ricky Lake?"

Marci laughed. "We're not here to expose your scandalous life."

Her smile turned radiant. "Good."

"We're looking for a girl," Jake said. "We thought she might dance here." He showed her a picture of Charm on his phone.

Her eyebrows drew together in vague confusion, and then she nodded. "The strawberry-blond hair threw me off. She's dyed her hair black since this picture. She was running around here with this creepy goth girl called Star who played violin as a gimmick." She gazed down at the phone again. "Anyway, I guess your friend wanted to look like her. They certainly seemed to be *very* close."

"Close, huh? Well, I know Star from a club in Atlanta. What was my lost friend calling herself onstage here?"

"Fallen Angel. She wasn't my idea of any angel. She and Star both shot smack, and I think the violin player got her into hooking.

I heard talk they'd go to Atlanta together to do escort work for some big wig."

I bet that big wig was Thorn, Jake thought. "So when you say 'very close' what exactly do you mean?"

She leaned forward, a conspiratorial look of relish coming over her face, a face of dirty secrets thinly veiling a sense of fear. "They were into magic and sex together. I saw them kissing in the dressing room and lights were rushing through them like they were aliens. It was bizarre. I'm not saying they were doing anything wrong, but I don't think I needed to see it. Other witches work here, but I've never seen anything going on like that...erotic but so fucking evil at the same time."

"Listen, there is good and bad in magic. We're good witches." His eyes flitted about. Everyone gave a Cheshire cat smile. "In theory, anyway."

She grinned, nodding. "I must say the two of them worked really well together. If they danced together for guys, they'd make a fortune. Sparks would fly from the violin, and Fallen Angel would twirl like a little gypsy around the table. It was a spectacle. I felt like they were working some kind of spell. The guys would be mesmerized." She lit a cigarette, her gaze far away. "Star was just that, a star. She was so good at playing violin she joined a band and quit here."

"I know all about it," Jake said. "So, when Star quit, what happened to Charm...or Fallen Angel, rather."

Her eyebrows stitched in hard thought as she blew a plume of smoke. "It seems like she worked another month after Star left. Then she found out she could make more money in a jack shop and went to *House of Dolls*."

"How long ago was this?"

She shrugged. "Six weeks."

Six weeks, Jake mused. *That's a solid lead.* "She could still be there."

***

House of Dolls was run in a small white cottage lit by a neon sign overhung by a canopy of Poplar trees. The stroboscopic purple lighting made the Spanish moss streaming over it look like pulsing alien creatures.

Across the street was a dive bar called The Shanty. At last call, guys would come over here as though lured by the silent cry of sirens.

Marci and Jake parked next to each other by the liquor store next door. The gang ran like misbehaving children to the charming spot of debauchery.

Inside, a muddy construction worker was being led by a girl in bondage gear to a backroom by a leash. "I'm about to experience the dark side, baby!" He whooped.

Two girls on a sofa just shook their heads, eyes planted on the gang who'd burst in the door.

"I love your hair," one girl said to Jake. "You have to have sex to get it to look like that."

"And never comb it," he said. Everyone rolled their eyes. The truth was he agonized over his fucking hair like a diva.

They wound up in a session room, having a ball with the girls. They threw money at them recklessly as though it were part of a sacrificial rite to sex goddesses.

"Ever seen this girl?" Jake asked after the show was over, holding up his phone.

The girl looked and shrugged. "She's hot. We just started, though. A lot of girls have worked here we've never met. Check out the photo album up front."

They flipped through several pages—college girls to leather clad femme fatales—before they spotted her.

A squatty manager with a keychain on her belt came out front, checking credit card receipts. She noticed Jake.

Why do gay women always check me out?

"You're too cute to be in here," she said, looking stunned. "Are you looking for your girlfriend?"

"In a way I am. I'm looking for...Fallen Angel." He tapped his finger on Charm's picture.

The manager's beady eyes went cartoon character big. "She's a spooky one. She went to work for an escort service specializing in girls who do *sex spells*, for lack of a better word. A guy called up here saying he'd had sex with that 'angel who did spells...'" She made quotation marks with her fingers, "and wanted to know if she was working. I heard that a few times before I asked her to leave. I told her about the escort service, however. I didn't just run her off."

"What's the name of this place?"

"Premiere One Escort."

He googled the name and called, asking for Fallen Angel. A receptionist told him she'd gone solo.

He then went through three local adult online magazines, hitting the jackpot in one called Back Stage. Under the Personals he found her ad: *Need a fun evening? Call Fallen Angel.*

Brice called her number and left a message on the voicemail: "I really want to meet you tonight. How about nine o'clock at *The Crazy Parrot* on Tybee Island? I can pay for you to spend the whole night with me."

Jake was impressed. He couldn't have done it better himself. Should he have called himself? No. She might not come. This would be like trying to catch a butterfly.

Jake raced Marci to Tybee Island, singing Jimmy Buffet's *Margaritaville.*

Even Brice knew the words. He turned up the stereo.

The Crazy Parrot was a small beachside bar boasting a back patio with a view of paradise meant for poetry and love songs. Marci loved this place and insisted they do the "tryst" here.

A radiant girl came out to take their order. They all ordered Texas margaritas and shots of Blue Nectar Anejo.

Zowie tossed back her shot. "I'll bet our fallen angel doesn't show up, not that we need her as an excuse to party." She put down the shot glass while leveling a thoughtful look at Jake. Salty air streamed through Platinum tresses. "You'd be better off if she didn't show up. You need to get focused on your illustrious rock career."

"I love caustic sarcasm." He downed his shot.

"Just what are you going to do now exactly? What's your vision?"

He leaned back, gazing up at the patio umbrella. "When I finish the novel, I'll do two things, try to get it published while I write a concept record based on it, a rock opera. Then I'll put my fantasy band together. I've got to find the right people for me, ones who know metal and magic."

"Dark Promise is perfect for now," Marci interjected.

"I know. They've been amazing."

Zowie regarded him thoughtfully. "You were really offered a record deal?"

"Can you believe it?"

She shrugged. "You're interesting. There's more to you than people think. What am I hearing? Your book is based on dreams of The Nephemera?"

His eyes narrowed. "It's some other world. And sometimes the dreams are nightmares. I'm certain the place is real, though. It's no figment of my imagination."

"And there's some deeper reason why you're searching for your fallen angel. Right? It's not just to find the drug dealer, is it?"

He pointed at the amulet. "I'm more obsessed with finding out what this is all about. She stuck me with it and ran. Just what is this fucking destiny of mine? I don't like being the chosen one." He licked salt from the Margarita. "Plus, I feel like I belong with her. She's...sanctuary to me."

"She seems more like trouble than sanctuary," Brice said.

"She's...beautiful chaos," Muriel added.

Cameo laughed. "You're not happy until your life is a fabulous wreck."

"There's truth to that. It's like I'm not satisfied until I have to bail myself out of a bad situation. I'm all about sabotage."

"When are you going to let yourself win?"

Brice smirked. "Yeah, winner. How can you always lose and become a star. You have to go up to be a star and stay there. You can't keep going down."

Zowie said, "I think you need to uncomplicate your life. Stop worrying about girls."

"That's going to be like getting me away from magic."

Brice's phone rang, a metal riff ring tone. "Hey, I bet it's that girl." He answered. "This is Brice. I'm looking for some fun."

There was a pause. "I know you're a Caster."

"So what if I am?"

"It means two-fifty an hour. And I'll have pimp daddy backup."

"I'm just passing through town and need some company. Can we meet?"

Another pause. "Where?"

"I'm at the *Crazy Parrot* like I told you."

A long pause. "You want to meet at *Oysters*... right down the road. Let's meet in two hours. I'll tell *everybody* to come. Maybe we can run around and have some fun." He hung up.

"How did it go, you silver tongue devil?" Jake asked.

Brice blushed. "She's expecting everybody. I think she knows you're here."

"Good," Marci said tartly. "Let's spruce up for the evening."

***

Back at the motel, they dressed to club all night—the girls in flowing velvet and low slung leather, thick studded belts, silver jewelry flashing in the city lights. Cameo was all curves and glitter. Brice was the outlier, wearing a faded hoody with old horror movie images on it and a dingy goth metal T-shirt with big fat letters in calligraphy.

Jake wanted to look dark and sexy for Charm. He dressed black de rigueur, a thigh-length leather coat over a tight top with a ring zipper, lace-up leather pants. His fingernails were black, too.

At Oysters, girls brought large trays laden with buckets of crab and steaming plates of oysters to tables of tourists and drunken regulars. Many gawked at them. Their appearance was too dramatic, hunters from a future world here on a bounty.

They took seats at the bar, surf music playing. A tan blonde bartender who could've been doing suntan oil endorsements walked up to him. She smirked. "Surfer guys don't normally look so dangerous."

"I'm actually a spy searching for a dangerous girl."

Her eyes went wide. "A what? What a story." Then she smiled like a cat. "I've been called dangerous."

"I always find somebody dangerous."

"I don't doubt it." An unspoken proposition danced in her eyes.

He told her how to make a Black Dahlia, and she made a round for everyone, improvising on the blackberry liqueur.

"How'd you get the name?" she asked.

"Uh, a dead actress."

"Oh. Why didn't stupid me realize that?"

She poured the dark elixir out of the tumbler into their shot glasses. "This girl coming in the door looks like she belongs with you."

He spun around.

It was *her.*

She had become her own goth counterpart. No more sunflower girl. Her makeup gave her a preternatural pallor, white chocolate vampire candy. She wore the same black lace-up Doc Martens, but the little girl dress was gone, replaced by a studded crimson top and a short leather skirt.

And the hair? It was jet black now—a shadow over the strawberry fields of his memory.

Charm's expression was a mélange of shock, anger, and exhilaration at the sight of him. She stalked toward him, deadly doll walk, as though to release superhero fury on him.

"You shouldn't be here," she said flatly.

He grabbed her arm and dragged her out on the patio, pain and desperation in his eyes. "I've met Josephine or Star or whatever you call her. She told me she knew you. Listen. Terrible things have happened to her. She's *gone*, Charm. She overdosed on a sex drug called Rapture. We're trying to find the drug dealer who's spreading it, but we're dealing with something else much worse."

Charm's eyes flitted about in speculation. "Felicity?"

"Well, indirectly. This crazy violin player in her band named Minstrel has summoned a demon to possess her spirit to bring her back to life...restore her physically through magic. I want to stop it." He took a deep breath, feeling as though he'd just confessed to a murder. Then his urgency shifted to passion as his eyes welled with tears. He reached out to run his fingers through her hair. "Even your dark side is beautiful."

A deep understanding of the situation filled Charm's eyes. "I take it she ran from Felicity."

"She did. I was trying to help her, and now all this. Felicity is coming Bonding Weekend to play. Minstrel is telling me she wants me in the band, too." He touched the amulet.

"Many are going to be after you for that talisman because it carries so much power. It's worth a fortune to the one who possesses it." Her eyes dropped down. She sighed. "And then there's the real problem."

"Are you about to tell me why I have the amulet?"

"You'll have a clearer understanding." Her eyes returned to his. "The Dark Lord will be hunting me very soon. I had to find the amulet and give it to you while I still had time. Only you can tap into its true power and face the demon."

He gave her a hard look, tears streaming down his face. "Who is this Dark Lord?"

"He and his fold are responsible for the Darkened. He was worshipped by the first Darkened covens all those centuries ago. You hold his magic within this." She ran a finger down the black snake on the amulet.

"Fuck this is creepy. Just tell me everything. I know there's more."

She nodded. "Yes, there's more, but you aren't ready to hear everything." Her eyes drifted away. "I can only tell you we are strongly connected. This is why the Dark Lord wants us both."

Riddles, he mused. He wished he could touch her and draw forth forbidden information. She had him blocked, though, like always.

He collapsed in a patio chair and threw back a shot of tequila. This was all too much. "What do you know about Felicity and her gang?"

"She mostly talked about Minstrel. Josephine made him out to be jealous of her but also obsessed with her. He wanted to be able to control her, but he couldn't with Felicity around. My guess is Minstrel was thrilled she managed to escape Felicity, so he could find her and run off with her. He wanted her for his own. And now she's dead. I can't believe I've lost her."

"We may have lost her, but we can avenge her death. Do you know who Thorn is?"

She rolled her eyes. "Oh yes. I don't doubt he's responsible for this. I'll tell you all I know about him and Josephine, but in the meantime, we should have a little fun."

"What? You're not going to just tell me more riddles and vanish?"

"Not this time. It's your reward for being crazy enough to track me down."

Jake told everybody they'd be partying without him that night. The gang cheered him on, but Marci ran her tongue in circles, tossing her hair.

Bonding Weekend

"If I ever see you again, you'd better have something to tell us besides sex stories," Marci snapped.

Jake ran off, laughing.

***

As it turned out, Charm had a client who'd let her borrow his Porsche. They zoomed about Savannah like Hollywood stars. She wanted to go to all the gay bars, so they wound up hanging out with drag queens and dancing.

"Have you ever read *Midnight in the Garden of Good and Evil*," he asked her while they drank. "Lady Chablis did a show around here. She helped write that book about that twisted love affair shooting."

"No," she said. "But I know great readers who've read *Gone With The Wind* in my world who would love to read a Savannah based book like that. Anything lurid from the past goes over well there."

"I am so fascinated with this dark world you're from. The book that I'm writing surely comes from dreams of it. Why won't you tell me more about it? Why does everything have to be a mystery?"

She smiled slyly. "Why don't I let you see the Nephemera through me?"

"How will I do that?"

"By spending the night with me," she said simply.

Jake's eyes flared wide as he slapped down money for the tab. "Let's go."

They booked a plush hotel room off the coast. After having drinks in the hotel bar, they went upstairs and ordered room service. They fed each other candy and drank champagne like a royal couple.

Sweets and booze finally waned to passion held back like a tide. They tore each other's clothes off feverishly, lips ripping at the other's as they collapsed on the bed.

They writhed in the sheets, tongues working erotic wonders, until she wound up on top, riding him like a bronco. Visions riding on sex magic surged through his mind like runaway trains. He saw leather-clad winged figures perched on neon signs, sexy girls dancing in holograms, vehicles like UFOs zooming over cobbled streets.

And then with a shared gasp, the sex and the visions ended like a book slammed shut.

"Oh no...no more of this," she whispered, sliding off him like a minx and curling next to him. In a snarl of sheets, they held each other tightly.

"Was that the Nephemera I saw?" He ran his thumb over her parted lips.

"Yes. I could feel you experiencing my world in your mind."

Those visions were just like all my dreams, he thought. *My intuition is correct about everything.*

He took in her beauty deeply, worry in his eyes. "You don't want to have sex again, do you?"

"No. We can't," she said softly. "I can already sense you're reaching for your dark side. Once you embrace that part of you, you'll never be able to go back."

He wondered what exactly that meant as they fell off the bed like tumbling playmates. Balled fists pulled satin to the plush carpet with them, the twisted luxurious sheets symbolizing their complicated relationship.

"I saw angels as humans on these streets that made Vegas look like nothing," Jake said.

"We have wings in our world. Those you saw could've been hunters or prostitutes," she whispered, strands of damp hair in her face, a medieval cross clinging to the hollow of her sweat-sticky throat. "It's time to tell you a little more about the amulet."

He told her what he'd read in grimoires and heard from others like Snow. She giggled like a perverted schoolgirl at his words, curled next to him on the floor.

"What's so funny?"

Hidden secrets danced in her flared eyes. Then her laughter gave way to the adopted air of a pedantic school teacher. She held up a didactic finger, the sheets puddled around her, black flowing vampire hair thrown over one bare shoulder. Candles made exquisite shadowy renderings of her on the walls, her lip ring glinting.

"Many think that the first chronicled Darkened coven head, Lekriel, was directly involved in the blood ritual to create the amulet, but he wasn't. He had nothing to do with the creation of the amulet although the piece does hold the power of the opposing magicals, the Darkened and the Estranged."

He was mesmerized by her storytelling, her voice belonging to a nymphet oracle. He drew closer to her, his pace quickening as though from a movie of suspense. "But you do agree the Estranged are those whose power stems from angels rejected by God whereas the Darkened have dark magic from consorting with demons?"

"Right. This is total angels verses demons, but who is wrong and who is right in all of this is anybody's guess."

He nodded. "Yeah. That's true. So, if Lekriel's blood isn't in the amulet, whose Darkened blood is in it?"

She blinked with thoughtful languor, running her fingers idly through her hair. "The Darkened blood within the amulet was from Merek's lover Perdita, who was in Lekriel's coven. You are the descendent of their only natural child. This was much to Lekriel's dismay and caused a rivalry that exists today, as you well know."

"Okay," he breathed. "I get this. Now, is the wild story about an angel in female guise putting an *angel seed* in Perdita's womb true?"

"Yes. Her name was...is Sephera. Perdita drank her sex-charged ichor as part of a blood ritual of retribution against the Dark Lord. Sephera, you see, was put under a spell and seduced against her will by the Dark Lord. She wanted vengeance." Her eyes had gone wild with the imagined fury of the angel, but then she released a long sigh, raven hair sliding from limp doll fingers to fall over a pierced nipple. She shook her head. "Oh, I am digressing. Sephera's ichor was the *angel seed*. Out of three souls within Perdita's womb, two became hybrid angels, the third born a human...a hybrid nephilim or *Nephalem*, to be exact, from whom you've descended."

"Now you know I don't get this. Why wouldn't one of the angels get the amulet instead of lowly me?"

After a moment of thoughtful silence, she answered with a sharp intake of breath. It took everything for her to divulge this arcane secret, all laughter leaving her eyes. "You hold the perfect balance between the dark and the light." She regarded him with angel awe, her fingers to his parted lips. "Ironically, the two angel-born don't hold this essential balance of power within them, although the Dark Lord's magic is within their ichor. Perdita and Merek's only natural child, a daughter they named Desmoria, held this precious balance of power within her. It has moved through centuries and souls to rest with you, the first-born male descendant. As Sephera's spell dictates, only you can truly tap into the dual magic of the amulet, holding the blood of Merek and Perdita along with Sephera's ichor, the power of three. You were meant to be the one who can stop the Dark Lord when he runs riot. Sephera wants you to defeat the demon who seduced her against her will. You are prophecy, her instrument of vengeance."

He groaned. "I don't want to hear any more of this."

"You've already heard too much."

"Let's change the subject. Why would Josephine run off with Felicity, knowing she was likely to become a slave?"

"She wanted to play violin, and she thought Felicity would help her go through her Darkening. She didn't realize what she'd gotten herself into."

"Could you have taken her through her Darkening?"

She shrugged. "I know little about these rites of passage. I'm just a haunted angel with great darkness within me."

He grinned, giving a faint laugh. "What a line: *I'm a haunted angel with great darkness within me.* Here's what I'd like to know. Didn't she make enough money stripping and hooking to bribe somebody to perform the rite?"

"Oh sure, but she never held onto enough money with all the drugs she did."

"I can certainly relate to that. So, how did she meet the freaky old man with the pink house?"

"She really hit the jackpot with that one." Charm laughed. "He answered an ad she'd placed. He was gay, but his fantasy was to be dominated by a goth girl involved in magic. He *worshipped* her. He became obsessed not only with her but the magic. He started collecting Darkened grimoires and amulets. He helped support her. He even rented out that dungeon so she could use it for other clients. She even had her own room there. Often she'd only dance on the weekends and spend the week at that house."

"Her very own gay sugar daddy retreat, huh? She had it made. What happened?"

"He drank, became possessive and violent, so she took off."

"There's nothing worse than a drunk queen," he quipped.

"She told me he was probably schizophrenic. He actually scared her. I think she left a lot of her things there in her haste to leave."

"I know she left a journal and spell books because I have them now. I met the guy and followed him home. In the journal, there's talk of a secret place where we believe her ashes were used in a demon-summoning rite to bring her back. Do you know where this secret place is?"

Charm's eyes took on a searching cast. "She told me she swung in the shadows of a burnt school and played violin for the dead children. She made it sound like she wished she could join them." She shook her head. "The things she told me were a lot like the poetry she wrote, beautiful and eerie but unclear."

Cryptic, he mused, thinking about the strange horror of it all. "I believe she knew in her heart she was going to die. That was why she was so desperate." He ran his fingers through her hair, candy tresses. "What do you know about Thorn?"

She sighed. "Did you ever go with Josephine to an attorney's house? Surely you've met that jerk Peter. She was always going to his parties. I went with her twice."

"Yeah. He's in the middle of this mess. He actually came to me to rid his house of Josephine's spirit."

"Uh huh. He's probably got something to do with her death. Peter was a major client of Thorn's. He went through Thorn to get drugs and girls. He'd know how to find Thorn. I've seen him once at that house. This guy wears a fur coat, bald, a nose that makes him look like a vulture. And his head is tattooed with thorns. He's quite a character...ruthless and evil."

Jake listened intently, running his fingers through her hair. "Have any idea where his crib is?"

"He had more than one and moved around a lot. Peter took us to a place he had near the corner of North Avenue and Spring Street. Who knows if he's still there, though."

"Can you remember anything else?"

"I was pretty drunk that night. I'm not sure. His place was just a few blocks from a crowded burger joint."

"Are you talking about the Varsity?"

"Yeah, that's it. We passed a strip joint along the way. That place was big, really hopping, valets and all."

"You're talking about *Pandora's Box* where Marci works." Jake groaned in exasperation. "So Peter could've helped us find Thorn, but he didn't do it. He didn't want his big connection in trouble."

"And he knows Thorn would kill him," Charm said.

Suddenly hostile Darkened energy rolled over them like invisible storm clouds. "Shit. There's fun coming."

Jake threw out his senses, saw a figure on a motorcycle. "Fat Boy has found me. Let me try an old trick and see if I can still do it."

An expression of apprehension came over his face. He was certain he still possessed the dark *flesh rider* gift Ariel's summoned demon had endowed him with, but using it would open old doorways of fantasy and addiction, his soul traveling to others' flesh to experience their pleasure and thrills. It was the scariest and most beautiful thing. The demon had severed ties with him after Ariel's demise but left him with this dubious power, a curse really.

Still, he could fight like never before in kick ass spectral form.

"Ascend," he whispered, and his spirit left his body on the floor. He rushed across the parking lot, a shimmer of roiling light circling the biker.

His voice was an eerie threat of disembodied sound. "If you work for Thorn, you'll go down with him."

Omen swung his flail through the rock-singer apparition and then roared off, cursing. The very mention of Thorn's name had freaked him out.

Jake surged back into his body, gasping, curled up in pain. "He swung that *weapon* at me. I feel like he really hit me."

Charm pressed her hands to his hard stomach, fingernails tracing a sensual path to his navel. The pain vanished.

When the phone rang, he snatched it up. "Hello?"

Zowie was on the roof, flowing platinum hair like silver fire. "Are you guys okay?" She was flanked by Moonshine and Marci, movie promo poses.

"Yeah, how'd you know we're here?"

"We followed you. We have a room nearby. We had a feeling the bounty hunter would come after you when you were separated from us. Are you with your fallen angel?"

"Yeah, she's fallen even further, thanks to me."

"We're going after biker boy."

All three girls dropped from the gleaming hotel roof, flipping, twirling.

***

In the shadows of an abandoned warehouse, Omen plotted, second thoughts poisoning in his mind. He didn't really care what happened to Thorn as long as it didn't come back on him. What he didn't need was Thorn's people looking for him in the belief he ran his mouth.

So why was he even here? Money? He'd already been well paid by that geek Benjamin.

No. It was about pride and credentials. Taking out Marci Stone would be a huge feather in his cap. He'd be the premier hunter in the southeast.

And if he got his hands on that singer's amulet...

Therein lay his motivation to give this one last shot.

Omen heard a faint clattering sound outside and gasped as he felt the girls' power boil over him. It was showdown time.

He revved the engine and took off, flail held high as the girls smashed through a cargo bay door, landing like alien acrobats, fists effulgent with magic.

He did shrieking daredevil circles around them, circus stunt mania, weaving wild figure eights. He slung tendrils of crackling light from the flail, but they were easily dodged by these nimble hunters. They hurled spell bursts and daggers back at him; the overwhelming attack caused him to lose his balance on the Harley.

Sparks flew as the bike skidded and shrieked into a concrete wall with a great earsplitting crash. He tumbled away from the bike, cursing as he rose like a barbarian who would fight on without his horse. Flail brandished, he charged at them with *we-will-die-for-the-dragon* fury.

He roared like a Japanese movie monster, swinging the flail in mighty arcs at his whirling, bounding adversaries. A barrage of silver stars and knives bounced off his enchanted leather and hexed tattoos, but finally a few strikes took purchase.

Screaming, he staggered against a wall, a star embedded in

his thigh, another in his chest, rivulets of blood running from torn leather. *Fuck this*, he thought, collapsing. It was in his eyes that he was giving up the fight.

"I'm done," he said in a flat tone, reaching for a pack of cigarettes in his pocket. It was as though he'd done too many takes for a scene in a movie and was simply over it.

"Is Thorn paying you to take us out?" Marci asked.

He blew smoke casually, blood dripping off leather, pooling around his boots. Wincing, he snatched out the throwing stars embedded in him and slung them onto the concrete. "Yes and no. Thorn's using the idiot who stalked that girl Josephine to pay me. The gamer dork got some kind of inheritance. Thorn told him he'd kill him if I or somebody didn't get you guys off his trail." He laughed. "Oh well. I tried."

"Benjamin?"

"Yeah, that's his name. Listen. I'm sorry I ever got involved in this in the first place. I'm done. Let me tell you this, though. When that fucking succubus Felicity comes to town Bonding Weekend, she'll most likely be in cahoots with Thorn. Be careful. Oh, and tell that cute singer punk I think he's got a great voice." He rose to his feet and lifted his bike up in a Herculean heaving motion and hopped aboard, cranking it.

Marci's fists flared with light. "Wait a minute. Not so fast. Don't you know where he is? You met him at least once, I'm certain."

"I met him in some dumpy basement bar downtown with Benjamin, but I don't think he actually hangs out there." He blew a long plume of cigarette smoke. "I get the impression the stalker dork is a lackey for a highfalutin attorney, based on overheard snippets of conversation. Now this hotshot attorney I've heard about *could* tell you all about Thorn. Check him out. Benjamin was just a pawn." He revved the bike. "This biker's off to new adventures." And then he roared down the ramp past the shattered cargo bay door. None of them could think of reason to stop him.

Back at the hotel, Marci chuckled about the whole affair. "He's done. He just said 'fuck it' and drove off. I kind of got a kick out of his attitude." She smiled at Jake. "Oh, he wanted me to tell you what a fan he is of your singing."

"Oh really?" Jake responded dryly. Then he broke out in a

dreamy seventies singsong voice, pantomiming playing a tambourine: "Everyone that loves me wants to kill me..."

"And you're gonna be loved by millions," Marci said. "Plenty of people will want to kill you." Then her eyes settled on Charm, who was standing there with her keys.

"I've gotten a call," she said, hugging Jake. "I'm heading out. We'll meet again. If not here, then in my world."

Those words sent shivers through him, tears welling in his eyes. There was no point in trying to stop her.

"Do you want me to walk you to your ride?"

She looked at him over her shoulder, eyes flitting about. Then she smiled faintly. "Yeah, that would be nice."

Marci watched them leave, rolling her eyes at Jake when he waved bye to her. Then she called Peter. It went straight to voice mail. "Mister lawyer man, this is Marci. We've got reason to believe you can help us find Thorn. Call me back as soon as possible."

She lowered her phone, frowning. This wasn't good. Any time she called him he answered right away. Maybe Thorn had already decided Peter was more trouble than he was worth.

***

In the hallway, Charm rushed to an elevator, got in, and the door slid shut behind her.

She's always running from me. Jake felt like a stalker.

Reaching the lobby, he ran like Tom Cruise past a majestic fountain, nearly hitting a bellboy as he raced out of the hotel. He managed to catch up with her as she was sticking her keys in the Porsche's door. He threw her on the hood of the car, and she shrieked with laughter.

"Why are you always running?"

"I like games. I wanted to see if you wanted me bad enough to catch me before I jetted out of here."

He looked deeply in her eyes, mane trailing on her shoulders. "Okay, I get that, but what if I never got to see you again?"

She sighed. "Oh, you'll see me again. We're bound in a way you can never be with a demon. Running is my way of feeling free of you. I need my alone time before it all begins."

He scoffed. "Before what all begins?"

David Raven

"The coming of the Dark Lord," she whispered.

"The coming of the Dark Lord?" he repeated musingly.

"Your future rival in the world of rock."

He shook his head, eyebrows drawn together. His rock rival? What the fuck did that mean? This was her real game—words. She always spoke in riddles leading nowhere but to feelings of aloneness, confusion, and dawning terror. He wished he could run from her the way she ran from him.

But it was impossible. She was always with him, her strange poetry doing circles in his mind.

He felt like strangling her as she slid free of his arms like a minx and hopped in the Porsche. "Bye, Jake. I will help you when the time comes."

She screeched tires in an arc and took off, leaving him with his mouth hanging open. *Why me?* he thought, watching her drive around the bend and vanish from his life again.

Chapter Twenty-Two

Jake was quiet during the drive back to Atlanta, but that didn't discourage the entourage. Brice took control of the car stereo, playing more punk music than Jake had ever heard in his life. Cameo thought it was hysterical—and enlightening as well. She'd never heard of Johnny Rotten.

It was nearly dark when they made it back to Nightmare Mansion, the perfect time to start a party. Debauchery waited to be born.

Snow stood on the porch, waving at them like a bored president, a martini glass in a languorous drooping hand. He came across like some giant lily after a heavy rain.

Jake rushed up to him and snatched up a bottle of vodka set on the swing. "Charm told me I should've been an angel, literally. What does that mean to you?"

Snow laughed, drinking like a dowager with nothing to lose in life at her age. "I love it. You found your fallen angel with whom you're so obsessed." His eyes went distant a moment as if he thought hard about Jake's unique existence. "Yeah. You're really lucky you even exist."

Jake's eyes narrowed as he chugged vodka, a great tonic to his anxiety. "Why do you say that?"

"Have you ever really thought about the delightful angel/demon fairytale? There would've been no human lineage from those three souls if Sephera had wanted her seed to host in all of them. It was her will for you to exist. You are a long-awaited prophecy."

"Oh, this is the most fucked up existential shit I've ever heard." Jake groaned.

Everyone was drinking on the porch now, and candles and incense were being lit. Cameo was so eager to speak that booze ran from her mouth. "Yet you're human and you're going to be a star.

Don't you feel like the hottest catch ever?"

He shrugged. "I feel cursed."

"*That* makes you amazing," Snow said.

"And the fact that you don't know you're amazing makes you even more amazing," Cameo went on.

His eyes rolled to heaven. "Spare me."

Muriel added, "The future is much more important than a vague mythical past."

"You're so deep it scares me," Jake said. "I was trying to get Charm to tell me who is really after the amulet, this Dark Lord of hers, but she answers in riddles."

Snow crooked an eyebrow. "My guess is you'll know soon enough. In the meantime, I'd like to tap into your powers of illusion. Everyone follow me." He made a flowing theatrical gesture then led everyone into the living room like a haunted house tour guide. In the middle of the room, he pointed at a circle of sigils on the floor. "Stand in the middle of the circle."

"What's going to happen?" Jake asked.

"I take it you've never used aural triggers to create illusion. Now we're going to really see if you have the magic touch."

"Do you want me to sing 'Lady of Spain'?"

"Just sing the lyrics of one of your songs."

"I feel ridiculous."

"You're too modest." He turned toward the gang. "Behold the fabulous Jake Reece," he exclaimed in a carnie, freakshow ringleader voice.

Everyone laughed.

He cleared his throat and turned back to Jake. "Start wailing."

Jake sighed, threw back his head, and sang a line with great power and vibrato: "She would never be mine. She would always belong to the shadows of the night."

Tapped from his mind, images swirled up from the symbols of a beautiful teenage girl making her way down a neon drag. The living room became a seedy street corner of hustling and prostitution and then it faded away like a dream ending.

"Fuck," Brice said. "Was that New York?"

"No. I wrote it one night near the Greyhound bus station. There were a lot of homeless girls hanging out, but—"

Clattering poltergeist sounds filled the house, and then wind rushed through it as though a storm were brewing within the walls. Spectral gossamer formed into three nebulous figures around Jake—a drummer, a bassist, a guitarist.

"Bring us back so we can play with you," one whispered urgently.

"We want to be in your band," another insisted.

"You'll need us," whispered the spectral guitarist. "How can you become a star in that world without a band?"

"*That world?*" Jake questioned, falling back on the sofa. The ghosts rushed toward him like insistent paparazzi.

"No one can play like us," one said.

"No one can party like us," another said.

"The Dark Lord will envy you! He'll never have a band like us!"

Jake covered his eyes. "This is crazier than what Charm told me!"

As they pressed on in appeal, gesticulating wildly, they faded away. Snow gasped. Everyone was astounded. Then they started clapping.

"Congratulations! You've awakened our ghosts. That's what I thought you'd do."

Mellifluously maniacal music met their ears. They went outside to find Minstrel playing in a cavorting frenzy.

Coat flapping, he lowered the bow. "She's coming. Oh, my fine singer, now's the time to choose your fate. Why not leave town with me?"

"I'm not singing for a mad fiddler or a bitch succubus," Jake shouted.

"You need to tell us where Josephine's remains are," Marci said, charging toward him.

He fiddled so frantically he disappeared in a burst of light, leaving Marci standing amongst a swirl of leaves and sparkles of magic.

In the night, a crazed melody could be heard.

***

Peter walked into *Pulse* a drunken wreck. He was delirious in his desperation, his anxiety a fever. He had no fucking idea what to do. Everything was going to fall apart. Thorn wouldn't hesitate to kill him if he thought he had anything to do with the singer and those girls finding him.

He just wanted to drink himself to death and watch Abbey dance. The girl didn't like him, but she was tight with Josephine. A pissed off stripper was all he had to remind him of a happier past.

He ordered a snifter of the best scotch the bar had and took a deep sip, plunging into his dark lonely world. He didn't even bother to speak to his power-tie buddies lounging around a stage side table, getting dances while they talked about cases. He *was* a case—a mental one. He didn't need to listen to them drone on and on, pontificating about case studies, courtroom drama, or anything else amounting to nothing but ego-centered venting.

Yet he envied them. He was so much more successful, but none of them had the problems he had.

Abbey was dancing to Rihanna's song *Umbrella* on a side stage, unaware of him. She was twirling an umbrella, cute and charming—not the girl who'd done girl-on-girl domination games and bi-sexual threesomes.

And she certainly didn't come across like she'd be mixed up in magic and the occult.

But if she were involved with Josephine...

Abbey spotted him, which quickened a look of alarm on her face. The confident vibrant sexuality she was projecting was dislodged by a disconcerted air, her eyes cast downward.

He strode to the stage, offering a crisp fifty. Shrugging, she watched him snap it under her garter. Then she flared an insolent eyebrow, all that girl-next-door hair air sliding over one side of her face in a contrived taunting way.

When she got off stage, she went over to where he sat, sulking, alone, murmuring song lyrics.

"You're more fucked up than usual," she said acidly. "I'd swear you were living on the street."

"I could be soon," he said. "Let me buy you a drink. I really need to talk to you."

Abbey pulled up a stool, a Cosmopolitan slid her way. "I can't wait to hear this."

He gave a deep sigh of exasperation. "This Josephine thing has gotten *really* crazy." He straightened up, as best he could, and gave her a hard soul-wrenched look that actors practiced for casting directors. "Do you believe in ghosts?"

Her eyes flitted about, and then she raised an eyebrow oh so slightly. "A girl's gonna have her secrets."

"Well, I've got a secret. I didn't murder Josephine, but she's haunting my house as if I did. I've seen her *ghost*, Abbey." He threw back the booze, burning away the pain inside him. Even in his state, he couldn't help but notice she wasn't surprised at all he'd seen Josephine's ghost. "A contact of mine got me with these *magic people* who could exorcise the house or whatever. Now things are goofier than before."

"Magic people?" she repeated, intrigued.

"Three girls and a rock singer."

Her eyes went wide. "Lost Angel? Jake Reece?"

"Yeah. He has these powers." He snatched up another scotch, gesturing to the bartender for one more. "I thought he was just going to rid me of my poltergeist, but he's running around with those girls on some investigation. Those girls are fucking demon hunters, and they've found out I know Thorn. They think he's responsible for Josephine's death. They want to shut him down."

She exhaled heavily, knowing eyes heavy lidded. "I have very good reason to believe that weirdo at your house got Josephine some spooky dope. That's what killed her."

His eyes narrowed. "How do you know all this?"

"Just trust me. My...intuition tells me Thorn supplied that loser without knowing what was really going on. From what I've heard, you don't need a notable death within the circles of magic coming back to bite you on the ass. You most certainly don't want to make Thorn look like a fool."

"God, I don't know what I'm going to do. He's already called me to warn me to stay far away from the singer and those girls. I could already be a dead man walking."

"I wouldn't be too worried. He's the reason your parties are such a blast, the drugs and the girls. He makes bank off you. Thorn trusts you."

"I'm not so sure about that. He's paranoid."

"Have you thought about leaving town?"

"Oh, yeah, like that's the answer," he drawled sarcastically and then sighed. "Can I ask you something?"

A smile played over her face. "Sure."

"Has she...come to you?"

Her eyes lit up with sardonic amusement. "Why would you want to know? Jealous?"

"No. I just wonder, well, if she would tell you anything. Her intentions, maybe. They're telling me her spirit is mixed up with a demon. I thought you might know what's really going on."

She shrugged. "Why? Josephine was a dominatrix. Masters rarely give up secrets."

"Stop playing games," he called to her imperiously as she got up. "Have you seen the damn ghost or not?"

Her eyes drew together sharply in derision as she laughed like a girl hard to get, flouncing off into the crowd.

Oh, she has secrets, he thought.

He knew this not because of her vague winsome air and conniving eyes, but because he saw faint burns on her wrists she kept trying to cover up.

After several drinks, he called his favorite person in the world, none other than the dashing gay hustler Dennis.

"Hi, old friend."

"Old friend?" Dennis laughed hardily. "Are you throwing a family reunion?"

"Is the spook squad looking for me?"

"I'm sure. You don't want to face this, do you."

"Face my life being over? No. Listen. There's no way I'm going home. Not now, anyway. Could you meet me?"

"Oh...why not," Dennis answered. "A first hot date. You'd make a great sugar daddy. Besides, every rich attorney needs a boy on the side."

"Knock it off."

"Actually, I have a busy night. Never mind. Why don't you just call Jake? They'll protect you until this is over."

***

Peter, in a massive groan of effort, called Jake. The singer was ecstatic. They decided to meet at *The Highland Tap* in Virginia Highlands. A heavy thunderstorm that had traveled from the Midwest to quench the dry streets of Atlanta fell like dark judgment. The thunder was like gods having a nervous breakdown.

The heavy oak door to the bar swung open, and a figure with

a flowing mane appeared, backlit luridly by the flash of lightning. It was a total noir drama pose. From the bar below, the silhouette would have appeared to be that of a cloaked hero searching the night for villains.

The door shut, snipping the sky pyrotechnics from sight. Candles reasserted their luminescent reign in the bar. The figure became mortal again.

Well, almost.

Armed with caustic wit and theatrical attire, Jake romped down a staircase plunging from the sidewalk to the shadowy bar below. He wore an East German riding coat over a Fates Warning T-shirt, lace-up leather pants, and shiny new Doc Martens. Each slender finger was adorned with a silver skull ring or some other trinket of a macabre nature. Not that Jake was evil. Oh no. He was just feeling evil tonight.

He skirted a knot of college students who gawked at him as he breezed by. He pointedly ignored them, feeling like he was always on stage. If he was ridiculed for being too outrageous, well, that was just part of the game.

He heard a ripple of laughter behind him and rolled his eyes. Why must he walk among lower primates?

He leaned against the burnished bar, his eyes sliding from face to face, candlelit and animated. Ah, there was his prey now at the far end. Poor Peter, sulking in the shadows pitifully.

Jake quickly glided past the stools to meet his opponent in the psychological arena. Peter's shoulders were hunched with tension, his head propped on a tightly balled fist. A spiral of cigarette smoke rose above his head.

Silently, he pulled up a chair next to Peter's, lit a cigarette and crossed his legs. He tossed his hair over one shoulder and cocked his head in a gesture of curiosity.

Peter heard the jangling of Jake's large silver loop earrings and turned to face him. He appraised Jake in drunken languor, giving a faint laugh. "Did you come from a comic book convention?"

"I found this coat in a Little Five consignment shop. I had to sport it. I'm always looking for cool stage stuff."

"Your life is a stage," Peter said.

Jake scoffed. "Yours is too. Besides, we aren't here to

critique me, now are we?"

"No we're not." His eyes shifted to the bartender, and he ordered two shots of Whistle Pig. "Who knows? This could be our last night of drinking together. Cheers." Then they threw back the shots like they were in a plane about to crash.

When the burning in his belly faded away, Jake said, "I guess you feel like talking to me is tantamount to suicide, but I want you to know I totally identify with you. Thorn is a threat to me, too. He can help Felicity when she gets here. It's not good when these succubi get their hands on these designer magic sex drugs. It tends to make them much more formidable. I feel sure she's coming after me, and you need to realize, if she plans to avenge Josephine's death, you could easily be on her list, too. See? Both of us are in this mess. The first step is getting Thorn before he can empower that crazy bitch. Okay? Nobody wants to torture you to get the information."

Peter ordered another shot, nodding ruefully. "Thorn has a loyal posse. Even if you get him, someone else could come after me. I'm dead already, if you ask me."

Jake nodded. "Just hear me out. Marci is well known in magic. I can't imagine anybody who knows she's after Thorn wanting you bad enough to risk messing with her."

He sighed. "I'll tell you what I can. First of all, let me give you Benjamin's number since I believe he's behind all this."

"Has he come back to the house?" Jake asked, typing the number in his *contacts*.

"Hell no. Nor has he returned my calls. I'm not going back either...until this is over."

"So, what do you know of Thorn's whereabouts?"

Peter sipped his drink. "We'd meet at bars but never go to his house. There is a motel, though, where we met at a few times called the Downtown Stay. It's a dump, riffraff everywhere. What may be of keen interest to you is that he always rents the same room..." An image of a door with the number 51 on it spread over Jake's inner eye and then fizzled away. "To do business. He told me nobody else ever rented it because of complaints that it was haunted or something creepy like that. One night I actually saw him draw weird symbols on the walls with light from his fingers. The symbols would vanish, but he told me the room was marked."

Jake nodded. "Spells. Triggers."

Peter rolled his eyes and took a deep sip. "It was definitely some kind of hocus pocus." He downed his drink, his eyes flaring with bold thought. He raised an eyebrow. "Would it do you any good to have his phone number, too?"

"Maybe, but phone numbers can carry dangerous spells. I'll take it, though. You never know."

Peter wrote the number on a beverage napkin. "Could one of your crusaders watch my house while I drink myself to death? You guys can throw all the parties you want. Just keep it safe."

"Dennis would love to watch it, but you'd never get the house back."

Peter laughed, shaking his head.

"He's no fighter, though, huh? I'll talk to the girls about all this." Jake gave him a dark speculative look. "What's the real reason you're staying on the streets?"

"I hope to run into Ben."

"And kill him? Where will that get you?"

Peter shrugged. "I ran into a girl named Abbey at *Pulse*. I guess you've met her."

"I talked to her about Josephine."

"She's...up to something. When I told her about your involvement in this, she lit up like she had the hots for you. Don't be surprised if she gets in touch."

Jake grinned like an imp. "Okay. I just have one last question about the motel. When you'd meet Thorn, did he give you any idea where he was coming from?"

"No, but he was always there fast as though he was right around the corner. Why?"

"A little birdy gave me a tidbit of info while we were in Savannah. Anyway, we'll watch the house." He got up to leave.

"Hey, Jake," Peter called over his shoulder.

"Yes, legal eagle?"

"What if I do kill Ben?"

Jake shrugged. "I'm certainly no pillar of morality. Just be smart about it. You don't need him haunting your house along with Josephine."

"I see your point."

Jake headed back up the staircase. Coat flapping in the night, a spattering of raindrops fell from the yawning blackness like the last tears of a short, hard cry wrenched from an empty soul.

***

It was around Midnight. A motel room door with the brass numbers 51 on it went end over end in Jake's mind. After a few drinks at *The Eleventh Street Pub*, he leaped in his car and headed for the motel.

Did he have the good sense to get Marci? Nope.

He found the Downtown Stay a few blocks off Tenth and Spring Street. Paranoid shadow-veiled faces peered from between cheap curtains. It was like a comically demented director's creepy peek-a-boo angle on incorporating the "Meet the Stars" concept of *Hollywood Squares* into a seedy indie film: *Welcome to Homeless Celebrity Squares! In the middle motel window square, here's the premier crack dealer of downtown Atlanta, watching every move your ass makes! Below him in room 24 is the number-one contender for top meth head in the motel! The night hustle is on!*

Jake parked and walked into a neon lit office, the flickering sign begging to be a horror movie promo poster. "I need a room," Jake said. "Room 51."

The black woman, more interested in her lottery tickets, snapped her head up. "Why that particular room?"

He grinned. "It brings back great memories of a torrid love affair."

She made a bloodshot bug-eyed cartoon face. "A torrid love affair? Oh really? Really? You'd have a hard enough time making a whore you paid stay there, much less an actual girlfriend. We call it Stephen King's room." She chuckled, raising a fat finger of warning. "You aren't getting your money back if you take that scary room. I'm telling you now."

He smiled like a sneaky cat. "It's a deal." He shelled out the whopping fifty dollars it cost for a night.

She handed him the card key. "You're too pretty for this place. Are you trying to film a porno?" She laughed.

"I just like adventure."

"Adventure you'll get."

He strolled down a long walkway and then went up a flight of steps. Room 51 was on the immediate right. He opened the door to the sparsely furnished room. Magic rolled out like incense smoke.

"Sight," he whispered.

Sigils appeared all over the stained walls. A vision shot through his mind of a swank den of sordid activity in the bowels of a squalid neighborhood. He sensed the place was nearby, maybe even blocks from here just as he'd suspected after talking to Peter. It was a nest of magic. He'd bet anything it was Thorn's crib, the place Charm had told him about.

Suddenly, a ghostly force slammed him against the wall. The sigils on the walls flared with effulgent light. Then the sink in the bathroom went on full blast along with the shower. The lamp overturned and the bed shook, dark spirit shakedown.

Spectral gossamer swirled around him. When he reached for the door, a ghostly hand clutched his wrist to snatch it back.

He made a sharp gesticulation in the air, magic streaming from his fingers in sparkling wisps. Shadows thickened as spirits rushed to the corners, bodiless but feral, watching and waiting. The great ghost tamer, mane flowing, took a quick look around and then bolted while escape was still possible.

His next death-defying act would be right up the street. He'd walk it. Besides he didn't really want to park his car in a dangerous area, attracting attention.

Head down low, he passed through a neon lit area of sex shops and dive bars before coming up on the Varsity. At the corner of North and Spring Street, he headed toward the Bluff.

Within blocks, he felt dark magic in the ether. He found the source a few blocks down a narrow shadowy road, radiating from a bungalow shrouded in ivy. This didn't appear to be any pimp daddy crib. In fact, it looked abandoned, but magic radiated from the place. A short black guy in a hoody walked by him, giggling maniacally at the sight of Jake heading toward it.

On the porch, beer bottles full of cigarette butts were everywhere along with dope usage detritus—needles, dirty pipes, copper strands. Psychic images shot through his mind of wild candlelit sprees and rowdy drinking, the house haunted by both ghosts and addicts. The dark souls of the chemically damned, though, could be much more disturbing than any vengeful spirit.

And Jake knew all about being chemically damned...and magically cursed.

The door was unlocked. He swung it open, and dark magic crackled over him, flesh lightning. He whispered an incantation, hands thrust out, pushing the dark force away.

Silence.

His eyes slid over shadowy forms.

If Jake was seeking a drug dealer verses the rock singer celebrity death match, it wasn't happening here. Magic was still active in the house, but Thorn was long gone. The place was trashed, beer bottles propped on overturned furniture, liquor bottles being used as candle holders. It was a home for trap house trolls.

Another step triggered a ghost defense spell that brought a Rob Zombie movie to life. A phantasmagoria of ghosts rushed at him, and he swore he saw dead Hollywood stars before the spirits morphed into nameless hideous forms.

He slung spell bursts at them, spheres of angel fire, and they shrieked defiantly as though at the holy words of an Exorcist. Wallpaper ripped from the walls. Bottles took flight and smashed there, too. Furniture rose and flipped. An apparition of Marilyn Monroe rotted before his eyes, and then the spirit storm ended. Dead overdosed stars vanished from the hallway. Jim Morrison sang a final line of *The End* and then melted into the floor like a witch in its death throes. Thwarted ghosts watched Jake from shadow-veiled corners, tittering.

Creeping down a hallway, he took a deep breath and opened a bedroom door. What was once a conference room was now a campsite. Baggies, needles, and bottles were strewn over empty book shelves, a desk, and an overturned credenza. It was like a virus of addiction had taken over the house.

An image rushed through his mind of a laughing bald figure collecting money. This was most certainly Thorn. He was surrounded by men with guns. Major drug deals had gone on in this room.

He went farther down the hallway, stepping on another trigger. Now he understood the ghosts' private amusement. Portals opened, hell doorways, and gargoyles emerged, winged monkey-like creatures of myth and nightmare taking candlelit flight. Shadows of horrific grandeur possessed the walls and ceilings of the house.

He wasn't certain if they were merely illusions or actual

gargoyles like the ones he'd faced in Ariel's sex mansion, but he wasn't waiting to find out. He raced for the front door to find one guarding it like the demon dog Cerberus guarding the gateway to Hades. It roared at him with a terrible hideous mixture of leonine and reptilian rage. No, the front door was not a viable option of escape.

He ran toward the back of the house, but the winged monkey devils were everywhere now. The wicked witch of Oz had nothing on this horror show.

Squatting, he slipped out a piece of colored chalk from his leather coat. He scribed a circle on the hardwood floor, drawing sigils around it as he frantically incanted.

The gargoyles struck the wall of magic, viscous rivulets of venom streaming down sparkling barriers from the fangs of bestial maws. *Why the fuck did I come here alone?* he thought. I bet this shit never happened to the Hardy Boys.

He threw out a psychic call to Marci, seeing her onstage within his mind.

***

While Jake was surrounded by gargoyles, Marci was surrounded by tipping men on a dance platform. A crisp fifty was being slipped into her garter when the psychic slam of Jake's desperate words reached her: Trapped...gargoyles...Trap house near Varsity.

Eighties dance music was playing, something like Cameo or Gap Band, which always made her a lot of money. With this set, she would clear three hundred. She had to get to Jake right away, though. Jake, her favorite struggling artist *slash* complicated love interest, always took precedence over racking up tips.

She was about to leap off stage when Zowie rushed up to her, pushing aside well tailored men. "Did you pick up on Jake's cry?"

"Yeah. Gargoyles. I'll bet he found Thorn's crib in the Bluff."

"Let me handle this. This could be my initiation since I didn't really beat that biker in Savannah. I specialize in destroying monsters, and I haven't played beast slayer in a while."

Marci's brows furrowed. "You think you can clobber these gargoyles on your own?"

"Just watch. I can track him easily from *The Varsity*."

Moonshine joined Marci by the side platform stage, watching Zowie stalk off to battle. Their expressions were a complicated mix of concern, envy, and fear.

"Let her spread her wings," Marci said, shrugging.

Moonshine sighed. "Then she can bond with Jake."

Zowie was out of the locker room dressed to kill in two minutes. She blazed off in her new Ferrari like a leather-clad super heroine hitting the perilous streets of a decadent noir comic book world.

Racing past *The Varsity*, platinum hair whipped by the night wind, she shuddered when ether, charged with dark magic, met her like a drug. She didn't even have to conjure Sight because the house was like a beacon of magic.

She screeched up to the house and leaped out. Gleaming metal rang as she slid her Katana free from a sheath fastened to her back with a studded leather harness. Runes glowed on it like molten lava.

Two screaming gargoyles bounded out onto the porch, shrieking as they took flight, soaring at her. She beheaded one, impaled the other, both constructs shattering into shards of glass.

She rushed into the house, relieved to see Jake was alright, protected in a circle. "They're just constructs," Zowie said. "We have to find the spell trigger to get rid of them."

"The hallway," he said, pointing.

Zowie ran down the hallway, the creatures swooping down at her with slashing claws. She swung her Katana with both hands in great arcs of fury, beheading three more of them. The others hovered or clung to the walls, throwing shadows like huge gothic candleholders.

Several came at her as she leaped and rolled toward her mark, slamming the Katana down in the middle of a configuration of sigils on the floor. The magic coursed up the sword, electrical venom, the gleaming steel holding it prisoner.

In the air, gargoyles shattered. Others just dissolved like creatures made of sand returning to a primeval sea or melted like wax into the floor, an acid head's dream.

Jake's eyes flitted about nervously. "That's it. Bye-bye monkey birds?"

She ran to him, leaping up and down like a cheerleader until he dropped the defensive field. "I can't believe you came here alone," she said, hugging him. She was almost in tears.

He nodded. His eyes were on the ceiling as he awaited hell to erupt from heaven. Faint tittering could be heard from the walls, evil ghost joy.

"Man, that's creepy," Zowie said, grabbing Jake's arm as she strode toward the front door.

"So those weren't real gargoyles?" Jake asked.

"Yes and no. They were constructs. When the spell's broken, they break. But until then, they are fucking real as shit."

Outside, here came the calvary. Marci and Moonshine weren't about to miss out on all this. The Miata was screeching up to the curb as the two victors scrambled down the porch steps.

"I take it we missed the fun," Moonshine said, honey-blond hair thrown to one side, sliding over the strap of a halter top.

Marci just looked confused. "What happened?"

Suddenly, a sleek black convertible raced by. There was a spray of gunfire, and knives were hurled from masked figures.

The girls whirled toward the street, slinging a barrier of psychic force. They stopped the bullets in midair, but a few daggers got by them, blades jutting from the porch like steel thorns.

One grazed Marci's arm. She clutched it, cursing. "Damn. I'm hit. The fucking knife was hexed, too. I'm poisoned."

Moonshine grabbed the keys to the Miata. "Let's get you to Sophia's."

***

It was deep in the night when they showed up at Sophia's. Moonshine and Zowie rapped madly on the door, the peaceful sound of wind chimes slowing Marci's racing heart. She was in a delirium that wasn't completely unpleasant with Dark Lust being one of the symptoms of Darkened toxin, but she was dying nevertheless.

Marci gazed down at her arm, laughing softly. "Look," she said with a detached air. "You can see the magic at work under my skin."

The Darkened poison trailed from the wound on her arm in a

tracery of swirling glyphs like glowing tattoos. Sophia swung the door open, took one look at her, and clasped her hand to guide her into the house.

"I'm always ready for knife poison. Come with me."

She had a potion made up that Marci drank like the most delicious ambrosia she'd ever had. Then she fell into a deep sleep.

"She'll be fine," Sophia said, charms tinkling in her silvery hair, incense floating around her. "The wound wasn't that serious."

Jake shook his head. "Well, I'd say we're hot on the trail of Thorn if he's sending cronies after us." A musing look came into his eye. "*The Trail of Thorn* sounds like a good book."

Zowie held up an admonishing finger. "This guy is no joke. If he's conjuring constructs, he's a very skilled Darkened practitioner. We're not dealing with any two-bit drug dealer who merely got his hands on a grimoire."

"And Felicity should be in town any time to meet him," Moonshine said, shaking her head.

Sophia waved theatrically for everyone to join her on the porch. "Well, while Marci sleeps off the poison, let's celebrate the present. We've got each other."

They gathered around a table where a big crystal decanter of red wine was set. The dappled shadows of oak trees played over the plastic figures of twirling faeries, the night wind coaxing music from the chimes held by their tiny fingers.

Moonshine proposed a toast. "Here's to Jake. Thorn or no Thorn, Dark Promise will win next weekend."

Wine glasses clinked, and Jake went on to say, "And we can handle any trick Josephine has."

But what if Josephine...?

No. He forced his thoughts from returning ghosts and drank deeply from his wineglass.

Chapter Twenty-Three

In the desolate downtown Atlanta Greyhound station, a bus pulled up, bringing a fresh smattering of tired lonely people to the streets of South Hollywood. Minstrel watched from the shadows of an alley. He wasn't concerned with the arrival of runaways with dreams of stardom.

He awaited his kindred.

In the meantime, he played his violin on the sidewalk, captivating the homeless who had nothing but shoulder bags of dreams.

"I wash windshields for money," one said. "I wish I could do something like play the fiddle. You give the street some class, bro."

Several toothless wonders were dancing a jig when a tour bus and two vans came around the corner and pulled into the parking lot.

Ah, what a spectacular entourage of misfits, Minstrel thought.

The tour bus door snapped open, and out came Heath, known as Heathen. The handsome strapping devil bore a glossy blunt cut of jet black hair, a beat-up studded black leather coat flapping around him. A barbell lip ring was caught thoughtfully between his teeth. A long scar crossed his cheek that magic never healed, even glowed when he fought, and did he ever have the attitude to go with the sexy imperfection. The inverted crucifix tattoo in the hollow of his throat, full lips and square jaw completed a street level look both sensual and imposing. He was not a musician, but both a lover and a fighter. Felicity valued him highly.

Next was Aurora. If the goth world wanted a sun goddess, she was it. All leather-clad curves, she headed down the steps with bouncy big cat grace, tough and sexy. Her vermillion tresses, Viking princess hair, bore blond and black streaks, evoking images of funeral pyres. She was the true warrior of the coven.

The last off the bus was Felicity. She wore a flowing silver glitter goth top with a velvet skirt, hip-slung studded belt and space-girl boots (Planet Janet would be envious of her outfit). Her long black hair was streaked pink and blue, and brightly colored cabalistic symbols punctuated the corners of each eye, runic rainbow tears.

"Look at how beautiful we are in this moment," she said, gazing at the homeless and the strip bar *Magic City* looming over the subway station.

Some sort of spell had been worked on her voice. It was so soft, distant, and eerie, that it almost seemed synthesizer-processed. Dark twisted thoughts were always on the tip of her pierced tongue, strange poetic cryptic passages that made those around her shudder.

She gestured at the bus driver to leave. The equipment vans followed to some posh hotel. "We stand like gods and goddesses over street swine. And soon the whole city will know our lust, talent, and power."

Her voice was cosmically forlorn, yet Minstrel just couldn't help but love it. His maniacal cackle filled the desolate night, and despite ulterior motives, he did feel victory in having them all together. Like a band, covens were fragile things, given to falling apart. He would certainly stay with Felicity until something better came along.

They came toward him in a phalanx that smacked of superhero assemblage, windswept, an air about them of dark grand purpose.

Heathen gave Minstrel a smirk of lecherous knowing. "So, how many young ladies have you snared with your...dulcet tones?"

Aurora wasted no time jumping in. "Heathen, you were sent here to bring back Josephine, not for sexual conquest." Then she smiled. "I'll bet you have had fun, though, you and that fake charm."

"No one fear," Minstrel said. "Josephine's talents will be returning to us in a way you'd never imagine." His eyes slid to Felicity, and he whispered, "Do they know she's just a demon-bound spirit?"

"No," she said. "I, too, want to see her return to the flesh."

Minstrel threw back his head in a hardy howl. "Trust me.

There is nothing to fear. I have a plan. For now we need to share wild tales. I will be no disappointment as a raconteur. And we need to drink, be merry, and carouse. We've been apart too long."

And drink, be merry, and carouse they did. Across from the Greyhound station, the gay bar *Apostasy* brought in great numbers of lost souls from the station, big dreams and hearts led by tired feet down dirty metal steps to hard Atlanta reality. Actors, addicts, musicians, molesters—they were all driven by fantasy. The spirit of an uninhibited gay bar, where no one had a clear identity, held huge appeal.

The minute they passed through the doorway, they stitched into the tapestry of divas, goths, gay hustlers, bikers, and bondage boys. It was also a notorious gathering spot for reckless wanton figures of music and magic, a fabulous place for a historical meeting like the one about to happen. This old concrete block building, once a mechanic's garage, had become a theater to the roles of magical prima donnas and powerful artsy libertines.

Dark burnished sloshing liquor, reflecting beer sign neon, came together in a hardy toast, glasses coming together like clattering pool balls. "Here's to love and war," Minstrel said, tossing back rotgut whiskey that blazed a trail down his throat.

Heathen smirked. "Let's sack this place like Roman soldiers."

Minstrel held his violin high over his head like an instrument of battle, and cigarette smoke drifted around it like gun smoke.

Heathen reached for a dagger strapped to his midriff beneath the coat, but Felicity stayed his hand. It was not time for such histrionics...yet.

Thorn swaggered in the door, dancing about to the disco on the jukebox and sweeping his fur coat about theatrically. When gays could go out drinking and watch a drug kingpin dance to Donna Summer's *Hot Love*, they were going places. Everyone applauded his grand entrance as he strutted toward them as though he were a guest on *Oprah*.

He snatched the shot glass out of Minstrel's hand and downed the remains. "Oh, we can do much, much better than this." He ordered two more rounds of top-shelf liquor for the table with an imperious circular gesture toward the waitress.

"This is awesome," Heathen said, grabbing a fresh shot off the tray before the poor girl could serve it. "Just keep dancing and buy shots all night."

Thorn cleared his throat in his debonair manner. "We will do much more than drink." He pressed a nostril of his big beak nose shut and made a snorting sound. "But first I must converse with your lovely and talented leader." He motioned with a stabbing finger for Felicity to join him in a back booth. After sliding onto the red vinyl, he lit a cigarette with the candle on the table. The flame under-lit his face luridly, his thorn tattoo like a trap waiting in the shadows.

Before he even spoke, he handed several baggies to her. "This is Rapture, a most powerful sex drug. It delivers euphoria you wouldn't believe. The grimoire cookbook with the secret recipe was lent to me by a very wealthy coven. They have it back along with the drugs I created for their Bonding Weekend sex party. The batch was meant specifically for them." He smiled deviously, eyes hooded. "I kept a little for myself, however. Bonding Weekend is a big market for exotic drugs."

She listened intently, her distant gaze in some other galaxy.

"It has become popular among Darkened in dormancy to take this to deal with their Calling, but you can't shoot it or it will kill you. The gamer geek who was obsessed with your bandmate, Josephine, didn't know all these details when he slipped it to her, but she should've known better."

Her eyes snapped back from space to focus on him. "Still, you are the author of her undoing. I could and should seek vengeance. The murder of a drug dealer is one of death's greatest prizes."

He flared a brow, punctuating his smug self-assurance. "I am the biggest drug dealer in the Atlanta Darkened world. Even if you win at the Festival, you'll never get out of here alive. My retinue is waiting for you to do something stupid. Now, I apologize for Josephine, and I gave you two thousand dollars worth of Rapture for free."

"Why?"

"You know why. I need the singer you want and those hunter girls off my trail." A smile spread across his face. "I know a certain ghost who'd love to join you in this world again. And play her violin for you. She could easily lure Jake to your services without you even having to kidnap him, and then the girls will be consumed with finding him instead of me."

"Yes," she agreed, nodding.

"Josephine has visited me in her current...uh, transitional form. The demon needs strong sex magic to bring her over completely to the physical plane. Rapture can do this. Josephine will most definitely present herself to you for a drug heightened sexual experience. Trust me. I know how succubus magic works with designer drugs. You will return Josephine to the flesh. Whether you catch Jake is up to you. Do you accept my peace offering?"

She nodded, her true ecstasy over the sex drug offering veiled by her hooded dark eyes. "Okay. Let's talk about your network of power. To beat these girls, I may very well need—"

"Gotcha. If you need backup, I'll gladly let you use them if need be. And I may even assist you personally in this affair." He blew a plume of smoke, regarding her thoughtfully. "I have a tidbit of information for you."

She frowned. "Go on."

"The hidden library at Ariel's mansion, which I've heard was discovered by that singer and his crew, most definitely holds several Necromantic music score grimoires that would greatly broaden your power." He smiled slyly. "And be a challenge to your virtuosity."

"Challenge to my virtuosity? There are no challenges."

"Okay. Sure. The point is you will uncover highly technical pieces that haven't been played in centuries. You will be able to command the elements, ghosts, and the dead like never before. And on Rapture you would be tantamount to a musical deity. Even your powers of illusion would be transformed." He appraised her with great relish. "You will need that singer to get through the wards protecting the library, though. I hear he really has the magic touch with that amulet he holds. He could get through the defensive spells." He gave her a speculative look and shrugged. "I can't stress enough how catching him would help both you and me."

She nodded slowly, wheels turning in her mind. "I have orchestrated a plan to capture Jake Reece." A vague smile played over her face. "I had already anticipated your offer of Rapture."

"I'm sure," he said, and after a moment's silence, he rose.

"Whatever you do, stay in touch. I'd like to be a part of your festivities and the capture of that pain in the ass pretty boy."

"You'll hear from me soon enough."

In the bathroom, everyone snorted Rapture. The euphoric rush was like gods swimming in their veins. Aurora had fire in her eyes like two blazing guns. Heathen felt like a panther on the prowl. Felicity needed her lust sated, her power of succubus growling.

Atlanta was about to burn again. Who needed Sherman when you had a coven led by a violin virtuoso succubus? And Joan of Arc certainly had nothing on Felicity's vision of sexual conquest.

They hit the clubs, masters of the sex game, searching for the unique strain of sex magic thrill seekers who'd arrived early for Bonding Weekend. These were true fiends who would follow sex festivals between the Darkened and the Estranged around the world.

By nightfall, these dark restless figures were prowling the underground bar scene, wary love hunters driven by a nameless fever to find a catch of delicious opposite magic. Their desires were no less than a mission, a quest of sexual obsession. They would stalk the streets like starving prostitutes until dawn, seeking a lover.

"The devil in me wants to fuck the angel in you," Aurora whispered to the first creature of pained desire she encountered in the night.

"Are we not merely celebrating where it all began?" Felicity posed under bright theater lights, strolling down Ponce de Leon. "Dark cities have replaced medieval black forests, but we can still follow in the steps of the demons and angels who dared to love one another. We're just following ancient history."

"We're just following ancient history. If I strip for you, will you strip for me?" Minstrel wailed, doing his best Adam Ant dance.

Heathen laughed at his flamboyant jig and then pointed at a neon sign of a giant red lipstick case. A *Lipstick Lounge* sign flashed beneath it.

Heathen gave the place a thumbs-up. "I'll start my sex campaign here."

Minstrel chuckled robustly. "Oh? You should find the leather boy of your dreams here."

"Or the lipstick lesbian of your dreams," Aurora said, smirking. Then she winked, flaming hair flowing.

"Whatever." He scoffed. "I sense pussy and massive sex magic rolling out of the place. Let's check it out."

"Yes," Felicity breathed. "Lonely sex slaves without masters await us, curled on leather and velvet settees in waiting."

Felicity's intuition was stunningly on target. By the time the DJ had played three industrial dance remixes, the coven had brought several thralls into their fold, lost souls driven by wanton desire.

Moving on to straight and gay bars, the seducers gathered their prey—saved them, really—from smoky dance floors, grim late night diner scenes, and the shadowy alleys of neon drags.

Felicity's entourage soon looked like an Avant-garde sex circus. Club kids rushed up to them, thinking they were in Cirque de Soleil. *Could I have your autograph?*

They found several hot tarts at *Club Opera* in Midtown. Minstrel bought drinks and played erotic complex pieces on his violin, evoking Dark Lust in the unknowing girls. It was as though an aural spider web had bound them.

Next was a gay cruise bar on Ponce de Leon. Heathen had no interest in any gay scene, but he found willing women nevertheless. He scoffed at the ease at which he orchestrated the seduction of several girls. Who needed dark lust violin spells when he was a gothic player like none other?

This traveling show was led to an S&M bar on Cheshire Bridge Road before crossing over to a swinger's club down the way. There was porn on television sets in every corner of the place, and orgies going on in rooms surrounding the juice bar. Nonetheless, the writhing foreplay of Felicity's sex regime all over the leather furniture easily upstaged the goings on in the sex rooms or the porn videos. The ether was charged with sex magic, hot flesh pulsing with light, glyphs swirling around lovers like jealous ghosts. Many were recording this spectacle of magic and sex on their phones, including the bartenders.

Still, there was a general consensus that the foreplay and voyeurism had been fun, but the mass orgy needed to be in a regal spot of debauchery.

"Where are we going for the main event?" Heathen asked, girls wrapped around him, a pierced tongue doing circles in the hollow of his throat. "This place is a third-rate dump." Then he grinned, snatching twenties off the floor. "The tips were nice, though."

"The old drag queen's house," Felicity answered softly, her heavy lidded kohl dark eyes distant with clairvoyant vision. "We'll make it our sex mansion."

Minstrel downed a glass of wine then reached for his violin. "It's funny you should mention that odd fellow. How do you know about him?"

"Josephine once told me about a gay sugar daddy and his grand mystery house of macabre antiques and secret rooms. She never actually told me his name, though. I'm certain I see this place in my mind. And you most certainly know where this beautiful chamber of horrors is, don't you, Minstrel." It wasn't a question.

He ran the bow across the strings of his violin a final time, chuckling warmly. "Oh yes."

It was deep in the night. The entourage arrived at the old drag queen's house via a caravan of cabs, the sex thrall express.

Minstrel was the first to leap from the cab. He rushed up to the wrought iron gates of the ivy-hung brick wall surrounding the property in his usual sweeping Broadway style. He raised his violin and began to play an aural spell to break the lock, but then—

"Fuck it," Aurora said, kicking the gate open, leather boot drama smash.

The Dobermans came like race horses around the house, barking, jaws snapping. At the sight of Heathen, though, the dogs became playthings, drawn to him like mindless moths.

Felicity placed silver-nailed fingers, glamour claws, on each of their heads. Magic starred from her palms, and the dogs made groans of feral ecstasy as their eyes became glowing orbs of demonic roiling light. They were no longer the pets of a crazy old man but beasts of magic—Felicity's familiars.

"Heathen and the Hellhounds." Aurora laughed, shaking a skull-tattooed fist. "You need to start your own band."

"Your wit is very sharp tonight, Aurora," Felicity whispered, cosmic hollow eyes far away.

Bonding Weekend

The sight of this assemblage approaching the huge pink Victorian house was comparable to torch-baring rabble laying siege to the castle of *Frankenstein.* What flew out the front door, though, was no Frankenstein's monster, but the drunken drag queen dressed in female garb so hideous he might as well have been a creature of gothic horror.

"Finally you've come for me," he cried in schizo-glory.

The insane queen was outrageously dressed for the occasion: a red wine-stained flowing white dress, arms outstretched, bloody butterfly sleeves fluttering in the night. The makeup was so morbidly garish, the cross dresser could've been the *Bride of Frankenstein* (Comparisons to *Carrie* go without saying). Really a dead tawdry hooker brought back to life through voodoo came closer to the truth.

In a fit of rapture, the deluded ragged-out zombie queen charged toward Felicity, hips swaying in work-it-girl glory. "Oh..." The old man gasped, beholding Felicity in wonder. "You are the cosmic violin master Star has told me so much about. She told me you can release me from my pain and bring me into your fold."

"I most certainly can," she said, eerily soft, and then she did a dazzling run, arpeggio telekinesis spell, on her violin, hurling her worshipper back into the house.

He slammed into a gilded mirror in the foyer and slid down to the marble floor. He spread out his arms in a brief spasm, a final drag queen performance of butterfly death throes. Shattered statuary lay around him.

She, angel of death, knelt down to press her fingertips to his lifeless body, drawing his life force out of him. She sighed, the ghost of a smile passing over her parted mouth. His spirit was a drug rush to the succubus, her bloodstream his eternal resting place. And yes, his pain was gone.

In the living room was a rocking chair surrounded by books on Darkened lore, grimoires, and bondage. Heathen lay the dead drag queen there like royalty on a throne, and Minstrel pulled a bottle of Kettle One vodka out of a sideboard and slipped it into his stiff hands like a scepter. He stared from soulless sightless eyes at the sex show as it began, the bottle jutting from his crotch.

The murdered host of the evening had a broad eclectic CD and vinyl collection, everything from big band music to Baroque masterpieces—Minstrel's favorite—to syrupy seventies music. He even had a Partridge Family record. His lust for David Partridge was most surely a well kept secret.

"Cheesy seventies pop is great cocaine music," Minstrel said, eyeing a Bee Gees disco record.

"Whatever," Aurora said, snatching the vinyl out of his hands and slinging it like a Frisbee across the room. "Hey, here's Abba and Cher. Loving these two is a prerequisite for homosexuality." She dropped the needle on the Cher record and *Gypsies, Tramps, and Thieves* came to life, the wind instrument music like a seventies porn soundtrack. She pranced in front of the rocking chair, twirling in a sensual gypsy dervish. Then she took a big swig of vodka before finding another old record of interest. "Hey, *The Lawrence Welk Show*. We could use that as our orgy theme music. I actually like some of that corny stuff."

Felicity thought hard, gaze far, far away, oh so disturbingly calm. "Don't you need bubbles? Lawrence Welk had bubbles on his stupid late night show." And then her eyes went even dreamier. "Perhaps we should have a bubble illusion spectacle for our show...brilliant in its light-hearted irony."

"Oh lord," Minstrel cried, laughing. "Let's just play something dark, sexy, and dramatic and get this orgy going."

That settled it.

He found a compilation of Brandenburg Concerti in a huge classical collection taking up one wall. Dark rich harpsichord-driven orchestral music met their ears, music meant for ghosts and disturbed geniuses of music and art.

They all slowly undressed, a show of Burlesque. He even added impromptu violin to the music, weaving Dark Lust into the aural tapestry.

A girl went down on him as he played an erotic flow of legato notes. Felicity lit banks of candles for this night of ritualistic pleasure, the thralls writhing naked in the lurid flickering light. Then she filled crystal china from a polished marble bar with vintage wine.

"All hail the revolution," Heathen howled, raising a sparkling goblet in a vainglorious goth prince pose.

Minstrel pushed the girl away from his crotch and went to cavorting around in the candle light. He played manically, drug-driven, his junk bobbing beneath the lace ruff of his unbuttoned poet shirt. It was all he wore, the girl having practically raped him.

Felicity lit candles throughout the house. Wind from open windows blew through her cosmic hair, whispering aphrodisiac spells. Covering the dark paneled walls were shadows of feverish fucking that would have been erotic mural masterpieces if time had seized them for all eternity.

Pleased with the sexual abandonment surrounding her, Felicity retired to an upper room like a saloon prostitute, taking only girls, pure lesbian lust. She loved many of them to death like any good succubus.

It was no surprise when a great wind carrying an addictive scent speaking of untold toxic pleasure rushed through the house. Ectoplasm formed near the curtains of the drag queen's bed.

The demon diva had arrived, the spirit of the violin virtuoso Josephine. Even in spirit form, she craved stardom.

Tonight was no exception. She wanted to be the main attraction of this show of sex and shadows and rightly so. All this debauchery had been orchestrated to draw her here. She would soon be back, her ghostly realm no longer a prison.

The spirit flew into Felicity's arms, straining for form and flesh. Her ghostly tongue was drawn into the cosmic girl's mouth, Felicity tugged at black tresses that were little more than inky mist, drawing back her head. The spirit gasped in ecstasy.

Deep passionate kissing, the thrashing of lips really, spearheaded foreplay so intense the spirit exuded sweat. Within moments, Josephine's lush midnight tresses were firmly in this world, and Felicity pinned her to the bed, lustrous hair wrenched in balled fists.

"Finally, you are mine again," Felicity whispered, her tongue tracing serpentine lines over the firm pallor of her stomach and breasts, her pierced navel becoming a toy in Felicity's mouth.

In flickering candlelight, an audience watched the spectacle of girl on girl (or girl on demon) in wonder. Vulvas became weapons of frantic scissoring, and orgasms conjured sigils of magic in the ether.

The sex became a brawl. They knocked over lamps and upended tables, and even the sex magic ran riot, lifting morbid oddities from the dressing table, antiques thrown about as though by psychic force. Even the bed floated above the floor.

The onlookers wanted to join the love bash, but they knew the show was a performance for succubus and ghost only. This surreal porn show was theirs exclusively.

Josephine gasped in the throes of ecstasy as her spectral curves became flesh completely, ghostly gossamer floating away like candle smoke. She was reborn, a demon in the guise of a virtuoso violin vamp.

She leaped from the sheets, slashing a bow across the strings of her violin, which she brandished in triumph. Her playing captured the ears of everyone in the house, Brandenburg Concerti be damned.

She moved in a regal stride downstairs, a demon debutante ready to show them her sexual prowess.

Aurora, who'd worn out two guys, welcomed the demon girl. Let the demon girl dominate her. The role was an escape.

Josephine, though, had other plans. She grabbed a whip mounted to the wall, and she whipped Heathen like a dog while his Dobermans watched all the while. The crowd cheered and clapped at the spectacle.

The ravaged living room became an S&M parlor. Overturned furniture became torture devices of pleasure, kitchen counters became sex-rite altars.

Upstairs, hallways and bathrooms became porn sets. Here Felicity waited patiently for Josephine to return for an encore.

Sated from the orgy, Josephine rushed upstairs like a storm passing through the house, and materialized into a black cat. The house was filled with maniacal shrieks of laughter as she morphed from feline back to femme fatale at the top of the stairs.

Rushing into Felicity's room, Josephine slid out of her dress, black panties vanishing into mist before hitting the floor. She leaped onto the bed, her tongue sinking into Felicity's mouth to taste liquor, drugs, and madness.

Felicity not only tasted Josephine but saw her hot and sweaty nights onstage. She saw her twirling from poles, wild nights at parties, violins playing and whips cracking and...

Journals?

"Oh no," she said softly.

Josephine had written down secrets she shouldn't have, and

her adversaries could use this against her. If the right connections were made, they would find Josephine's ashes and break the bonding spell with the demon.

Felicity couldn't allow that.

Josephine sensed something was wrong. "Will I be with you forever," she asked, voice trembling.

"Yes, forever. I will never let our enemies reverse the spell, my dear Josephine. You must remain loyal to me, though. Without me, you can't remain flesh. The devil inside you needs my magic."

A faint smile played over Josephine's face, her raven hair splayed over Felicity's breasts. "Then feed the devil inside me if it means being beautiful and talented for all eternity...if it means *life*."

Felicity's eyes rolled upward in relish as she reached up to caress her ghost lover's face. "Oh, I will, but first can you tell me where the journals with all your secrets are?"

A heavy thoughtful pause led to a deep rueful sigh. "Jake has them, but he'll never understand the poetic veil of riddles."

A comet of hope streaked across the galaxy inside Felicity's head, a silver fingernail brushing over the parted lips of her demon doll. "And when I have Jake, the journals will be mine, as well."

Chapter Twenty-Four

It was last call at *My Hot Sister*. A drunk college girl was playing Katie Perry and Lady Gaga songs over and over. Her girlfriend finally snatched her up and took her home. Another couple was trying to mock the erotic poses of the faeries in the murals. Others just had a few drinks and then headed out to the late night Atlanta club scene in secret Midtown hideaways.

It was a typical night.

Jake was placing the last case of Night on Ponce I.P.A. brew into the cooler when Abbey strolled into the bar.

Surprisingly, she wasn't dressed like a stripper. Tonight she wore a football jersey tucked into a pair of faded jeans, knee ripped artfully, and her hair was pulled back with silver barrettes, a girl-next-door playboy fantasy. She was even more striking than she looked onstage.

She gave a quick hug to a strapping tattooed guy who would've loved to spend the night with her, but she moved on, making her way to the bar. She took a stool in front of Jake, smiling with dreamy languor. Glassy eyes dilated, she was feeling no pain. He was in the middle of making six Kamikaze shots. He gave her an amused speculative look, wondering what she was high on.

"What brings you here to meet a singer without a band?" he asked, handing out the shots to a gang of Buckhead girls.

Her smiled broadened, a long errant strand of blond hair punctuating the curve of her mouth. "From what I hear from Peter, you're much more than a singer without a band."

"So you've talked to him since we met."

"Yeah. He's a mess, totally desperate."

"He's got a reason to be desperate."

She sighed. "I know. And I'd like to talk about everything. I wish we could hang out. I know I don't look that great tonight. I'm sorry."

He couldn't believe it. He actually had a beautiful girl apologize to him. Could this be a sign of the apocalypse? "Don't be ridiculous. You look fantastic." He took her hand, her fingers curling slightly in his palm.

She cocked an eyebrow and grinned.

He flared a brow. "Whatever you drink is on me."

She nodded approvingly. "I definitely want a dry dirty martini. Up."

"Okay. How about a Black Dahlia shot?"

"A Black Dahlia?"

"It's named after Elizabeth Short, the old Hollywood actress who was murdered. I'm obsessed with anguished struggling artists who meet ruin."

"Oh? Does Josephine make you think of this girl?"

"You know it. Let me ask you something before I forget. Do you know where this secret place is she went to write poetry?"

Her eyes of glass caught fire, secrets igniting in crystal balls. "I've heard her talk about it." And then she cut her eyes away.

He took her hands again. An image of old brick buildings surrounding a playground raced through his mind. "Where is this playground I keep seeing?"

Her eyes went wide. "So part of your magic is psychic visions?"

"Oh yeah. I'm a clairvoyant."

"She took me to that place once. I was *so drunk*. I just remember her reading poetry and..."

"And?" He was hinged on her next words.

"The place was haunted. There were ghosts everywhere. I think they were children who died in a fire. A girl appeared when Josephine played violin. I was so scared I ran and caught a cab home."

"Can you remember a main road? A clue? Anything?" He felt certain there was something she just didn't want to admit.

"I think the buildings were a school," she said after a long thought.

He recalled the passage of poetry about kids burning. It made sense that he was looking for a place like that. "I've got reason to believe her death is connected to a dealer named Thorn. Have you heard of him?"

She took on a guarded restless air. "Uh, I've run into him. That's not somebody I'd fuck with."

He changed the spout on a vodka bottle, regarding her thoughtfully. "I don't know whether you like Peter or not, but Thorn will probably try to kill him. I'm trying to stop this guy. Do you have any clue where Thorn's crib might be?"

Her searching eyes flitted about. "There's this place near the corner of North Avenue and Spring Street, but I don't think he's there anymore."

"I'm acquainted with that fun house. How did you know he's moved on from there?"

She shrugged. "Somebody told me. I think Josephine was there for a final party."

He added olive juice to her martini and slid the glass to her. Then he feigned a look of shock. "You don't want to try my signature shot?"

Her eyebrows drew together in mock offense. "Sure I do. You're too busy playing detective for me to get a word in edgewise about it."

He made a big show of making the shot with the secret blackberry liqueur. "Here's the favorite shot of a murdered actress."

She laughed, reaching over the bar to playfully push back the hair from his face. "Listen. I really don't have the answers about Thorn and all. I came here to have fun with a hot guy."

Jake made a magazine pose, hair over one eye, sexy and mysterious.

She rolled her eyes, shaking her head. "You are *sooo* full of yourself. Oh yeah. I'll take a Night on Ponce, too, since you just stocked it. Somebody's gotta drink it up."

He popped the top off of the craft beer and set it on the bar. Their fingertips touched briefly as he drew his hand away, the sensation like a paint brush coloring the canvass of his mind. He saw images of her body as she danced next to a bed. For a brief moment he saw a dark-haired figure watching her from the shadows, and then the mind show vanished.

Abbey held up the shot, the artsy beer can in the other hand. "Cheers. Welcome back to Earth from wherever you just went, great psychic. Here's to all you anguished artists."

She did the shot, which she raved about, and then nursed the martini and Night on Ponce. Hours went by, and the night came to a close. It was too busy for them to talk, but he was acutely aware of how she watched him, her interest in him deeper than she would admit.

"Let's get out of here," she said with a sassy toss of her hair. "We're young and alive and free. No more talk about dead girls and asshole drug dealers."

Oh really? Here we go. "Do you want to go clubbing?"

She made a wincing sexy expression. "Oh hell no. Why don't we just go back to my house? I have all kind of liquor, and I think there's food in the fridge." Her full lips spread into a sly smile of unspoken promises. "We could just drink and listen to music. Let's talk about your next band and this book stuff your doing. Okay?" She took a deep swig of Night on Ponce. "Hey, I paint by the way. Do you want to see my paintings?"

"What kind of paintings?"

"Oil and acrylic. I've actually sold a few. I'm no Rembrandt, but I love doing it."

He couldn't believe he'd met a cool girl who was an artist. "Okay. Give me about an hour or so to clean this place up."

She waited for him, quiet, texting furiously as regulars paid and left. Eerie goth electronica pulsed from the speakers, setting the tone for the late night.

In the kitchen, Jake propped against a rack of dishes, pondering Abbey's sudden appearance. Why was his spidey sense tingling? This awesome night just seemed so strange.

***

The fog was thick that early morning. Jake felt like he was making his way through London as he followed Abbey's Corvette through a series of narrow Midtown streets.

Finally the brake lights flashed, and Abbey zoomed up a steep driveway. He pulled his hippy-stickered Toyota dream machine up to the curb and parked.

The quaint small house was marked by several huge Magnolia trees and a beautiful terraced garden. Wind chimes hung from the trees above. A carpet of English Ivy snaked down to the sidewalk, thick tree roots bulging through it.

"I love this place," he said. "I can see where this would be a great place to paint."

"Oh, it's a wonderful place to paint," she said, locking the door to the car with her remote. "It's a great getaway from the dancing. I have my own little world."

He made a face that reflected he was impressed. "Reading and music is the ultimate escape, and painting, in your case."

"And sex," she added casually, unlocking the door.

His eyes flared as her words registered. "And sex. Silly me."

"Josephine loves games, you know."

"She sure did. I noticed you put that in the present tense."

She put a hand to her mouth. "Did I? My mistake." And then she slipped inside the house.

The wind gusted, and he swore he heard a voice on the wind, the chimes ringing louder and more resonant. Leaves rustled madly. Frowning, he closed his eyes and leaned against the side of his car. He supposed he was hearing things again.

He trudged up the steep yard, English Ivy crunching beneath his feet. He wondered with a slight shudder what spirit was veiled by the greenery, watching him and teetering. Oh, his imagination was at it again.

He went through the doorway to find Abbey standing in the middle of the living room, smiling winsomely, dream girl hair thrown over one side of her face. Two votive candles were burning on a glass coffee table beside two sparkling snifters of Grand Marnier.

On the far wall hung a huge black and white print of the Hudson River, the New York skyline beyond it. Placed next to it was a framed poster of a singer bound with leather straps.

"I love that poster, but I don't even know who it is."

"David Lee Roth." Jake laughed. "He was a big star in the seventies and eighties. He was the singer in Van Halen. He could do a high kick I'll never do."

"I think I've heard of Van Halen. I just thought he was hot."

There was also an array of porcelain Harlequin masks arranged in an arc over a stereo system that looked like a rocket-ship console. Next to it stood three towers of CDs, and on the other side was a young girl's pink plastic seventies record player covered with pop star and TV show stickers—*Charlie's Angels* and the *Land of the Lost.*

"Don't you need to be six to have this?" He laughed. He wandered over to the record player and lifted the top. "I wonder how many *Partridge Family* records were played on that. And look, it has three speeds."

"Just like a little toy I have," she quipped, smiling slyly. "No seriously. I bought the cute kiddie record player on impulse, but I only collect good seventies music, not bubblegum."

He dropped the needle, and Ziggy Stardust—David Bowie—came alive through cracks and pops decades old. He held an imaginary microphone to his mouth, imitating Bowie's flamboyant onstage presence.

All of her furniture was retro stuff. Curvy vinyl furniture filled the house along with lave lamps and old pop star posters.

"This is cool as shit. Where did you get this stuff?"

"Thrift stores up and down Ponce and Moreland," she said. "Do you collect anything?"

"I collect books and comics. I have a ton of CDs, too."

He went through the short stack of old vinyl singles—most of it glam rock—Queen, the Baby's, etc. He did find a yellowing copy of *Unchained Melody* by the Righteous Brothers, though. *When was this? '65? What a find.*

Abbey burst through a beadwork curtain from the kitchen, carrying more booze, but that really wasn't what he noticed. She'd taken her jeans off, the oversized jersey covering half of her thighs.

She caught him staring and smiled. "What's wrong?" Candlelight flickered over her face.

"Have you returned from the kitchen to seduce me?" He smiled broadly.

"No. Don't get hasty. I went in my bedroom and put on my Daisy Duke shorts." She pulled the jersey up to reveal the country girl cutoffs.

"Oh darn. Hey, I didn't realize you had a tattoo on your hip. That looks just like Josephine's."

She stretched out a tan thigh. "This is true." It was a black dragon with green eyes trailing down her hip to her thigh. "We went together and got it in Little Five Points," she said. "We did a lot of things together...*a lot of things.*"

We did a lot of things together, too. Erotic images of three-ways and girl on girl washed over his mind, but with them came an eerie sense of something strange happening. He couldn't place a mental finger on it.

What is Abbey hiding?

"You know, Josephine was very fascinating to me," he said. "I'd seen her in visions before I met her. She's even influenced my book. I've really grown obsessive about her."

Abbey set down the liquor bottles. "She had that effect on men. She was so exotic and...captivating with her poetry and violin. She always kept a diary. In fact, I have a journal of hers that has inspired many of my paintings and sketches. Her poetry was very erotic...and very visual."

He lifted a brow. "What do you mean by *visual*?"

Abbey licked her lips, sticky with Grand Marnier. "You obviously know how erotic she was." She cut her eyes away before secrets could leak out. "She reveals a lot about her fetishes and her lust for girls in the diary."

"I have *some* idea." He moved closer to her, touching her gently on the hip. Her eyes were hooded, dark memories like shadows flickering inside them.

"Yeah, she...liked girls and games," Abbey whispered, redolence of incense wafting through the living room.

He grinned. "Would you like to share what you mean exactly?"

She blinked slowly in sexual languor. "Her thing is bondage."

"You mean it *was* her thing."

She didn't answer as she pulled the barrettes out of her hair. The spill of playboy blond tresses unleashed his imagination as though she'd executed a hex. The girl-next-door became a porn star.

Lust and apprehension twined within him. Did he need to get involved with a girl who'd been so close to Josephine? She seemed obsessed with the dead stripper, too. Sure, Abbey was hot, but the whole idea of being with her was almost creepy.

Well, maybe not *too* creepy.

Now was not the time to dwell on such things, though. There were stories to hear about the violin vamp.

Sighing, Abbey filled two brandy snifters and then fell back in a bean bag chair. Her nipples jutted from underneath the jersey.

There was something timelessly beautiful about her. She wasn't as boldly exotic as Josephine, but there was a classic beauty about her that made him see her from many angles. Abbey captured the mystique of women who came alive in history books. She could have been a Welch witch or a maiden struggling on the prairie of early America. She could have been an alluring intellectual hippy of the sixties, or she could be what she was now, an artsy girl with dark sexy secrets. He'd met a classically trained ballerina like her once who'd completely molested him. Oh beautiful memories...

Anyway, regardless of who this old soul had been in another incarnation, she couldn't have been any more breathtaking than she was now.

"Close your eyes," she said.

He heard the soft impact of clothing drop to the floor. Then a vinyl record began to play.

As *Suffer Kid City* by Ziggy Stardust filled the air, she said, "Now open them."

Oh this is fun. What kind of game is this?

When he opened his eyes, she had her jersey pulled up just below her breasts. Her forefinger was doing a spiraling trail down her stomach, circling her pierced navel. Her restless fingers headed for the elastic of her floral lace panties. He noticed how the silver loop in her navel would move slightly when she tightened her taut midriff. She obviously hit the gym. He loved it.

"Open the top drawer in the couch side table," she whispered.

He did so, discovering an elaborately detailed dragon candle holder made of pewter and studded with jewels. It had been placed between two stacks of romance novels. He pulled the dragon free, candlelight flashing off it.

"Light the black candles," she whispered.

With the lighter in his coat, he lit candles embedded in the tail and sinuous arched back, and then he placed it on the coffee table. The pewter beast looked like a flying demon from hell.

Abbey continued her story: "Josephine was very passionate about music, but there were three other things that she loved that come to mind right away. One was dragons. I bought her this. She kept it here for our...games here. That's also the reason why I put a dragon tattoo on my hip to match hers." His eyes slipped down her body. The dragon seemed alive in the flickering light, ready to take flight from her flesh for nocturnal adventure, only to return by morning, a prisoner of Abbey's beauty and a part of it. "The second was rosaries. Josephine had a very special one that her mother had given her. Her mother was Catholic, you see." Abbey's face became grim. "Someone stole it from here."

His eyes grew wide. "Someone broke in here just to steal a rosary?"

"She had stalkers. I bet somebody from the club followed her here. Leatherwear of hers and other toys disappeared, too."

The weirdo who bought her Rapture, he mused. *He would be obsessed enough with her to do this. He was crazy.*

Abbey pressed a forefinger to his lips and then raked a nail over his bottom lip. The jersey fell to the floor. All that blond hair spilled over her shoulders, hard nipples jutting from beneath beach fantasy tresses.

He still kept his hands off her, wanting to hear more. Lurid stories before sex. How could he beat it? "What was her third great love?"

"She loved dungeons...namely, bondage gear." She cleared her throat. "Why don't you take your coat off?"

He slipped it off, and she pushed him down on the sofa. Then she yanked the Black Veil Brides T-shirt over his head and tossed it on the floor.

She began to slowly trace a winding path down his chest with her fingers.

He closed his eyes. *Atlanta is about to burn again.* "So, how did you feel about Josephine?"

She unbuckled his black leather belt. "I honestly thought she was crazy, but I loved her. She...was difficult to break away from." Abbey was silent a moment, a short period of time where dark speculative thoughts could fester, and then she sprang up girlishly. "What would you like to hear? You see I've got a thousand CDs."

Then he smelled it.

The sweet ritualistic scent of Josephine's perfume.

The telltale tingling of spectral presence rushed through him, sending shivers down his spine, and then passed. "Do you wear Josephine's perfume?"

"No, but I wear something very close, Jake. Very close."

"What does that mean?"

"Details, Jake. You're complicating matters."

Oh this is strange.

"What about the music? You never answered me."

"Unchained Melody."

Seconds later, he heard the pops and cracks of the old vinyl record, and then the romantic piano introduction struggled through the petulant noise, a great overture to a long night of passion.

He thought of a sexual encounter with a country girl who went by the name Bobbi. He'd met her while visiting his grandmother in Cogdale, Georgia. He met this rocking babe the summer he ran away from San Diego, leaving his parents and life behind.

He discovered her out strolling like a nymph that had dared to leave the Georgia forests for adventure. They sat on the porch swing and listened to her country music, pop crossover music really, sung by girls as hot as she, watching a world beneath pecan trees slowly go by.

After about an hour of honky-tonk songs about keg beer and parties in the woods, she found an oldies station on her boom box and took him behind a big fig tree. There she planted the most passionate kiss on him he'd ever had in the shadows of swaying boughs, wasps, and a cloyingly sweet scent in the air.

He'd never forget that afternoon, lying among the leaves and roots, the radio playing *California Dreamin'* by the Mamas and the Papas. To this day, he'd played that song with its awesome harmonies on the jukebox wherever he was tending bar.

Abbey came slinking around the coffee table, twirling deliriously, flinging her jersey about like a burlesque dancer. "Open your mouth." And then she stuck a pill of Ecstasy on his tongue. She smiled devilishly. "I want you to close your eyes while I leave the room a minute."

"You are driving me out of my mind." He closed his eyes, listening to the sound of his shallow breathing and the record. The popping and cracking had become much worse, but the record's beauty and charm made its way around the flaws, turning it into a rough-cut diamond. He heard Abbey's footsteps and the clatter of something metallic. Still, he kept his eyes shut for fear of ruining her erotic performance.

The clatter became louder, and then he felt her hair fall over his face. A thick sunshine-blond strand rested on his lips.

"Stretch your arms out."

It was a command, not a suggestion. He didn't really feel he had a choice. Something cold curled around his wrists like two serpents—handcuffs.

She'd run the chain behind a heavy floor lamp. Candlelight and romance was out the window.

"Open your eyes."

He gasped softly. There she stood in sheer black lingerie, leather stacks, garter belt and all. She should've been doing endorsements for Victoria's Secret.

He tried to imagine his San Diego high school sweetheart dressed like a seductress and tying him up. He giggled at the absurdity.

"What's so funny?" she asked, eyebrows arched.

"I was just thinking of an old girlfriend who would be shocked by this."

"Oh?" She flared a brow, pulled off his pants, and traced a line with her fingernail down his chest to his groin. He felt the first hot flash from the sex drug kick in, and his heart began to pound even faster. Her every touch was deliciously amplified.

Straddling him, she kissed him deeply. She tasted of Grand Marnier. The perfume in the air was like racy island fruit, sex magic rippling across his skin. Her hair covered him like a veil as she gently bit his lower lip, her tongue darting teasingly.

"Josephine was beautiful, but she was twisted, bitter, and very strange," she whispered in his ear. "She once told me that she often played violin alone because spirits listened to it."

"What about the dragon?"

"She said one day a dragon would swoop down to pick her up and take her on a ride across the universe. She would have a bag made of silk to collect whatever struck her fancy, a star that enchanted her or a comet streak. It was fun to listen to her stories. Then she'd turn around, though, and be so cold or jealous. I never knew what I was going to get from her."

"Oh, the vagaries of an eccentric stripper violinist."

"What?" She laughed.

"Uh, count on musicians to be weird and unpredictable."

She smiled, hair stuck to her lips like strands of syrup. "Yeah. She had a lot of contradictions. As sophisticated as she was, she was still childishly selfish. She had to have her way. Always."

"That's some friend you had there. How did you deal with her complications?"

"We were much, much more than friends, Jake. There were all sorts of...outlets to deal with complications."

Then she went down on him.

In his ecstasy, he didn't notice the candles throwing shadows where none should exist. Nor did he hear the breathing of a third person. The perfume belonging to a sex rite became much stronger.

A music box from her bedroom suddenly began to play. The ballerina melody was the bedtime story dreamy kind often laced into techno and dance pop. The shadows appeared to be writhing to it, sensual stripper writhing, inky spectral gossamer was floating through candlelight. It vanished, though, never thickening to flesh.

Was it Josephine or shadows?

Sliding off her thong, Abbey pushed his face to her groin. It was the eeriest fusion of submission and conquest. She dropped the crop stick she was holding and groaned as his tongue went to work. Oh the sense of power. He felt like he was giving head to the whole world.

She rode him in his bound state. He felt like a powerful caged animal or a crazed fan who couldn't quite reach the front of the stage of a rock show he'd waited years to see.

When the sex game was over, he was sweaty and exhausted. She unlocked him, and his sentence was done. She lay beside him, handcuffs held to her chest like a cherished toy.

For the longest time he just lay there, listening to himself breathe. The drug rolled through his veins, euphoria sex trundle. It was silent, the crack and popping of vintage records long over.

For a while he just enjoyed his high, eyes closed. When he opened them, she was painting.

He crept up behind her and watched her dip the brush in various pigments, light strokes creating shadowy suggestions of a curvaceous girl.

She peered over her shoulder at him, grinning. Her lingerie was back on, and her hair was tucked up in a poet's cap. "You like it?"

"Oh yeah. Who are those shadows of?"

The wind blew, dappled shadows of tree branches dancing over the canvass. Magnolia leaves cleaved to the open window, others rushing in.

"No one in particular," she said offhandedly. "If you would like to see some other paintings, there's a stack by the sofa."

He went through several that were interesting. Many showed a naked girl who was part shadow. Another depicted a whip coiled over a violin in a twist of sheets.

Déjà vu, he thought.

He got dressed, noticing her phone on the coffee table. He couldn't resist checking out her photos, and she was too caught up in painting to notice.

He went into her photo gallery. A series of very recent pictures were taken of the bed.

"Sight," he whispered, and vague forms appeared on the photo: vague impressions of black tress ectoplasm, a hint of milky white leg, and green eyes without a face like the eyes of a cat when lightning strikes.

He checked the videos, and the real show began. There were several sequences of Abbey bent over as though being whipped, but no one was there. She was tied to a bedpost, writhing to an invisible force. If he focused, though, he could make out the ghostly gossamer of a girl with long midnight hair.

This invisible force was most certainly Josephine. Abbey was still getting it on with her in ghost form. The spirit of Josephine was probably waiting on Jake to leave so she could have Abbey to herself!

Watching...

Waiting...

Tingling washed over him and slithered down the channel of his spine. He laid the phone down, joining Abbey again. She was so engrossed in the painting, she never noticed anything. "I've got to get my day started." He placed a hand on her shoulder.

She nodded silently, mixing colors, her high driving her to create. Then her eyes moved across the walls as though she heard something.

"Can you tell me anything else about Josephine's secret

place?"

"I just know if you find the secret place, there'll be a swing set and a girl waiting there, wanting Josephine to return and read poetry to her."

"A ghost?"

She shrugged. "I sure thought she was. That's why I ran."

He sighed. He'd heard enough riddles. He hugged her as she painted with an air of anxiety. She ran her fingers down the side of his face, toying with his hair, and kept painting.

"What's wrong?" he asked.

A pause for a brush stroke. "Nothing's ever wrong. I'm just a bad, bad girl."

...*who needs a spanking*, he finished.

Abbey's eyes moved over the walls again, watching shadows.

Whatever she was waiting for, he didn't want to know. Without another word, he left.

Chapter Twenty-Five

What a night. He was making so much money at *My Hot Sister* he was probably going to quit *Final Destination*. He might not even call *Medusa's* back. He was a liquor bottle twirling icon, rock's answer to Tom Cruise. His signature Black Dahlia shots were a huge hit everywhere.

The Indigo Girls were playing on the internet jukebox, spurring acoustic guitar sing-a-longs. One girl from Agnes Scott College brought in her guitar. She played on a stool, surrounded by friends.

During slow periods he'd work on *Spell Island*. A train would rattle by, metal lummox, the heavy trundling a soundtrack to his heavy thoughts. He felt darkly ambivalent about life, but he certainly wasn't bored. His life had become a metal song, a horror story and a Southern Gothic novel spliced together (He thought Sophia should summon the spirit of Faulkner or Poe and ask them what to do).

Jake was reaching up for new bottle of Jägermeister when Minstrel paraded in the door. His nimble silver-ringed hands flew over the violin with a virtuosity that astounded Jake.

"My dear boy, the time is at hand," Minstrel said, pointing the bow at him. "It's our last chance to run off like vagabonds in the night together. We'll start a band and know freedom like never before. Girls will come to us as though we're the incarnations of gods." Clapping and sounds of mock awe came from eye-rolling college kids at cocktail tables.

For a moment, Jake stared at him in consternation. "If you want to get away from Felicity so bad, why don't you run off alone?"

"My fine singer, I can't succeed alone. Don't you see? It's time to choose a road. Have you ever read Robert Frost's *The Road Not Taken*? You don't want a road that leads to Felicity. You can't turn back."

He sighed. "Just why do you want me so bad?"

"I know how powerful you'll be if you go through your Darkening. You'll be a hybrid nonpareil."

He regarded the violinist with weary disgust. "I'm not going through any stupid Darkening."

"Sooner or later, I don't think you're going to have a choice. Your Darkening is the only way to open your powers of Incubus. You'll be even more powerful and talented than Felicity."

Jake slammed a liquor bottle down and charged around from behind the bar. "If you want me so bad, you'll tell me where Josephine's ashes are buried."

"Oh no can do." Then he strolled out the door, making a *tsk-tsk* sound while playing a sad melody.

When it was a little after last call, a breeze blew into the bar, carrying a scent that could belong to no other, the redolence of forbidden paradise. His demon alarm, a mad rush of tingling, went wild.

Josephine.

She was very much on the physical plane, green fire in her cat eyes. Was she ever breathtaking, wearing silver bangles, black leather and a lace-up corset. Long black hair was fanned over alabaster skin, a jewel pendant resting in the hollow of her milky white neck.

How should he feel? Should the sight of her, however ravishing, inspire terror? His confusing mix of feelings would never stop him from wanting her, be her a demon, girl, or ghost.

Yet was he ever scared, nearly shaking. Just look at her, the embodiment of sex, full moons, and midnight.

She reached out to him, fingertips pressing together, and then they clasped hands. That's all it took. A frisson of Dark Lust shot through him like an injection—a touch was all it took. Stragglers still there at last call watched this as though it were a stage performance.

"Minstrel's spell really came through," he said.

"Yes, I'm finally back," she breathed, sensual lips parted. "But the spell might not last forever."

"And then you'll go back to only being a ghost?"

She lowered her eyes, sighing. "It's possible."

"How long will you be here?"

"Who knows?" She took his hand. "My time could be short. I want to run around and have some fun before I take you to bed."

He was speechless. He was about to have a night on the town with a ghost. The notion was both erotic and terrifying yet appealing to his sense of adventure.

And he knew the sex would be great.

She had the fantasy of a rock star being her submissive, so he went for it—even though the chain and slave collar were a tad much. How could he argue with a girl who might only have a short encore of life left?

First, they went to *The Dungeon*. Hex spotted them right away through a laser light pierced cigarette haze. He watched with an envious amusement. Jake was embarrassed. He looked like the girl's bitch.

Josephine was bold, head held high, jostling her way around the bar. If she weren't a gothic diva, someone may have snapped on her. Instead she garnered looks of awe.

"We thought you were dead," a bartender said. "Where have you been?"

"I've just been lying low." Nobody questioned her.

She led Jake into the restroom. Girls *oohed* and *ahhed* over him. One squeezed his crotch. Another jerked him around to kiss him deeply, his ass pressed against the sink. Josephine put a stop to that fast.

"Make no mistake. He's mine," Josephine asserted, but then she offered the blushing girl a bump of coke. It was all just a game, her bluster like a pro wrestling promo.

After doing thick white lines in a bathroom stall, they headed back out. He thought they were going to the dance floor, but no. The lioness paraded around with her rock singer acquisition. Buckhead couples, Midtown strippers, and backstreet leather boys offered big money to have him for the night.

"No thanks." Jake laughed, but they still groped and playfully pulled at his mane in an attempted overture to sex. "I'm not a gigolo."

"Are you sure?" Josephine smiled like a cat. "There's quite a sex bounty on your head, hot stuff. We could make a fortune."

"Prostitution is not my thing."

She winked. "That's good to hear. I wouldn't share you with these people, anyway."

Then she took him to the dance floor. He danced with her to a Rob Zombie remix. She twirled like a misfit schoolgirl, her heavy silver jewelry all a-clatter. Her vibrancy made Jake think of a young Madonna.

The DJ moved from metal to nineties goth music, a Type O Negative song ushering in the darkly sexual shift. Her essence returned to her eyes when the eerily erotic keyboard intro to *My girlfriend's Girlfriend* filled the chamber. It was like peering into a dark forest holding nymphs with wild dangerous allure.

Swaying hands went in the air, laser lights raking over them. The dancing became more of a sensual sway. Josephine was like a black rose in a night breeze. Jake just bounced his shoulders, fending off sex requests.

Finally, they came together and kissed deeply. Just the tip of her tongue poured Dark Lust into him. He shivered from the onrush, eyes rolling upward.

He sensed a distant psychic force reaching for his mind, but it was too late to worry about such things. After dancing to the eighties Cure song *Fascination Street*, she led him out into the night. They hailed a cab, and she directed the driver to the drag queen's house.

In his rapture, Jake laughed. "I don't think that crazy old drag queen will be thrilled to see me."

"He won't mind at all. He has gone away."

Jake didn't know what to think of that, but events were moving too fast for questions. The cab was there in no time, and the gate was open. She headed up the driveway as though she owned the place, yanking Jake along.

"I see we aren't starting the party," he remarked, struggling to catch up like a drunken prom date.

The air was charged with sex magic, ready to explode. Furniture was overturned from the throes of mindless lovemaking. Exhausted lovers watched them from shadowy corners with languorous glassy eyes.

He was marveling at this tableaux reenacting Roman orgiastic overindulgence as an image of murder came into his mind. He saw the old man reeling backward and sliding down the wall.

"What happened?" he muttered deliriously as she led him upstairs.

She looked back, grinning deviously. "Whatever do you mean?" Then her eyes grew wide with lust and excitement. "Let's do it in here."

It was the drag queen's bedroom—Felicity's new love nest. Handcuffs hung from the posts of the four-poster bed.

She unhooked the chain from the thick ring on the choker, the chain coiling like a snake on the floor. "You've been a good sport about the collar." She ran her fingers through his hair.

"I know I've been a good sport. You need to stick to the violin." He gave her a hard appraisal. "What exactly is going on?"

She sighed, eyelids hooded. "There's no further point in games. Now that you're in this house, you can't run off anyway."

Fuck. It was a trap.

As she ripped off his shirt, he heard lines from *Hotel California* by the Eagles in his mind. *You can check out any time you want, but you can never leave.* He needed to run, but his Dark Lust was so intense that, even trapped, he wanted her.

At her touch, though, visions of figures getting off a bus filled his mind. Who were these people? Was she entangled in their cabal?

She sunk her tongue into his mouth, slinging him on the bed. She didn't use handcuffs, no bondage, but the passion was all it took to ensnare him. She gripped him by the wrist and hair, riding him like a pioneer heading into a brave new land. It was the kind of rough sex where he felt used, but the pleasure rendered those feelings negligible.

When they were exhausted from lovemaking, orgasms riding waves of magic, he fell into a deep sleep. The Dark Lust faded away like a dragon pacified by fresh kills and new treasure.

He woke to the hypnotic dulcet tones of a violin. Josephine was playing in her thong. He watched her private concert a moment, and then reality hit him hard.

Time to get the fuck out of here, he thought, leaping up. How could he have let her drag him back to this *House of Usher*?

What was even more frightening was that he didn't really know what was going on. Fear of the unknown was always worst. He was certain, though, he'd know soon enough.

Derisive amusement played over her face as he dressed hurriedly and rushed for the staircase. "Just where are you going?" she asked.

Then everything hit certifiable nightmare status.

He froze on the steps at the sight of two Doberman's morphing into winged hellhounds, the twin spawn of Cerberus. They roared like small dragons, saliva dripping from dinosaur jaws. The viscous acid-drool pooled on the hardwood floor in front of their monstrous paws, sizzling like grease.

"Come to me, my loves," a voice called in an eerie tone of affection, Lily Munster love.

He gazed across the living room to behold Felicity for the first time. She was a living video avatar—a goth/glam goddess of war, cosmo-bondage Barbie.

She wore a leather choker festooned with heavy rings around her neck. A cropped studded top exposed a creamy mid-riff where a G-clef note was tattooed over her navel, pierced with a barbell ring. A loosely worn studded black belt accented a voluminous blood-red Victorian velvet skirt, slit to be provocative, flowing in the wind from open French doors. Leaves floating in tumbled about her lace-up leather boots.

She smiled faintly at Jake, her iridescent nebulae hair reflecting candlelight. The dogs ran to her, leaping about like happy children.

On the polished dinner table lay a cornucopia of fruit, cheese, and a bottle of Pinot Grigio. "Join me," she said softly. "Aren't the dogs beautiful?"

He cleared his throat and walked down the stairs like a talk-show guest. "Oh yes. Just *precious.*"

She played a dazzling piece on her violin, and the amulets on the dog's collars flashed. They shifted back to monstrous form.

"I'm swooning with Rapture," she said in her cosmic delirium. "It's made me feel like regaling. Just look at what I've done for you." She gestured eloquently at all the sex victims, passed out from exhaustion, sprawled around the dark-paneled, elegant house.

Lowering the violin, she stepped over a sleeping body and sashayed toward him, her hand reaching out for his amulet. Sparks flew, yet still she smiled with profound relish, her black eyes half-lidded.

Her face went through a series of expressions: lust, contempt, and awe. "Oh, you most certainly are the direct descendent of Merek...the hybrid everyone speaks of in hushed tones." Her voice was eerie in its whispery soft malevolence. "You know where a huge collection of books are in Ariel's mansion. We must go there. I want the book collection."

She wants me to play Scooby-Doo, he thought. *Well, I've been used before.* "Why does everyone want those books so badly?"

"All sorts of hunters have reasons to want the invaluable collection of treasure maps leading to priceless jewels, untold powerful spells, history books of long forgotten lore. There are even grimoires with brilliant spell music for violin that I seek. Most of all, there are old brittle books with the key to opening doorways to the Nephemera...pages that haven't been read in centuries. Did Ariel have any idea that this hidden library of great arcane secrets was there?"

"Uh, yeah. She was obsessed with finding it, but I beat her to it."

"Ah, yes," Felicity said, those shiny black eyes of druggy enchantment reflecting candlelight. "I have heard tales of a demon summoned from the Nephemera turning her to stone. There are also rumors her ghost haunts that mansion now."

Oh great. The bitch haunts the place, waiting on my ass to show up again. "You want me to deal with this ghost?" he asked incredulously.

"No. I'll deal with Ariel. Just get me into the library by using your unique gifts."

"Why don't I just tell you where it is, and then you can let me go."

"No, it is not that simple." Her soft spacey voice made him shudder. "I am a Succubus of Illusion. With you, I can put together an act unparalleled in the world of magic. I, too, am a hybrid. If you go through your Darkening, we'll have chemistry like none other. I can't let you go."

"I don't know anything about illusion. This is ridiculous."

"You don't understand. The girl who protects you... Marci Stone. She hasn't explained anything to you about your dual power because she doesn't want you to go through your Darkening. She doesn't want to lose you. You have a voice that could move millions. If you tap into your true dual power, your mere voice will carry spells and illusion. It is time for you to discover your true nature and join us."

"Who is '*us*'?"

"You'll join the three of us onstage. Minstrel, myself, and Josephine."

He flared a brow. "Josephine?"

"I have every intention of holding onto her...forever. We'll have an Illusion/Goth act that will take the world by storm."

No wonder Minstrel wanted to get away from this crazy controlling psycho bitch. He should've just run away alone. "Why do you want to go to the Nephemera so bad? Isn't it dangerous there?"

"Yes. There is great power there, too. I know an Illusionist who made it there and back. Demons and angels walk there in human form, many of them prostituting themselves." She tilted her head thoughtfully, eyes like the night. "This dark Eden is divided up by nine concentric rings, nine worlds of fantasy and sin on a single island. Just the airborne magic will transform my power of illusion."

He shook his head, scoffing. *How could this be real?* "So you're obsessed with reaching this angel world."

"How else can I reach the next level?" she asked. "And truth be told, you're obsessed with it, too."

She has a point. "Is taking me to bed part of your plan?"

"Oh no. I have no interest in men. Josephine must be your lover so that I can tap into your power through her. I wouldn't mind if the three of us were together, though."

Fantastic, he thought. He could look forward to an eternity of three ways with a violin succubus and a ghost girl submissive. This was crazier than Ariel's scheme to be the queen of a hybrid race.

He had to escape her, but how? He felt sure the house was warded.

Down a long hallway stood Aurora, and behind her was Heathen. "I'm in the mood for a little game," she called out, eyes full of wild delight falling on Jake. "You get a tour of our new party house."

Felicity ran the bow across the strings of her violin, nodding her consent to her fiery minion.

It was the first time Jake was able to really see the house. The mansion was filled with morbid exotica, priceless weapons of antiquity, and instruments of torture. On the walls were mounted battle axes, civil war muskets, and maces of barbarians. On bookshelves rested rusty lanterns from long lost pirate ships, bejeweled daggers and encased gold doubloons. A Scottish Claymore rested against an armoire, flanked by suits of Gaelic armor. The old drag queen even had an Iron Maiden and other nameless torture devices set out amongst wingback Victorian furniture.

It got weirder.

Mannequins were set about the house garbed in beautiful Victorian dresses. One mannequin wore the bondage attire of Marquis de Sade, complete with a whip and big wooden dildo. Most rooms served as huge closets for the old man's dresses he wore on stage in his cabaret shows.

"Nice, huh?" Heathen smirked.

Jake didn't say anything.

They moved on. Finally, Aurora chose two swords of antiquity from the walls. "Care for a duel?"

"Do I have a choice?" Jake asked.

She slung furniture out of the way and tossed him a sword. What was this? *A broadsword? It was heavy as shit.*

Jake was no swashbuckler from an Alexander Dumas novel like *The Three Musketeers*. This was survival.

Aurora toyed with him while Heathen watched intently in amused thrall. Jake flailed wildly at her, but she easily parried the strikes.

He was relieved to see this fight was not serious. It was more like a sword fighting scene with Gomez and Morticia of the *Addams Family*.

"Stick to singing, pretty boy," Aurora said.

Heathen clapped and howled on the sofa, loving it.

Jake, a long cut across his mesh shirt, was forced back against a suit or armor, her sword point to his chest.

"You can't sing either if you're impaled with my sword." Aurora pressed just hard enough to draw a bead of blood. "Unless dead singers can sing."

"The band doesn't need another ghost," he said.

For a few long heavy seconds Aurora gazed at him like a cobra, and then a voice came from downstairs. "I've found Chardonnays of impressive vintage. Some bottles must be over a hundred years old. All of you must simply come drink with me."

Aurora smiled slyly. "Let's go drink wine. You can die another time."

Jake followed them downstairs. *Let's go drink wine. You can die another time. Those are great lines for a song.*

Felicity poured glasses for everyone, a shiny red apple from the bowl in her other hand. The wine tasted like oak and apricot mixed with a spring breeze. Jake drank two bottles while Aurora danced to seventies disco music, swinging her sword about as though she were doing a show in Vegas. Finally, Felicity took the helm, swaying to scratchy vinyl orchestra music, chewing her forbidden fruit. Juice dripped on the floor like spilled ichor. Her shadows on the wall were like mindless cult members formed from darkness. Heathen got sick of it all and left.

As the dawn painted the sky with magenta pigment, Felicity headed upstairs. Josephine materialized on the staircase behind her in flowing Victorian elegance.

Nothing like morning sex, Jake thought and passed out.

***

Felicity had money. For their jaunt to Ariel's mansion in the mountains the following afternoon, only the best would do. She rented a four-seater Porsche 911.

They were quite a sight—Jake, Felicity, Aurora, and one of the two dogs filling the car like bizarre yuppies. Jake was in the back with the faithful demon pooch. Aurora drove while Felicity played her violin, improvising melody lines to the symphonic metal music playing on Sirius XM radio. She coaxed brilliant accompaniment from her cosmic soul, heightening the grandeur of Epica, Nocturna, and Night Wish.

Felicity took the best liquor and several bottles of vintage wine from the house, tossing it all in the backseat for the dog to guard like a dragon. Off they went to the little town of Wylon where big dark arcane secrets nested in the forested mountains.

Jake made the most of his captivity, swigging wine like it was soda pop. By the time unincorporated rural oblivion spread out around them, he was just short of blitzed. He sang Miley Ray Cyrus songs, wailing metal falsetto style (*It's the cliiimb!!!*) as cornfields, farms, and rusty tractors on sprawling land slipped past him. Felicity played Blue Grass on her violin. Aurora made redneck jokes, howling like a banshee while she did shots of Whistle Pig out of a QuikTrip cup.

"Play Hayseed Dixie," Aurora shouted over her shoulder. "They actually do all those metal songs on Banjoes."

So Jake played Hayseed Dixie's version of *Hell's Bells* on his phone. Felicity loved the toothless sounding shit, adding her manically magic fiddle.

Eventually, a narrow lost highway, the kind where spirits gathered in the dead of night to watch headlights, led them to a nowhere dump of a convenience store. A wooden sign shaded by a swaying Pecan tree read: *Tommy's Food Mart.* A painted sign over the storefront touted: *Yes we have pig's feet here.*

Homeless drifters, more lost than the spirits in the woods, gaped at them in puzzled awe from corners of the store. Inside, a fat clerk with a face like a plum reached for a shotgun under the counter the minute they burst in the door.

"Hey," the clerk bellowed, "no crazy big city cult needs to be bringin' a damn dog in here! I will call the pol—"

The Doberman leaped up on the counter, morphing into a winged abomination. The owner shot wildly as he ran out the back.

"Fill the trunk," Aurora whispered, burping up white wine, and she plundered the place like a Viking princess. "Join the fun," the wild crimson haired warrior yelled at Jake, laughing. She was juggling beer and doing flips down the aisles.

"Sure," he said, living out an unspoken fantasy to rip off a liquor store. It was like a scene out of Stephen King's *The Stand,* outrageous behavior born of apocalyptic desperation.

When they were done, the trunk wouldn't even close.

A police car pulled into the parking lot. The cop got out, bemused, a regular Barney Fife. Jake shook his head from the backseat. Aurora up front, giggled. Weed had her flying.

Felicity stood next to a gas pump, playing her violin, glitter-goth hair flowing in a breeze carrying the fresh country scent of cornbread and turnips.

Jake couldn't fucking believe it. *Oh, oh, he's walking over to fuck with her. He's going to think she's an alien here to abduct all the farmers. We need to get the hell out of here.*

"Are you playin' the fiddle for money, ma'am?" He chuckled. "There's a shelter in the next town where—"

"We aren't homeless, you idiot." Aurora leaped from the car, a sphere of roiling azure light forming in her palm. "You might want to worry about your cute cop car."

Terror filled the hokey cop's eyes as the hurled spellburst shattered the windshield, setting the squad car ablaze. Aurora laughed hysterically, watching the cop run like an escaped criminal down the road.

Felicity looked vaguely amused yet annoyed. "I was going to play a beautiful piece for him. You shouldn't have run him off before I played, my fire child."

Aurora laughed. "Come join your fire child in the car." She held up a liquor bottle. Moonlight and whiskey sloshed about together, an argent rippling glow on amber fluid. "I'll find you a real cop to entertain."

She floated over to the car with no sense of urgency like an overmedicated psychopath who'd effortlessly escaped a mental ward for an evening stroll. Once she was in the car playing again, Aurora shrieked onto the highway.

Jake just closed his eyes, lay back and laughed. The dog had a look like he wanted him to just shut the fuck up.

The Porsche raced past a trailer park, a farm, and a plantation house before hitting a stretch of highway meant for nightmares. That's when a B-movie motel came into view.

Felicity ceased playing her violin. "I want to stay in that *dump*," she said in a singsong whisper.

Aurora screeched into the shadowy parking lot like she was filming a chase scene in an indie film. They certainly looked like the stars of an underground classic.

A stringy-haired woman used to freaks coming to the place handed them keys with a vague shake of her head. She did smile when she saw the dog. "I love Dobermans. My neighbor used to raise 'em."

"This is my first," Felicity whispered.

The clerk's eyes flared in wild speculation and then went back to her business.

The room looked like a party had just ended. The bed was made, but the maid had left beer bottles. Needles were in the bedside table drawers. Broken glass from a meth pipe was strewn about the bathroom sink.

"So, homey," Felicity said softly.

Aurora took a deep swig of Jack Daniels. "Yeah. Our very own weekly rental trap house." She sat on one of the two beds, smirking. "We'll think fondly of this place when we're in the bowels of that fucking house in the hills."

Jake had his own bottle. If he couldn't escape them, he could sure as hell drink with them. "If Ariel wants to kill anyone, it's me. You two are Darkened. She might think of you as kindred and let you escape."

"Make no mistake, she'll want us all dead," Felicity said, raising her wine glass in a toast. "Here's to our guest of honor, Jake Reece. His magic is the key to opening the doorway to the hidden library...and ultimately the door to the Nephemera."

"Aren't you excited?" Aurora asked, flaring an eyebrow. Her long ropey red hair was thrown over an alabaster shoulder bearing a tattoo of a hooded skull.

"Uh, cheers," he said, cutting his eyes away from the symbol of death. *Don't Fear the Reaper* by Blue Oyster Cult played over and over in his mind, haunting and ominous.

***

They drank for several hours before heading back to the car for the mission in the mansion—the case of the hidden library. On the winding dirt road leading to this huge gothic edifice, Jake spotted a few spectral lights within the surrounding forest. *Yep the ghosts have been waiting on our arrival.*

Come out to play...

Felicity played a complicated Bach piece, watching the headlights pass over orb webs spanning the road, spider eyes glittering in them. "I love playing for ghosts."

"And I'm sure they love it, too," he answered dryly.

The silhouettes of spires and turrets set against the moonlit sky slid out of the darkness. It finally struck Jake how much this place made him think of the Ellen Rim Rimbauer house—The Thornewood Castle. This was a mansion of madness, too.

Felicity loved it, gasping in awe. "This is no house. This is a castle. No...a work of art."

Aurora groaned. "Yeah, we don't have to cross a god damn moat to get to this big old gothic god-only-knows-who-died-here place, do we?"

"Uh, no. Moats are the least of our problems."

Aurora parked next to the vine-shrouded wall and everyone got out of the car. Jake closed his eyes, throwing out his senses. He expected to hear Ariel's threats riding the susurration of windswept trees. He didn't, but he did feel a presence he couldn't quite define.

Puzzled, he strolled to the open gates, closing his eyes again. When he pressed his splayed hands to the wrought iron bars, he gasped. A strong surge of impressions led to a chilling realization.

Spirits that had been waiting for years and years, a hundred or more, to escape the forests and takeover the mansion were reveling in Ariel's death. They were free at last to roam. If she were there as a spirit, she was not powerful enough to hold back the great numbers of specters who hated her and wanted the house back.

And there was something else.

The spirits had brought with them a wild magic so powerful that it was causing nature to flourish preternaturally. The air was charged with it.

"You're leaving that damn dog here?" Aurora asked Felicity, who'd gestured for her new familiar to remain behind.

"Yes, my new friend will do us no good against ghosts. I'd rather he guard the car. That way I can see through his eyes if we have unexpected guests."

Jake was impressed. The crazy violinist was no idiot. He'd noticed before that genius warred with insanity within her mind. The dog, in winged form, watched them walk through the gates, perched on the front of the car like a huge hood ornament. *Nobody* was fucking with that car.

He knew what he would see before he began leading his captors up the dark lamppost-lined driveway. The magic in the ether had turned the place into Eden. Vines with huge succulent alien flowers grew luxuriously over everything, draping oriels and stone gargoyles, blanketing the cobblestone driveway and surrounding terraces. They'd even overtaken the mythical statuary and the fountain, shrouding a fused pair of stone lovers rising above the dirty water.

The group stood in the moon shadows of steep gables, beholding the grandeur of the house. The fire Jake and the girls had escaped after dealing with Ariel may have caused some damage, but the house was very much intact. It felt sentient...alive.

Passing the gargoyles flanking the arched doorway, he opened the heavy door which squeaked petulantly, rusty caterwaul. His hands searched frantically for light switches in the darkness. Sure enough. No electricity.

In the foyer, they lit a bank of pillar candles and carried a few of them along. He led them through the house as though he were a tour guide.

The interior had been overtaken by nature, as well. Huge ropey vines boasting waxy flowers like giant tea cups had spread over the velvet-flocked hallways, the flashy theme rooms, and the polished bars. The grandeur of the house, though, still asserted itself through the intrusion of nature run riot.

He pointed at the calligraphy above an archway that read *Paradiso*. "I'm sure you heard the concept behind this sex mansion/nightclub is based on Dante's *The Divine Comedy*."

"Yes," Felicity said. "Ariel was brilliant in her insanity."

The singer smirked, candlelight making his face a Halloween mask. *Talk about the pot calling the kettle black.* "You admire her, huh?"

Felicity didn't respond, gaze far, far away.

He took them up the curving staircase to the sex rooms in *Paradiso*, the dance floors of *Inferno*, the lounges of *Purgatorio*.

Even Aurora was impressed. "Fuck. This beats anything I've seen in New York or L.A. Why did she want to live in this hick town?"

"Seclusion," Jake said, thick dripping candles lighting the way past gargoyle newel posts. "Plus how could you find a cooler house than this to throw raves?"

"Yeah, I get it," she said, holding her candle up to go-go cages and platform stages.

Felicity remained silently thoughtful.

"Okay, now its time for the grand finale," Jake said. "We're headed to the main dance chamber that leads to the wine cellar...and the statue of Ariel if she's still there."

"Yes," Felicity breathed. "The hidden library is in the wine cellar, isn't it?"

"You guessed it."

The huge chamber had the worst fire damage—blackened rococo rugs, the burnt remains of velvet furniture and tattered curtains, tall floor candelabras overturned and sooty—but the DJ booth with its spiral staircase and the chamber's huge bars were still there, unscathed. Pyramids of liquor bottles awaited another rave. The place refused to die.

A wave of tingling washed over him, the telltale sensation of a spectral presence. He threw out his senses, expecting to see a dab of ectoplasm as ghosts watched candlelight carved shadows.

What he saw, though, was breathtaking. The place had become a crowded ballroom, full of ghost guys and dolls. Swing music was playing, the dancing spirits having a total blast. Laughing girls twirled, bright dresses swept about. Leading men dipped and flung their dance partners, swaggering, fedoras tilted rakishly.

Wow. Was this a scene out of The Titanic?

On the velvet furniture, sequin-dressed damsels drank martinis and smoked with long stem holders. Specters in pinstriped suits threw back scotch and slapped down cards. It was a paranormal noir film feast.

Did they care the place had been burned?

Nope.

Suddenly the spirits rushed away in a ghost raid panic. Jake felt a new presence, possessive and vengeful.

"We need to make our move," he urged.

Felicity's eyes slid languidly over the vaulted ceiling. "Yes, time is of the essence," she said in her spacey way.

Aurora's eyes went wide. "Let's grab what we can and get the fuck out of here."

Jake motioned for them to come behind the bar and gestured toward a huge oak door. "That door leads down to the cellar. It's show time."

He gazed down the dank stone steps, raising his candle to light the way. With the *clump-clump-clump* of bootheels behind him, echoing in this small space, he felt like he was being led to the gallows. He wanted more light, but the candles had melted away in the gargoyle sconces, now festooned with gauzy sheets of cobweb.

He found himself holding back a nervous titter. No one was going particularly fast down the steps. His captors were just as afraid as he was. The *clickety-clack* of bootheels behind him came at a wary measured pace.

Two thirds of the way down, he held out the dripping candle, illuminating a statue of beauty and anguish at the bottom of the steps.

It was none other than succubus Ariel Celique, still there after her final battle with the demon she never should've summoned, captured in stone forever. Even her pet spiders had been turned to granite on her curvy body, perched on the deep folds of her flowing garb. Vines were wrapped around her like pythons, wanting not just her body but her soul, big waxy blooms mocking her.

A faint smile played over Felicity's face. "The demon truly captured her beauty."

Whatever, Jake thought. "She wanted to be the creator of a new hybrid race and now look at her."

Aurora smirked. "She's gonna wind up in somebody's garden with bright gay windmills and a Buddha statue. Somebody would pay a lot for that at Home Depot."

Felicity's eyes went black as she gazed up the staircase. "We should proceed in haste, I think."

Jake couldn't have agreed more, throwing himself into the task of finding the library doorway. He felt the magic radiating from the walls, rippling across his flesh.

His eyes slid over the wine-rack-lined walls, filmed with cobweb. He invoked Sight, pulling out the old bottles until he found an arcane symbol. Tearing away strands of web, he finally exposed a circle of elaborate sigils visible only to his preternaturally heightened eyesight.

"This is where it all starts," he said in a low storyteller voice.

He shuddered as magic crashed into him like a tidal wave, roiling through him. It wasn't from the wall, though.

Ariel was here. Her magic charged the ether like a storm,

electrical pheromones.

"No, this is where it all *ends*," a menacing voice called from the top of the stairs.

A wind whipped through the cellar, carrying leaves, and then shadows gathered like curtains, morphing into the specter of Ariel Celique. She was nearly flesh, milky white, voluptuous in a studded leather corset, hair like streaming blood thrown over one shoulder.

"Fuck. She looks like *Carrie*," Aurora said, forming a spell in her hand. "All she needs is pig's blood all over her prom dress."

Felicity remained in silent wonder.

Ariel floated down the stairwell, a velvet skirt dragging over the dank steps behind her. The ghosts of spiders crawled up her arms and midriff, dangling like Egyptian jewelry. She held out one of her pets, silver crosses on a black leather bracelet clinking against the candlelit wall. "You have no business here in my house," she stated imperiously.

A thickening spell roiled in the palm of her hand. She was just shy of reaching the physical plane, her skin so supple yet not quite real.

She hurled the spell at Aurora, who leaped and spun, dodging it. Aurora then slung her own magic with thrusting tattooed palms.

The burst shattered Ariel like glass. Black shards dissipated into inky effluvium, then morphed into shrieking ravens. The birds of dark lore soared up the stairwell, vanishing.

What now? No more ghost. No more birds of Poe poetry. The house was silent, deathly silent, but for how long? Jake's eyes moved about. He kept expecting this place to start breathing.

No way had she given up just like that, he thought.

"She's trying to freak us out with mind games. Let's deal with this bitch before she traps us in this holding cell." Aurora bounded up the steps while sliding a broadsword free from a back harness.

Just as she reached the head of the steps, a spectral force, ghost comet, rushed down at her from the DJ booth. She swung the sword wildly at the juggernaut, glowing runes on polished steel making brilliant streaks in the darkness.

An apparition, a hideous demonic caricature of Ariel, hovered just beyond the reach of the weapon. The shimmering creature gazed down as though from a mythical mountain of gods, casting judgment. Then the ghost dissolved into squid ink gossamer, floating through candlelight and then fading away.

More silence. Only the faint sound of dripping candle wax could be heard.

Felicity raised her bow and began to play, conjuring ghosts of her own. The French doors slammed open, and a torrent of spiritual force rampaged through the chamber. Jake felt like he was in an X-Men movie.

They stood in the eye of this spirit maelstrom. Felicity's black eyes reflected the violent swirl of spirits, portals to her private cosmic hell. "My dead kindred will guard us during our visit here."

Jake was speechless. Ariel's vengeful spirit was nowhere to be found, dispelled.

His captors watched intently as he pressed his palms to the sigils on the walls and closed his eyes. The amulet around his neck flared to life as he incanted what mindlessly poured from his mouth.

He was aware defensive magic coiled within the walls—spellwork that could go off like a bomb—but the power he was conjuring threaded around all of it, unimaginably powerful and sentient. He was a regular hex hacker.

He lowered his hands from the walls, releasing a deep sigh. He was happy to just be alive. The sigils were glowing, but what did that mean?

There was a heavy pause, a jury judgment pause. A tarot card flipped through Jake's mind of The Hang Man. Fate was up in the air, suspended.

Aurora shifted from one leather boot to the next, eyes flitting about in bewilderment. Then Felicity's eyes rolled upward. She released a sigh of pleasure that was pure orgasmic validation.

"Oh yes. The time is now."

The wall turned to darkness and melted away. Inside was a room lined with shelves and pedestal tables laden with grimoires, treasure, and tomes of history.

Jake walked through the magical doorway first. The power he'd invoked melted away protective spells over the bookshelves. Everything was for the taking.

He closed his eyes a moment, seeing magical history unravel

behind his eyes. There were several robed figures performing protective spellwork and sealing the wall.

"A coven lived here over a century ago," he whispered in awe. "They created this hidden room and performed all manner of sacrificial rites on this property. That's much of the reason there's so much magic here...so many ghosts."

"And now all this is ours," Felicity breathed.

"Uh huh sure," Aurora said, nodding sarcastically. "Let's grab this shit and go."

Jake and Felicity each carried a stack of books while sassy fire girl grabbed up silver coins and exotic oddities. The spirits Felicity had conjured still roared through the house, a paranormal hurricane, but the ghost din was beginning to die down. Her violin spell was about to run its course. Then Ariel would return with all her fury.

They hustled out through the gates to find the dog soaring about as though auditioning for a circus. At the sight of Felicity, the beast flew to the ground and ran to its master.

She really loves that monster, Jake marveled. *She's like Lily Munster.*

They all jumped in the car, Felicity playing dulcet soothe-the-savage-beast music on her violin. He just shook his head. *That dog is gonna wind up in bed with her and Josephine—and it'll be doing more than eating Scooby snacks.*

Back at the motel, it may as well have been Halloween.

"Trick or Treat," Aurora howled, flinging the door open for another small-town coke dealer.

The traffic to the room had become ridiculous, but the motel clerk was too terrified of them to call the town's hokey cop brigade. Just let these freaks party their asses off and leave.

And party they did. It was a big deal they'd survived that haunted house. This was their farewell blast.

Aurora chugged vodka as she tossed another century old silver coin into the hands of a hick hustler. The mythical dog beast leaped around behind her, wings unfurled. Amulets from the arcane stash and sparkling beads hung from the party animal's neck. The creature was only missing beach shorts and flip flops now.

"I think we should name the dog Witch Doctor," Aurora said,

tugging him playfully by the beads.

"No," Felicity said in her eerie distant voice. "The dog needs an exotic name." Her disdainful gaze fell on the guy at the door. "Get the rabble to move on. I'm trying to read."

The motel dealer handed Aurora the dope with trembling hands, his eyes as big as saucers. "I take it ya'll do magic."

She smirked, bottle to her mouth, and then answered with her best southern accent. "We damn sure do."

The nervous kid smiled faintly, his friends behind him frozen in awestruck terror. "I'll bet dis coin is worf uh fortune."

"It's damn sure worf more than the nose candy," she laughed mockingly, tossing back hair like wildfire. "Seriously, some lucky fucking coin dealer will give you bank for that. You've only given us an eight ball. You're lucky I'm even paying you. We could just take the shit."

He nodded emphatically and took off, his entourage trailing behind him like *The Little Rascals*.

Aurora shut the door and divvied out the dope on a scrying mirror. Felicity was oblivious to Aurora's hayseed mocking debauchery, lost in lore and spells written in exquisite flowing cursive. Her silver fingernails brushed sensually over the gilded leather covers of timeless masterpieces.

On one of the beds, Jake wrote music on a Moog keyboard synthesizer Felicity had insisted they bring and stashed it in the Porsche's trunk. Next to him were lyrics Felicity had written. She'd even given him a recording of violin music his composition was meant to accompany.

This song would open their show at the Bonding Weekend festival. With him in the band, how could she lose the battle of the bands?

His friends in Dark Promise certainly wouldn't beat her—not if she had him singing and playing keyboards.

Fuck.

How was he getting out of this? Was Marci trying to reach him with her mind, throwing out desperate messages? He didn't know because he'd blocked her out psychically in fear of Felicity picking up on it all.

There just wasn't going to be a simple way out of this predicament.

Deep in the night, Felicity lowered a gilded tome, saying in an urgent whisper, "I've found a doorway to the Nephemera. At dawn, we head back to Atlanta."

"Sure, Felicity," Aurora said, doing another line. "Whatever."

The partying, despite Felicity's fiat, went on until about noon. Doubloons and dope were exchanged, and even Felicity abandoned her reading to join the fun.

Eventually everyone collapsed in a heap, sleeping a few hours before finally leaving the next day at dusk. Then they took back roads to slip out of the nowhere town.

Chapter Twenty-Six

It was nightfall in Atlanta. The gables of Nightmare Mansion were set starkly against a sky bruised by twilight. Spindly Bone Tree branches filled the sky with tracery, turning the coming night into a celestial window.

Muriel was propped on the railing of the wrap-a-round porch, a balmy breeze whipping her long earthy hair. She was reading *Frankenstein*. The tension around her eyes tightened as she read a horrifically poignant part. To be half man and half monster...

But wasn't that what the Estranged were? With angel blood in their veins, were they—nephilim—any different?

She lowered the book, considering her existential questions. Snow and everybody else had gone to Veggie Land, thrilled to hear they were putting turkey in the veggie sandwiches instead of pork. God forbid Snow put a pound on his lovely waist. She supposed she should join them.

She strolled under the Bone Tree, capillary moon shadows thrown over her hair. She scowled, wrinkling her nose. Riding the bonfire breeze was the sweet putrid smell of that BBQ sauce plant up the street. If she didn't love this house, the coven, and the cemetery, she would leave Grant Park.

Oh, who was she kidding? This neighborhood was in her blood. Where would she go?

Veggie Land was on the corner of Cherokee and Memorial across from the Oakland Cemetery. The old brick walls of the industrial chic building bore colorful paintings of dancing vegetables. Despite the fun atmosphere, seriously sophisticated clientele came here for the chef-driven preparations.

There was a bar, though, bringing a crowd from the party circuit to the hip healthy place. The joint had been a dive bar and an even dumpier diner before its current incarnation. The counter that had served as both a bar for drunks and a truck driver's forum for road story bitching sessions now held an assemblage of vegans, wannabe vegans, and Casters—all of them strange, difficult, and peculiar. Who was the worst mixture of all these traits was anybody's guess.

Snow was the first to spot Muriel coming in the door, *Frankenstein* held to her chest like a second heart. "There's our literati leader. We wondered when you would show up."

"I read," Brice interjected, scowling. "Not everybody here is so into themselves they can't take time out from the mirror."

Snow primped an eyebrow. "I'm just jesting. I love to read. I just don't flaunt it. I read biographies."

"Of hairdressers," Brice finished.

Snow rolled his eyes, tossing his cocaine-colored hair. "Whatever, you miscreant."

Cameo was leaning against the counter, hipshot, all blond hair and glitter, like some otherworldly Cinderella of prostitution. "You guys need to stop arguing. We need more solidarity. We're too much like the Brady Bunch."

Snow laughed. "You'd be Jan. Swing that hair, girl."

Muriel joined in at the counter. "Hey, our idiosyncrasies are what keep us interesting...and together. Think about that."

Everyone agreed silently, turning their eyes toward Snow for whatever profound or caustic remark he might have about the state of affairs. While Snow had been called a cocky fop and much uglier epithets, he was wise beyond his years. He'd seen a lot go down in the world of magic, making him ruthless and cunning. And the vanity he was notorious for truly intensified his wit.

Muriel cleared her throat. "So let's get a booth and discuss the concert. How do you think we'll beat Felicity at the show?"

"Our illusions are better," Snow said simply. "And we have a trump card in Jake." He chuckled faintly. "I got a call that he was parading around town with some hot goth dish. I guess he got laid. Have you heard from him?"

Muriel's face darkened. "I haven't seen him. That's one of the reasons I came here. I was hoping there was a good sex story to be heard."

"He's probably just running around," Cameo said offhandedly. "I'm sure *My Hot Sister* is packed with festival people who just got here. It would be easy to be led...astray."

Snow groaned. "I'd like to think he'd have better sense than to run around when Felicity could already be on the prowl for him."

Muriel's eyebrows drew together. "Maybe he's with Marci. Let me text her." She went into contacts on her phone, her fingers gliding over the keyboard. A response came back right away. Muriel nodded ruefully. "She's coming. I think she has bad news."

***

Marci stormed into the diner with the ravaged look of someone who's had a nightmare of dire portent. Her stormy hair clung to the side of her face. Her skin held a waxy pallor.

Behind her was Zowie. Her face was dark with concern, but amusement played vaguely over her expression. "I know Marci looks like she's got the plague, but she'll be alright."

"They've got him," she gasped, walking up to the bar. Her eyes were glassy portals to Jake's soul.

"Are you sure?" Snow asked.

"Yes. He just sent me a very faint telepathic message. He was trying to tell me something about Josephine luring him to Felicity, but his voice just..." Her eyes narrowed as she tried to grasp the horror of it all, "faded away."

Muriel made quotation marks with her fingers. "So this *ghost* is definitely in league with our enemy."

"I'd say so."

"Why do you look like you just gave birth?" Brice asked, always a wise ass.

Marci tried to smile. "Brice, you wouldn't understand." She threw her arms around Muriel and muttered, "I've got a bad, bad case of Dark Lust."

"I see," Muriel said, astounded. She could see why Zowie wanted to laugh. "Did you have sex with a succubus?"

Marci cut her eyes to the floor and then closed them. "No, but Jake either fucked one or fucked someone who just fucked one. He and I are connected on...many levels."

Muriel smiled knowingly. "I bet."

Cameo leaped up joyfully. "Things are going to get better. Let's just make a plan. We're smarter than who we're up against. Come on. Let's get a booth where we can properly unite."

It looked like a scene from the *Breakfast Club* when they all slid into a back vinyl booth, curved like a horseshoe. Cameo took photos of the group, showing them off.

"I think this photo should be the first CD cover," she said, holding out her phone.

"No," Snow said flatly. "Stick to your porn director dream."

Their server was a thirty-year-old chunky hip mom everyone called Tequila Sheila. Her hippy long auburn hair, worn in a plait, was slung over a Grateful Dead T-shirt. She smoked more weed than anyone else they knew and thought the magical gang was cooler than shit. One of her major life goals was—if she could afford a decent babysitter and escape motherhood for a night—to get high at Nightmare Mansion, hoping to see the ghosts.

"What ghost sightings have I missed?" Her eyes settled on Marci a moment, but she didn't say anything.

"None," Cameo said. "But our big Bonding Weekend house party is coming up."

Tequila Sheila was ecstatic. "I can't wait."

"Yeah," Muriel put in. "Come join our world of wild partying, dancing, and ghosts. There'll even be inter-magical romance."

"The Darkened and the Estranged get together, huh?"

"You know it."

"We also have a kidnapping to solve," Cameo said, immediately sorry she'd said a word, based on the withering looks.

"It's nothing," Snow said dismissively. "Even if you don't come to the house, go see our show. The battle of the bands is going to be like a cowboy showdown. Or a Japanese horror flick. We're going to blow away Felicity, musically and magically."

Brice scoffed. "You guys want life to be a soap opera. I think this whole Bonding Weekend thing is a load of shit."

"That's because you're a dork," Cameo fired back. "You need to get laid."

"I don't need anything but to be left alone." He stormed off to the bathroom.

Snow made a gesture like he was brushing away a fly. They pattered back and forth with Tequila Sheila a few more minutes before she scribbled their order and darted off to another table.

Snow turned to Marci, shaking his head ruefully. "I wonder

how Jake got in this mess."

"He usually walks into it. He just seems to love trouble."

"Where do you think he is? Tied up in a hotel somewhere?"

She shook her head. "He sent one more thought to me I haven't mentioned: *big pink house*. Does that mean anything to you?"

Snow's eyes shifted about searchingly and then grew wide with stark realization. "He's talking about the fucking drag queen's house, that crazy old man who tries to play sugar daddy to the strippers. Josephine was living with him, doing bondage work in a dungeon room there."

Marci snapped her fingers. "That's right. Jake was telling me about it. Do you know where it is?"

"Fuck. I never asked. You'll find it in due time, I'm sure. I wouldn't worry about Felicity killing him because he's too valuable. He's probably partying with her."

"I think it's time to crash Felicity's party."

"Yeah. I have the feeling she's the reason I'm so hot and bothered. When I catch her, I might just fuck her to death."

"We'll have to get Jake back by the time of the show," Cameo said. "Then the Bonding Weekend party will really start."

"Ah, victory..." Muriel smiled. "I just want to win the battle of the bands and then read a good book. All of you can run around like fools."

Brice came back, overhearing the last snippet of conversation. "I think this weekend could mean the end of some lives."

"Oh, doomsayer." Cameo laughed. "You're going out with me this weekend even if I have to drag you along."

"You two together?" Muriel scoffed. "That's scary."

Snow hummed the theme to *Dark Shadows* as Brice glowered at them all.

***

Atlanta was another day closer to Bonding Weekend, and Felicity felt her plans coming together. As dusk approached, she strolled through the murdered drag queen's house, lighting candles. She texted back and forth with Thorn until the terms of their agreement were satisfactory to both parties.

She lowered her phone and took a deep sip from a red wine

glass. A night was being ushered in, holding great purpose.

The debauchery in the house had cooled to mulling and plotting. Minstrel played a dark hypnotic piece, nimble fingers dancing while books and candles floated around him.

Heathen and Aurora had already hit the streets, looking for love or a fight, whichever came first. Felicity's sex quest wouldn't start until she'd explored this house.

She pulled another book from a tall bookcase, nodding in approval. "These are very old spell books that he acquired. They must have come from Europe. Rare. Very costly."

Minstrel gazed over at the rocking chair where the old man had turned to ash. "He was quite erudite. We really should bury our little scholar."

"No. His ashes should be used for spells."

"I didn't think of that."

"By the way, Josephine shared a little secret with me. Look at what I found behind these books on Marquis de Sade, Houdini, Cabalistic magic, and Sadomasochism."

She released a latch behind a polished bookcase, pushing it open to reveal a sex parlor. Inside was an X-frame, altars festooned with straps, ceilings hung with chains. On a pedestal rested a sex magic grimoire.

She ran her fingers through the ashes on the chair. "There was demon magic in his veins but not enough to bring about his Darkening. He was obsessed with becoming a Caster, but it was pointless. He couldn't transcend the human condition."

Minstrel nodded ruefully. "And yet so many of us see our condition as a curse. We're deviates God won't recognize. It's such a pity. I love my eternal life, making love, playing music, casting magic. What else could ever matter to my crazy heart?"

"We love you, fool that you are. I will be as lighthearted as you, once I find Josephine's journals."

He played a final flourish. "There's no telling who has them. Jake could've given them to anybody."

"I'll find them," she whispered, floating off like a ghost.

Jake was listening to this as he practiced music in a library room lined with leather tomes of insanely esoteric subject matter. The dog was curled asleep next to his keyboard. If he tried to escape, the pooch would morph into a drooling ravenous nightmare.

Nevertheless, he had to roll his psychic dice. It was telepathic risk time. He sensed Marci had gotten his last message even though she was dealing with Dark Lust. She was going to kill him for having sex with Josephine.

He threw out another message: *She's coming after you...the journals...trapped at pink house.*

The dog woke, growling, and then went back to sleep.

Jake took a deep breath to still his racing heart.

Chapter Twenty-Seven

Moonshine was a fun-loving person with a lot of country spirit. She was a sexy girl in her Daisy Duke shorts, but could she ever cook like Mama.

The smell of turnip greens boiling in an old pot and cornbread baking in a cast iron skillet filled the loft apartment. She stirred garlic into the mashed potatoes as she gazed down at the Oakland Cemetery through the wall-length windows. A gothic wedding was taking place near Margaret Mitchell's grave. Marci wondered whether the *Gone with the Wind* author could cook like her partner.

"It's almost time to chow down," Moonshine announced. She was frying up pork chops and had pulled a squash casserole out of the oven—home cooked ecstasy.

"I feel like I live on a farm," Marci said.

Zowie's battle-loving eyes softened. She was on the verge of tears. "You're doing this for me?"

Moonshine spun around to face her, flinging long honey-colored hair. "You better believe it. And we've got sweet tea, too."

"I love all this, man. Muriel would make fun of me if she knew I wasn't eating just vegetarian stuff. I used to sneak to a country buffet in Cabbage Town."

"You're about to forget all about some Cabbage Town diner dump." She flipped a pork chop, eyes flicking toward Marci, whose expression had darkened. "Are you okay?"

"Jake is trying to reach me." Her eyes narrowed, searchingly. "She's coming...journal...trapped."

Muriel sighed. "He's in some kind of predicament. My guess is that he's been kidnapped. I need to go by *My Hot Sister*. I'll bet that's where all this started."

After eating Moonshine's feast, they went to *My Hot Sister*. A barback had overheard a conversation between Jake and a sexy leather-clad stranger.

"Did Jake leave with her?" Marci asked.

"Yeah. I bet they hit the town. Jake was going to be her *submissive* or some weird shit like that."

"Oh really? What could you tell me about her?"

"She looked like a stripper, long black hair, and she wore leather." He smiled. "Kinda dangerous looking. She kept talking about how great it was to be whole again and play her violin."

Oh, the stripper ghost has returned to the flesh. "Do you have any idea where they may have gone?"

He scowled, thinking hard. "I just heard she was determined to get a bondage collar on him and *show him off.*"

Think, Marci, think. Should I go to the Dungeon next and talk to Hex? On impulse she called Sophia.

"Sophia, Jake's been kidnapped."

Sophia was silent for about thirty seconds as images spread out behind her eyes. "I see a house full of weapons and books. He's there...yeah, against his will." She was silent another moment. "Whoever owned that house is dead. They killed him. And something terrible has happened to his two dogs. They're under a spell."

Two dogs, Marci mused. "The old man who was Josephine's sugar daddy had two Dobermans. Do you know where the house is? I believe I'm looking for a big pink Victorian house."

"Go to *Final Destination*. That's where the old man hung out."

Marci nodded. "Alright, let's go everybody."

***

Marci parked a few blocks from *Final Destination* next to Piedmont Park, the girls turning heads as they moved like cats of prey down the sidewalk. They were ushered into the club like stars, tipping everyone at the door fabulously.

Type O Negative pounded from the speakers, setting the stage for a night of dark sensuality. Strangers made out in shadows and corners. Old friends argued at the bar in front of everybody. Booze flowed, and drama unfolded.

The dance floor was tantamount to a vaudeville sex show. Leather-clad guys danced as though they were a choreographed act while goth girls swayed around them in woozy oblivion. Couples from the mainstream parts of town danced in drunken mockery. Strippers undulated and cavorted on platforms, turning the spectacle into a stage production.

At the main bar, Constance was hanging on Mitch. He was bragging about a huge tip he'd gotten off a local television newscaster lady who'd come in the salon.

When he spotted Marci and the gang, he rushed to them with hugs. "You girls look flawless." Then his face shadowed with concern. "Have you seen Jake?"

"Not recently, but we have a pretty good idea where he is," Marci said, extricating herself from Mitch's effusive embrace. "We need your help. Where is that old drag queen's house?"

He waved at Jazz, who headed over with a pool stick in his hand. "Hi. Where the fuck is Jake? Did he find the girl of his dreams and run off to paradise?"

"I don't think he's in paradise right now," Marci responded. "Do you know about Josephine?"

"Oh yes. He's messing around with one of her friends now."

Leave it to Jake, Marci thought. "We've got reason to believe Jake is at that creepy old man's house where Josephine used to hang out."

Jazz gave a knowing smile, all pearly whites. "The girl he's screwing now would know where that house is."

"She's dancing at *Pulse*," Mitch offered. "Her name is Abbey. I don't know her stage name."

"Okay. We'll pay her a visit."

They all did shots of Grand Marnier together, and then the girls left for the strip club *Pulse*.

Once again, the hunters were treated like royalty. Bartenders came at them like they wanted autographs.

"I feel like we're on the Tonight Show," Zowie said. "Does everyone know you guys are hunters?"

Marci glared at her. "Fuck no. We are a covert operation."

Moonshine grinned, tilting her head. "You'll get used to the attention. It's because there's three of us, and we're all hot. We look like we're a band or something."

"*Charlie's Angels*," Marci interjected. "Or those girls on *Charmed*."

Zowie nodded, impressed. "Yeah. The power of three."

Marci liked how she thought.

They ordered martinis while checking out the scene. The fawning bartender told them Abbey was in the back, but when her set came up, she didn't come out.

"Is there a problem?" Marci asked.

The bartender shrugged.

"Go in the back and tell her we'll pay her two hundred dollars for a table dance."

The bartender whispered the message to a dancer. The girl rushed to the back, looking a tad jealous. Minutes later, Abbey emerged from the dressing room. "Is this about Jake?" she asked, arms folded defensively.

Marci flared a brow, lowering her Martini to the glossy bar. "So, you know he's missing in action."

She sighed heavily, rolling her eyes like a teenager. "I knew something weird was going on. He came here with Josephine about two days ago. It freaked me out. I thought she was...dead. I'll bet they went to that weird old man's house."

"Do you know where it is?" Marci asked.

She nodded. "Right across from Inmann Park. It's this big pink cat-in-the-hat looking gingerbread house."

Marci regarded her speculatively. "Have you been there?"

"Once. It was bizarre. Roman Empire shit and battle axes on the walls. And he has two dogs that scared me to death."

Sophia had nailed it.

"Were sex games the only reason he was interested in her? He seems—"

"Obsessed? It has more to do with magic. He collected all sorts of spooky books. Josephine told me he thought she could awaken some sort of power within him. She always thought he was nuts, but she trusted him. Even after she got an apartment, she went by there constantly. He had a room set up for her. She's probably got stuff over there still."

"I'm hearing this creepy old man's in trouble, too...probably dead."

"You know, I haven't seen him at *Final Destination* the past few nights, but he started hanging out less and less. I guess he kind of had a nervous breakdown when she disappeared. He told me her ghost haunted the place. Who knows? He drank a lot, on top of being nuts."

Intriguing, Marci thought. "What else can you tell us about Josephine?"

Her expression became very guarded. "You need to go see that attorney Peter. He knew all about her...lifestyle."

Marci smirked, nodding. "I need to check with Mr. Playboy, anyway." She texted Peter and then called Dennis, who was babysitting the attorney's house. "Hi, Dennis. How's life at the den of iniquity?"

"Nothing new." Dennis laughed. "I feel like a bored museum curator. Peter called me once from a bar, though. He was *very* drunk. He might do something *crazy*."

She sighed. "We're about to do something crazy, too. It appears the glorious pink drag queen mansion is a lair for Felicity and her coven. We think the bitch is holding Jake there, so we're about to crash the party."

Dennis pursed his lips. "I'm jealous that I don't get to go. My intuition tells me the party you're about to crash is one *hell* of a party."

***

The gang zoomed into Little Five Points in Marci's Miata. After pulling up to the curb next to a Hookah shop, they leaped out and headed up the sidewalk like typical partying night goers. They passed a tattoo parlor, the Yacht Club, and an Indian restaurant.

A potbellied drunk with a *Duck Dynasty* beard gazed their way in wanton awe. Zowie gave him a withering look, so he staggered off, dejected. The three of them ignited male fantasy. They could be spies, assassins, porn stars. Really, they were all three, bound by magic and sisterhood.

The air was redolent of cumin and garlic emanating from the Indian restaurant. The sound of congas from a Latin club across the street infused the night with a sense of exotic festivity. Wind lifted hair off their shoulders as they moved with an easy sexy manner in their leather gear.

They garnered stares when they streamed through a big crowd at a popular southwestern bar and grill hotspot. A brawny girl with cutoff jeans and a bicycle chain bracelet poured them massive Lemon Drop shots with Grey Goose vodka the minute she spotted them.

"Killer shot," Zowie said, licking her lips.

Neon light played over platinum tresses, flowing electric filaments. Her nose stud sparkled like a disco ball. She was like an exotic biochemical creature.

"You know, Marci," Moonshine said. "This could be a trap. Felicity and her crew could be waiting for us."

"They might be waiting, but I bet they aren't ready for us."

"No way," Zowie said, and they punched fists together in unity.

One more round, and then the girls headed back out onto the bustle of the sidewalk where bohemian goods were being hawked. A hippy tarot card reader slapped down cards revealing the future to a high school girl who wanted to know if she should forget her boyfriend and go abroad for college. Skater punks zipped by so fast their trundling wheels sounded like furiously slung bowling balls. Marci tried to remember the last time she went rollerblading as she pulled out into traffic.

She cruised into the neighborhood surrounding Candler Park. McClendon Avenue was lined with Victorian Ginger Bread houses too extravagant for this century, anachronistic grandeur. Interlaced branches of maples and oaks were silhouetted against a moonlit sky. At this time of night, no one was in the park.

She spotted the pink house befitting a Dr. Seuss story. It looked like a house children would love, but she knew the pink house held nightmares.

They leaped over the brick wall. Huge swaying trees threw shadows that evoked the feeling of gothic vampire cinema.

She threw out her mind, searching for Jake. The house was warded to block psychic invasion, but she believed she vaguely sensed him.

That's when they were enveloped in dark magic.

"Oh fuck, look up," Moonshine said.

Winged beasts were perched atop the house, monstrosities of myth. The devil dogs bounded downward as though to protect the gates of hell.

Marci slung two swirling spheres of light at the front door. She felt the resistance of wards, but her magic was stronger, shattering the wood. Rushing past the colonnaded porch, she bounded into the foyer, the others following suit.

They were at the head of the staircase when scrawled symbols flashed on the floor like pinball machine lights, and the foyer became a stage of illusions. Walls vanished. The hallway stretched to nightmarish length.

And then the girls saw Felicity for the first time. Her eerie beauty, a place where horror and exotica met, was breathtaking.

"Welcome to my sex mansion." The voice came from all around them like the call of a mothership to a destroyed city, echoing throughout the house, alien and droid.

The illusion vanished, and then a torrent of spirits emerged from the walls like demons, flying at them with such force they were thrown to the floor.

They lay there watching in awe as the ghosts raced around, unleashed. Nebulous faces depicted pain, fury, and menace with chilling eloquence. She even spotted the hateful gazes of children, murdered maybe, who would love to see everyone die with them.

From deep in the house, Marci heard wickedly frantic piano playing. It sounded just like what Jake would play when he was drunk. The crazed music set the tone for the ghostly frenzy.

That's Jake, Marci thought. *He's alive. And he'll play that very same music onstage with Felicity if we don't save him.*

They attempted to charge down the hallway from which Jake's drunken ululations could be heard, but the spectral storm pitched them out onto the porch as though vomited from the maw of the house.

They thought of going back in, but the hell beasts perched on the steep gables of the spirit-infested storybook house were already bounding downward, fangs bared.

They rushed for the brick wall and leaped over.

"Let's go back," Zowie exclaimed in frustration. "I'll have both heads of those devil dogs." Her sword rang as she slid it free from a studded-leather back harness.

Marci nodded no emphatically. "There's no way to beat her at this illusion game, but he's safe. They need him for the big concert, but, believe you me, I plan on being the show stopper."

Chapter Twenty-Eight

Friday finally arrived—the first official night of Bonding Weekend. It epitomized being young and enchanted, closing chasms between the Darkened and Estranged centuries old. Many would share carnal ecstasy befitting a forbidden drug, but was not forbidden love really the same?

The nexus for this wild time in Midtown was Piedmont Park. Bands played. Leather-clad girls danced in cabarets, doing sword fights and juggling balls of illusory flame. On one stage, a girl writhed while illusory snakes slithered over her. A telekinetic lifted lions into the air, along with Ferraris.

Around the stages, tents were set up for selling amulets, grimoires, potions, and artwork. Tarot card readers told hard truths to those who'd listen and told teenagers exaggerated stories of money, college glory, and sexual adventure. Tattoo artists created ink that could protect a person from bad spirits.

Prostitution ran amuck, particularly in the gay bars surrounding the park. Drugs ran riot. Most of it was just for fun and thrills, but serious business lay behind the scene in terms of power and sex. Some became sex gods, drug lords, and rock icons while others were ruined.

Back at Nightmare Mansion, Cameo couldn't wait to begin a night she hoped would never end. She grabbed Brice by the hand. He rolled his eyes as she led him off the porch. They raced off like eloping lovers, runaway Romeo and Juliet.

For Cameo, normally into glitter, sex was the color of black. She wore a little black dress and patent leather boots, fishnet hose, glitter on her face, eyes darkened with Kohl. Brice wore a black leather coat over a dark grey turtleneck with designer black jeans and lace-up boots, the svelte hipster.

They hit dive bars first, dropping by *The Escape* where they were *oohed* and *ahhed* over by their buddies before heading to

Midtown. There was a sprawl of clubs that would be teeming with Darkened looking for the pleasure of Estranged love, but the proper place to start seemed to be *Paramour*.

They slipped out of a cab on Crescent Ave and came across like the sexy scandalous children of corrupt politicians, the kind tabloids chased, shaking hands and giving hugs. It was all social artifice covering up deep dark sexual motives.

The attention was all very nice, but that was the whole problem—it was all just very nice. No magic could run wild in this situation of social protocol.

Cameo felt like a prom queen who wanted to get rid of her handsome but boring date to quench her night passions with someone dangerous. Brice, despite his looks and charms, was nothing but a place of safe co-dependency. She wanted to go on a true hunt.

Brice felt much the same. She could be his sister. For this night to be any fun, filled with crazy stories they could share, it needed spontaneity free of guilt or obligation.

They ordered drinks on a terrace overlooking the city and talked briefly about who they'd like to meet.

"You need to find someone who'll tie you up and scare you a little bit," Cameo said, sipping an Expresso-tini. "You've been bored for too long."

He shrugged. "I'd just like to find someone like you."

"Now that's really boring." She laughed. "Find a girl who's nothing like me. I want stories when we return to the house."

"Stories?"

Suddenly Cameo pulled Brice to her and kissed him deeply, leaving him in a state of shock. "I'm going. Don't just sit here and sulk like a dork."

She headed to *The Dungeon*. Every perverted story in her mind could find its first sentences in this birthplace of dark fantasy. Even gay guys ogled her as she weaved her way to the bar, all that blond hair thrown over one shoulder. Here the ripe debutante waited and watched.

Brice had slipped in behind her furtively, hiding in a crowded corner. Truth be told, he didn't want anyone. He just wanted to see where the night would take Cameo.

***

Heathen had hit the streets sooner than anyone else. Like some gothic imp born of Dionysus' imagination, sex had never been anything but a game. He didn't need a festival to orchestrate a night of sex-capades.

Still, he had goals for the weekend. A three-way with Felicity was an unrequited fantasy. Oh, she'd do it. He just needed to find a third party.

Hours of trawling had brought him to *The Dungeon*. Gays came up to him, offering drinks and their beds. His lust was running high, but not for boys. He rarely swung that way, but occasionally a guy would fit the night's script.

He was almost ready to give up for the evening when he spotted Cameo, giving off magic-pheromones that drew him straight to her.

***

Cameo loved gay bars. It meant cooler people, stiffer drinks, and better music. She liked misfits, people living on the dark side of life who don't belong in mainstream reality. Men who traded power-ties and suits for whips and harnesses...

She wouldn't even mind hanging out with a gay guy tonight. Sometimes they appreciated a beautiful girl more than these straight baboons she met with no charm or wit. And certainly no fashion sense.

Still, she needed to get laid.

The music played as she drank and waited for someone to make her feel like a gorgeous plaything.

***

Heathen watched her for a while, a predator, a lover, a desperate soul. He needed her as much as she might possibly want him.

The fragileness of this situation drove him crazy with exhilaration. Could he capture her heart? When he came up to her, would he see her eyes come alive with his reflection in them? Oh, Heathen, lean tattooed body covered in leather and mesh, ready to shatter like glass when beheld by her.

He commenced the journey across the bar, every slow motion

step a major life decision. He was counting on having a single cosmic point in time when the stars were aligned in his favor.

Taking a deep breath, he touched her shoulder. He pulsed with her magic. "You could be my answer," he said simply. "We could fill each other's hearts and souls with magic."

For a moment, she took him in. The possibilities were endless with someone so gothic but tough. He could be her *Anti-Christ Superstar*, the duality of glamour and evil embodied.

"I've never seen you before," she said warily, flaring an eyebrow. "Are you new in town, cowboy?"

"I'm used to roaming, so I'm new to any town," he said. "I've only recently joined a coven. Regardless of what my coven leader is after, I'm only after lust and adventure. I believe in the pleasure principle. What else is there?"

Now her curiosity was truly aroused. "Just who is your coven leader?"

"I can only tell you she's a violinist."

Violinist? Was he talking about Felicity? "I'm Cameo. What's your name?"

"Heathen."

Even his name sounds sinful. She drew back a moment, assessing him. How could she turn him down? So beautiful and sleek. And she loved his spirit and attitude—a wild animal roving the night.

She was so aroused. Her nipples tingled as her skin rippled with his magic. This was like being high—no, better. The sex would be out of this world.

She had to tell Muriel about this, poor studious girl. Muriel, an erudite enchantress, wanted to wait like some scholarly siren for a Darkened boy to come to the house party she could seduce with meaningful literature before her body took over.

What Muriel needed to do was join the sex quest.

She reached for her cell phone, but Heathen caught her arm. She looked up, and he assailed her mouth with a rough passionate kiss. She threw her arms around him, enthralled by his desire. Magic poured through their bodies in manic circulation, shared eroticism like a storm system.

"Come with me," he whispered. "I'm staying in a beautiful house where I can make all your dreams come true."

She was swooning with Darkened magic. All thoughts of calling anyone were gone.

She just wanted him—the focus of her rapture.

He took her by the hand, and they passed through the crowd together. Her senses were deliciously heightened. The brush of an arm was erotic. The breath of a drunk became the sigh of a lover. The stares of onlookers became gazes of sensual languor. Even the most mundane objects became beautiful in the fascination they stirred within her.

And music...

It was like she'd never heard a sound before.

Her desire to dance endlessly vied with the calling to mad sex. Her skin thrummed with the aural caress of electronic effluvium, her heart racing to catch up with the beat.

He was ahead of her as they walked out the door. There was victory in merely escaping the crowd, their two hearts and desires able to bond, unhindered by loud conversation and commotion.

They were whisked off in a cab as though they'd left a Broadway musical. All of this was just so magical...

"You can be mine forever if you so wish," he promised.

And at that moment there truly wasn't anything else she wanted, just Heathen, her gothic Romeo, forever.

The dead drag queen's house was quite a sight upon arrival. The pink Victorian house astounded her—not just because of its magnificence but because of the spectacle of those coming and going like it was a gingerbread trap house.

Passing through the gates, Cameo felt as though she'd entered some erotic heaven. Even the two dogs, Felicity's new familiars, came at her not like vicious hell gateway guard dogs but loving beasts.

And was there ever wine and carnality to be partaken of in this grand nest of debauchery. The orgiastic scene before her must have come from the mind of Marquis de Sade, but the comical abandonment came closer to being a stage performance for the play *Springtime for Hitler* in *The Producers* movie.

Ah, what a mockery had been made of the poor crazy old man.

Freaks had ransacked his closet, fulfilling every female impersonation fantasy imaginable. Prom queens, Cher look-a-likes, and Gestapo girls pranced around on an insane plateau of feminine glory.

There were even those dancing with mannequins. They howled with banshee laughter, flinging them about, lifeless legs and arms smashing into armoires and china cabinets.

Others had found whips and flails, flogging those who were fucking. Others bounded throughout the house in search of an even greater spectacle. One reveler was so high, he was pouring hot wax on a mannequin strapped to a dungeon room X-frame.

As for sex, the house had become a porn stage of epic scale. Felicity played her viola in serene detachment, the aural magic of the hypnotic tones acting like a sex drug on the wanton revelers. Some fucked on the grand piano while others tangled each other in damask curtains, ripping them from walls with feverish intensity. Someone was even using the coffee table as an altar for bloodletting.

Felicity ceased playing, watching all this like some dark goddess beholding the fall of Sodom and Gomorrah. She smiled in rich delight and secretive knowing when Heathen burst on the scene with Cameo. "Oh, you'll be the first to know."

Her cryptic remark gave Heathen chills. "Know what, my dark mistress?"

"The dungeon room is now much more than mere housing for devices of pleasure and pain."

Heathen grabbed Cameo's hand and drew her into the library, then shut the door behind her. There at a piano sat Jake. He met eyes with her only fleetingly before cutting them away. Swooning on Darkened magic, Cameo did the same, confused by the situation.

"I have created a doorway to the Nephemera with this priceless grimoire." Felicity pressed the tome to her leather corset. "Soon I'll make love to an angel, and my playing will reach unimaginable heights."

Heathen looked stunned. "No one knows if such a place even exists."

"Surely you jest," she said softly. "I feel this beautiful world calling me like a siren."

Felicity led them through the secret bookshelf entrance into the dungeon. She ignored the candlelit submissive being flailed on an altar by a teetering dominant. In their rapture, they ignored her, too.

She drew back a velvet curtain to reveal a huge circle on the wall surrounded by elaborate symbols. "Let's go," she whispered. "Our heaven waits. Open the door for us. The circle can only be used once, so we should consider ourselves very fortunate."

The spell can only be used once, Jake mused. *Great. We're about to get trapped in hell.*

The truth was, though, he was burning with curiosity. Would this be the world all his visions came from—the stuff of his novel? He couldn't wait to see.

"Okay. Let's give this a shot." Jake held his splayed palms to the sigils around the circle, eyes closed, focusing. Incantations rolled like movie credits down the back of his eyelids. As he whispered the arcane words, the symbols flared with light.

The wall dissolved like candle wax to reveal...

Everyone stared in quiet awe for a moment. *Fuck. This is real,* Jake thought, heart racing.

Huge platforms of shiny black rock floated in mist over a bottomless chasm like giant diamonds. Whether they were magical constructs or actual rocks was anybody's guess. These formations served as a bridge to take "new guests" to the other side of the abyss...

And into the Nephemera.

The platforms were laden with burning pillar candles, turning them into floating altars. *That would look cool in my stage show,* Jake thought.

Winged figures perched on craggy outcroppings on both sides of the hellhole abyss. Other winged forms spiraled around the walkway of floating rocks like birds of prey.

Flanking the main bands of obsidian-like platforms were two male angels. They were clad in studded leather, black dusters flapping in the wind of an eternal night. They held swords with runic markings in one hand and pillar candles in the other.

The beings themselves seemed to be made of wax, their pallor vampiric, eyes as black as the rocks beneath them. The candle flame heightened the ethereal yet ghostly horror on their faces.

One angel with blood-red Viking hair spread his enormous

wings and hovered over the platform, sword brandished. Candlelight threw giant Japanese monster movie shadows of this video game avatar over the outcroppings. The creature was a video designer's dream brought to life.

"We are the gatekeepers of the Nephemera. Join our world if you dare," he called to them. "Just remember. Our world even strikes terror in the hearts of angels."

"Dreams can become nightmares here," the other added.

"And pleasure and pain can be one and the same."

There was a dramatic pause, and then they said together, "Enter the realm."

And enter the realm they did. All fear was overridden by an overwhelming sense of quest.

They treaded warily at first. The formations were close together so there was no need to leap from rock to rock like daring heroes, but a fall would be a timeless nightmare plummet through a roiling bed of mist into oblivion. Even Felicity crept along like a crippled woman at first, but their courage and determination grew as they advanced across the formations.

Suddenly, Felicity jumped to a separate floating platform as though taking the stage. She raised her eyes to the timeless acrobatics of guardian angels under a gunmetal grey sky pulsing with colored light. Drawing in a deep breath, she coaxed long dramatic notes from her violin tantamount, in eerie grandeur, to a Sci-fi/horror movie soundtrack.

Jake felt a ragged admiration for the bizarre virtuoso. They were experiencing otherworldly horror straight out of H.P. Lovecraft, and she was detached enough to calmly put music to it.

She loves this place, Jake thought, almost laughing. *Freaky bitch.*

Then like a gothic Joan of Arc, Felicity moved forward, beckoning to them with her glittery silver fingernails. They followed like a cult.

Beyond the final platform, the mist thinned to reveal trees befitting Middle Earth. The huge boughs swayed, old creaking sentinels, watching and waiting. Salty wind blew through the doorway, carrying a racy scent Felicity recognized as wild magic.

Everyone knew this was perhaps the point of no return, but no one seemed to care—especially Felicity. The desire to see this world chronicled in centuries of lore was too great.

Felicity played a manic flourish on her violin, then leaped from the rock. The two lovers followed her like children with eyes of wonder. Jake was last.

Their rite of passage was completed.

Behind them, the chasm of angelic guardians vanished, replaced by a torch-lit beach that would've been the envy of California tourists. It was paradise. Even the apocalyptic sky came across like an erotic light show.

The beach led to a lush forest. Bars lined the edge of the forest, beach beauties cocktailing everywhere. *These girls belong on a cruise ship,* Jake thought as a windswept calendar girl in a pineapple skirt and a lace crop top approached him.

"Are you going into the Forest of Souls?" she asked.

"The Forest of Souls?" he repeated, confused.

"They say spirits haunt those woods. I've even heard stories of demons appearing in human form. It's dangerous. Anyone who goes in there and comes back with pictures of the first wall of the Nine Rings gets to drink free for a week."

Jake laughed. "You get a whole week of drinking for fighting evil spirits and demons, huh? That sounds like an even trade. How did you make it here? You didn't go through a doorway in time, did you?"

"Oh no. That's for you magical types. I took the bridge from New America."

"New America?" Felicity questioned.

"That's what the United States was named after the third world war. This Island is all that's left of what was California, thanks to the bombings and earthquakes. The island holds what was Los Angeles in the old world and another chunk of California. It's big. Anyway, the supernaturals took it over. They say in the middle of the island these angels live in a place called the House of the Fallen. Magic books say God condemned them to exist there. Who knows? You'd have to travel through the nine rings to get to it, but I'm here to make money and have fun, not get killed. Anyway, there are all kinds of magic books written about this place. Creepy spell books call this place the Nephemera, but the official name for it is Little California. Tourists often call it Magic Island or Sin Island because it sounds cool. It's like Hollywood and Alice in Wonderland rolled into one. And is it ever wild there...sex shows and prostitution."

Jake nodded. "I see. Where do you stay if you aren't going into any of the *nine rings*?"

"I've got a hotel room on the coast about a mile down the beach with several of my girlfriends. None of us want to go into the rings because kidnapping is huge. Girls get drawn in by the strip bar scene and all the glitz. They wind up being prostitutes or slaves for sex shows, but they might get to have sex with an angel. I've got to get my courage up."

"So, this island is like Vegas separated into nine rings," Jake said.

"Except there are no codes or ordinances. A castle might be right next to a sex shop. A Victorian house straight out of a monster movie might be next to a strip joint. It's surreal. And there's no real law. Crime lords run it all, so be careful."

They headed toward the forest. A statue of an angel with outstretched wings stood before the trees. It gestured with robed arms at the forest beyond it.

"This is my Eden," Felicity whispered.

"More like the Holy Roman Empire," Cameo said. "Look over the tops of the trees in the far distance. That's a fucking castle."

"I hear rumors of a demon king living there," the girl said, following them. "Like I said, be careful."

Jake gave the castle a hard look. An image flashed through his mind of a figure in a top hat surrounded by tawdry girls. He was no mere demon king, but rather a goth pimp demon god, used to sex and servitude.

Was Jake somehow connected to this demonic mad hatter?

He was astounded. "This forest makes me think of Dante's Inferno, but I don't think Virgil is anywhere to be found."

"Stop speaking of literary classics," Felicity said. "This is no book. This is our destiny."

Once again, she led the way, shadows devouring them. Everyone could feel the forest teeming with spirits.

As they trod over the gnarled roots of towering trees, faint laughter could be heard. The wind picked up, carrying faint whispers. Jake even felt the eerie caress of fingertips brushing over him. One spirit actually tugged at his hair.

Felicity thought of this as paradise. Perhaps it was a dark haunted counterpart, hell's rendering of beauty. Huge menacing trees bore succulent fruit like nothing from their world. Vines boasted enormous flowers radiating moonglow magic. Hovering around them were spectrally diaphanous insects of pulsing alien beauty. These enchanted creatures were nearly spirits themselves.

Heathen reached out and plucked fruit from a thick gnarled creaking bough that should've been the arm of an ogre. He bit into it, swooning with sexual euphoria.

He handed it to Felicity. She took a bite then handed it to Cameo. She took the dripping piece of fruit in both hands and brought it to her mouth as though she were kissing it.

As Cameo lowered the fruit from her candy lips, Felicity thrust her tongue into her mouth. They shared chunks of fruit, tongues entwined.

Cameo dropped her clothes like they were emotional baggage. She was free in this exotic world to live out one of her fantasies—a ménage a trois with two Darkened.

Felicity played her violin as Cameo reached under her velvet skirt to pull off her thong. Heathen hurriedly undressed her as Cameo's tongue went berserk on Felicity's dark mound.

Thick vines, sentient and jealous of the spectacle, joined the orgy, creeping over them, seeking love. Huge flowers blossomed before everyone's eyes, a miracle of magic and nature fused. The three became a work of art brought to life for Jake to behold.

Heightening the eroticism were the spirits watching like voyeurs from dappled shadows. A girl materialized in flowing lace and leather, rushing up to Jake. Her spectral doll face showed great urgency.

"The castle...the Dark Lord is coming for you very soon."

"You must beat him to become a star," whispered another voice from behind him.

Spectral fingers brushed over his lips, caressed his jaw, and ran through his hair. He thought he might have his own orgy if these ravishing spirits reached the physical plane. These girls had no charms, spells, or demons to call flesh, though.

After the promising sexual overture, they vanished to join the forest again, leaving him burdened with wind-laced magic and disappointment.

Oh what drama. Questions spiraled in his mind. Who was in the castle? What was this about beating a Dark Lord to become a star?

The figure in the top hat cavorted in his mind, holding up a scepter with skulls on either end. Then he was gone just like the ghosts.

As for the three-way gang, their collective throes of rapture were torn apart by the echoing roar of distant beasts...

...or maybe not so distant.

Felicity was the first to separate from the snarl of ecstasy. They dressed hurriedly.

"Fuck. We're about to get eaten," Cameo shrieked and then giggled, drunk on sex magic.

"I can soothe the savage beasts," Felicity said, smiling with great relish. Then she played a flashy piece that sent glyphs of magic through the air. "That will hold them at bay."

Of all of them, Heathen looked the most frightened. "How do we get the hell out of here?"

Jake closed his eyes. He felt spirits all over him like panicking forgotten lovers. "The doorway...it's still on the beach."

They headed across the sand. With his Sight, he spotted the shimmering doorway just beyond the crashing waves. Sigils in the ether flashed like fireworks when he leaped through the circle, followed by the entourage.

The chasm awaited them again. This time they encountered two female angels wearing thigh-high boots, vinyl hot shorts, and sword harnesses strapped over leather crop tops with ring zippers. Had they escaped heaven to live the roles of porn stars doubling as hunters? Regardless, they held vigil over the bridge between time.

"We'll see you again, Jake Reece," one said, blond hair spilled over a leather strap.

"Yes, our star will return," the other added, smugly self-assured. She was gazing down into a crystal ball, sword propped on her shoulder.

Riddles-riddles-riddles. Jake was ready to lose his mind. "I'm getting the fuck out of here and never coming back," he called out, and he was met with quiet knowing smiles.

His outcry was completely lost in Felicity's cosmic world. "I hope to be by your side," she whispered, and that scared him more than the cryptic remarks of the sexy winged sentinels.

They all leaped from the last candle-laden platform and landed in the sex dungeon. With sex magic thrumming in their veins, they rushed out of the dungeon and into the library. They felt like deities that pagan girls would dance around in a sex rite.

There Minstrel stood, astounded. Felicity spoke to him alone.

"Heathen found the beautiful young blond while he was trawling the streets. How do I tell him that I wish she were my thrall?"

"My dear mistress, she doesn't need to be a thrall. She needs to be held for ransom. She's in Snow's coven, and he's the guitarist in Dark Promise."

"And we could use her to get Josephine's journals."

"Why not?"

"Oh, the enormous possibilities." She gasped, raising her violin. "Great sex makes me want to play violin. Everyone get ready for rehearsal."

From the shadows of the candlelit library, Josephine materialized, pushing Jake on a desk to ravage him. "I would have gone with you, but the angels would never let me go over. I'm not supposed to be in this world at all, which is why I must love you while I can."

And then they had mad sex. As he thrust into her, all he could think of was how much her desperation sounded like Charm's. The island, call it what they want, was a glorified prison without chains.

Jake was soaked in the sweat of ghost sex when rehearsal began. High on dark magic, Jake improvised wildly like a demon freed to play once again. He weaved piano lines through the virtuoso chops of violin as though possessed by Litz.

Cameo twirled to the music, betrayer ballerina, unaware of the painful irony of this crazed rehearsal.

If only Snow knew she was there, dancing her heart out to the music of Darkened enemies and the kidnapped singer he swore he'd protect.

***

Snow and Muriel were rehearsing down in the studio when

Brice arrived in a manic scramble as though monsters were chasing him.

"Oh, it's our drummer," Snow said archly. "We'd hate for you to stop trick or treating on account of us and our stupid little rock group."

"Where is Cameo?" Muriel asked.

"She met a guy and ran off and left me," Brice said, resentment in his voice. "I followed her to this big funky psychedelic house." He shrugged. "I guess there's a party going on there. She was just wild about this guy she met. She ran off with him like she wouldn't care if she ever came home again."

Snow snapped his head toward Muriel, rolling his eyes. "We should've forbidden her from going "boy shopping" until after the show. This whole bonding thing is going to make her too irresponsible and reckless."

"I hope she's not in trouble. She's not answering her phone," Brice said.

Snow gave him a weary look. "You know that doesn't mean anything." Then his expression darkened. "Wait a minute. Where was this house?"

"Grant Park. This demented pink house."

"Oh no. That's where Marci and her girls were attacked. Felicity has taken over that house." He quickly called Marci. She picked right up. "Hey, gorgeous, I've got bad news."

"Let me guess. Jake's running for governor."

"No. We believe Felicity has Cameo now, too."

Marci cursed under her breath. "You watch. Felicity will have them both in her show. She'd better make the most of it because it's the only show she'll do with them. *Ever*."

Chapter Twenty-Nine

Ten bands participated in the Bonding Weekend battle of the bands contest at Piedmont Park that Saturday. A panel of judges sat before the concert stage. There would be a grand prize, based on music and spectacle of illusion.

The first act was a progressive/speed-metal band that doled out double bass drum fury as illusions of dragons roared over the stage. The lyrics, sung with banshee grandiosity, were high-flown and heraldic. They should've done the soundtrack for the movie *300 AD*.

The next few bands were mediocre at best. The showing for these bands was sparse, but as nightfall came, the crowd thickened with fans of Dire Portent and Dark Promise. There were also a lot of Lost Angel fans arriving, mostly girls, who wanted to know what the hell had happened to Jake.

Marci searched through the crowd, hoping to spot him, maybe hiding in some clever way, but it was pointless. He wouldn't escape Felicity that easy.

The lights went down for Dark Promise, and her thoughts went back to the Lost Angel show. What a night. Jake was on the verge of getting signed. Now he was in the hands of enemies.

Still, the show must go on. Snow's ego couldn't handle canceling their show over Jake.

And who could blame him? Even without Jake, they were far better than the bands before them. They'd made some calls and found a dancing girl and keyboard player to fill in for the missing members.

The Dark Promise show was met by a roaring crowd. The stage illusion spells were unbelievable. Roiling orbs of light exploded like fireworks, sparks raining down on hovering apparitions that morphed into monsters and then band members.

The music started with a song called *Statuary Shadows*.

Classical piano ushered in a power chord slam, and then Muriel sang of introspective midnight cemetery strolls, a raven her only company. Lush sheets of synthesizer sound covered Snow's chunky riff like mist. Muriel's bass line was a brooding plod, pinning down Brice's complex syncopated rhythms. The ensemble effect was beautifully morose but hard hitting.

The dancer girl swayed and twirled, streaks of glittery stardust trailing behind her. She held a roiling sphere of light in her hands. The sphere held scenes of seedy neon nights as though it were a crystal ball foretelling a future of dark addiction.

Spectral ribbons rose from the spheres, video ghosts, developing into erotica and sweaty dance floor scenes. The visual effluvium swirled over the drummer's throne, wreathing around Brice as he pounded out a thunderous beat and trundling cascades of percussive sound.

The goth crowd moved up front. They thrived on the ethereal feel of the music. Many mimicked the dancer, some wanting to know where Cameo was. Nevertheless, they had the largest crowd so far.

The judges were very impressed. Marci was certain they'd still win the contest.

She was searching through the crowd again for a sighting of Jake when she spotted Cameo, a gorgeous goth hoodlum at her side.

As she forced her way through the crowd toward them, Heathen spotted her with druggy eyes, nudging Cameo. The cosmo-blonde waved languorously, oblivious to Marci's sense of urgency.

"He's with meee," she crooned in ecstasy when Marci rushed up to them. "Isn't he beautiful?"

Marci's eyes shot from her to the pretty punk. Cameo wasn't in her right mind, addled on sex magic.

It took everything for Marci not to grab her and shake her. "They're looking for you. They had to do the show without you."

"She's one of us now," Heathen said smugly, running a silver ringed thumb over the hollow of her glitter-coated throat.

"Snow doesn't need me," she said with bitter resolve, eyes glazed. "He never needed me."

"You've lost your mind," Marci said. "You need to get back

to the house before the night is over."

"This night will never be over," Heathen assured her. "She will be with me forever." Then they stormed off indignantly.

In frustration, Marci returned to the stage to watch the rest of the show. There was a long encore ending with a girl in white riding a black stallion through a forest. To great applause they left the stage before the illusion faded away.

Now it was time for Dire Portent to come on.

The lights went down, and a robed monk-like figure went about the stage, lighting candles. With each new burning wick, a glyph flashed on the stage.

Finally seven candles burned. Two figures joined Felicity and raised their bows. Glyphs on the violins flashed, and the symbols on the stage pulsed with life.

Felicity took her place behind a viola and then spotlights shot down to reveal first her, then Minstrel, and then finally Josephine.

Wearing a corset and a skirt of flowing black, Felicity coaxed long smooth notes from her instrument. Stage triggers gave birth to illusory scenes of gypsies and medieval bondage. Then Minstrel and Josephine weaved intricate lines around her playing. The debauchery of Marquis de Sade met symphonic grace through Minstrel's legato runs. Dark sensuality met virtuosity with Josephine's acrobatic arpeggios.

Plumes of mist rose from stage glyphs, solidifying into the oceanside palisade strolls of ravishing damsels. The scene morphed into a vision of dancing maenads cavorting around a burning pyre, wine skins held high.

Haunting keyboards joined the rich sound. Marci would recognize Jake's playing anywhere. He wore a tight mesh top and lace-up crimson vinyl pants. He did the show justice, flinging his thick mane of hair, crazed with passion. He was a slave to music long before Felicity kidnapped him.

He whispered words of erotica, triggering glyphs inscribed on the keys of a grand piano. As he played frantic trills and runs over racing electronica, illusory porn scenes rose like wraiths over the stage.

Marci moved toward the stage. Now was the time to unfold her plan. Wards would be around the stage, but up top...

Jumbo-trons showed the band's performance to the huge

Piedmont Park crowd. Two screens flanked the stage, a third above it.

She bolted into the shadows of stage lighting, an exotic feral thing, making her way behind the stage. She scrambled up a series of thick wires and metal poles, reaching the top of the screen within seconds. Stage lights threw her shadow dramatically, turning her into a cinematic super heroine poised to strike. When security noticed her, it was way too late.

Marci jumped from the top of the stage, landing next to the piano. Jake, wide eyed, continued to play like mad. The crowd cheered. *This is great!* Was it part of the show? Would she sing with him?

It was an ironic role reversal, Juliet there to save Romeo.

Aurora burst from backstage. She strode in big purposeful steps of fury toward Marci. Her sword sang as she slid it free from a studded harness glinting in stage light.

Was this all orchestrated? This was better than professional wrestling. She looked like a Viking princess warrior out to defend her tribe. *Monday Night Raw* couldn't have done it better.

She swung the sword in furious arcs, Marci leaping and ducking, bounding over the piano in a series of flips. All the while, Jake played, illusions of dirty sex flowing upward in lurid gossamer sheets, mist porn for the masses.

Aurora charged like a lioness around the piano, managing to grab a handful of Marci's hair before she could evade the barbarian babe. She slung Marci across the stage just like a mauled wrestling diva. She skittered and slid into a stack of amplifiers as the trio deftly drew forth dulcet drear with slow measured movements of their bows. It sounded like they were playing a gothic version of a James Bond soundtrack to the stage action.

The crowd loved this extravaganza. What theatrics. *Music meets illusion meets violence.* Felicity's show was the arcane package deal.

"What a show!" Omen laughed from the crowd, knowing the truth. He was relishing every second of this, thrilled he'd stayed in town.

Marci sprang to her feet, gladiator girl bouncing back. The crowd applauded. Her adversary lunged at her, sword poised to impale. Marci leaped and whirled, slinging silver stars right into

Aurora's face.

The Valkyrie screamed, falling from the stage.

On the trio played, the music synced to the action like Pink Floyd's *Dark Side of the Moon* with *The Wizard of Oz*.

Marci raced like a busted cat burglar across the stage, snatching up Jake. Illusions of tossed wet sheets and wild thrusting vanished from the night. The trio played on.

She leaped from the stage, holding on tightly to Jake. They fell into the crowd, tossed about by fans, before falling to the ground.

"Thought you'd drop by, huh?" Jake laughed deliriously.

"Hey, what can I say? I wanted your autograph."

"I should've known you were stalking me."

"You're so intuitive."

Clutching his arm, she led the way through the concert crowd. Her Miata waited on Tenth Street, parked in an alley.

Chapter Thirty

At Peter's playboy house, a good time was underway. The pool was a long stretch of water reflecting shimmering moonlight. Seventies disco played around the swimming pool, retro-hipsters doing lines of blow to Cher and Andy Gibb.

Most of the crowd was Dennis's buddies. The dashing drug dealer had successfully turned Peter's house into a disco night gay club.

Moonshine strolled through a sliding glass door to the pool area. "We would've come in our bikinis if we'd known about this." Marci and Zowie were right behind her.

Dennis sat at a poolside bar, sipping a drink embellished with an umbrella. He should have been in Hawaii. "I'm having a ball holding down the fort, but the real party is at Nightmare Mansion. I'm ready to go. Have you heard from Peter?"

"No, but we have Jake."

Through the bank of sliding glass doors he could be seen sprawled like a torpid frog on a sofa, swigging straight liquor. Dropping the bottle of vodka on the sharp angled glass coffee table, he wiped his mouth like a wino and joined them outside.

"Are you through feeding?" Zowie asked.

"Thanks for all the sympathy. You're a great replacement for China."

Moonshine chuckled. He was right. "Let's all do some shots and get the hell out of here. Trouble could be on the way."

Suddenly, a roaring sound like a mechanical dragon drowned out the disco beat. *Bye-bye Bee Gees. Here comes Omen.*

He screeched through an open gate in a grand entrance like Rob Halford of Judas Priest, sliding to a halt by the pool. From the roof, Aurora lunged, doing a series of flips before landing like a cat poolside. In a whirl of motion, she slung daggers at him that bounced off his burly form, skull and snake tattoos on chunky arms flaring with protective magic.

A mace materialized in his hand. She circled him, sliding a sword free from her back harness. In a bounding leap, she plunged her sword down at him, bent on impaling him. He caught her with the flail, thick chain wrapping around her leg, and hurled her like a bag of trash into the water.

She burst out of the water, furious sun goddess mermaid, and rolled to her feet by the lip of the pool. Sword leading the way, she lunged at him, making wide slashing arcs.

In her reckless rage, she slipped on the wet tile, and that was her fatal mistake. He roared by her, swinging the flail mercilessly, and the spiked ball slammed into her head. She smashed into a cocktail table on the way down to the deck.

There the dead sun girl went nova and turned to ash. Splattered blood spilled poolside sizzled and vanished.

The party people had run for their lives although the fight was over so fast it was like a movie trailer.

The girls stood there, hipshot, watching. Zowie had her sword brandished in case he meant more trouble.

He scoffed like he was spitting tobacco, scorned country boy sound. Then he waved dismissively. "Listen. I'm here to talk. I might have a little information you can use before I leave town."

"Oh really?" they chorused.

"You're looking for a guy named Thorn, right?"

Marci nodded. "Go on."

"I've gotten word he thinks I know too much and plans on having me taken out, so fuck it. Let me help you. I know where his East Atlanta crib is. I've met him there."

Jake regarded him curiously. "I'd love to know what Thorn would have you killed over."

He sighed, lighting a cigarette, laughing a little. "This whole thing is over a punk loser named Benjamin Crow. He was the geek stalking Josephine. She never would've had anything to do with him if he hadn't manipulated her with drugs. He bought some Rapture from Thorn. I still can't believe a hot shot Darkened dealer like that would sell to him, but he gave it to her, and as you know, the shit killed her."

Jake swirled the name Benjamin Crow around in his mind, seeing a shadow-veiled figure going through a book in a panic.

"Okay. Is this the guy who was living here?"

"Yeah, I think so. He was this tortured gamer genius type who never could get off the ground because of a drug problem. Like I said, people who are too smart for their own good wind up being losers."

"Where is he now?" Marci asked.

"In hiding. I know Thorn wants to kill him. He caused a big noise for a wimpy poseur."

Jake was reeling mentally from this info. He didn't know whether to laugh or scream. Poor Josephine, with all her talent, latent power, and *big* plans, fell prey to the fantasies of a gamer dork.

"So where is this crib?" Zowie asked.

"Follow me," he said with a hardy smirk. "I could go for a brew in East Atlanta before I leave town."

Omen led the caravan to East Atlanta. Jake parked his Toyota behind Marci's Miata in the parking lot of a bar called *The Library*. Here one could get drunk and check out literary classics. They did a round of Premiere Anejo tequila shots together, and then Omen gave them the address for Thorn's place.

The bungalow was much like the sketchy spot off Spring Street. It could easily be another crack house, abandoned by Thorn after he'd been there a few months.

Marci rushed onto the porch and slung magic at the door. There were wards, symbols flashing on the porch, but they weren't strong enough to hold back her spell bursts.

She leaped and rolled into the house, thrusting out a barrier of magic, a silver star in the other hand. Crouched by a leather sofa, she waited.

She was met by silence. It was so quiet, the raucous noise of a nearby bar could be heard faintly.

The place was swank. The chic leather furnishings were comparable to Peter's décor. Beautiful paintings of Greek and Roman monuments filled the walls. The house could've been a fine dining Italian restaurant.

Jake and the other girls came in to find Marci inspecting two open briefcases on a coffee table. "This is a fortune in coke...just left out. He was in a hurry to get somewhere."

The singer pressed his fingertips against the suitcases, and an onrush of images filled his mind: sweaty dancers swaying to goth music, candlelit orgies, gargoyles gazing from velvet-lined hallways.

He gasped, opening his eyes. "He's at Ariel's. There's a rave—a big fucking rave. What a perfect place to have the biggest underground Bonding Weekend party."

He called Snow. "Hey, man, I do believe that the rave of all raves is being held at Ariel's."

Snow was silent a moment. "God. That's the secret party I've heard about. Of course. That's perfect for the mother of all grand finale parties. So you're off to the slaughter."

"No time like the present. Plus I wouldn't miss this rave for anything."

"We will keep the party going here until you're back. Cheers." He held up a shot glass of Whistle Pig on his end of the phone line. "I've got some great bourbon waiting on you, so come back alive."

Jake grinned. "And I've got enough coke to kill an elephant, so just you hang tight."

Grabbing a few party favors at QuikTrip, the gang raced off to Ariel's house in the mountains of North Georgia.

***

Benjamin Crow rushed into a downtown Atlanta fleabag motel. He'd been trawling the streets, clinging to his sanity. His Flash T-shirt stunk of booze and body odor, and there was dirt in his dyed shock of black hair from sleeping in a park.

A stoned receptionist with a bull ring and dreads thought he'd seen everything until this haunted goth outcast staggered in the door.

He took the money from the guy's shaking hands, smirking. This was a bona fide nut job. He wasn't sure he should've let him check in here. Oh well.

In the room, ol' Benjie boy tossed the dirty gym bag he was living out of on the bed along with the stained army jacket he'd stolen from a thrift store. He snatched out a bottle of Jim Bean and a grimoire from the bag.

He drank deeply, nectar of the gods, flipping through pages until he found the spell to ward off ghosts.

He uttered the incantation, grasping the amulet he'd bought for big big bucks from an occult shop.

What was he going to do? He couldn't go back to the halfway house in this shape, and Thorn—the devil himself—was after him.

He was a dead man.

All over a fucking girl.

He turned on his portable CD player. *Sweet Sister Mary* by Queensyrche filled the room with eerie flowing choral sound. He reached for the baggy of coke in his coat and made lines on a bedside table.

Despite his gut wrenching anxiety, he tried to think like a survivor. He still had inheritance money. He'd party all night, get some girls—yeah, that escort service—and then he'd leave town. He'd go to California or something. Surely the demon ghost wouldn't follow him there.

Right?

He curled on the bed, eyes flitting around in the dark. The talisman was clutched like a lifelong cherished possession in his hand.

In the bathroom, the reflection of Josephine, a masterpiece of scorn and gothic beauty combined, passed across the cracked mirror. She smiled in it briefly before dissolving into shadows.

Chapter Thirty-One

Marci and the gang's trip down the interstate to Ariel's mansion was like a Six Flags ride to hell. Rave-bound drivers screeched from lane to lane as though driven by a psychotic breakdown. Couples hung out of cars, making out like this was Mardi Gras. There was even sex in a van for interstate voyeurs. The back doors were open like flapping beetle wings to display the live traveling porn show, the van going at a speed meant for the autobahn.

Needless to say, these revelers made it to the rave first.

Upon their arrival, the little town of Wylon was actually quite peaceful. They quickly made it to the long dirt road that led to the sex mansion of arcane secrets.

Marci parked her Miata off the road, watching everything in amused awe. Jake pulled up behind her.

This was the Fat Tuesday's of Bonding Weekend. Sex was everywhere—in the woods, on the statuary, even in the cobblestone driveway leading to the mansion.

Submissives were tied to trees and the robed arms of granite gods. Candle wax ran down torsos in hardening rivulets. Others were flogged into a state of ecstasy.

Others were so high they just wandered lost through the grounds. Dominants found many of them and made pets of them with chains and collars.

Tikki torches were set all over the place, throwing shadows of turrets, steep gables, and vine hung oriels over the mythological statuary surrounding the house.

The water fountain in front featured two lovers fused eternally. Torch flame was brilliantly reflected off the water's surface, turning this monument into a blazing pyre meant for damned witches of the Inquisition.

The great arched doors to the house were open, and raucous

partying could be heard deep within it. There was no security or cover charges. This party was as underground as it got.

"There's not even any electricity," Jake said, gazing at the house.

"Abandon all hope ye who enter here," Marci whispered, quoting from Dante's *Divine Comedy*. "Why didn't she just call the place Ariel's Inferno?"

"I know," he said. "Remember how she has the place divided into heaven, hell, and purgatory? Those sex fantasy rooms are hard to forget."

"I sure haven't forgotten it," Moonshine said.

"You guys stop reminiscing," Zowie said, sliding her sword free from a back sheath. "Let's go. I've never seen the place. I feel deprived."

They followed her through the doorway into a foyer lit with tea candles spread everywhere. It was as though trolls lived here now. Elegant portraits of Ariel flickered in the trap house light.

The gang strode down a long hallway lined with velvet flocking, gargoyle sconces watching them. After a few shadowy twists and turns they reached the main dance chamber. *Inferno* was inscribed in calligraphy above the arched entranceway. This was the heart of the party.

Jake recognized the pounding ethereal symphonic metal of Night Wish when he entered the room, lush regal keyboards wrapped around sinister sexy riffing. A big crowd filled the dance floor, but they weren't dancing—they were watching a spectacle. The gang jostled through the crowd to discover the most bizarre sex show ever.

There was a bed in the middle of the dance floor with lovers taking their turn with Ariel.

She was flesh.

Nearly.

Above her, Felicity played her violin, glyphs of magic swirling over the bed.

Minstrel had a front row seat, watching the spectacle in horrid disbelief. "Felicity used a seduction spell to conjure Ariel for a sex rite like she used on Josephine to bring her back to fleshly form. Even an angry ghost like Ariel can't turn down a chance to be whole again."

"Why would they want to bring back Ariel?" Jake asked.

"Her blood," a voice called behind him. It was Heathen with his arm around Cameo. "Felicity wants her blood to make more Rapture with Thorn. She's already high on shit Thorn made with his own blood to sell here."

"Where is Thorn?"

"He's staying at a motel near here called the Do Drop Inn. There's a hole in the wall bar in front of it where they might be partying if the place is still open this late."

Jake's eyes passed over the faces of the entourage. "If she takes Rapture made with Ariel's blood she'll finish losing her mind. And then Thorn will start selling it on the streets. If we don't stop him, partiers are going to die."

Heathen made a vague dismissive gesture. "I'm out of this mess. Cameo and I are leaving town."

Marci gave Cameo a hard look of appraisal, eyebrows drawn. "You need to tell Snow you're running off."

Cameo shrugged, cutting her eyes away.

"She's going to call him," Heathen assured them. "She just needs to get her head straight. We both do." He pointed down a hallway. "The guy that threw this party is crazy, too. You all need to run before he finds you."

Suddenly, swords and all sort of nasty magical weapons were directed at them. It was none other than the council of the Darkened.

"I think we should have a little fun," a short robed figure said.

"I'm putting my money on the four of them!" a voice screeched from the crowd, spurring on an uproar of applause.

***

A big betting crowd gathered in the *Purgatorio* chamber. The rabble eagerly awaited the first battle.

The three girls and Jake were all being guarded in separate fantasy rooms at the top of two winding magnificent staircases. In these rooms of bondage games and role playing, they imagined what horror awaited them.

Through huge arched doors came a monstrosity, part scorpion, part man. The half beast hybrid swung its tail like a club. This creature was encircled by men with swords.

"We brought this shape shifter all the way from the Nephemera just for these games," a Darkened council member told Jake as he was led down a grand staircase to the crowded floor. "The hunter was paid a handsome sum to capture him, so we need your victory. We've bet on you."

His eyes shot across the chamber to his brand new buddy. Oh fuck.

"He's a shape shifter?"

The councilman chuckled. "They take a drug in that world called Morphoria. It causes them to morph into whatever creature's venom or blood was used to make the drug. Extremely addictive. It turns them into...monsters."

He was dragged through the crowd into a huge circle surrounded by magical wards. The crowd gathered around it, along with luminaries of the magical world sitting on velvet sofas, settees, and wingback chairs. The place had become a small arena for bored Darkened royalty to watch death.

Jake was forced into the circle, wards on the hardwood floor flashing behind him. He gazed at the thing across from him and groaned. *You have got to be fucking kidding me.*

The creature charged at him, the crowd roaring, its tail dripping venom. The thing swung its tail, pimp slapping him across the circle. It laughed like a drunken ogre, looking toward the crowd for approval.

The singer formed a spellburst in his hand, but before he could sling the spell, the tail curled around him like a python.

The stinger was in his face, giant thorn, venom oozing like melting wax. *Oh shit.* The creature tossed him like he was a ragdoll toward the crowd, raising its arms victoriously. Wards crackled. Jake screamed from the Darkened jolt of magic and staggered forward.

What am I going to fucking do? There was no way to win a physical confrontation with this abomination. On impulse, he squatted, amulet in his grasp. "Rise," he whispered, and his spirit separated from his flesh.

An apparition of Jake landed in front of the scorpion man. The thing swung its tail at him, stinger ripping through spectral gossamer. The hybrid being ran about in a frustrated mania, thrashing its tail as Jake appeared and vanished.

Jake became calmly logical. What could he do here? An emperor of Rome wanted to see a lion devour a victim. A king or queen wanted to see an opponent get beheaded.

But in this case...

He threw all of his magic into an onsurge of spectral force. He slammed into the creature's tail. The stinger broke away.

In semi-physical form, he caught the detached stinger in midair to great applause.

Now what? He thought of Medusa being defeated by seeing herself in a mirror. Narcissus was turned to stone from gazing at himself in a lake.

Did this thing need a taste of its own poison?

Plummeting downward, he thrust the stinger into the torso of the creature. The thing shrieked as it flailed its blunted tail. It collapsed, writhing in its death throes, pulsing with inner light.

Jake rushed back to his body. There he was curled on the floor with the stinger in his grasp, the prize from his projected form.

The roar that ensued belonged to a Roman coliseum. A robed council member entered the circle, gazing down at the stinger. It, too, turned to ash.

"You may be a rock singer extraordinaire, but you are also a clever resourceful fighter," the Darkened leader said with a raspy reptilian voice. "You have beaten the odds and made me a fortune. How would you like to be set free so you can enjoy the rest of your evening?"

"How about releasing my friends?"

He came up close to Jake, a thick monarchal finger extended. "The girls aren't up against what you just faced. Their matches are busy work while you take care of a little task."

"What is it?"

"You need to take care of Thorn."

"This is over Rapture, isn't it?"

The hooded figure shook his head. "He had no business using our grimoire recipe to mass produce such a dangerous drug. Bring me all the dope you can find and that damn fur coat to prove you killed him. Then I'll release your friends. Good luck with your band if you live through this."

Bonding Weekend

***

The pilgrimage to the mansion had reached epic proportions. Jake made his way across the mansion grounds, feeling like he was in Times Square. Goth girls rushed up to him, wanting his autograph and much more. Drunks ran into him. Spirits called his name.

He beheld a fascinating vaudeville of sex shows as he rushed toward the gates of this infernal place and ran to his Toyota. As he pulled onto the dirt road, hipsters passed him on their way to the mansion. They were unaware of watchful specters materializing around them.

Ghosts of vixens and vagrants floated up to the car as he gained speed. They were either pleading with him or wanting to divulge some secret. Were they murdered here by Ariel? Were they just lonely? One glitter goth was actually beating on the car as Jake hit the gas pedal, leaving the ghost scene behind.

"Don't leave us," he heard on the wind.

That was all he needed to stomp the accelerator and get the dirt road of the damned behind him.

Back in town, he found the bar that fronted the motel where Thorn was supposedly staying. The honky-tonk joint was called *Pierson's Place.*

He parked behind a convenience store down the road and ambled toward the bar in the role of small-town drifter.

Would the bar even be open this late? With all that was going on in town, there was a good chance. Thorn may have even paid off a bar owner to stay open later.

Jake rounded a bend, and *Pierson's* lit neon sign came into view. Beneath it was a marquee. The country band Rough House was playing next Friday.

The lights were on in the bar, and romping music played on a jukebox. Jake peered through the glass window to behold a character he felt certain was Thorn. The guy belonged in the panels of a Marvel comic. He swept his fur coat back and forth, gesticulating flamboyantly, thorn-tattooed bald head gleaming in the ceiling lights. He had his imperious beak of a nose in the air, rapturously lost in laughter and rowdy discourse with a table of hot country girls in cutoff jeans and crop tops.

A bleach-blond waitress who could've been hooking at a truck stop brought a tray of shots to the table. Thorn tossed big bills on the tray like money was nothing. Jake recognized the old sugar daddy song on the jukebox as *Come to Papa* by Bob Seger. For this party scene, the song was apropos.

Jake swung the door open and their eyes met. Time stopped. All that mattered to the universe was the showdown.

It was on.

Jake slung telekinetic force at Thorn, hurling him over a pool table. His flashy nemesis sprang to his feet, thrusting bejeweled hands at scattered pool balls. They rose in the air and flew across the bar like a mini-asteroid belt.

Jake slung a spell burst at the barrage, shattering them in midair. Shards rained down on cocktail tables, big chunks clattering to the floor.

The girls ran out the door; the bartender hid behind the bar.

Jake was poised for another strike, magic swirling around his fingertips. "Does Batman know you're at large in Gotham City?"

Thorn flared a needle-thin eyebrow. "That's impressive, Mr. Elvis." Thorn scrawled a summoning circle in the pool table felt and made conjuring gestures over it. "But my power is not from any comic book. It's *real*. You're the one in dreamland, and I am about to send you where there are no dreams."

Dark spirits rose in a spectral stream of inky gossamer and surged toward Jake. He leaped over the bar, slinging streaks of magic, whispering a spell. The warded off grotesqueries swirled just beyond the barstools like impatient ghostly boozehounds wanting service. Jake had to think fast—the spell wouldn't last long.

Thorn was running toward the back door when Jake heard a besotted slurring voice behind him. "I reckon I'd go beat the shit out of him with a liquor bottle if I wuz you." It was the bartender hiding behind a huge box of limes. He chugged whiskey in glassy-eyed fear. Jake took one look at the bearded mountain man and—

The liquor bottles...

He thrust splayed hands at the backbar of colored bottles, incanting as he made a slinging motion toward his escaping adversary. The liquor bottles became glass missiles.

Most of them smashed into the walls, but as Thorn reached

the back door, two clobbered him in the back. A fatal third shattered against his head. He was hit with such force his head slammed into the door, cracking the burglar-proof glass. Blood dripped from his mouth as he slid to the floor. The spirits streamed back into the scrawled summoning circle on the pool table in an effluvium of outrage.

Jake leaped over the bar and rush to Thorn's prone form. He tugged the coat off him and darted out the back door. Behind him he heard the bartender applauding.

Okay, what now? He needed to find Thorn's motel room fast and get the dealer's dope.

There was a path beyond a back parking lot that led up a hill to a desolate strip of motel rooms. Next to the strip was a decrepit old house with a flickering *Do Drop Inn* sign hanging from the porch. If lightning had flashed, he probably would've seen Norman Bate's dead mother from *Psycho* in a rocking chair, staring out an upstairs window.

He trudged up the path, expecting escaped lunatics to leap out at him from the surrounding trees. The wind blew and an owl hooted, heralding horror, but nothing emerged from the shadows.

At the top of the hill, he stalked the length of the motel, passed room after room, his senses thrown out to detect magic. Nothing. He headed around back to the rooms on the other side.

He felt the wards right away.

Room 11.

Here we go.

As his fists starred with magical light, Felicity's hellhound pets smashed through the windows. The creatures swooped and dived with all the vengeance of hell. He slung a spellburst at the beasts, but they darted away in demonic aerial grace, his magic dissipating like falling fireworks in the night.

They flew circles over him like vultures, jaws snapping, demon beast slobber dropping and sizzling. They appeared to be plotting his death, the whole idea of it even more terrifying than their appearance.

Crackling magic arced between his hands as he leaped up from the ground. *What do I do? If I run they'll snatch me up like a fucking rabbit.*

The creatures glided upward in tandem, choreographed

monster moves, and then plunged downward. Jake's eyes grew wide in terror but he would not run. *Fuck this.*

Magic rose from his palms, luminous gossamer. He squeezed his eyes shut and threw out the barrier he used when deflecting bullets, a trick Marci taught him in magic training. This wasn't a move of brilliance but survival.

The kamikaze creatures slammed into the barrier, and the amulets around their necks shattered, the dark spell broken. Wings thrashing, the stunned creatures tumbled to the ground, their form morphing between dogs and demons.

Magic swirled around Jake's hands. He conjured orbs of fiery light and like a death-dealing sorcerer threw them at the enraged beasts. Roaring like dragons and writhing in throes of agony, they disintegrated.

Jake gazed at the horrific spectacle of their ashes and then laughed in delirious triumph. *Fuck. I feel like a dragon slayer.*

He caught his breath and went back to the task at hand. Using the fur coat as a blanket over the glass shards, he crawled through the shattered motel window and dropped into room 11. There on the bed lay two suitcases. Opening them, he found several bags of Rapture. He stuffed them into the fur coat pockets, used the door to exit, skirted the motel, and made his way through the surrounding woods toward his car, fur coat now slung over his shoulder like a deer hunter's trophy.

***

Jake felt like Dorothy in *The Wizard of Oz* when he returned from his quest—the fur coat his witch's broomstick. Nobody was outside because everyone was deep in the bowels of the house where rave music pounded like a racing heart.

He rushed up the steps to the porch, and the arched doors swung open. Out came the council and their entourage.

"I take it you knew I was coming," Jake said, breathing heavily. He handed over the fur coat and the dope bags. "Thorn is dead. So are Felicity's guard dogs."

"Oh yes," came a whisper from within a cowl. "Felicity."

Jake would know that voice anywhere—that hideous voice. It was the Darkened councilman who'd made the deal with him.

"She has wandered off into the woods where she will pass

through Rapture's gates of delirium to enter the realm of death." He lowered the cowl, revealing a bald head, fleshy frog face, and a big smirking amphibian mouth. It was as though Gollum had become a gameshow host. "Release the girls," he rasped like a creature from Middle Earth, gesturing imperiously with a fat hand.

From the shadows of the house emerged the three girls. They burst through the council retinue to hug Jake.

"Our hero," Moonshine said, running her fingers through his tousled mane. "In my eyes, you are already a big star."

Zowie shook her head, grinning. "You just never know who's going to be a hero."

The frog man leader gave a loud raspy laugh, hideously robust. "There is money to be made if you get back in the games."

"We ought to be paid for what we've done already," Zowie snapped.

Frog man made a face of exaggerated cartoon sympathy. "I understand." He was handed a stack of hundreds by a tattooed aide standing beside him. "Split this up amongst yourselves."

The leader barked his signature lizard lord laugh as Marci snatched up the money like a pimp.

"We're moving on. It's been real." She gestured for everyone to head toward the gate.

Frog man shrugged. "You've won tonight, Jake, but there is much ahead. You have started a chain of events toward the opening of a door to the Nephemera. Your presence has resonated throughout this island of the future. Friends and enemies from that world will be seeking you for grand and desperate reasons. There is even a prophecy about a performer who rises to fame but must face a great, great demon. You might be that person. You just might need my help one day. So why not come be a part of the festivities inside?"

Jake did his best mocking lizard voice. "Because the festivities inside will get us all killed."

"It is true that discretion is definitely the better part of valor." Frog man watched them leave, his laugh a maniacal shriek.

Jake cranked his Toyota, thrilled with thrum of the old engine. *Ah, new beginnings.*

He was following Marci down the dirt road to freedom when his phone rang. It was Peter.

"I've got the son of a bitch," he barked into the phone.

"Who?"

"Benjamin Crow. Hear him confess for yourself." There was a pause filled with heavy breathing. "You tell Jake what you told me or I'll blow your god damn head off."

"Jake..." A pathetic trembling voice came on the phone. "Josephine used to buy heroin at a trap house across from an abandoned school. She'd take her stash to the playground, get high and write poetry."

"And this school is where?" Jake asked.

"It was so late that night. And I was drunk...nervous about getting caught following her. I-I remember being on Moreland and passing over Memorial Drive. I recall an old church next to the trap house. The homeless slept on the steps like they thought God was coming to pick them up."

An image shot through Jake's mind of sleeping forms covered by the shadow of a cross and then it vanished. Was he seeing the church? A shelter? He needed more to go on.

"Fuck. I can't believe I've just told you this. I think—"

Bang!

Jake's eyes grew wide as he bounced over bumps in the horror house road. "Hey, Benjamin!"

The line went dead.

He called Marci, who'd already reached the highway. "I just got the ultimate *Tales from the Dark Side* phone call."

"What?"

"Get this. Peter was holding that stalker Benjamin hostage. He forced him to tell me what he knew about Josephine's secret sanctuary by gunpoint. I think Peter pulled the trigger."

She scoffed softly. "Well, that's one less loser to worry about while I take a much needed shower." The other girls whooped and hollered in wholehearted agreement.

Chapter Thirty-Two

The gang got motel rooms off the interstate and drank until they collapsed, sleeping hard until late afternoon. They then found a country restaurant where they shoveled bacon, scrambled eggs, and grits into their mouths like starving school children as they traded war stories of scorpion gods and half-lizard barbarians.

Zowie chopped up avocado and egg white (a health nut even in hick land), appraising Jake. "I wonder how much money that councilman won over your victory—ripping the stinger off that son of a bitch and killing it." She swilled rich Jamaican coffee.

He shrugged, tapping a spoon on a coffee cup like he was playing the drums. "I have *no* idea, but even if he'd paid me any to go after Thorn, there's no just compensation for fighting flying devil dogs."

Moonshine smirked, lowering her cup. "You *Beast Slayer*."

The girls laughed.

Jake rolled his eyes then covered his blushing face with his hands.

After going over and over their crazy stories (*Who did what and who shouldn't have done what and what else could we have done?*), they tossed uncounted bills down beside greasy plates and rushed out the door.

A wary waitress who'd listened intently to the bizarre conversations snatched up the money like it was a historical moment. Realizing her sudden windfall, she raised up chunky hands with the twenties fisted in glory, jumped up and down, and howled with glee. Regulars watched her, stunned.

The gang was oblivious to the uproar, ready to get back to Nightmare Mansion for the time of their lives.

Tonight would the final night of Bonding Weekend.

The grand finale of debauchery!

Once they were a few blocks from the house, they all speculated wildly on the upcoming night's events. In ten minutes, they'd be parking just beyond the shadows of the Bone Tree.

It was nightfall, and the crowd at Nightmare Mansion was getting big. The sky was stained with pensive colors. Snow was strumming an acoustic guitar, posing like some American folk hero while Muriel took pictures of him. He was playing *The Milky Way* by The Church.

After snapping the photos, she went back to reading Frankenstein out loud. A group sat around her on the swing and railings.

The front of the house had become a misfit greeting card scene. Candles had been placed all over the wrap-around porch as though to mimic the star-strewn night. Music pulsed from the house: *In the Shadows* by the goth band Dark.

Snow put down his guitar and took up bartending duties at the outside bar. The oval porch booths were filled with revelers. Snow had already started his tricks, glowing martini glasses doing spirals in the air, hovering, doing flips. Jägermeister shots morphed into black serpents trailing along the bar.

When the gang screeched up, a crowd ran down the porch steps to greet them like paparazzi.

"Snow!" Jake laughed, hugging him. "We've got quite a story. Are you interested in a pack of refugees?"

"Are you kidding? You're who everyone is talking about."

The crowd followed Snow back into the house where he continued his showy bartender duties. Liquor morphed into butterflies and collected in a tumbler to become a colorful drink.

"We all want to hear about your great exploits," Snow said. Shots of bourbon became rusty skeleton keys with a flourish of his hand. "Do we have some dead enemies to show for your being late to my party?"

Moonshine patted Jake on the back. "Thorn is most definitely dead. Our boy here saved us all by bringing Thorn's goodies back to the Darkened council."

Marci cleared her throat, nodding ruefully. "We also saw Cameo with the boy-band punk she'd found."

Snow rolled his eyes, laughing. "She'll be back when the guy's sperm runs out...or the drugs run out. I must say I don't appreciate her consorting with the enemy camp, but I doubt she knew what she was doing."

Snow's cell phone rang, the ringtone featuring a snippet from Marilyn Manson's *Heaven Upside Down* CD. It was Dennis. And who did he have with him but Peter. The two were spilling from an Uber out front. "I take it the party has already started," Dennis exclaimed, parading in through the door.

"Oh, a party can never really start here because a party never really ends," Snow said.

Dennis grinned. "A continuum of debauchery."

"Exactly! Come listen to music and drink yourself blind."

The drunken attorney came right at Jake as though he were a forgiving priest. "I didn't shoot him. He grabbed my gun and shot himself. I-I just called the police and left."

Jake handed Peter a glass of McCallan 18. "So what? Nobody cares about that freak. His clues helped us, but I need something more to find Josephine's ashes. Do you know anything about a secret place where Josephine wrote poetry?"

Peter shrugged, drinking deeply. "I never even knew she wrote poetry. I wasn't someone she confided in."

Jake had no problem believing that, his thoughts settling on Abbey. He called her, getting the voice mail. He hung up in resignation. The party was in full swing, and a dead stripper was the last thing on anybody's minds. Everyone was talking about music, sex, and power.

Snow directed his playful barbs at Peter. "Isn't there a song about killing all the attorneys to make the world a better place?" he asked, breaking out more liquor bottles.

"The Eagles, I believe," the drunk attorney answered. "I believe they're right. I'm a dirty dog. I need power."

"It's like my dancing," a stripper sprawled on the sofa said. "I feel like it's what keeps me from being ordinary, yet it's nothing but drama. Why do I want to do it?"

"Magic is the same thing," Muriel said. "It's a curse, yet we love it."

"We are all just who we are," Jake said. "It's like a plot in a book. Nobody planned it. It just *is*." He was going into a philosophical tangent when his phone rang:

"It's me," Abbey said, crying. "I can't take it anymore. The demon will come see me again tonight. I'm tired of the long nights with...*her*. I want to help you find where Josephine is buried."

She showed up with a sketch she made the night she went to the playground with Josephine. She didn't actually draw the playground. She drew an old church made of stone across the street.

The historical gothic edifice looked like something of out *The Hunchback of Notre Dame*. She'd even drawn the homeless sleeping on the steps.

"Oh, this is what Benjamin was talking about," Jake exclaimed in revelation. "I've seen it. It's famous for looking like a medieval church, but it's used by junkies. They call it Junkie Cathedral." He threw back a shot, burning away anxiety. "It's time to put Josephine to rest."

He headed toward the front door without telling anyone his plans.

But they knew.

"Bye, Jake," Marci called out. "Thought you'd go banish that demon all by yourself, huh?"

He looked over his shoulder. "The succubus is going to come to me most likely, wanting sex. I do want to be there for that."

She shrugged, looking hurt.

"I'll be back after I break the demon spell."

Snow was shaking a tumbler. "You better come back alive because a big crowd is coming, and they expect a show. Your old band mates will be here."

"Yeah. We love you," Moonshine shouted as Zowie smirked at her side.

"We all love you," Abbey added softly, wiping her eyes.

He smiled. If he was killed tonight, he wondered if he'd be a popular cult figure. He wanted to die by flying off a bridge in a Porsche or some other glamorous death, but he feared he'd just overdose in a trashy motel one crazy night.

Giving hugs and high-fives, he headed down the porch steps to this secret sanctuary burning for so long within his mind.

***

Jake wasn't certain where the church was on Moreland Avenue, but he felt sure it was a mile or so off Memorial Drive.

Singing along to the *Queen of the Damned* soundtrack he bought in a Little Five Points record store, he passed a rundown Blues bar, a big thrift store, and a homeless shelter with a group of guys propped on a pickup truck. They laughed and smoked. Life was just an object of derision.

Just beyond a wash of neon light from a liquor store, he spotted the ornate old church with its gothic cross high in the air and a rusty bell in a slender tower. All it needed was a gargoyle perched on the spire.

Junkies were hanging out on the steps. What had Benjamin said? It looked like God should come pick them up? Yeah. The dead stalker was right, but there was no abandoned school across the street.

He slowed down to check out the scene, changing his music to New Years Day, *Victim to Villain*, vocalist Ash Costello belting out lyrics of vengeance to pulsing techno-metal. A few hustlers slipped out of streetlight-carved shadows between the church and the trap house to darkly appraise Jake as he cruised to a stop and rolled the window down. "Hey."

"Need something?" one guy asked.

"Is there an abandoned school around here?"

"Yeah. Just go down that road." He pointed at a shadow-shrouded backstreet beyond a small grocery store.

"Got it. Thanks." He drove the backstreet past a block of woods before arriving at a complex of graffiti-riddled brick buildings with shattered windows. He parked at the litter-strewn curb and got out.

From the woods emerged a toothy derelict wearing a knit cap. He smirked. "You ain't goin' in there, are you?"

"I'm looking for something."

"Well, somethin' might find *you*. This place is haunted. There was a fire in one of them buildings. I've seen ghosts of the children. It freaked me the fuck out. Now I won't crash in there, even if I'm desperate."

"Thanks for the warning."

The man just shook his head and kept walking, a book bag bouncing on his back. Jake watched him amble off into the night, a silhouette with a drifter's defeated slouch.

Jake headed warily down a cracked walkway overrun with

weeds. He shivered, sensing spirits, but kept moving. The playground had to be in the middle of these condemned school buildings.

A swing set came into view just as dark magic rolled over him like storm clouds crackling across his flesh. He spotted sigils throbbing with crimson light like angry wounds on the side of a vine-covered building.

Fuck. I'm an idiot. I just walked into a trap.

The ether crackled with the birth of a spell, seeds of Necromancy, swirling sheets of inky darkness coalescing into constructs drawn from a demented mind. Jake's fists starred with magic as spectral light became skeletal beings with hollow eyes burning with the fires of hell. The dead hissed, a demon chorus, the tattered dirty remains of clothing hung on rancid decomposed bodies. Dark blood ran in thick dripping rivulets from toothless rotting mouths.

The school yard was now straight out of *House of the Dead.* He felt certain this was Felicity's artwork.

The creatures shambled toward him, brandishing axes and knives. He slung a spell burst at one, deflecting an axe going end over end toward him. *Oh, this is no fucking video game*, he thought, mind racing near panic. *We aren't scoring game points here.*

He thought how he'd dealt with the scorpion man. It was a huge drain on him to leave his body, but what else could he do?

In spirit form, he shot through the night, doing crazy comet spirals before throwing all his paranormal force into the rotting belly of one zombie. The thing exploded like a bag of trash; splattered guts dissipated in the ether, gore gossamer at its goriest. All the others went down the same way, flailing weapons to no avail.

Soul and flesh once again, he ran to the playground. There in a swing sat a little girl, watching him. Then a dark flowing figure materialized next to her.

It was Josephine. She held open a book of poetry. The ends of her long black tresses pooled on the pages of elegant script, dark secrets captured. Her lip piercing glinted in the moonlight. The dappled moon shadows of windswept leaves danced over her.

She was erotica personified.

"Felicity's magic is still with me," she whispered, but Jake could see her clinging to flesh, life force disappearing.

"I know you want to live, but you're nothing but Felicity's sex slave. That's what Ariel wanted to do to me. There has to be another way."

"But Felicity gave me new life."

"You'll never be free of her," he pressed on. He wanted to reach out to her, but he was afraid she'd reject him.

He gasped as he felt Felicity's magic rippled over him. She separated from the shadows on a partially collapsed walkway and glided toward them—no, floated toward them like an apparition, cosmic hair aloft. She raised her hands high in conjuring fury as lightning raced across the sky.

Jake regarded her in awestruck horror. *She is high out of her fucking mind on Rapture. And her power is jacked up bigtime. She's gonna hit me with all her crazy bitch wrath.*

The wind rushed with biblical force through the school grounds infested with screaming spirits. Felicity had raised a spirit storm.

He attempted to form a protective circle around himself, but there were so many desperation-fueled spirits that he was thrown to the ground. Huge branches came at him like a nightmare phantasmagoria, battering him like a condemned witch.

He thought of leaving his physical body, but what would happen to his spirit in this maelstrom? He was drained and could be torn apart, never to return to the flesh.

"Where is Thorn's grimoire?" Spirits hissed with an accusing fury, flowing ghostly grotesqueries, hags out of *Hamlet*.

"The Rapture recipe," another hissed.

Fuck. All she can think about is more Rapture?

He slung magic at the spirits, repelling them long enough for him to leap up and make a run for the school like all hell was chasing him—and actually, it was.

He flung a petulantly squeaking door open, raced down a long surreal hallway transplanted from the funeral home in *Phantasm*. All the while, he threw spells at the grimy walls, wards to hold back the spirits.

At the other end of the hallway, Josephine materialized. Now he really did feel like it was Labor Day horror movie night at the

Starlight Drive-In. She floated toward him, wearing flowing black, a gothic prom queen gone mad.

"I need you, Jake," she whispered. "Fuck me on a desk like a bad schoolgirl. I need your love...your magic. I-I'm losing my hold on..."

Outside, the spirits watched like voyeurs wanting fleshly pleasure. Josephine slowly dropped her clothes, ghost tease, coming closer...closer...closer. Those eyes, those wounded dark demon eyes. "Don't you want me?"

The wards had no effect on her. She kept coming, slowly, creepy cat.

Felicity's power of illusion and construct realism took on proportions tantamount to world building. She was playing the violin with all her drug-addled virtuosic passion, her imagination running amuck.

The hallway morphed into a velvet-flocked passageway. A room full of needles and beer bottles became a posh den of debauchery. The smell of incense was intoxicating...an overwhelming aphrodisiac.

"This is our heaven," Josephine whispered, reaching out to take his hand.

She led him into a luxurious boudoir and pushed him back on a four-poster bed. She was unbuckling his belt when he decided to take a crazy risk. He sensed the wards around the playground were psychic barriers so strong they blocked Jake's clairvoyant reach. Maybe he could fortify the spell to hold back other paranormal forces.

He pushed Josephine away and made a break for a door at the end of hallway, racing back toward the playground. Spirits rushed at him like an angry wind, a spectral hurricane. He slung spell bursts, knowing his magic wouldn't hold them back long.

Where did Minstrel set the wards? I don't have time for an Easter egg hunt.

He threw out his preternatural senses to the night, a huge tree appearing behind his eyes. *Where? Where? The damn ghosts are waiting to get my ass.*

His eyes went beyond the fenced-in playground area to rest on a huge oak tree next to a crumbled walkway, gnarled roots bulging through crack-heaved concrete. He leaped over the fence to check it out.

There on one of the shards of the sidewalk upheaval was an elaborate spell drawn with chalk. Surrounding it was a pentacle, enclosed by a circle. *Oh yeah, this is where he bound Josephine to the demon.* The spell was complicated and powerful, throwing out a psychic barrier like none other. He had never seen one that could hold back his mind so completely.

Would Minstrel's masterpiece of spellwork embrace his hybrid magic?

Lady Luck, don't fail me now.

Pressing his splayed fingers to the sigil, he uttered an incantation, infusing his magic into the more complex spell orchestrated by Minstrel. He felt the spells dovetail and click together.

A smile of dawning victorious realization spread across his face. *Yeah, man. My spell is live!*

After a few moments of silence, creaking school building doors opened to let Josephine out into the night. *Here comes my girl!* The windswept femme fatale moved like a wary cat toward the playground.

Then she stopped, frowning, moon-shadows playing over her. Tears streamed down her semi-corporeal face.

She couldn't get through the barrier.

She stood in flowing black before the gate, gazing at him in sorrow. Forlorn spirits hovered behind her, looking like rock fans that couldn't get tickets. This show was sold out.

"*Please* don't take away my friend," the schoolgirl whispered from the squeaking swing. Josephine's book of poetry was in her small ghostly hands.

Oh no, he thought, cringing. *I trapped the little girl in here with me. This is total Tales from the Crypt.*

"She wants me to stay forever," Josephine whispered, her spectral black tresses becoming an inky effluvium, melding with the night.

She dropped her velvet dress and slid off her panties, telling him what she'd do to him. "Let's have sex on the merry-go-round. I want to be on top."

He sighed. *Oh boy.*

Vines grew up the fence around the playground before his

eyes. Huge black flowers bloomed befitting a devil's paradise. The vines crawled up her body, turning her into an erotic tarot card.

Her violin solidified from darkness, and she played a sad dulcet piece. "If you lose me now, you'll lose me forever. You'll only fuck me in your dreams."

This is too much. He could feel the music working on his willpower. He staggered backward, pressing against the fence; shadows from swaying oak tree boughs slid over him.

I need to find her ashes and get this over with.

He went to work, removing concrete shards from the bulging roots. Even the tree itself emanated necromantic magic. The prize had to be here beneath the sigil-scrawled shards.

He scrabbled through small shards, tossing bigger ones aside. Sure enough, lodged beneath a massive root, rested a silver box most certainly containing Josephine's ashes.

He held it tightly like a child. *This is what's really left of her, not that demon girl.*

Lightning flashed across the sky as Josephine made elaborate hand gestures in the night. A doorway opened.

"I am leaving this world," she whispered. "Come join me." She dissolved into spectral gossamer and flowed into the ethereal doorway.

The shimmering doorway shrank to a sparkling point and vanished. *She's gone to that dark angel world*, he thought, *the one filling my book and my dreams.* It was a desperate demon's last hope. No ritual to free Josephine's spirit mattered now.

"Is she gone forever?" the schoolgirl ghost asked.

"I'm afraid so."

"She used to read poetry to me every night...so beautiful. Now I'm alone."

She rose from the swing, and tears streaming from her eyes, she dissolved in the darkness.

How terribly sad, he thought. *This is like a gothic soap opera. What a timeless friend must mean to someone whose life is over.*

Somewhere on the school grounds, Felicity was playing feverishly. The violin runs ebbed and flowed as she moved about as though working the streets of Vegas for tips.

Out of the shadows, she appeared, playing with unreal technical wizardry, fueled by Rapture. Spirits surrounded her, an ectoplasmic posse.

She'd beaten herself. He saw it in her eyes that she was a star burned out, ready to overdose, implode.

She played a marvelous extinction burst of notes and then collapsed like an abandoned puppet. The bow slid from her trembling hand, violin clattering and then going still by her sprawled body.

She flashed with pulsing light and then turned to ashes, the wind blowing her remains over the violin as though to bury it like a treasure.

He released a long shuddering sigh. *Man. The road to death can be highly pleasurable for someone so powerful.*

The rooster that gets its head chopped off...

He walked to the swing, wishing he had the book of poetry the little girl was reading earlier. She never returned, though. The lonely windswept night was all his. His only friend was the darkness.

He swung a while, a kid himself really, wondering if Felicity had joined the ghost children of the burnt school.

Then he thought of Josephine in that dark other-dimensional world.

Would he meet her again?

He refused to entertain himself with an answer and rose to leave.

***

Nightmare Mansion had taken on the appearance of a carnival. Magicals and mundanes were all over the place. Even the homeless had come to join the debauchery.

The members of Jake's last band Lost Angel were setting up to play in the backyard. The crowd was growing, many arriving from the festival. They gathered around the living room bar, watching Snow turn liquor into serpents and vodka into doves.

Muriel, in the meantime, read classics to a porch crowd, this time Charles Dickens. She was an amazing raconteur, auditory threads of illusion becoming a tapestry of dirty London streets, starving orphans, and cruel curmudgeons.

Tonight, she would also tell the ghost story of the murdered rock band. "They may very well show their spectral faces this evening."

This is when Jake showed up with the silver box after his hard candy victory. Muriel screamed for Snow to come out on the porch as Jake ambled up the steps.

"What happened?" Muriel and Snow chorused. Marci and the girls rushed out behind him.

Everyone wanted to hear a lurid story of victory. Jake told them about the spirits and zombies, the seductive illusions and Felicity's eerie death.

"Here are Josephine's ashes," he said, shrugging.

"Did you free her spirit?" This was Abbey, who wanted no more ghost sex.

He sighed. "The demon slipped away to that Island world in the future, but she's through haunting this world. Your night visits from her should be over."

Abbey sighed with relief.

Snow patted Jake on the back. "I'd say your cup is way more than half full. It's impossible to solve everything at once."

Marci wrapped her arms around his neck, squeezing him to her.

A bevy of fans were standing out front, watching it all. Snow called out to them like a demanding English school master. "Everybody head around back if you want to hear Lost Angel."

The backyard became a crazed concert theater. Shadow Basher was the opening act, a goth metal band packing killer illusions. Visions of crucifixions appeared behind the drummer's throne. Salem witches burned as guitars wailed, bass drums battering. Huge bats formed from shadows, whirling about before assuming liquid form in shot glasses.

The crowd was revved up, and the guys in Lost Angel were ready to play. Now the only problem was getting Jake to come out and sing.

Snow found him writing feverishly by candlelight as though trying to capture the passion of a historical literary figure—Bram Stoker straining toward the end of *Dracula*.

"Alright, mister rock god gone nerdy author, your public awaits you. Everyone is wondering where you are."

Jake dropped the pen. "Why is everyone so worked up about this? I blew it. I'm the reason there's no record deal. I can't believe those guys even showed up to play."

Snow closed his eyes, nodding knowingly. "The real reason you don't want to sing is because you'll realize how bad you want to be onstage again...up front."

"Where are the guys?"

"They're waiting for you *onstage*."

A walk that seemed like a never ending dream through the smoky, creaking house brought him to a clamoring audience. He felt like he was the guest star on a local television station talk show—a washed-up singer who needed exposure for a comeback.

He'd been promised a surprise, and boy did he ever get it. Auditory illusion triggers had been placed around the band, invoked immediately when the music began.

The dramatic dark swell of a keyboard brought on inky streaks of mist. Vocals about a midnight rendezvous conjured an illusory overlay of motel rooms with writhing figures in twisted sheets. The song *Damsel in Distress* brought in a hero on horseback who galloped through the crowd.

Jake proved he still had it even after a night of fighting foes. He didn't have time to primp. He'd just slipped on a gauzy tight black shirt. His mane of streaked hair flowed in the night wind. He sang with great power and vibrato, belting out lines meant for a bard, crosses dangling from his bracelet-beaded wrist as though he were a warlock.

The band, especially guitarist Nick Dryden, was on point. Arrangements were tight, as though they'd rehearsed all weekend. They played several encores. Nobody wanted them to leave the stage, but they did finally finish, announcing this would be the last Lost Angel show ever.

Now the crowd certainly had the Woodstock spirit. Deep kissing had begun in the audience, and some had already taken to the rooms upstairs.

Now it was time to boogie down. Club music pulsed and pounded—everything from industrial dance like Ministry to psychedelic-disco like *My Life* with the Thrill Kill Kult.

Muriel and Snow went about the crowd, pouring liquor into wanting mouths, alcoholic baby birds. Illusory spells on walls flashed in sync with the techno/goth pound, swirling illusions drawing from the sensual thoughts of revelers: visions of canopied beds, sex on couches and pool tables, bathroom stall porn scenes. The DJ went on to play music by the goth band Dark and nineties music like Sisters of Mercy and Nine Inch Nails. What was a party without NIN's *Pretty Hate Machine*?

At midnight, Muriel read from Jake's rough manuscript, much to his protest. A story came to life in illusion of a druggy boyfriend's search for his girlfriend who'd become a slave on Jake's *Spell Island*. Club scenes, Victorian sex mansions, and neon-lit misty scenes floated around the porch, candlelight flickering. Jake wound up enthralled.

Then the ghost story came. Everyone, holding candles, gathered close to hear about the band murdered by the Bone Tree.

As she gave a haunting account of the jealous shooting, three figures appeared under the tree. The ghost band!

"We have until dawn to dance," a shimmering long-haired figure called out. "But we will soon play by your side forever." He held a guitar high in the air, a true rock star pose.

Jake leaped down from the porch to face the ghosts. "What does that mean?"

"Doorways will open soon," the second said.

"There'll be three angels..." the third added.

"One for each of us," they chorused.

"I'm so sick of riddles," Jake exclaimed.

And then they vanished, leaving behind the moon-cast shadows of craggy branches.

Epilogue

The Bonding Weekend party was over, and Jake wrote furiously in his room as the sun came up. It would take him three days to finish the novel, writing nonstop. How would he end it? He had no idea.

One thing was for sure. His rock opera would be based on this novel. He fell back on his bed, candles guttering after a long night, like exhausted lovers. He mulled over the name of the fantasy metal band he always wanted to play his rock opera live.

Almost asleep, he listened to Freddie Mercury singing about Marie Antoinette. It came to him before he slipped into a long awaited dream.

His band would be called *Queen's Fury*.

David Raven

About the Author

David Raven lives in Atlanta where urban culture and the stripper/club scene has greatly influenced his novels. His background is in the hospitality industry, i.e. waiting tables and nightclub work. He listens to goth/industrial bands like Thrill Kill Kult, Type O Negative, and Rob Zombie, and classic heavy metal like Yngwie Malmsteen, Mercyful Fate, and Queensyrche. He's a fan of indie films, B-horror films, and anything involving psychics, ghosts, and the occult. Educated at Georgia State University, his hometown is Waycross, Georgia, where there is nothing but the Okefenokee Swamp, the railroad, and wonderful small-town childhood memories.

https://www.facebook.com/davidravenbooks.
https://www.twitter.com/davidravenbooks
Https://www.instagram.com/davidravenbooks

Enjoy more short stories and novels by
many talented authors at

www.twbpress.com

Science Fiction, Supernatural, Horror, Thrillers, Romance,
and more

www.ingramcontent.com/pod-product-compliance
Lightning Source LLC
Chambersburg PA
CBHW051134030726
47504CB00004B/867